PRAISE FOR

The End Begins
"The first book in Davison's Seven Trilogy grips the reader from page one and holds on until the very end... Thought-provoking, relevant, and suspenseful, *The End Begins* is a must-read."
— *ROMANTIC TIMES*, 4½ Stars, *Top Pick*

The Darkness Deepens (formerly *The Dragon Roars*)
"Sara Davison's second book in The Seven Trilogy brings together all the essential elements of a good suspense read—compelling story, fast-paced action, and believable characters... Readers will not be disappointed in Davison's second book in the trilogy; it delivers!"
— LUANA EHRLICH, Author of *Titus Ray Thrillers*

The Morning Star Rises
"Another thrilling read from Sara Davison. Thrust into the midst of intrigue, terror, and a heartrending love story, you will sit on the edge of your seat..."
— BONNIE LEON, Best-selling Author of the Northern Lights series

Vigilant
"In *Vigilant*, Sara Davison has created deep characters and a story that will grab your heart and keep you on the edge of your seat. Days after reading the story, the characters are still on my mind."
— Patricia Bradley, Memphis Cold Case series, Winner of Inspirational Readers' Choice Award

THE ROSE TATTOO TRILOGY
BOOK ONE

LOST DOWN DEEP

SARA DAVISON

THREE DREAMERS
PRESS

Lost Down Deep
© 2020 by Sara Davison

Three Dreamers Press
Guelph, Ontario

ISBN: 978-1-7770646-0-0

The Author is represented by the literary agency of WordServe Literary Group, Ltd, www.wordserveliterary.com.

Cover Design: Roseanna White of Roseanna White Designs
Formatting: Polgarus Studio

To Keith ~ for having the courage to come back home.

Welcome to

THE MOSAIC COLLECTION

We are sisters, a beautiful mosaic united by the love of God through the blood of Christ.

Each month The Mosaic Collection releases one faith-based novel exploring our theme, Family by His Design, and sharing stories that feature diverse, God-designed families. All are contemporary stories ranging from mystery and women's fiction to comedic and literary fiction. We hope you'll join our Mosaic family as we explore together what truly defines a family.

If you're like us, loneliness and suffering have touched your life in ways you never imagined; but Dear One, while you may feel alone in your suffering—whatever it is—you are never alone!

Subscribe to Grace & Glory, the official newsletter of The Mosaic Collection, to receive monthly encouragement from Mosaic authors, as well as timely updates about events, new releases, and giveaways.

Learn more about The Mosaic Collection at
www.mosaiccollectionbooks.com

Join our Reader Community, too!
www.facebook.com/groups/TheMosaicCollection

Books in

THE MOSAIC COLLECTION

When Mountains Sing by Stacy Monson
Unbound by Eleanor Bertin
The Red Journal by Deb Elkink
A Beautiful Mess by Brenda S. Anderson
Hope is Born: A Mosaic Christmas Anthology
More Than Enough by Lorna Seilstad
The Road to Happenstance by Janice L. Dick
This Side of Yesterday by Angela D. Meyer
Lost Down Deep by Sara Davison

Coming soon: novels by Johnnie Alexander and
Regina Rudd Merrick

Learn more at www.mosaiccollectionbooks.com/books

Fear not, for I have redeemed you;
I have called you by name, you are mine.
When you pass through the waters, I will be with you;
and through the rivers, they shall not overwhelm you...
(Isaiah 43:1-2)

CHAPTER ONE

The house should have been completely quiet. Still, Summer Velásquez stirred in her sleep. Prying her eyes open slightly, she brushed her long, almost-black curls out of her eyes and glared at the offending red numbers on the clock radio beside her bed. 11:10 a.m. Way too early for someone who'd worked all night and only managed to crawl between the sheets three hours earlier. She flung an arm over her eyes to block out the thin rays of sunlight that stubbornly worked their way around the edges of the wooden blinds covering her bedroom window.

A muffled sound from downstairs, like the soft squeak of a running shoe on the gray slate tiles in the front entryway, drifted up to the second floor. Summer bolted upright. *Someone's in the house.* She reached for the phone on her bedside table and punched in 911. No time to talk to anyone. If something was about to happen, hopefully the dispatcher would be able to hear it and would send the police to her home.

She slid open the top drawer of the nightstand. A ring box beside the clock caught her eye, and she swept it and the phone inside and closed the drawer, hoping that would block out the voice of the dispatcher. Flinging back the covers, she threw her legs over the side of the mattress and pushed to her feet. She tugged the strap of her tank top into place as she tiptoed, nearly soundlessly in her bare feet, across the wooden floor to the dresser that lined one wall of her room. Not wanting to give away either her presence in the house or her location, she gripped both knobs and slowly, slowly slid open the top drawer.

The harsh click of a Beretta safety sliding off froze her in place. "Don't."

Summer let go of the knobs and lifted both hands slightly in the air. Her stomach twisted into a painful knot as she struggled to keep her breathing slow and even. Who was in her house? In her room? And what did he want?

"Step back."

She complied. *Ten calma. Stay calm.* She took another step back and slowly turned to face him, keeping her hands where he could see them.

A tall, broad-shouldered stranger in black dress pants and a steel-blue shirt stood in her doorway. His clean-shaven face might have been handsome if the eyes focused on her weren't so hard and cold. Summer repressed a shudder. The man pointed the pistol directly at her chest, holding it in his gloved hand in a way that suggested he was familiar with guns and knew exactly how to use one.

She swallowed. "What do you want?"

A mocking smile turned up one corner of his mouth. "What do you think?"

Despite having immigrated to Canada ten years earlier, traces of the Spanish Summer had spoken exclusively during the first eighteen years of her life in Mexico still clung to her words, even more thickly when she was flustered. "We have no thing of value."

"I seriously doubt that is true."

In her tank top and shorts, Summer felt incredibly vulnerable. And if there was anything she hated, it was feeling vulnerable. She lifted her chin. "Whoever you are, you have no right to break into my home and—"

The spark that flashed in his eyes stopped her. The man took a step forward, the gun still trained on her. "I don't have a right?" He pushed the words out through clenched teeth. "I have every right to be here, to come after the diamond."

Her eyes narrowed. *He thinks I have something that belongs to him. Why would I?* "Look, I don't have any diamonds." She kept her voice low and even in an attempt to keep from antagonizing him further. "But I would be happy to give you what you want if you tell me what it is."

His laugh was as cold as his eyes. "Oh, you'll give me what I want, all right, chica." He took another step closer and reached out with the gun.

Summer forced herself not to flinch. Any sign of weakness would only add fuel to his boldness. Did this have something to do with her work? She wracked her brain, trying to remember if she had seen this person before, but nothing came to mind.

The man slowly ran the barrel of the Beretta down her cheek. "They told me you were beautiful. I thought they were exaggerating."

Who told him that? Who had been talking about her with this man and why? The cold steel sent shivers of apprehension racing through Summer's body. It took everything she had not to swipe the weapon away. *Espera tu oportunidad. Wait.*

Her eyes locked on his. Neither of them moved for several seconds, until the gun slipped slightly down her cheek. *Now.* She bent her arm and brought it up sharply, knocking the gun away from her face. Grasping his wrist, she twisted it and bent forward, sending him sprawling over her and onto the floor. Summer leapt over the prone body and ran for the door. Just before she reached it, strong fingers closed around her ankle, and she lost her balance and fell onto the wooden floor with a thud.

She flipped onto her back and bent her knee, then drove her free foot into the man's face. His nose gave under her heel with a sickening crunch. The man howled and let go of her ankle. Summer shoved hard against the wooden floor with both feet, propelling herself backwards. When she reached the doorway, she flipped over onto her hands and knees and scrambled to her feet.

3

She made it as far as the top of the stairs before an arm circled her waist and lifted her up. Summer kicked backwards, landing one solid hit to the man's shins, but he didn't loosen his grip.

Cold metal dug into her temple. "Stop." The gun pressed deeper and she winced. "Are you going to keep fighting me?"

She shook her head slightly and the man set her down. Summer whirled to face him. Blood dripped from his nose and onto his chin. Keeping the gun aimed at her face, the man swiped a gloved finger over his top lip and glanced down at it. He cursed loudly as he gripped the pistol in both hands.

Piensa. Think. Everything in Summer screamed at her to run, but that would only guarantee a bullet in the back. She did take one small step backwards then stopped and raised both hands again. "I'm sorry. I did not mean to hurt you. I got scared. Tell me what you came here for, and I will do whatever I can to help you get it."

The man stepped forward. "Too late for that, sweetheart. A little cooperation back there..." he jerked his head toward the bedroom, "... might have saved your life. Now I'm going to leave my message and get out of here."

Her forehead wrinkled. Leave a message? For who? How did he plan to—? His finger tensed on the trigger. Heat coursed through her. *Do something. Now.* Focusing all her rage on the man in front of her, Summer ducked below the gun and launched herself forward, ramming her head into the man's stomach.

The breath emptied from his lungs with a whoosh, but he managed to bring the butt of the weapon down on her head as he stumbled back, driving her to her knees.

For a few seconds, Summer concentrated on drawing in air, blinking to clear the vision that had gone blurry. A stabbing pain shot through her head from her neck to behind her eyes. Grasping hold of the railing at the top of the stairs, she hauled herself to her feet. The man swore at her and lunged forward. When he hit her, she lost her grip and they both tumbled down the stairs. The man managed to grab the railing and stop himself part way down, but when Summer reached frantically for one of the posts her fingers closed around air. She continued to fall, hitting the stairs violently several times until she landed on her back at the bottom and her head cracked against the gray stone tile. Hard.

Dios, sálvame, she breathed as, unable to move, she watched the man slowly descend the stairs, one deliberate step at a time. *Would* God save her? No one else could now. The smile on his face slid in and out of focus. One of Summer's arms had landed beside her head and a warm, sticky liquid lapped against her skin.

The man reached the bottom of the stairs and shoved the gun into the back of his dress pants as he crouched beside her. "Well, look at that. You did help me after all."

His voice, like his body, wavered, as though she was seeing and hearing him under water. Summer licked her lips. "H... how?"

"You've enabled me to leave my message." Using the glove that didn't have his own blood smeared across it, the man dipped two fingers in the pool and scrawled something across the wall at the bottom of the stairs.

"What...?" She couldn't finish the sentence. The word she had been grasping for was gone, lost in the thick fog swirling through her mind.

Far off in the distance a siren wailed. The man glanced toward the door. "What message?" He stopped writing and stepped over her, heading for the entrance. "You, chica. You are the message." The front door clicked behind him.

Summer pressed her eyes shut and opened them again, willing away the darkness that crept across her field of vision. *It's so cold.* A numbness started deep inside her and spread through her chest and stomach and down her arms and legs. The wail of the siren grew louder.

They're too late.

Her entire body had already gone numb, as if encased in ice. She blinked, trying to make out the words on the wall. The letters danced a macabre waltz across the white paint and the effort it took to try and still them sent another stabbing pain shooting through her head. An inky blackness fell over her vision, as though the power had been cut in the house.

Summer closed her eyes.

CHAPTER TWO

One month later

Summer's mother punched the pillow on the hospital bed lightly to fluff it up, her movements stiff and awkward.

Summer touched her elbow. "Estoy bien, Mamá. I'm fine."

She wasn't fine. Being stuck in this bed for two weeks after waking up from her coma was about to drive her out of what was left of her battered mind. "At least, I will be fine when I can go home." The thought sent a twist of pain through her. *Where is home?*

When she'd asked her parents about the place where she'd been injured, they'd been vague, something about a house she'd moved into a couple of years ago that they had never felt was right for her. The way her mother crossed her arms and spoke with a hint of smugness in her voice suggested that her accident had only proven their point. The scant details they'd provided her didn't sound right or familiar. How could she have lived in a place she didn't even remember?

She was able to recall every detail of the home she'd grown up in, the pale blue carpeting, the striped wallpaper in her room, the expensive antique furniture she was barely allowed to use for sitting, let alone lounging or climbing on. Her dorm room at the University of Toronto remained vividly entrenched in her brain. Even now she could close her eyes and picture that and the apartment she'd moved into after she graduated. How could those memories be so clear when everything that had happened to her in the last few years had simply been erased?

7

Retrograde Amnesia, the doctor had called it. He was cute—she had no trouble remembering *that* little fact—with dark hair and dark eyes and an accent that confirmed his Hispanic heritage. Summer had no idea whether he had been intentionally assigned her case for that reason, or whether it was pure luck that he had been able to communicate so effectively with her parents, offering them information and hope in a calm, soothing voice. Not that they appeared to need soothing. Summer had rarely seen either of them express emotion. Even now, in the face of the extensive injuries from her fall, they remained implacable, if a little impatient with having to spend so much time in the hospital over the past month.

The doctor earned more of her mother's attention than Summer did. When Dr. Lopez stood at the side of her bed, explaining what had happened to her—the damage that had been inflicted on her brain when she'd fallen down the stairs and cracked her head on a marble floor—she'd felt her mother's eyes on her. When Summer's gaze had flicked over to hers, her mother had inclined her head slightly in the doctor's direction.

Summer had glanced away quickly, but she couldn't stop the rush of heat that flooded her cheeks. Had the doctor caught her mother's gesture? Honestly, didn't she have enough on her plate right now, recovering from a traumatic head injury and trying to capture the memories of the last few years, without her mother trying to match-make?

The doctor's words—that it wouldn't help her to recover her memories if she stressed out about it, or tried too hard to grasp for them, that the best recourse was to get on with her life and allow them to come back to her in time—were nearly lost in the buzz of humiliation shooting through her.

Her father had been gazing out the window, but he came over to stand beside the bed now. When he spoke, his words had a hint of steel woven through them. "You will leave this place tomorrow. Mamá and I are bringing you home with us. Once you are there, with your family in a familiar place, you will recover quickly."

A shiver rippled through Summer. That did make sense. She shifted on the bed. *So why doesn't it feel right?* "I'm grateful for all you and Mamá have done for me, Papá. But I should go home. I must have bills to pay and a mortgage."

He shook his head. "You do not need to worry about that. It is all taken care of."

"But—"

Her father raised his hand, the signal that he had spoken and would hear no more about it. Summer clamped her mouth shut. He tapped the top of the bed rail with his palm. "You sleep now. Do not think about anything but getting better."

Her mother nodded curtly before replying, in Spanish, "Sí, you rest. We will pick you up in the morning to take you home."

Summer studied her. People often mistook the two of them for sisters. Her mother had been twenty when Summer was born, but she didn't look more than a decade older than her daughter. Her eyes were dark with long lashes, and she worked out in the gym in the basement of their home daily, keeping herself in peak condition. Men turned and watched her when she walked down the street, but she only tossed her head—sending the long, dark hair that flowed down her back in thick waves tumbling over her shoulders—and offered them such a look of disdain that most turned away quickly. Summer had always thought she looked far more like a spy than the accountant she actually was.

The buttons on her black shirt clicked now against the bed rail as she leaned slightly over it.

Summer tensed. Was her mother about to hug her? While her parents had provided for her every material need growing up, physical affection had rarely been doled out. Had the accident softened her mother's heart? Her mother grasped the starched white sheet in both hands and tugged it up to Summer's chin before straightening. "Buenas noches."

"Good night." A slight ache in her chest, Summer watched as her mother gathered up her purse and the bag she always brought with her to the hospital. She had no idea what either contained, as she didn't think her mother had ever opened them in her presence. Mamá switched off the reading light above the bed so that only the dim fluorescent lights set into the ceiling remained on. Summer waited until the door had shut before closing her eyes and snuggling down farther under the blanket with a sigh.

She was nearly asleep when a sharp rapping on the door jolted her awake. Summer clutched the sheet to her chest with both hands. "Come in."

A woman in a navy jacket and trousers strode across the room. Her blonde hair was pulled back in a neat bun, adding to the aura of professional confidence. She stopped next to the raised railing that ran along the side of the hospital bed. "Ms. Velásquez?"

Summer let go of the sheet with one hand and rested her arm near the edge of the bed, close to the call button. "Yes."

The woman pushed back her jacket to reveal a badge clipped to her waistband. "Detective Holmes, Toronto P.D."

She frowned. Why on earth was a detective coming to see her, especially this late at night? Was she in some kind of trouble? "What can I do for you, Detective?"

The woman nodded at the chair in the corner of the room. "Do you mind?"

"Of course not."

While the woman retrieved the chair, Summer gingerly sat up and switched the light on then adjusted her pillow so she could lean back against it. *What is this about?*

The woman sat down and crossed her legs. "I'm sorry to bother you, Ms. Velásquez, but—"

Summer waved a hand through the air. "It's Summer, please."

"All right, Summer. We've been waiting for your doctor's permission to speak with you, and he finally let us know this evening that it would be okay to question you about the assault."

Summer's head jerked. "Assault?"

The detective nodded. "Yes. I know you have no memory of either the attack or the perpetrator, but—"

Summer held up a hand. "I think there's been a mistake, Detective. I wasn't attacked, I fell down the stairs. It was an accident."

The woman's forehead wrinkled. "You did fall down the stairs, yes, but it was not an accident. And the man who did this to you is still at large. We're hoping you might be able to remember at least some details, however minor, that could help us locate..." She leaned back in her seat and contemplated Summer. "You have no idea what I'm talking about, do you?"

Summer shook her head then winced at the pain that shot up from her neck. Had she really been attacked? If so, why had no one told her? Dr. Lopez obviously knew, since he had given the detective permission to talk to her. A stab of betrayal shot across her chest. Her mother could forget about anything happening between Summer and that man.

Although he likely assumed her parents had filled her in on what had happened. She bit her lip. Did her parents know? Surely they wouldn't have kept such vital information from her. Summer's jaw tightened. Of course they would. Growing up, she had often felt as though she were being kept in a cage, if a gilded one. Her parents had rarely shared what was going on in their lives with her, only providing her with information they deemed absolutely necessary for her to know. As she had no brothers and sisters, that had led to a pretty lonely childhood. But it was one thing for them not to share details of their own lives with her—this was Summer's life. Her grip on the sheet tightened. What else hadn't they told her?

The detective glanced toward the door. "Didn't you wonder why you have around-the-clock security outside your door?"

"I have a guard?"

"For your protection, yes."

"I haven't left this room. I had no idea." Summer let go of the sheet and clasped her hands over her stomach. "Obviously vital information has been kept from me, Detective. As I am nearly thirty, and not a child, something my parents appear to have forgotten, I'd appreciate if you could tell me everything you know about what happened to me."

The woman tugged a notebook from the inside pocket of her jacket and flipped it open. "Of course. The morning of January 3, shortly after 11 a.m., you were upstairs when someone broke into your home. A neighbor reported seeing a man leave the premises and drive away in a black car, but she was too far away to be able to provide us with the licence plate number or a description of him. From the evidence we gathered at the site, it appears that, before he left, he confronted you either in your room or right outside it and the two of you struggled at the top of the stairs. You fell—or were pushed—down the stairs, and you struck your head on the tile at the bottom, which rendered you unconscious."

Summer's insides twisted into knots. *Who would do that?* "And then the man what, simply left? Did he steal anything?"

"He left, yes, likely because we received a 911 call from your address and one of our squad cars was approaching the house with the siren on. And no, robbery does not appear to be the motive. The attack seemed to be more... personal."

"Why do you say that?"

"Because whoever he was wrote a message on the wall at the

bottom of the stairs in your blood." Her voice was cool, detached—the tone of someone who had seen such horrific things in her line of work that the use of human blood as a writing medium did not even faze her.

Summer grimaced. "What message?"

The detective glanced down at the notebook. "It said, *my patience has nearly run out.*"

CHAPTER THREE

Jude McCall stood in the dark alleyway across from the hospital, one shoulder propped against the cold brick wall, his breath coming out in spurts of white fog in the frigid February air. He stared up at the window of Summer Velásquez, watching as her parents moved around the room. His jaw tightened. How was it those two had unlimited access to Summer, while he was kept out by the armed guard stationed at her door?

Heat coursed through him. He was the one who needed to talk to her, to finish...

A silhouette filled the window, and he ducked back into the shadows. If they saw him, they would call the cops and he might never see Summer again. He needed to be patient. She had to get out of the hospital soon, and when she did, he'd follow her home and wait for her to finally be alone. According to his source in the Toronto PD, she had no memory of recent events, so she wouldn't recognize him. It should be safe enough.

The light spilling from the window dimmed as a lamp was switched off. Her parents must be leaving. Five minutes later, the couple came out the front doors and made their way down the sidewalk toward the parking lot. Jude pressed his back against the wall and held his breath as they passed by him on the other side of the street. After ten seconds, he slowly let his breath out. *Too close.*

He gave them another minute to reach their car before shifting around to face Summer's window again, tugging the zipper on his winter jacket a little higher. A cold wind swept between the two buildings, sending empty take-out bags and paper cups cart-wheeling through the alleyway like tumbleweeds in the desert. The light flicked back on as someone else came into the room. A woman, it looked like. His muscles relaxed a little. A doctor maybe, although from watching her the last few weeks he was pretty sure her doctor was a man. A nurse then.

Jude kicked at the wall with the toe of his running shoe. *This is ridiculous.* He had to stop trying to guess what was going on with her and find a way to get closer so he could see for himself. Reaching behind him, he fingered the pistol he'd stuck into the back of his jeans with numb fingers. Maybe he should shoot his way in and carry her out.

Great idea, Jude. A shoot-out in the hallway outside her room would be the perfect way to get her to go with him. Not to mention that, even if he did succeed in storming his way in there, grabbing her, and getting them both downstairs, the place would be surrounded by cops by the time they emerged from the building.

Blowing out a deep breath, he slammed his back against the brick wall. Something had to happen soon, something that would make it possible to get to her.

He was tired of waiting.

CHAPTER FOUR

Summer pulled on jeans and a light green sweater and stuffed the rest of her clothes into the bag her parents had brought her. When she pulled her long dark curls back and fastened them with an elastic into a loose bun, her head throbbed and all she wanted to do was turn out the light and crawl back under the blanket and sleep. She'd spent a restless night on the narrow bed. Questions about what had happened to her and why her parents had lied about it assaulted her weary brain, keeping her from settling. About the time weak rays of winter sunlight battled through heavy gray clouds to fall across her bed, she made a decision. She wouldn't stay here waiting for them to come and take her to their home.

The hairbrush on the table beside the bed clattered to the floor when she reached for it. Her fingers trembled and she dropped it twice before finally clutching it firmly enough to shove it into the bag. Nothing else sat on the little table. Why had no one sent cards or flowers? Didn't she have any friends who cared about what happened to her? Or had her parents refused to allow any of those items to get to her?

She gritted her teeth. How could her parents have kept the truth from her? Her entire life they had drilled into her how important family was, that it was everything. Was that what family meant to them? Controlling and manipulating each other? They had to have known the police would come and talk to her, or did they assume they would be there and could intercept them when they showed up, talk to them on her behalf as though she were a helpless child? Summer grasped the zipper and nearly drove it off the track as she ripped the bag closed. Even if they hadn't lied to her, there was no way she could go to their house. Her attacker was still out there somewhere, and there was a good chance he was coming back for her. Even if her parents had betrayed her by keeping her in the dark, she couldn't put them in that kind of danger.

The words the detective had spoken drifted through her mind. *My patience has nearly run out.* Summer felt for the lump at the back of her head and winced. Patience for what? And what would he do to her when it had run out?

She sank down on the edge of the bed. Where could she go? And what about the guard outside her door? Summer pushed back her shoulders. She'd worry about where to go later. For now she had to figure out how to get out of the hospital. She reached for her purse and dug around for a moment before pulling out a set of keys. Hmm. She must have a car somewhere. Would it be in the parking lot?

Summer started to shake her head then remembered how it had felt the last time and stopped herself. Of course it wouldn't be here. She obviously hadn't driven herself to the hospital while unconscious, and no one else could have driven it since she still had the keys. So where was her car?

Biting her lip, she rummaged through her purse and pulled out a worn purple wallet. After riffling through the cards stuffed in the bill section, she tugged out her driver's licence. She didn't recognize the address on it. Her forehead wrinkled. Must be the house her parents had briefly mentioned to her. And if she had lived there, her car must still be parked there.

She pushed herself off the bed and slipped the strap of the purse over her shoulder. Grasping the handles of the bag she had packed, she strode across the room. Cautiously, she peered out the window. All she could see were the crossed legs of someone in a navy uniform sitting to the left of the door. With a hiss of frustration, Summer pressed her back to the wall at the side of the door. Would there be a shift change soon or had the person guarding her settled in for the night?

If she had to, she could slip out of the room, catch him by surprise, and take him out before he could prevent her from leaving, but that would draw far more attention to herself than she wanted. Summer frowned. What made her think she could do that, anyway? The guy was pretty big. Still, something told her she could take him on, if she needed to.

She tapped her fingers against the wall before pushing away and looking out again. A large paper coffee cup and a water bottle sat on the floor beside the chair. *Perfecto.* Whoever it was would have to take a washroom break at some point, right? And when he did, she would be ready.

CHAPTER FIVE

The silhouette of a man appeared in the opening of the alleyway, and Jude shoved himself away from the wall. His instinct was to reach for the gun, but he waited, muscles tensed, as the man strode toward him, garbage crunching beneath his feet. In the dim light of the moon and the lamppost out at the street, the man's handsome features—dark, slicked-back hair and even darker eyes—gradually became clear. As did the hatred radiating around him like an aura. Jude swallowed. Summer's father.

He stopped a couple of feet in front of Jude, a scowl twisting across his features. "¿Qué estás haciendo aquí?"

Jude lifted his chin. "What do you think I'm doing here? I'm keeping an eye on Summer."

The man kicked a tin can with the toe of his thousand-dollar Italian-leather shoe. It clattered against the brick wall a couple of feet from Jude, and it took everything he had not to jump. When Summer's father spoke again, it was in English, but with a thick Spanish accent. "I told you when you tried to get to her in the hospital that I did not want you anywhere near her."

"I'm on public property. You might be able to hire a guard to keep me from seeing her in there, but you can't control what I do out here."

"Can I not?" The man reached into the pocket of his Brioni suit coat.

Jude's hand inched behind his hip. If her father pulled out a weapon, he wouldn't hesitate to grab the Glock. Instead, the man took out a phone, tapped the screen, and held it up. A couple of seconds later, voices spilled from the device. Jude listened a moment. It was him and Summer, arguing. His stomach twisted as he met the simmering gaze of Mr. Velásquez. "How did you get that?"

"It does not matter how, only that I have it." He hit the screen again to silence the phone before sticking it into his pocket. He stepped forward, stopping so close to Jude that he could feel the man's hot breath when he spoke. "This recording makes you a prime suspect in the attack of my daughter. I am working closely with the police to find the evidence to prove it. Already it is mounting. Your fingerprints are all over the house, so they know you were there." Venom flowed through his words like sap through a tree. "If you try again to see her, or if I catch you anywhere near her, I will hand over this recording to them. I am sure they will be very interested to hear that you had a motive for the attack, as well as the means and opportunity. This is the missing piece of the puzzle."

"And yet you haven't given it to them. Because you know I didn't do it."

"I know no such thing. I am biding my time, waiting for you to push me far enough that I have no choice. I have already told my daughter that I believe you are the one who did this to her, so she wants nothing to do with you. I strongly advise you to stay away from her. Far away. Or I will see to it that you are locked up so tightly and for so long that you will never be able to get to her again. Do I make myself clear?"

Jude's heart sank. Had her father really told Summer Jude was the one who attacked her? If so, the chances of her ever being willing to talk to him were pretty much non-existent. He'd have to come up with another plan entirely if he hoped to be able to reach her.

Her father took a step closer, until his chest was nearly touching Jude's. The butt of the gun pressed into Jude's spine when he leaned away slightly. He could grab it, force the man to back off, but if he pulled it out he'd use it, and the last thing he needed was another death on his conscience.

Still, everything in him screamed at him to fight. He clenched his fingers into fists, itching to forcibly remove the smug look from the man's face, but he knew from past experience that would only make things worse. And he couldn't take the chance that Summer's father would turn that recording over to the police. Jude had to stay out of prison long enough to figure out a way to see Summer. The man held all the cards at the moment.

"I asked if I had made myself clear."

Jude gritted his teeth. "Yes."

"Bien." Mr. Velásquez stepped back and brushed his hands against each other, as though swiping off any contact with Jude. "Then do not ever let me see you again. The moment I do, I hand that recording over to the police." He spun around and stalked out of the alleyway. Jude stared at the opening long after the man had disappeared around the end of the building. Then he stooped down, snatched up an empty beer bottle, and sent it hurtling toward the bricks. The glass shattered with an angry crash, depleting a little of the fury and adrenaline coursing through him.

He slumped against the wall. *Think, Jude.* The confrontation with Summer's father had been a setback, nothing more. The stakes had been raised, but that wouldn't deter him from his mission. He *would* find a way to get to Summer.

Even if he risked going to jail for life to do it.

CHAPTER SIX

Summer waited, her head turned so she could see the blue-clad legs outside her room at all times. After twenty minutes, the person sitting on the chair in the hall uncrossed his legs. Every muscle in Summer's body tensed. Was he getting up? For a moment, the man didn't move. Then he stood and she was able to see the back of him as he stretched both arms to the ceiling and stomped his feet. He was medium height, probably five ten or so, and his short hair was light brown. From her vantage point, she couldn't make out any other features.

How long had he been sitting there with nothing more happening than the odd wheelchair rolling by or a nurse pushing a cart past him with a curt nod? Poor guy. And how did the staff feel about having someone on their floor who needed guarding? What about the other patients who shuffled by in their blue gowns, backs hanging slightly open? Had they been scared to fall asleep at night?

Summer pressed the fingers of her free hand to her temple. What a lot of trouble she had caused, without realizing it. Fresh anger, directed at her parents, coursed through her. And at the man who had attacked her. Her grip on the overnight bag tightened. Who would want to hurt her and why?

She pushed back the thoughts that crowded into her mind. *Concéntrate.* The guard lowered his arms, glanced in both directions, then strode down the hallway. Summer counted to five in her head before gripping the knob and slowly tugging open the door. She peered out the opening in time to see the man disappear into a room on the far side of the nursing station. One woman in pale pink scrubs sat at the desk, head bent as she wrote something, likely filling out a chart. It was now or never. Taking a deep breath, Summer stepped into the hallway and headed in the opposite direction. A door at the end of the hall was marked *Stairs*, and without a backward glance, Summer pushed through it and started down. She passed the third and second floor landings before marching through the doorway onto the main floor.

No one moved to stop her as she traversed the maze of corridors, following the bright red exit signs. At last she reached a door to the parking lot. Summer paused and stared out a large window beside the door. No shadowy figure appeared to be out there, watching for her. Tugging the phone from her pocket, she found the number for a local cab company and called it. She made arrangements for someone to come as soon as possible to pick her up, then ended the call and dropped the device back into her pocket. Ten minutes later, as the yellow vehicle drove up to the door, she lifted her bag and, as nonchalantly as possible, strolled out the door.

Jude's phone vibrated and he snatched it up and scanned the screen. She'd used her phone to call a cab. His eyes widened. She was leaving the hospital? Alone? He couldn't believe the guard would allow that. A grim smile crossed his lips. Somehow she'd slipped by him. Which made his job that much easier.

Where would she go? Home? If she'd been going to her parents' place, they would have driven her, she wouldn't have called a cab. That meant she likely wasn't planning to follow through with the plans to stay with them, so her home made the most sense. He grabbed his jacket from the hook behind his office door. It didn't matter. As long as she had her phone with her, he could track her movements. And if it did occur to her to lose the device, he had a back-up plan. No way he was going to lose her again.

Still shoving one arm into a sleeve, Jude flung open the door and headed out into the cold February night.

The cab driver had been chatty. Summer had answered his questions as briefly as possible, trying to convey that she was not interested in a big discussion without seeming rude. The fifteen-minute drive to the address she'd given the man felt a lot longer, but at last he pulled up in front of a two-story home and stopped at the curb. "Thanks." Summer handed him a couple of bills, fumbled for the door handle, and hopped out of the back seat. She closed the door behind her and waited until the vehicle had driven away before starting up the path to the front door. The house wasn't fancy, but it was a nice gray-stone building maybe twenty years old. A large maple tree stood sentry in the front yard, and the tops of more trees in the back hovered above the roofline. Nothing looked familiar, but this had to be the place she had lived, the place where someone had broken in and...

Don't go there. If she thought about what had happened, she wouldn't go in. And maybe taking at least a quick look around before she jumped into the small red Corolla parked in the driveway would jog some kind of memory for her. Plus she could see if she had a winter coat here, since she hadn't been able to find one at the hospital.

Before she could second-guess her decision, Summer pulled the keys from her jacket pocket, hit the button on the remote to unlock the car doors, and tossed her bag and purse onto the passenger seat. After closing the door and locking it, she strode to the front door, pausing before inserting the key. Was he waiting for her inside, even now?

She swallowed hard before shoving the key into the lock. Of course she would be careful, but she couldn't live her life in fear either. She couldn't let that man, whoever he was, have that much control over her life and happiness.

The thought sent fury coursing through her, and she shoved open the door so hard it crashed against the wall behind it. Summer winced. So much for being careful. If he was inside, or anywhere nearby, he now knew she was here too.

Pushing back her shoulders, she stepped into the opening. A wooden staircase curved up to the second floor directly in front of her. Although the tiles in the entryway had obviously been cleaned, pale stains remained both there and on the wall at the bottom of the stairs, and she swallowed hard. The faint smell of bleach hung in the air. For a moment she stood in the doorway, straining for any small sound, any hint that someone else was in the house. She heard nothing. Finally, summoning every ounce of courage she had, Summer stepped inside and closed and locked the door behind her.

Since her key had worked, this must actually be her place. On slightly weak knees, she made her way up to the second floor, gripping the railing tightly. The last thing she needed at the moment was another tumble down these steps.

She paused at the top. Which room was hers? The master? Did anyone else live here? For some reason, that thought hadn't occurred to her. Did she have roommates? Was she boarding with someone else, a family maybe? From the way her parents had talked, she had assumed she lived alone, but now that she thought about it, they hadn't actually come right out and said that.

Given the silence, and the fact that her car was the only one in the driveway, if someone else did live here, they didn't appear home at the moment. Hopefully they wouldn't arrive before she had time to look around quickly and head out.

Summer walked into the large master bedroom and paused, one hand on the dresser to steady herself, giving her eyes a moment to adjust to the dim lighting. A thin layer of dust coated the furniture and hung in the air, visible in the weak rays of sunshine that filtered around heavy wooden blinds. The queen bed was unmade, but otherwise the room was neat. Three doors led off the main bedroom. Two closets and a washroom? Were the closets his and hers?

Striding forward, she grasped the knob of the first door and pulled it open. Women's clothes hung on the rack. An overnight bag sat on the shelf and she snatched it down and tossed it onto the bed. After grabbing a couple of outfits, two pairs of jeans, and several long-sleeved shirts off the hangers, Summer closed the closet door and headed for the dresser. She retrieved socks and undergarments from the top drawer and a sweater and a hoodie out of the bottom one and tucked them into the bag before zipping it closed.

A car door slammed outside and her stomach tightened. Time for her to go. She stole a last look around the room. Nothing, not the book on the bedside table, or the pictures hanging on the wall, not even the sweater thrown over the back of an armchair in the corner released any memories from the tightly locked box in her mind.

Biting her lip, she slung the bag over her shoulder and crossed the room. At the bottom of the stairs, she stopped and peered through the window in the door. A woman with a paper grocery bag in each arm walked up the pathway to a house across the street and two doors down. The car door. Some of the tension released from Summer's shoulders. Better not press her luck and stay here any longer though. Sliding doors set into the wall caught her eye, and she dropped the overnight bag on the floor and pushed them open. A red Columbia jacket with faux fur trim on the hood hung on a hanger, and she snatched it off and tried it on. Perfect fit. She pulled black gloves from the pocket and tugged those on, too, before grabbing the bag and heading for the front door. She waited until the woman across the street had gone inside then glanced up and down the street. Seeing no one, Summer opened the door and slipped through and out onto the front porch.

Mi celular. As much as she hated to lose the cell phone her parents had brought to her in the hospital, along with a bag of clothes and toiletries, she didn't want anyone using the GPS to follow her. Even she didn't know where she was going, so no one else did either. Until she knew who had attacked her and whether or not he might return, she would really like to keep it that way. She took the device out of her pocket, stepped back into the entryway and, with a sigh, dropped it into a vase of artificial flowers sitting on a small table inside the door. She could pick up another one once she had settled somewhere away from here. Preferably far away. Far enough to be safe, anyway.

If such a place existed.

CHAPTER SEVEN

Jude stood behind the door in the guest room, taking slow, shallow breaths even after he'd heard the front door close behind Summer. He'd debated with himself the whole time she was in the house, wondering if this was the time to confront her. In the end, given what her father had told her about him, he'd decided to leave it to chance. If she came into the guest room and saw him, he would have no other option than to try to keep her there long enough to finish the conversation they had started the last time the two of them were in this house together. And to prevent her from calling the police and alerting them to his presence before they could. His fists tightened.

When she'd started up the stairs, blood had pounded in his ears. Turning his head slightly, he'd caught a glimpse of her through the crack between the frame and the door and he'd almost stepped out of the room to face her. He'd stayed put. He would only have one opportunity. The timing had to be perfect.

Jude had jumped at the sound of the car door slamming. Summer had obviously heard it too, as she came out of the bedroom shortly after and headed straight down the stairs. He had forced himself not to follow her but, when he'd heard another door slam and the sound of her engine roaring to life, he'd inched out of the room and descended to the main floor. By the time he reached the door and peered out, her car was gone.

He tugged the phone from the back pocket of his jeans and opened the app. Scanning the screen, he frowned. The GPS still showed that she was in the house. He whirled around. How was that possible?

She's dumped her phone. The question was, where? He bounded back up the stairs, taking them two at a time. As far as he could tell, she'd only come in, gone up to the bedroom, and headed back outside. How many places could there be for her to leave it? Jude pulled a pair of gloves from his jacket pocket and slid them on. If there was a chance there was any evidence on it, video or audio recordings of her attack, he couldn't leave it for the wrong person to find.

After carefully pulling open every dresser drawer—including the top one he'd grabbed the Glock pistol out of last time he'd been in the house—riffling through items on the closet shelves, and checking under the pillows, he dropped to his hands and knees and searched under the bed. Nothing. With a frustrated grunt, Jude clambered to his feet and stalked out of the room. With every second that passed she was slipping further and further from his grasp. He had to find that phone and get out of here now. He stopped at the bottom of the stairs and turned in a slow circle. What could she have done with it? The vase of flowers by the door caught his eye and he strode over to it. He turned the vase upside down and the phone clattered to the table along with the fake orchids. *Yes.*

Jude snatched up the device, shoved the flowers back into the vase—the fewer signs he left that he'd been in the place, the better—and slipped out the front door. He'd parked his black Miata around the corner so she wouldn't suspect anyone was in the house. Thankfully, at this time of day most people in the neighborhood were either at work or in school and no one that he could detect was around to see him as he made his way to the car and slid behind the wheel.

Yanking his phone out of his pocket again, he opened up another app and waited a few seconds before the data he was looking for flashed onto the screen. With a grim smile, he dropped the device into the empty cup holder and shoved his key into the ignition.

Time for Plan B.

CHAPTER EIGHT

Summer wheeled her car into the parking lot behind a gas station and put it in park. The car felt strange, as though she'd recently bought it and had to figure out where everything was. On impulse, she leaned over and opened the glove box. After rummaging through it, she found a small blue folder, pulled it out, and flipped it open. The ownership and insurance information. Sure enough, there was her name in black and white. Summer Velásquez.

With a sigh, she replaced the folder and closed the door. What now? She had to get out of the city, but where could she go? She had no family anywhere else in the country. A stab of pain shot through her chest. Her parents had lied to her. At the moment, she couldn't depend on family anyway. Did family keep things from each other? Show each other such little respect and honesty? For now, she would have to carry on as though she had no family. The sharp edge of that thought carved out a hollow, empty space in her chest. Summer gritted her teeth. If she was going to survive this, she couldn't trust her family or anyone else. Not for a while. She was on her own.

So where should she go? She had no phone and no GPS, although she wouldn't have any idea what destination to key in if she did. Could she get a map in the gas station? Did they even make maps anymore? Wouldn't hurt to ask. Worst case, she could grab a coffee and something to eat while giving whoever worked there a good laugh when she told them what she was looking for. With a wry grin, she shoved open her door and made her way around the building. A large man in grease-covered overalls nodded at her as he came out and held the door.

Summer flashed him a quick smile and ducked inside. The store was small. Before she could even ask, she spotted a rack containing books of maps. So the world hadn't gone completely digital yet. She walked over and stopped in front of the rack, slowly spinning it as she read the titles. She'd never been on the run before. What was the protocol? To get as far away as possible from where you were? Stay relatively close and hope your pursuer, if you had one, assumed you would be farther afield?

Her options were limited, at least on three sides. From where she was, just east of Toronto, an hour or two south would take her into the States. As she had no passport with her, that wasn't an option. Because of the Great Lakes, to go very far west, out of the province for sure, required driving south into the States or hours and hours north, up long stretches of isolated highways winding through a rugged landscape of rocks, trees, and lakes. The population there was sparse, the main inhabitants being deer, moose, bears, and wolves. She repressed a shudder. Not a good place to get stranded, especially when she had no one to call to come help her.

Summer reached for the purple wallet and tugged it out. As discreetly as possible, she opened it and counted the cash. Slightly over a hundred dollars. She glanced at the ATM in the corner. Should she risk one withdrawal? Whoever had attacked her knew she was in the Toronto area, so she wouldn't be revealing anything new. She just wouldn't be able to use any kind of plastic after this.

Summer tugged her bank card out of a pocket in the wallet and stared at it. Did she know her password? If she'd had it longer than six or seven years, it might come back to her. Staring at the small plastic card did not summon any combination of numbers into her head. After a couple of minutes, she replaced the card with a frustrated sigh. A hundred bucks then. Her gas tank was full, thankfully, but her traveling options were now even more limited. She'd have to try to find a place within a couple of hours' drive and somehow get a job as soon as she got there with no resume and no clue what her last few years of work experience might have looked like.

She shoved the wallet into her bag. Well, it always worked out for the girls in those cheesy Christmas movies, fleeing overbearing parents trying to set them up with the wrong man or demanding bosses in high-stress careers. Real life worked like a Hallmark movie, didn't it?

With a grimace, she turned back to the rack of maps. That *had* given her an idea. The heroines in those movies always landed in a small town somewhere, where people were a little friendlier and less concerned about pesky things like credentials and references. Where could she find a place like that?

Summer snatched a book labeled Southern Ontario off the rack. With spring still more than a month away, it was comforting to think about going to a place with the name southern in it, although southern Ontario wasn't much warmer than the rest of the country at this time of year. Still, psychologically it sounded appealing. She flipped idly through the pages. *God, lead me. Show me where to go.*

She blinked. Where had that come from? Did she have a faith? Although they both had a Catholic background, her parents hadn't taken her to church when she was growing up. Still, the prayer that had sprung into her mind felt right, somehow. She'd have to mull that over, maybe while she was driving. Search her soul, so to speak, to find out what she believed and what, exactly, her relationship was to the God she'd cried out to.

A picture caught her eye and she stopped flipping. An old mill sat at the edge of a narrow river, water flowing over small falls next to it. Something about the mill and the row of neat, cottagey-type houses with flowering vines climbing stone walls and trellises in backyard gardens spoke to her. Called to her even. Was this the place? Could it be the answer to her prayer?

She searched the page until she found the name. *Elora.* The word flowed over her like the water over the rocks in the picture. It sounded like something out of a fantasy novel, a kind of fairy village. A definite possibility. She whispered the name, something about it resonating with her deep inside, like a bird fluttering its wings slightly before settling back into its nest and tucking its head under a wing. She checked the location. About an hour and a half drive, which shouldn't be a problem in terms of fuel. Was it far enough away, though?

Summer, sé valiente. Yes. She needed courage. Also a job and a place to stay. But courage first. And coffee. Tucking the book under her arm, Summer wended her way around shelves of chips, groceries, and cleaning supplies to a coffee machine. After filling a brown paper cup and splashing in a dollop of cream, she snapped on a plastic lid and carried the cup and the book over to the counter.

A young man with straggly, shoulder-length brown hair punched the items into the cash register and grabbed her money without taking his eyes off the video game on the tablet on the counter. That was one benefit of their technology-obsessed society—fewer people would take the time to really look at her, let alone attempt to engage her in conversation. Of course—her eyes shot up to a cobweb-draped camera dangling from the ceiling in the corner of the store—electronic eyes were on her constantly, even if human ones weren't. Should she dye her hair? Get glasses? Try to change her appearance in some way like they did in the movies?

Summer almost giggled at the thought as she dropped her change into her wallet and picked up the book and coffee. *This isn't funny.* She sobered immediately. Of course her situation wasn't funny. Someone could be watching her even now, waiting to follow her. Could she be leading him straight to a small, innocent town whose friendly, unsuspecting citizens had no clue what havoc was about to descend upon the normally peaceful place?

God, please protect me. Protect anyone around me from any harm that might come to them because of me. The muscles that had tightened in her shoulders relaxed a little. All she could do was be as careful as possible and trust that God would watch over her. She had no idea where that trust had come from, but she felt it suddenly down deep in her bones. However it had come about, she *did* have a relationship with God. He was with her, and he would watch over her, wherever her journey took her.

Breathing a prayer of thanks for that assurance, Summer pushed open the door with her elbow and stepped into air so cold her breath came out in puffs of white clouds.

When she reached her car, she unlocked the vehicle with the remote and slid behind the wheel. After setting the coffee in the cup holder and tossing the book onto the passenger seat, she shut and locked the door. For a moment she sat, gripping the wheel with both gloved hands, gathering strength. Then she slid the key into the ignition and started the engine.

It was time to hit the road and see where it took her.

CHAPTER NINE

Jude drove through the parking lot of a coffee shop and wheeled into a spot. Snatching his phone from the cup holder, he studied the screen a moment, his brow furrowing. Where was she going? An hour ago she had driven through Toronto, heading west. Did she have a destination in mind? As far as he knew, Summer had no family outside of Toronto, other than back in Mexico. He'd been monitoring her bank and credit cards and she hadn't attempted to use either, which meant she had a limited supply of money and gas. So, what was her plan?

Feeling the need to stretch his legs, Jude climbed out of his car and strode into the coffee shop. He grabbed a coffee and a ham and cheese sandwich at the counter and headed back to the vehicle. No rush to keep up with her as he could monitor her movements as long as she was in her car, but he didn't want her getting too far away from him either.

Jude took a bite of his sandwich, drumming his fingers on the steering wheel in an attempt to dispel a little of the excess adrenaline pumping through him. What if she dumped the car like she had her phone? It was the last connection he had to her. The only way he could track her down.

And if she didn't, but stopped somewhere and found a place to stay, what then? Could he arrange some kind of "accidental" meeting? What if her memory suddenly came back? He stuffed the rest of the sandwich in the bag and tossed it on the passenger seat, too worked up to eat. He'd deal with each of those possibilities if and when they came up.

For now, all he had to do was figure out where she was and where, exactly, she was going.

Summer turned onto the road that led into Elora and crossed the metal bridge leading to the heart of the little town. It was as picturesque as it had appeared in the map book, even more so now, covered in a thick layer of snow. After the bridge, she turned left, drove down a block, then pulled over to the curb and turned off the engine. Ahead of her and across the street loomed the beautiful Elora Mill, the building that had attracted her interest in the book. For several minutes she gazed at the old stone structure, a hotel and fine-dining establishment, and the smaller building beside it, an elegant spa. She glanced down at her fingers and winced. What she wouldn't give for a manicure right about now. Or a pedicure. Or a massage. She rested her head against the back of the seat. Maybe one day. Judging from the look of the place, she'd need to make a bit of money first.

People wandered past her on the sidewalk, many with bags clutched in both hands. According to the book she'd bought, Elora was a popular place for tourists in the summer. Even now, weeks from spring, the quaint shops and pubs that lined the street on both sides appeared to be doing a steady business.

Which boded well for her and her job prospects. Summer grasped the handle and pushed open the car door. If she was going to stay here for awhile, it would be good to acquaint herself with the town, maybe see if any of the stores or coffee shops were hiring. She climbed out and closed the door, absently reaching behind her and hitting the lock button on her key fob as she started across the street. On her way to the Mill, she slowed, gazing at windows filled with high-end kitchen supplies and breathtaking artwork. After meandering to the end of the street, she reached the long stone wall that enclosed the towering limestone mill. The wall, covered in dry, brittle vines, extended past the building, and she wandered along it, letting her palm brush against the cool surface.

When the wall curved around the back of the building, she traipsed along the small footpath running beside it into a strand of trees. Once in the shade, she stopped and zipped her jacket up a little higher. Probably should have worn the gloves she'd taken off and tossed onto the seat with the map book while she was driving, but it was too late now. Fifty feet ahead, the path swung to the right. Summer stopped at the curve and leaned against the stone wall that followed the shape of the path, this section of it clearly designed to keep children and wayward tourists from venturing too close to the edge of the riverbank. Her head throbbed and her feet felt as though they were weighted down with bags of sand. In addition to the head trauma, a month of lying in a hospital bed had weakened her to the point where every step was an effort.

The sound of rushing water filled the air, and she gazed over the wall at the small waterfall she'd seen in the picture. Chunks of ice clung to rocks and tree limbs, and thirty feet past the waterfall the river had frozen over completely, the ice glistening in the thin February sun. A wonderland. What was it about this place? It felt familiar, somehow. Had she been here before?

She couldn't remember ever setting foot in this town, but somehow, as she gazed out over the rooftops of the houses on the far side of the river, she was filled with a sense of something she couldn't quite identify. Home, maybe? Perhaps the place reminded her of somewhere else she had been. Or maybe—she pressed a hand to her chest—maybe she had been here in the last few years and the memory of the town was one of the countless others that had been erased from her mind. She turned and sagged against the stone. If she had been here, did she know anyone in town? Would someone recognize her? If so, maybe she wasn't as safe as she'd hoped.

Summer lowered her hand and pushed herself away from the wall. She was here now and, for reasons she couldn't explain, she felt safe. Unless something happened to make her feel otherwise, she was going to stay put.

An acrid smell wafted on the air. Summer looked down and frowned. Someone had tossed a cigarette butt into a cleared area beneath a tree. A dry, rust-brown leaf curled beneath the still-burning butt, tendrils of smoke winding up around its edges. She frowned. The tree could have caught on fire. How could anyone be so careless? She strode over and stomped on the leaf and the cigarette, grinding both deep into the ground until she was certain any chance of a flare-up had passed. Summer glanced around. She hadn't noticed anyone else on the pathway, but someone had clearly been in the area in the last few minutes. A cool breeze skimmed her cheeks and she shivered. *Get a grip, Summer. No one knows you're here.* The news the police detective had given her had rattled her more than she'd realized. If she was going to hide away in this town and concentrate on getting her memories back, she'd have to get over it, stop jumping at every noise and looking for danger where none existed.

Drawing in a deep, steadying breath, she retraced her steps out of the trees and back to the row of little shops, searching each window she passed by to see if any were advertising for help. At the end of the first block, she sank down on a picnic table set up outside an ice cream shop. What was she doing? First, she needed a place to stay. Even if someone was hiring, and she hadn't seen any signs yet, no one was likely to give her a second look if she didn't have an address or phone number to give them. Bad enough she didn't have a resume and couldn't tell them about her work experience.

She frowned. What *was* her work experience? She was 28 years old—surely she'd been working the last few years. But at what? What kind of skills did she have? She'd waited tables to put herself through university, she did remember that much. Her final year was a bit fuzzy though, and she couldn't remember anything after that. What had she done with her education? What did one do with a degree in political science? Politics seemed like a good bet, or some kind of diplomatic job. Summer clenched her fist and pounded it lightly against her forehead. *Piensa. Think. Who are you and what do you do?* As Dr. Lopez had warned, straining to remember did nothing but intensify the throbbing in her head.

Why hadn't she asked her mother and father? The last week had been so filled with tests and conversations with her doctor and with thoughts of leaving the hospital that it hadn't occurred to her to think much beyond that. Until last night, she'd assumed she would have all the time in the world to talk to her parents and get them to fill in at least part of the gaping black hole that was the last few years of her life. Especially since she'd thought she would be living with them for a while.

And speaking of her identity, was it safe to give out her real name while she was here? What if a prospective employee Googled her or somehow put it online that she was here in town? She bit her lip. Googling herself was actually a good idea. As soon as she could get to a computer, she would do that, maybe get some answers about who she was and what she did.

In the meantime, what name should she give herself? Something a little more Spanish than Summer would be believable. She had asked her mother once where her name had come from, as it wasn't a common one in Mexico. Her mother had told her that she and her dad had been looking for something different, so they'd settled on Summer, her mother's favorite season and the time of year Summer had been born, since her birthday was in August. Valid reasons that made sense. At least growing up she didn't have any other girls in the class with her name.

Summer's best friend all through grade school was Ana. Summer had loved her friend's name and often wished it had been hers. Maybe it could be—temporarily, anyway. It was an interesting concept, naming yourself. How many people got to do that? She managed a wry grin. There had to be one or two upsides to the situation she found herself in, didn't there?

What about a last name? Garcia was one of the most common surnames in Mexico. If she went with Garcia, maybe whoever Googled her would give up before making it through the long list of names that popped up. Summer tapped her nails on the table. Or maybe she should make it a little easier than that for someone to find her alterego. An idea formed slowly in her head and she opened her bag to retrieve her phone. Maybe she didn't have a paper resume, but she might be able to produce something every bit as good—better, even—if asked by a prospective employer. All she had to do was create a LinkedIn profile with the name she chose for herself and a few years of manufactured work experience and she'd be all set.

Summer wrinkled her nose. Other than a few glaring holes—the fact that she would be lying and misrepresenting herself to someone looking into hiring her, and that she would actually have to be able to perform whatever workplace duties she claimed to have experience in, when in all likelihood she didn't—it was a perfect plan.

She searched through her bag for a few seconds before remembering she no longer had a phone and closed the bag again. She flicked a straw lying on the table and watched it spin around in a circle before dropping between the wooden slats. Summer didn't move for a few seconds, until her conscience got the better of her and she slid off the bench, crouched down, and retrieved the straw. After depositing it in the nearest garbage can, already overflowing with empty cups and napkins, she brushed off her hands and trudged back to the picnic table.

Now what? There had to be a library in town. Would they have computers available for public use? She should go and search to see if there were any rooms or apartments for rent in town. Although the possibility of finding one that didn't require first and last month's rent and a credit check was slim. Summer sighed as she propped her elbow on the table and rested her head on her hand. Trying to stay positive when at every turn she hit a wall as solid as the stone one she'd walked along moments before was exhausting.

Maybe she should go back to the home she didn't recognize as hers and take her chances that the man who had attacked her there had been bluffing and wouldn't actually come back to finish the job that he had started.

CHAPTER TEN

Díaz propped a shoulder against the stone wall that ran along the side of the Elora Mill, down to the river, and pressed the phone to his ear, waiting through three rings. He was shivering, although he had no idea whether that was because of the light dusting of frost clinging to the wall or apprehension over his impending conversation. Both, maybe. Finally, the call connected, and a deep, raspy voice on the other end barked out, "Dígame."

"She's in Elora."

"Excelente."

"You want me to bring her to you?"

"No, todavía no. Solo obsérvala."

"Just watch her?" Díaz shrugged. "You're the boss. Shouldn't be too hard. She has no idea I followed her here."

"¿Que hay del otro?"

"Kendrick?" Díaz shot a nervous look toward the street. "No sign of him yet. I don't think he knows she's here. I'll watch for him though."

"Dame cualquier información inmediatamente."

He scratched his eyebrow with his thumbnail. "Of course I'll let you know everything that's going on. That's what you pay me for, isn't it?"

His boss chuckled. "Eso, y otras cosas."

Díaz winced. A few other things was right. Truth was, he did a lot of things for his boss. Things he never thought he'd do. He had to take care of his family, though. "I'll call when I have news. Let me know when you want me to move in." He stabbed the disconnect button before the voice on the other end could issue any further instructions. If he didn't hear them, he didn't have to carry them out.

Díaz leaned against the wall and watched the water tumbling over the dam until the cold of the stone seeped through the arm of his jacket and he pushed away. Shoving the phone into his pocket, he shot one more look toward the river. Then he went to do his job.

CHAPTER ELEVEN

From halfway down the block, Jude watched Summer as she sat at a picnic table, seemingly oblivious to the people passing by. A pair of binoculars lay on the seat beside him, but with all these people milling around, he didn't dare use them. When she rested her head on her hand, he frowned. She'd only been out of the hospital for a few hours—was she exhausted or in pain? Or was it hitting her all of a sudden that she had no place to go, nowhere to stay? All three, most likely.

Would she give up and go home? He actually preferred her in a small town where it would be easier to keep tabs on her. Although, to badly misquote Humphrey Bogart, of all the small towns in all the provinces in the country, why did she have to wander into this one? Any town would have been better for him than Elora. What could have enticed her to come here, of all places? He wiped away the beads of sweat that had formed on his forehead, despite the cold day, with the side of his hand.

At least she was out from under the influence of her meddling parents. It had been impossible to get close with the two of them hovering around her all the time, filling her head with lies. Now that she was away from them, nothing would stop him from getting to her. He just had to keep her from leaving town so he could choose the time and place.

Jude grabbed his phone and did a quick search for rooms for rent in the area. A couple of them were way out of her price range—and his—but the third one on the list caught his eye. He scanned the details before hitting the phone number in the ad. The woman who answered sounded friendly enough, and he made arrangements to come over right away to look at the room. That done, Jude shot one last glance down the street. ˋSummer hadn't moved. If his plan was going to work, she needed to stay put for the next half hour or so. Given the lines of fatigue grooved into her face, chances were she wasn't going anywhere.

He pulled onto the street and stopped at a bank where he made a withdrawal from the ATM before driving the few blocks to the address the woman had given him. The street the house was on was lined with tall, overhanging trees, and the homes were large and looked to be at least seventy or eighty years old. Jude pulled up to the curb in front of the one in the ad and turned off the car. The house was one of the biggest on the block. Although it hadn't been kept up as well as it might have been—the paint was peeling in spots and the curling shingles suggested the roof could definitely stand to be replaced—the word that sprang to his mind when he looked at it was *stately*.

The white clapboard house was nestled far back on the property and surrounded by towering maples. A stone walkway wended its way from the sidewalk to the double front doors. Large windows graced both stories, which meant the inside would be bright and warm. Jude shoved open the car door and half-jogged up the walkway.

Before he could reach the front doors, they both swung open. A tall, thin woman stood in the doorway. She looked to be in her mid-sixties, with long, red, frizzy hair that was doing its best to escape the clip at the back and spring up all over her head. She wore some kind of flowing navy dress covered in flowers nearly as bright as the grin that spread across her face as he approached. She stuck out her hand. "Nancy Snodgrass."

That fit. Jude grasped the cool, bony one in his and shook it firmly. "Nice to meet you. Thanks for letting me come by."

"My pleasure. You said you were looking at the room for someone else?"

"Yes, actually. A woman who arrived in town today and has nowhere to go. I thought of her when I saw your ad."

Nancy let go of him and swept her arm through the air with a flourish. "Come on in. You can tell me a bit more about her while I show you the room."

The smell of a roast cooking filled the air, and his mouth watered. When was the last time he'd had a home-cooked meal? Pushing back the thought—and the sudden surge of nostalgia—Jude followed her across the spacious entryway and up the Gone-with-the-Wind-style staircase. Like the outside, the inside of the house showed its age. The wooden floorboards creaked when he stepped on them and the carpet on the stairs was worn thin in spots. Still, everything looked neat and clean and antiques graced every shelf and table in sight.

At the top of the stairs, he followed Nancy down a long narrow hallway to the last room on the left. When she opened it, Jude nodded. This was the place. A four-poster bed took up half the room. The rest was filled with a tall dresser that lined one wall, a wardrobe, and a rocking chair in a corner by the window, a wool blanket tossed over the back of it invitingly. A round, plush carpet covered almost the entire floor. The walls were white and the sheer curtains were covered in pastel flowers. The room was perfect.

"How long will your friend be staying?" Nancy crossed the floor and pushed open a door.

"I'm not sure. I can pay you for a month up front, if it's okay to go month to month." Jude stuck his head into the small washroom with the clawfoot tub and washbasin sink.

When he stepped back, Nancy leaned against the frame, crossed her arms over her chest, and tapped a foot. For a long moment she studied him, as though assessing his intentions.

Jude met her gaze steadily. She had to agree to let this room to Summer. Although that would be the easy part of his two-step idea.

"What's her name?"

He hesitated. Was Summer using her real name now that she was on the run? She'd been smart enough to lose her phone, she'd likely think of that too. "I'll let her introduce herself to you, if you don't mind."

The landlady shrugged. "Does she have a job?"

"Not yet. But she's a hard worker. She'll be out first thing tomorrow, looking for something."

Nancy pursed her lips. "And you say she has nowhere else to go?"

"That's right. It was a spontaneous decision, coming here. She didn't have time to make plans."

"Hmm." She continued to study him as though he were a piece of art hanging in a museum she felt compelled to interpret. When he was growing up, Jude's mother had watched a lot of re-runs of the sitcom *Alice*, about a waitress in a diner called Mel's. Nancy reminded him of another of the waitresses in the diner, Flo. Could have been her sister, actually. He half-expected her to pull a pencil out from behind her ear and point it at him. "Running from the law?"

That stopped the smile that had been about to cross his face fast. Jude blinked. "No, of course not. She wouldn't jaywalk if someone paid her to."

Nancy huffed out a breath. "All right then. I don't know why, but I'm inclined to trust you to vouch for her. She can stay one month, and we'll see how it goes."

"Excellent." Jude tugged the wallet from the back pocket of his jeans. "I do have a favor to ask though."

She tilted her head and more red curls sprang loose and boinged around her ears. "What's that?"

"She can't know that I've paid for her room. She's kind of proud and independent. Any chance you could tell her that she can pay you at the end of the month, to give her time to get a job and earn the money?"

"I'm not in the habit of lying, mister."

"And I'm not in the habit of asking people to. But I know her, and I'm pretty sure she'd sleep on the street rather than take this room if she thought I was somehow involved in getting it for her."

"How's she going to know about the place then?"

Jude took a deep breath. This was the tricky part. "I, uh..."

She planted a fist on one flowered hip. "Spit it out."

"Well, I was sort of hoping you might be willing to go downtown and, if she's still where I saw her last, kind of bump into her, start a conversation. Somehow work around to the fact that you're looking for someone to take the room you've got for rent. That way she'd think it was coming from you, not me."

He hadn't realized she was chewing gum until she snapped it loudly. Exactly like Flo. "Got it all figured out, don't ya?"

It felt like a rhetorical question, so Jude held his tongue.

After a few interminably long seconds, Nancy pushed away from the frame. "Lucky for you, I blocked out the afternoon to show the room to potential renters, so I've got a little time on my hands. And I happen to be in the mood for a challenge."

Jude let out a breath. "That's great, thanks so—"

She held up a hand. "I haven't done anything yet. I might not be able to find her. Even if I do, she may not agree to come home with me, a perfect stranger. Hold off on any thanks until we see if this cockamamie plan of yours even works."

He pulled four one-hundred-dollar bills out of his wallet and held them up. "I'm willing to bet this much that you'd be able to talk anybody into doing pretty much anything."

She hesitated before reaching for the bills. "Takes a smooth talker to know one, don't it?"

Another rhetorical question. Jude grinned.

"How will I know her?"

He found a picture on his phone and handed her the device. Nancy studied the screen for a moment before handing it back. "I guess I can see why you're so willing to help her out."

Heat coursed through his chest. "It's not like that."

"Sure it ain't." She snapped her gum again and started back through the bedroom. "Let's go then. If she's the kind of person you described, she likely won't sit around doing nothing for long."

That was true. Jude caught up with Nancy in the front foyer and touched her arm. "Thanks again for doing this. And could you do me one more favor?"

Nancy bent down and tugged a pair of boots on over her knee-high striped socks. When she straightened, her green eyes met his. "Seems you've about used up all your favors for one day."

"I know I have. But would you mind pretending you don't know me if I show up here at the house? I really don't want her to figure out I had anything to do with her finding this place."

Nancy tugged on a wool coat and pulled open the front door. "Since I don't know you, not even your name, that shouldn't be a problem."

Jude suppressed a smile as he followed her out the door. Yes, Nancy was going to do just fine as a landlady. Now all he had to do was pray that Summer would think so too. Otherwise it would be on to Plan C.

CHAPTER TWELVE

I can't sit around here all day. Summer closed the map book with a snap. Except that she had no idea where she should go. She rubbed her hands together, trying to keep the circulation going. *God, could you show me? Give me some kind of sign? I really have no—*

"Excuse me."

Summer looked up, shading her eyes with one hand and trying not to wince at the pain the bright light sent shooting through her head. A woman wearing a beige wool coat over a floral dress, curly red hair poking out beneath a cream-colored knit hat, stood on the other side of the picnic table clutching a paper takeout cup. The rich aroma of chocolate drifted on the steam that curled out of the hole on the top.

"The other table is taken. Do you mind?" The woman gestured to the bench across from her.

"Of course not." Summer grabbed the book and her purse and started to get up. "I was about to leave anyway."

"Oh, please don't rush off on my account. I'd enjoy a little company while I drink this."

The hint of wistfulness in the woman's voice stopped Summer and she sank back down on the bench. *Where do I have to be?* "I can stay for a few more minutes."

"Wonderful." The woman lifted the skirt of her dress with her free hand and swung one leg over the bench. When she was settled, she reached across the table. "Nancy Snodgrass."

Summer's mouth went a little dry. Could she do this? She grasped the woman's hand. "Ana Santos." The surname slipped off her tongue before she had a chance to second-guess it. Too late now. She had committed to being Ana Santos for the foreseeable future. Better get used to it.

The woman nodded and let go of her hand. "Beautiful name. Spanish, right? Where are you from?"

"Mexico. Although I've lived in Canada for ten years." *No dés tanta información. Way too much. Keep your answers brief.* She swallowed. Living a double life was going to take a bit of getting used to.

"And how long have you been in Elora?"

Summer licked her lips. "About an hour. It's a lovely town."

Nancy glanced around. "It is that. One of the prettiest in Ontario. We're quite proud of it. Are you passing through?"

She hesitated. Something about this woman invited trust. Which could be dangerous. Summer shifted on the bench. "I'm not sure yet. I was thinking about maybe staying awhile, but I'll have to see if I can get a job."

Nancy took a sip of the hot chocolate and wiped a smudge of whipped cream off her upper lip. "Where are you planning to stay?"

Summer let out a nervous laugh. "I haven't quite figured that out yet."

For a long moment the woman studied her. A drop of melting whipped cream slid down the side of the cup before she made a tsking noise with her tongue. "Well, you can't sleep on the street. This might sound a little crazy, but I have a room for rent."

Alarm bells went off in Summer's head. A complete stranger happened to have a room available in her home?

Nancy tugged a napkin from the pocket of her coat and swiped it over her fingers. Then she pulled a phone from the large yellow purse she'd set on the bench beside her. "I can see what you're thinking. A perfect stranger offers you a place to stay, out of the blue. Likely running one of them rings you hear about on the news, right?" She typed something into the phone and turned the screen toward Summer. "I don't blame you—pretty girl like you can't be too careful. Not that there's a lot of that sort of thing happening in our little town. That I know of. But to set your mind at ease, here's the ad I placed this morning."

Summer scanned the screen. Sure enough, a woman named Nancy had placed an ad for an available room. But the monthly rate, while reasonable, was a lot more than she had access to at the moment. She shook her head. "I don't have a job yet. I'm afraid I wouldn't be able to pay you."

The woman slid the device back into her purse and zipped it closed. "I'll be honest with you. I rent out the room less for the money than to have another human being in the house. I never want to become one of those crazy old women who talks to their cats and no one else. So I only have one cat—you aren't allergic, are you?—and I let out one room so my voice isn't the only one echoing off the walls of the old place."

Summer struggled to keep up with the stream of words coming from the woman. Clearly she *was* in need of someone to talk to. The room must have been empty for a while. She repressed a smile. "No, I'm not allergic."

"That's good. As you can imagine, I'm a little particular about who I share my home with. I've been putting off advertising because I didn't want to have to sift through the hordes of people answering my ad to try and find the one I'm looking for. I always do know, you understand, when I see her. And I ain't been wrong yet. Leastwise, God hasn't failed me yet. I always pray before I start looking that he'll bring the right one along and that I'll know her when I meet her. Thing is, I knew the moment you looked up and smiled at me that you were the one. You'd be doing me a huge favor if you saved me the time and aggravation of interviewing a long line of people traipsing through my house."

"But..." Summer's mind whirled. The woman had prayed about the room? Was this God then, working everything out? Or was she being naïve and walking straight into some kind of dangerous situation? She almost laughed. The woman across from her didn't look like she would hurt a fly. Surely Summer could trust her. She repressed a sigh. Frankly, she didn't have a lot of choice.

Nancy reached over and covered Summer's hand with her slightly sticky one. "I know you don't have the money right now. But I peg you for a hard worker. I reckon you'll get a job quick enough. I'm more than willing to wait a little, end of the month even, to get the money."

"But do you really want me living in your house? You don't even know me."

Nancy squeezed her hand before leaning back on the bench. "I'm not sure I understand it myself, but I'm not sure when the last time was that I was so sure about anything."

Summer blew out a breath. "Well, if you're that sure"—she offered the woman, her new landlady, apparently, a wry grin—"then thank you. I accept."

"Good." Nancy took another sip of the hot drink and wiped her lips with the napkin. "Let's go home, shall we?"

Those were words Summer hadn't dared dream she would hear for a long time. She gathered her things and stood. God had answered her prayer, more quickly and beautifully than she could have imagined. If her faith was the only thing she ever recaptured from her life over the last few years, that just might be enough.

CHAPTER THIRTEEN

From his vantage point a block away, Jude watched as Summer got into her car and followed Nancy's beast of a vehicle down the street. So his *cockamamie* plan had worked. About time one of his plans went the way it was supposed to.

His phone jangled and he glanced at the screen. *Moser.* Jude snatched it up and pressed it to his ear. "Yeah."

"Did you find her?"

He ran his fingers through his hair. "Yeah, I found her."

"Are you gonna bring her in?"

His stomach tightened. "Not yet."

He waited through the long pause that followed, until Moser broke the silence. "The boss man isn't happy about you taking off like this. How long are you planning to stay gone?"

"As long as it takes."

Moser released his breath with a hiss, and Jude moved the phone slightly away from his ear. "What do you want me to tell him?"

"Tell him this is something I need to do. I'll come back as soon as I can."

"With her?"

"That's the idea."

"He wants you to bring her to see him."

"I'm sure he does. It's going to take some time though. I have to move slowly, get her to trust me before I can make a move. I have no idea how long that will take."

"Well, I recommend you get your tail back here sooner than later, or you may not have anything to come back to."

"Not gonna lie to you, Mose, none of that really matters to me at the moment."

"What about your clients?"

He slumped against the back of the seat. "Let them know I'll be back as soon as I can. If they need anything, they can contact you or Joe."

"Look, Jude." Moser's voice softened. "I know you're going through a hard time, but think about what you're doing. Do you really want to throw away everything you've worked so hard for?"

"Of course not. But this is something I have to do."

Another long silence before Moser sighed. "Keep in touch, okay?"

"I will." Jude hit the end-call button and tossed the phone onto the seat beside him. He glanced down the street. Both vehicles had disappeared, although a cloud of the thick black exhaust belching from the tailpipe of Nancy's old boat still hung in the air, dissipating slowly to drift over the wall surrounding the mill. Jude shook his head. That ancient Impala of hers had backfired twice when he'd followed her downtown. The first time he'd nearly driven up over a curb. No doubt it would freak Summer out too, after everything she'd been through.

He blew out a breath. Nothing he could do about that. She was in the fire-engine-red-finger-nailed hands of Nancy Snodgrass now. Jude turned the key in the ignition and pulled away from the curb. Now that he'd found a place for Summer to stay, he needed to figure out his own plans. From what he could remember, there was a cheap motel on the outskirts of town where it wasn't likely he'd run into anyone he knew. Jude turned down a side street, drove two blocks, then turned left. He slowed his vehicle as he approached a house on the right with gray siding and black shutters framing every window. A lump rose in his throat that he could barely breathe around as he pulled up to the curb and stopped. For thirty seconds he stared at the place. The driveway was empty and there were no signs of life behind the white lace curtains hanging in the main floor windows.

Just as well. Jude shoved the transmission into drive and pulled back onto the street. Twenty minutes later he'd checked into the Wayside Motel. He grabbed the remote, flopped onto the brown and orange floral bedspread, and pointed it at the TV screwed into the top of an old scratched wooden cabinet. He flipped through all twelve available channels. Nothing but soaps and daytime talk shows. With a groan of disgust, he turned off the TV, tossed the remote onto the bed, and clasped his hands behind his head as he stared up at the water-stained ceiling.

Now what?

CHAPTER FOURTEEN

Summer sank down onto the yellow bedspread, her legs about to give out. Was this actually happening? Twenty-four hours ago she'd been in a hospital bed. Now she had moved into the home of a complete stranger. Of course, pretty much everyone she encountered was a stranger these days, since she couldn't remember anyone she had met in the last few years.

A calico cat leapt up beside her and brushed past Summer before settling himself in a ball at the foot of the bed. A loud, purring sound drifted from him almost immediately. Summer ran a hand over the multi-colored back. "What a sweetie."

"His name is Charles Dickens. And that confirms it." Nancy pushed her way into the bedroom with an armload of clean, folded, mint-green towels. "Here you go, hon." She plunked them down on the dresser.

Still stroking the soft fur, Summer tilted her head. "Confirms what?"

"That I made the right choice. Charlie is an excellent judge of character. Clearly he's as convinced as I am that you are the roommate we've been looking for."

Summer studied the cat, eyes closed as though he had already settled in for a long nap. "Well, I agree with you both. This place feels like home already."

"Good." Nancy gripped the white post at the corner of the bed. "I'm going to finish making dinner now, so you have time to settle in before you join me. Let me know if there's anything else you need, you hear?"

Summer smiled. "I will, Nancy. Thank you so much."

"It's my pleasure, darlin'. I'm happy for the company."

"Can I help you make supper?"

"Not tonight. First day's a freebie. After that we can work out a schedule, take turns cooking and cleaning up. Sound good?"

"Sounds perfect."

Nancy flapped a hand in her direction before disappearing into the hallway. Summer stretched out on the bed and stared up at the ceiling, white stucco framed by eight-inch crown molding. She only had a handful of things to unpack—she could take a few minutes to rest and attempt to process everything that had happened in the last twenty-four hours. *And what will happen next.*

Which reminded her, she still needed to set up her LinkedIn profile. She just needed a few minutes to gather up the energy to move... Thirty minutes later, she forced herself to swing her legs over the side of the bed and sit up. Her head hurt a little less, but exhaustion still weighed on her like one of those aprons the dentist spread over her before she had an x-ray done. She had to keep moving, though. Had to get out her tablet and set up that... Her shoulders sagged. She'd left the tablet her parents had brought her in the drawer of the little table beside her bed in the hospital. Maybe that was for the best, though. If someone wanted to find her badly enough, they could probably use the IP address to track her down. Summer swallowed. It was next to impossible to hide in this age of electronics, but she was going to give it her best shot.

She padded down the hallway and descended the wide staircase. Nancy was chopping vegetables in the kitchen when Summer walked in, but she looked up and pointed a carrot at her when she entered the room. "You must be used to those instant, microwaveable dishes you kids eat so much of these days. Takes me a bit longer than that to prepare dinner since I make it all from scratch."

Summer laughed. Kid? She hadn't been called that for a few years. "Oh no, I'm not looking for dinner already. I was wondering if there's a library in town."

Nancy glanced over at the rooster-shaped clock on the wall. "There's one on the main street, but it won't be open now. Closes at three on Saturdays. Were you looking for something to read? I've got a few shelves of books in the study right down the hallway past the dining room and to your right." She gestured with the carrot, tiny peelings spraying across the counter.

"Actually, I was hoping to use one of their computers, but I can go tomorrow."

Nancy shook her head, red curls flying. "Not open Sundays at all. Small towns, you know. It'll open at ten on Monday, but you don't need to go all the way over there for a computer." She set the carrot down on the board and wiped her hands on the red and white polka dotted apron she'd tied around her waist. "I've got one out here in the dining room you can use."

Summer frowned. "I don't want to impose any more than I already have."

Nancy waved away her protests. "I barely use it myself. I only have it because my son insisted on getting it for me. I do check it once in awhile for emails, but mostly the poor thing sits in here gathering dust." As if to prove her point, she scooped up the bottom of her apron and swiped it over the screen of the ancient desktop monitor before jabbing a skinny finger at the power button. The monitor crackled and hummed as it struggled to turn on.

Oh dear. Better post that profile as soon as possible, while the poor thing still had a bit of life in it.

Nancy tapped the back of the chair. "You sit right down here and do whatever it is you wanted to do. Until you start making enough money to buy one for yourself, we'll make this the house computer."

Summer slid onto the chair. "All right, if you're sure."

"I'm as sure as... well, do we need to go through all that again?"

"I suppose I could save us both some time and assume that, if you say something, you're sure about it."

Nancy patted her on the shoulder. "Now you're getting it. You do your thing and I'll go finish with dinner."

It took a few minutes for the old machine to warm up, but Summer was relieved to find there was Internet service. After shooting a quick look at the kitchen, she typed her name into the search bar. The only item that appeared on the screen that appeared to have anything to do with her was a brief news article on the attack. Clearly the police were keeping a tight lid on any information they had gathered, as the journalist shared fewer details than the detective had when she'd come to see Summer.

She switched to Facebook. Although she couldn't remember her password, she did a search for her name. Lots of profiles popped up, but none with her picture. A search of other social media sites yielded the same results. If she had been active on any of them, she no longer was. Had someone gone through and erased her from the sites? Or had she been so influenced by her intensely private parents growing up that she'd been reluctant to share any part of her life online? Either way, from a virtual standpoint, it was as though she had never existed.

Repressing a sigh of frustration, Summer created a LinkedIn profile for Ana Santos, complete with a history of waiting tables and serving coffee because she did remember doing both during her university days. It had been hard work, but she didn't mind that. In fact, the harder the better as it might keep her mind off of her parents' attempts to control her life and the ongoing threat of a dangerous stranger showing up at her doorstep.

Shoving away the anger that threatened to rise, Summer spent a few minutes searching various sites for job postings in town. A couple of ads looked interesting—one for a waitress and another for a store clerk—and she made a note to drop into the establishments on Monday before powering down the computer again.

Ana Santos had an online presence now. Her new life had begun.

CHAPTER FIFTEEN

Díaz rolled down the window of his car to let a little fresh air waft through the vehicle. He'd been watching the big white clapboard house for two hours and no one had come or gone. Maybe he'd call it a day. He knew where Velásquez was staying, and she'd likely be here for a while. He hadn't received the order to move in yet, so he could come back tomorrow and stake out the place for another few hours. What did he care? It was on the boss's dime.

And so was dinner. He glanced at his watch. Might as well go grab something before checking into the Torchlight Inn, which sounded like a fancy establishment but was actually a fleabag motel, one of the few in town he could afford on his budget.

A blue Impala drove past him and Díaz straightened. Was that the redhead? He rolled up the window and slumped down in his seat. The vehicle turned into the driveway of the house he'd been watching. A few seconds later, the woman he'd scoped out the day before when she pulled into the driveway ahead of Velásquez popped out of the driver's side door, red frizzy curls flapping against her neck.

Díaz rolled his eyes at the tree-hugger get-up she had on. That one could be trouble. He knew the type. All soft on the planet and animals and people too, if it came to that. She might take it upon herself to be some kind of protector over her new boarder. Maybe she even owned a shotgun. He could see it, her storming out of the place, aiming a massive weapon at him and ordering him off her property.

He grunted. Never underestimate the eccentric, that was his motto. You never knew what they were going to do. Unpredictable.

And if there was anything he hated, it was unpredictable people.

Of course, Velásquez was no pushover either. Díaz's gaze followed the landlady up the walkway until she disappeared through the door. When he'd waited fifteen more minutes with nothing going on, he straightened and turned the key in the ignition. He'd have to carry out his boss's orders, no matter how many crazy, unpredictable women tried to get in his way. If he didn't, his family wouldn't eat.

Failure was not an option, so when the boss gave the order, he was going in. Shotgun or no shotgun.

CHAPTER SIXTEEN

The town was small, but by Summer's third day of traversing the downtown streets, including the steep one that led up through the center of downtown, her legs shook. Almost everyone she had encountered when she'd gone into the stores and businesses had been friendly. Unfortunately, their good will did not extend to hiring strangers off the street to work in their shops.

She'd inquired at thirteen of them over the last couple of days but had been politely rebuffed at each. Three of the managers had encouraged her to come back in a couple of months, when tourist season was starting up again, as they might have something for her then. Problem was, Summer didn't have a couple of months. Not if she hoped to stay in Elora and avoid returning to her parents' home, pleading forgiveness for leaving so they'd allow her to stay and take advantage of their charity.

Which is exactly what it would feel like at this point. Charity seasoned with humiliating defeat. Given the way her parents had manipulated her, that would crush her spirit more than anything that had happened in the last few days. She shook her head. More important than her ego was the fact that it wasn't safe to return to her parents'. If someone was still after her, that was the first place they'd look, which would put not only her but her father and mother in danger. As much as they had angered her by treating her like a child, she couldn't do that to them. She had to figure this out on her own.

Nancy hadn't even bothered asking her at dinner the night before how the job search was going. Obviously Summer wore her frustration like the only job-hunting-worthy outfit she'd brought with her—a short black and red plaid skirt, black tights, and long-sleeved red sweater.

A door to the shop she was passing by opened at that moment, and a cloud of the most delicious aroma Summer had ever smelled wafted outside, accompanied by the sweet tinkling of bells, like something out of a movie. Maybe she actually *had* ventured into a scene from Hallmark. She wouldn't be at all opposed to the idea at the moment, since it would mean she was destined to find her happily ever after here.

Taking a slow, deep breath, Summer closed her eyes, tipped her head back slightly, and analyzed the tantalizing smells like a connoisseur would the bouquet of a fine wine. Coffee, fresh-baked bread, and... She took another sniff and let out a sigh of pure bliss. Chocolate. That combination had to be what heaven smelled like, didn't it?

Her sagging spirits buoyed, Summer followed her nose through the door and into the small bakery. A cup of coffee and even a tiny taste of whatever was emitting that fabulous chocolate scent and she might have the energy and the courage to carry on with her search.

A young man had hopped off his bike while she'd been standing there. He locked it into the metal stand in front of the bakery and pulled open the door so she could go in. Summer smiled and nodded at him as she entered the warm, cozy bakery, the aromas inside even headier than those that had drifted out the door.

The place was small, with a stool-lined bar running under the front window and six or seven small round tables scattered across the wood-hewn floor. Brightly-colored paintings covered the walls, a sign describing them as works done by local artists. Wooden shelves filled with books filled the wall space above and down both sides of the mantel of a fireplace that was likely gas but looked remarkably real. It was one of the most welcoming spaces Summer had ever been in. Once she had her life figured out a little better, she was definitely going to spend a lot of time at the—she glanced at the sign on the wall behind the cash register—Taste of Heaven Café. She grinned. Obviously she wasn't the first person to liken the little shop to paradise.

Overwhelmed by the long counter covered by platters of baked goods of various kinds, she waved the biker ahead of her in line. He stepped to the counter and ordered a large black coffee and a nut and seed health bar. Seriously? Who had the self-control to walk out of this place carrying the sum total of about a hundred calories? She rolled her eyes. Somebody who could look like that in athletic wear, that's who. And who rode his bike when the ground was covered in two feet of snow.

Not that she was going to worry about that today. She'd had a rough few days—few weeks, actually—and she was definitely going to treat herself to something sinfully decadent. She scanned the row of goodies and knew as soon as her gaze landed on the pastry what she wanted. Summer strolled to the counter. A woman about her age grinned at her, deepening the dimple to the right side of her round, freckled face. "What can I get you?"

"Large coffee with double cream and a chocolate croissant, please." Just saying the words sent a thrill of anticipation through Summer.

"Coming right up." The woman, whose name tag identified her as Daphne, rang up her purchase, handed her the change, and went to retrieve her drink and pastry. In less than a minute she was back, handing Summer a large steaming cup and a plate with the croissant on it.

"Thanks so much." Summer accepted both from her and took a few steps toward an empty stool at the front window. On impulse, she turned back. "You aren't by any chance hiring, are you?"

The woman tilted her head, her blonde ponytail brushing her shoulder. "Not officially, no."

Not officially? What did that mean? "So, unofficially then?"

The woman laughed and looked around the room. Summer followed her gaze. Three women sat at one table, deep in conversation punctuated by rounds of laughter. Four other tables were occupied by people working away on laptops or staring at their phones. No one had come into the shop since the guy in front of Summer had breezed out and jumped onto his bike. The woman nodded toward the front window. "Why don't I grab a coffee and we'll chat for a few minutes."

"Great." Her heart rate picked up as she wended her way around a couple of empty tables and settled onto a stool. Was it possible the woman would consider recommending that her boss hire Summer? Working in a place like this would be a welcome respite from everything that was going on in her life at the moment. *God, if this is where I'm meant to be, help the owner or manager or whoever makes those decisions to see that.* She contemplated the brief prayer. It still shocked her how easily the words came to her, but it comforted her too. Although she couldn't remember how she'd come to have a faith, it felt more real and true than anything else in her life, a huge missing piece of the puzzle the last few years had become.

Even if it didn't work out to get a job here, she'd enjoy her croissant—still warm where it rested against her thumb as Summer set the plate down on the bar—maybe make a new friend, and then be on her way, having discovered a haven she could come to whenever she needed to get away from the chaos around her.

The woman, an apron tied around the long pink shirt she wore over brightly-flowered tights, set a large blue mug on the bar and plunked herself down on the stool beside Summer. "I'm Daphne, as you can see." She pointed to her name tag. "Daphne Cook."

"Ana Santos."

Daphne picked up her mug. "I haven't seen you in here before."

"I've never been. Although I definitely plan to become a regular."

"That's good to hear."

Summer shifted on the seat to face her. "I'm new to Elora, actually. Which is why I asked if you were hiring." She shot a glance at the kitchen entrance. "Should I talk to a supervisor or the owner?"

"That would be me, hon. My husband and I bought the place eight months ago. He's the baker, and I handle the front counter." She sipped her coffee and set down the mug. "I know, I know, Cook the baker. I've heard all the jokes so you can save yourself the trouble." The dimple flashed again.

Summer grinned. "I wouldn't dream of it." Not after she'd faced Summer jokes during all the other seasons of the year since moving to Canada. She couldn't share any of those with Daphne, of course.

"What brought you to Elora?"

Her chest tightened a little. Dangerous territory. "I needed a new start."

"Man trouble?"

You have no idea. "Something like that."

Daphne picked up her mug again. "I get that, honey." She glanced over at the kitchen. "Not now, of course. Thankfully I emerged from the swamp of pathetic, flopping fishes clutching on to a good one, but I definitely do get it."

Summer laughed at the image. She herself had wallowed in that pond more times than she cared to remember. A thought struck her and she stilled. Had she been in it recently? Did she have a man in her life that she didn't even remember? Panic gripped her and she looked down at her ring finger. Bare. Her shoulders relaxed. If she did have a man, he'd have to be one of those pathetic ones Daphne had referred to, since he hadn't even come to see her in the hospital. She gave her head a little shake. The dart of pain that shot through it reminded her she still had a ways to go in the healing process. Likely on more levels than just physically. Cheeks warm, she lifted her head and met Daphne's gaze.

The woman was watching her, a thoughtful look on her face. "Everything okay?"

"Yeah, just experienced a few flopping fish flashbacks of my own. I think I need a bite of this to recover." She lifted the croissant and bit into it, flakes of pastry sprinkling her sweater. She moaned in pleasure as the buttery dough and warm melted chocolate swirled over her tongue.

Daphne grinned. "That's the response we hope for. I'll pass your approval along to Shawn—he'll appreciate it."

"Please do." Summer set the croissant down and wiped her mouth with a paper napkin. "So I'm curious about what you meant by not officially hiring."

Daphne wrapped both hands around her mug. "Well, Shawn and I decided when we bought the place that, start-up costs being what they are, we'd go as long as we could with only the two of us working here. Thing is, the business has done a lot better than we expected it to at this point, all credit to him and his incredible baking skills which"— she patted her slightly chubby belly and offered Summer a rueful look—"I am far too acquainted with. The last few weeks I have been thinking it would be nice to have another person around to help me. I never get a day off, can't even leave the shop during business hours as no one would be here to help customers, so it's been a bit more of a tie than I'd anticipated."

Summer clasped her hands in her lap, hardly daring to hope. "So you know, I fell in love with this place the second the door opened and I smelled all the delicious odors wafting out. I have waitressing experience and, judging from this croissant, I won't have any trouble extolling the virtues of your husband's wares to any and all customers who wander in. Not to mention that I am available immediately and my schedule is wide open, so I'd be happy to take as few or as many hours as you wanted to give me. I'd say that I would be willing to work for pastries, but I do need to pay my rent, although I wouldn't expect more than minimum wage."

Daphne gazed at her over the rim of her pottery mug. "Goodness, that's quite a spiel. I suppose I should look at a resume if you have one, and of course I'll have to talk to Shawn, but something tells me you and I would have a great time working together."

"I completely agree." Summer unclasped her hands and nabbed a croissant crumb from the plate with her finger. "Unfortunately, I don't have a computer here yet, so I don't have a hard copy of my resume, but you can check out my..." She hesitated. Daphne was studying her with such an open, guileless look. Did she really want to start out their friendship with a lie? It was too dangerous to share her real name, but the manufactured background? She blew out a breath. "Look, here's the truth. I recently suffered a head injury and can't remember anything about the last few years of my life." Her Spanish accent always thickened when she was flustered, and she nearly tripped over the English now as it came out of her mouth. "I do know I waited tables in university, but can not remember what I did after that, so I created a fake LinkedIn profile for myself to show employers. The thing is, I do not feel right about using it, so there you go." She lifted both hands, palms up. "I can't tell you what I've been doing the last six or seven years, although I wasn't lying about having experience waiting tables. I do remember that much.

"In any case, I completely understand if you can't hire me when I have nothing to offer you to prove to you that I have any recent experience that would enable me to do this job and contemplated making something up. In fact,"—cheeks burning, Summer slid off the stool and stood—"lo siento. I'm sorry I took up your time. Although I can not say I am sorry I came in here since it is such a lovely, cozy place. I'll be sure to come back soon and try—"

Daphne stopped her with a hand on her arm. "Whoa. Slow down."

Her bright blue eyes twinkled. "You not having a resume wouldn't have stopped me from hiring you, although finding out you'd lied to me might have. So I'm glad you chose to be honest, because I've decided that I would really, really like to work with you, Ana Santos. Pending Shawn's approval, I think we can work something out."

"Really?"

"Yes, really. Now hop back up there and finish that croissant. My husband takes it as a personal insult if customers leave a crumb on their plates."

"Well, I certainly wouldn't want to insult the baker." Summer climbed back up and reached for the croissant. She stopped with the treat midway to her mouth. "Thank you, Daphne. Even if your husband doesn't agree, it means a lot to me that you would want me to come work here. I admit I was a little discouraged when I was passing by your bakery this morning, but you've made me feel a whole lot better about things. Well, you and this gooey chocolate." She dipped a finger into a splotch that had landed on her plate and stuck it in her mouth. "How does your husband do it?"

Daphne lifted her shoulders. "I have no idea. I'm perfectly content to let him bake for me without asking him any of his secrets. If he shares them, he might expect me to start making some of the things myself, which would upset the delicate balance of responsibilities we have achieved both here and at home."

"Smart woman." Summer took another bite of the pastry and washed it down with the rich coffee. "Do you have any kids?"

"Shawn has a son, Cory, who's great. You'll likely see him around here from time to time when he's on a break from college." A slight glumness settled on her face. "Shawn and I don't have any kids together, though. We'd like them, but we've been married four years and it hasn't happened for us yet. We thought it was going to, last year, but we lost the baby right before Christmas." Brightening, she elbowed

Summer in the arm. "We're sure having fun trying again though." She clapped a hand over her mouth then lowered it, her round cheeks pink. "That's TMI, isn't it? Shawn's always telling me I give out too much personal information to people. I can't help myself, though. I believe everyone has a story, and I want to hear it so badly sometimes I forget they might not want to hear every detail of mine." She reached over and covered Summer's hand with hers. "I can tell you've got an interesting one that you're not quite willing to share yet. That's fine." She patted Summer's hand before pulling back. "Whenever you're ready, I'll be here."

"Gracias. Thank you."

"De nada."

Summer raised an eyebrow.

Daphne smiled. "I fell in love with Mexico during a family trip to Acapulco when I was twelve."

"That's where I'm from! Well, not Acapulco, but Mexico."

"Really? That is so cool." Daphne inhaled sharply. "I've been practicing for years and have gotten pretty fluent, but it's hard when I have no one to practice on. Maybe you could help me polish it up a little?"

"I'd love to."

"And you can help me teach Shawn too." Her eyes twinkled with mischief. "There's nothing sexier than a man who speaks another language." She pressed her lips together and glanced around the shop. "Oops. Probably shouldn't talk like that. Our pastor comes in here for coffee sometimes, and while he likely wouldn't care, Shawn might not appreciate me talking like that in front of him."

"You go to church?"

"Yes. Do you?"

"I think so."

Daphne cocked her head again. "You think so?"

Summer ran a finger around the plastic rim of her coffee cup lid. "Yes. I didn't have a faith growing up, but something must have happened to me in the last few years, something I don't remember, because I know I have one now. I've been praying and it feels very real and natural, like God is right there with me."

"Which he is, of course. Hey, why don't you come to church with us on Sunday? Everyone's really friendly—it would be a great way to get to know people in town."

Summer felt a little dizzy. Partly the on-going effects of her head injury, but also because everything was happening so quickly. "I'll definitely think about it."

"Great." Daphne hopped down off the stool. "Come say hi to Shawn so he can put a face to a name when I talk to him later."

Summer followed her behind the swinging door and into the kitchen. Her blonde ponytail swinging, Daphne barreled toward a bearded, linebacker-sized man in a full-length black apron scooping a cup of flour out of a bag.

"Oof." Her husband groaned when she hit him, flour spilling onto the counter and filling the air with dusky clouds. "Daph, for goodness sake." He set down the cup, gripped both her shoulders, and planted a kiss on her lips. Despite his words, he didn't seem to mind at all that she had interrupted him—forcefully—in the middle of his task. When he let her go, she stepped back and fanned her face with one hand.

Summer suppressed a smile. How much fun would it be to run a business with a spouse you were so clearly head over heels in love with?

"You could walk into the kitchen like a civilized person and say my name if you want my attention, you know."

"I know, but that's not nearly as fun."

"I suppose not." Shawn tapped her nose, leaving a dusting of flour across it. His gaze lifted above his wife's head, as though he'd only now realized someone else was in the room. "Hi there. I'm Shawn."

Summer stepped forward and held out her hand. "Ana. First time customer and now your biggest fan. The chocolate croissant I demolished a few minutes ago was the best I've ever had."

The big man beamed as he gripped her hand in his flour-covered one. "That's what we like to hear."

As he let her go, bells jangled softly in the coffee shop. Daphne slid a hand through the crook of Summer's arm. "Better get back to work. Just wanted to introduce you to Ana, who has graciously offered to start helping me out front. Well, see ya."

She tugged Summer toward the exit. Summer caught a glimpse of Shawn standing behind the counter, covered in flour, his mouth hanging slightly open, before the door swung shut behind them. Daphne leaned in and, in a conspiratorial whisper, said, "Best to plant the idea and let it grow awhile. I'm sure it'll take root, but I'll have to let you know what he says. Do you have a number I can reach you at?"

Summer gulped. She had no phone, no number, no way for anyone to text or email her. How had she thought any prospective employers might contact her? "I'm sorry. I... I haven't gotten a phone yet."

"No worries. Why don't you pop back in for a coffee tomorrow morning, and I can let you know what he said. That will give me the night to... you know, convince him."

Summer pressed her lips together to keep from giggling. "I'll do that. Thanks so much, Daphne."

"My pleasure. See you tomorrow." Her new friend winked at her before turning to greet a woman who stood at the counter, a baby tied to the front of her in a sling. Summer sobered. What was that like for Daphne, waiting on mothers who came in with babies and small children when she didn't have any of her own? It certainly had to be a painful reminder of the one she had lost. *Todo el mundo tiene problemas. You're not the only one who's suffered hardships.* That helped put things in perspective.

Summer gathered up her garbage and dumped it in the bin on her way out the door. Had all of that really happened? She bit her lip. Daphne Cook might share too much personal information, but Summer had never felt drawn to anyone so quickly. If Mr. Cook the baker agreed—and given the way he looked at his wife, Summer had a pretty good feeling about that—nothing would make her happier than working with that woman, surrounded by all those glorious smells all day long.

A taste of heaven indeed.

CHAPTER SEVENTEEN

The dark, stone staircase descended sharply in front of him. Jude clutched the flimsy wooden railing so tightly his knuckles cracked and whitened. *Where is she?*

"It's only fifty-nine steps. You can do it." Her voice came to him, drifting through the gathering twilight, laughing, teasing. Jude stared down the rough stairway, carved into the side of the rock face. He knew how many steps there were. How many times had they counted them as they'd scrambled up and down them as kids? But that had been in the summer, in daylight. This evening the stones were covered in ice and a dusting of snow marred only by her footprints.

He'd had a long, hard day at work, and all he wanted to do was go home and crash in front of the TV. He called her name, hoping she would come, knowing she wouldn't. It had never been possible for him to talk her out of doing something once she had an idea in her head, no matter how crazy it was.

He peered through the trees growing out of the rocks, barely able to see her making her way along the rough shoreline. He called her name again. She didn't turn, but her laughter wafted up to him and his jaw tightened. Seriously?

He was going to have to go after her. He stomped down onto the first step and paused. *Really don't feel like doing this.* It wasn't so much the fifty-nine down he objected to but the fifty-nine back up.

A loud crack shattered his thoughts, followed by a scream that turned the blood flowing through his veins as cold as the ice spider-webbing beneath her feet. *No.*

Jude scrambled down the stairs, stumbling and slipping on each one until the fifty-nine felt like hundreds more than that, only managing to keep from tumbling down head over heels by grasping the wooden railing and sliding his hand forward until slivers dug into his palms. He called her name, but no sound broke the silence that had descended over the river, thicker and deeper than before.

Crashing over rocks and fallen logs that littered the pathway, he made his way to the spot where, fifteen feet from shore, a black hole in the ice gaped like the mouth of some hideous predator. His chest clenched. Why had she gone out there? They'd been strictly warned not to go anywhere near the ice. What was she thinking?

He groaned. She'd been thinking what she was always thinking— that rules were made to be broken. Only this time more than the rules had been broken...

Shoving back the fear that threatened to overwhelm him, clouding his thoughts, he took a few running steps out onto the ice, lowering himself to his belly and crawling toward the hole when he was a few feet away. Nothing broke the surface of the water, no flailing hand, no one gasping for air or trying to climb out. The water was as still and dark as if the surface of it had never been breached.

Frantic, Jude shoved an arm into the hole, chunks of ice breaking away beneath him. He called her name again as he dragged his arm through the frigid water. His fingers touched nothing but icy liquid. He lost track of time as he slashed through the water over and over, only stopping when a large chunk of ice broke away beneath his shoulder and he had to scramble away from the hole or he'd go in too.

It was too late.

Flipping over onto his back, Jude let out an anguished scream, his numb, dripping arm flung over his eyes. She was gone. And it was all his fault.

A siren shattered the stillness and Jude bolted upright in his bed, his damp T-shirt clinging to his torso. For several seconds he concentrated on drawing in one ragged breath after another then he flung the floral bedspread off himself and swung his legs over the side of the bed. Where was he?

Dazed, he lowered his face into his hands. Gradually, his heart rate slowed enough that he could lift his head and look around. Oh yeah. The Wayside Motel. He was back in Elora. His Ninevah. The place God had been telling him to go for a long time and he'd been resisting. Even though part of him had really wanted to go. That part that, until now, had been outmuscled by his fear. The siren outside the window had nothing to do with him. Not this time, anyway.

Light flowed around the edges of the heavy brown curtains and he glanced at his watch. 9 a.m. Summer was likely already out, pounding the pavement again the way she had the last couple of days. Better drive around town a bit, see if he could find her. And maybe he could scrounge up a decent cup of coffee while he was at it.

Jude stumbled across the room to the dingy washroom. Gripping the porcelain sink with both hands, he stared at himself in the mirror. His hair was disheveled and two days' worth of stubble dotted his chin and cheeks. He looked like what he was—a man on the run. From himself as much as anything else. A man haunted by his past.

He looked away from his reflection and reached for his toothbrush. Unfortunately, since he'd returned to the town he hadn't been sure he'd ever see again, that past was very aggressively asserting itself into the present.

CHAPTER EIGHTEEN

The heavenly aroma she'd inhaled when entering the bakery the day before wrapped around Summer now, helping to settle the fluttering in her stomach as she walked inside.

"Ana!" Daphne rounded the counter and came toward her, arms outstretched. After seeing her approach her husband the same way, Summer braced herself, but Daphne skidded to a stop inches in front of her and flung plump arms around Summer in a tight embrace. "You came back." She stepped away but didn't let go of Summer's arms.

A few patrons—a man in a business suit who'd been tapping on a tablet with a stylus and a woman in a black wool sweater reading a book—glanced over, but otherwise no one paid much attention to the two of them. Did Daphne greet so many of them that way that they no longer took notice? If so, she had a real gift with people, because she had definitely made Summer feel special.

Daphne let go of one of her arms, but kept her grip on the other so she could tug Summer to the counter. "First of all, what can I get you?"

Summer would have preferred to start with an update on the job situation, but she tamped down her impatience. "I'll have a coffee and," she stepped back to survey the counter, "an apple-cinnamon muffin, please." Hmm, if she did end up working here, she'd have to be careful not to consume Shawn's amazing offerings too often. Or maybe she'd keep walking up and down the steep main street every day to burn off the excess calories.

Daphne handed her the coffee and muffin and nodded to the bar where they'd sat the day before. Summer meandered over to what she was already coming to think of as her stool and settled onto it. When she bit into the soft, crumbly muffin, she couldn't repress a sigh of appreciation, in spite of her angst. "So good."

Perched on the stool beside her, Daphne beamed and smoothed the apron over her thighs. "Good. Now down to business. Shawn has agreed to hire you part time—at least twenty hours a week—until April. After that, business starts to pick up so, no promises, but we'll try to give you full-time hours at that point." She clasped her hands in front of her chest. "What do you think?"

Summer set down the muffin and brushed cinnamon and sugar off her fingers. The offer wasn't exactly solid, but it would give her an income she could likely live on for the next few months. She smiled. "When can I start?"

Daphne unclasped her hands and clapped. "I was hoping you would say that. And by the way, I might have hinted to Shawn that your presence here will increase the male traffic through the door, hope you don't mind. So how about starting right now?"

Her new boss apparently had a habit of slipping potentially unwelcome information into a conversation and then either abruptly leaving the room or switching topics before the other person had time to react.

As long as Summer's new employers didn't expect her to encourage anyone to keep coming back, she could live with it.

Summer's head started to spin again, but she straightened on the stool. *Sé valiente. Have courage.* "Now is perfect. Let me finish this amazing muffin and then I am at your service."

When the bells jangled again, Summer glanced over. The sound might become annoying at some point, but it still sent shivers tingling across her skin, as if a moment of magic in a movie was occurring. And speaking of movies... The man who walked in could have been coming straight off a set himself. She looked away quickly and busied herself wiping down the counter as he stood, hands in the pockets of his leather jacket, gazing at the menu board behind her.

His light-brown hair was short and slightly disheveled, the kind that guys could simply run their fingers through and look amazing, which drove Summer crazy. When she tossed the cloth under the counter and lifted her head, a pair of hazel eyes met hers, his intense look—was that sadness? anger?—sending the words she'd been about to say tumbling from her brain.

Head injury. She excused herself, a little lamely, for her momentary lapse of concentration and cleared her throat. "What can I get you?"

His eyes cleared as thoroughly as though the emotion had been swiped off like chalk from a blackboard. "What do you recommend?"

It seemed imprudent to tell him she'd only sampled two of Shawn's concoctions, so Summer settled for, "The chocolate croissants are the best I've ever had."

One side of his mouth turned up slightly. "Sounds good. I'll take one chocolate croissant and a cup of the strongest black coffee you have on tap."

In spite of herself, Summer couldn't help returning his grin. That was a new one. She ran her finger down the menu taped to the counter to find the cost of each item and punched it into the cash register Daphne had quickly shown her how to use before dashing out to get her hair cut. Thankfully, it was the simple, old-fashioned kind that only required the cashier to punch in the price of each product and hit enter to get a total. "That will be 4.25 please."

He tugged a wallet from the back pocket of his jeans and pulled out a five dollar bill. "Keep the change."

Summer blinked. She hadn't been expecting anyone to tip her for handing them a pastry and a cup of coffee over the counter. She grabbed three quarters and held them out. "No, please. It's no trouble."

He held up a hand. "I insist. I hate carrying change around."

"Well, all right. Thank you." She slipped the coins into the pocket of the red apron Daphne had given her. As soon as she had a chance, she'd find a jar to use for tips. That way, if anyone else gave her money, she'd drop it in there and make sure it got to Shawn, who deserved it far more than she did.

Summer grabbed a large paper cup and filled it nearly to the brim with steaming coffee. Whatever kind Shawn and Daphne used was one of the most incredible she'd ever smelled, and she inhaled the aroma as she carried it over to the counter and set it down. "Would you like a lid?"

"No thanks." He inclined his head toward the table in front of the fireplace. "I think I'll drink it here."

"All right." Summer waved a hand. "Go sit down and I'll bring you your croissant."

"Thanks."

She tried not to let it, but her gaze followed him as he wandered over to a table, set down his cup, and pulled a laptop out of the bag slung over his shoulder. Her inhibitions seemed to have lowered greatly in recent weeks. *Head injury.* Summer grabbed a plate and headed for the platter of croissants. How many things was she planning to blame that on now?

When she carried the plate over to the table, he moved the computer out of the way so she could set it in front of him. "Thank you."

"You're welcome. Enjoy." Before he could say anything more, she strode away, retreating behind the counter. Didn't he work? What guy his age had time to sit around a coffee shop in the middle of a

Wednesday? *No te metas en lo que no te importa.*

That was true. It wasn't her business. What was her business was her new job. And she needed to concentrate on it, and on remembering the last few years so she could tell the police who had attacked her.

And with apologies to Hallmark, that was all she planned to think about until the trouble she was in had been resolved.

Jude slumped against the back of the chair. Although he'd watched her face carefully as he'd approached the counter, Summer had given no indication that she recognized him. That was probably for the best if what her father had told Jude was true.

He shoved the last bite of chocolate croissant into his mouth. He wasn't a huge sweets person, but Summer was right—it had to be the best baked good he'd ever tasted. If he was going to come in here often, he'd have to resist ordering one every time. He swiped a napkin over his mouth and reached for the coffee. How often could he come in without anyone becoming suspicious? Or recognizing him? Jude blew out a breath. That was a chance he'd have to take. He needed to lay the groundwork, gradually get Summer to trust him, so he could get her back to Toronto.

Part of him was tempted to simply take the gun out of his bedside table drawer at the Wayside Hotel, wait in an alleyway as she walked home from work, and use it to force her to come with him, explain everything later, but pulling something like that would not end well. Summer was a fighter, as he well knew, and she would either be able to resist him or draw an awful lot of attention to the two of them in the process.

Jude opened his laptop, studying her surreptitiously over the top of it. A blonde woman had come into the shop and gone straight behind the counter, patting her hair in a way that suggested she'd had it cut and wanted Summer's opinion. Summer said something and the two of them laughed. His chest squeezed. When was the last time he'd heard that sound from her?

Focus, Jude. Stay the course. He tore his gaze from her. If his plan was going to work, he had to stick to it. Be patient. Slowly build a relationship with her. Woo her, even. See if he had any more success with that tactic. Jude played idly with a napkin as he sipped his coffee. His boss's impatience aside, he was willing to take his time and make sure he did it right this time.

He'd let her slip through his fingers once. He had no intention of doing it again.

CHAPTER NINETEEN

Summer swept the floor behind the counter, over and over the same spot as her gaze strayed continually to a table by the window. A woman in her sixties, white hair styled in a short, elegant cut, sat there. Her daughter—the young woman who had stood at the counter, her young son strapped to her chest, the first time Summer had been in the shop—had settled across from her.

The two women had come in several times during the first couple of weeks Summer had worked there. Every time they came in, they each ordered a cup of peppermint tea and shared a piece of pastry. They stayed an hour or so, taking turns holding the eight-month-old boy, Jamie, and talking and laughing together non-stop.

Summer finally gave up on the sweeping and propped the broom in the corner. Grabbing a cloth, she began wiping down the counter, her attention still drawn to the threesome by the window. She had no recollection of ever sitting and chatting with her mother, let alone laughing. Daphne came up behind her and leaned in to whisper, "That's sweet, isn't it?"

Summer stopped wiping and contemplated her new friend. Judging from the wistfulness in her voice, her relationship with her mother wasn't that warm and fuzzy either. "You don't get along with your mother like that?"

Daphne scrunched up her freckled face. "Definitely not. I'm not sure my mother ever stopped yelling at my dad long enough to say more than a few sentences to me. I honestly can't remember ever hearing her laugh. And I haven't seen either of them for a few years now. Their choice."

That hurt Summer's heart. How could anyone treat adorable, sunny Daphne that way? Summer touched her arm. "I'm sorry."

"I'm sorry, too, for you."

She blinked. "What do you mean?"

"I was watching you watching them. You don't have that kind of relationship with your mother either, do you?"

It was going to be awfully hard for her to keep anything from Daphne. That thought bothered Summer less than she thought it would. "No, I guess I don't." The memory of her parents' betrayal stabbed through her again, and she tossed the cloth under the counter. "Do you mind if I take my break now? I could use a little fresh air."

Daphne's smile held sadness. "Sure. But if you ever do want to talk about it, I'm here."

"Got it. Gracias."

Summer shoved open the door with her shoulder and stepped into the back alley. An icy breeze swept down between the two buildings, sending clouds of snow swirling around her legs. Slumping against the stone wall, she let out a long breath.

An acrid smell drifted on the breeze and she glanced around. No one appeared to be in the alley, but a cloud of smoke definitely hung in the air between the two buildings. Whoever had been smoking had been here in the last couple of minutes. Why would they be hanging around the dumpsters behind the café? She shook her head. Probably kids, or maybe someone cutting through the alleyway to get downtown.

Summer strolled out to the sidewalk and around the block, praying as she walked, each step easing a little of the angst Daphne's caring comment had stirred up inside her like silt from the bottom of a pond. When she came back around to the back door of the bakery, calm had replaced the angst. *Thank you, God.*

Bells jingled as she returned to the counter. She glanced over and her face warmed. It was him again. Movie star man. He'd been in several times since she'd started working. He had to be new in town too, since Daphne had told Summer she'd never seen him before.

"Hey," Daphne hissed at her, "es tu novio."

The flush of heat spread down Summer's neck. The man was certainly not her boyfriend. They only talked briefly when he came in. That intense look she'd seen in his eyes the first day hadn't reappeared, thankfully, but still she kept their exchanges brief and professional. Summer shot her friend a warning look before turning to the man. The first couple of times he had come in, she'd tried to pawn him off on Daphne, but her friend would have none of it, so now she didn't even bother. "Good morning."

He grinned. "Morning."

"What can I get you?"

He answered the same way he always did. "What do you recommend?"

Summer had begun to take it as a challenge. She tilted her head and contemplated him. What did he appear in the mood for today? "Cinnamon-raisin scone?"

As always, he nodded, once. "Sounds perfect."

She forced herself to look away and grab the tongs from beneath the counter. Shawn's scones were almost perfectly symmetrical, but she still found herself looking for the biggest, most perfectly golden one to give to the man. He deserved that much as one of their most faithful customers, didn't he? After sliding it onto a plate and setting it on the counter, Summer filled a paper cup with black coffee and pressed a white plastic lid onto the top of it. "Anything else?"

"Actually, yes." The man tugged the wallet from his back pocket and withdrew a five. "I'm new to the area, so I was wondering if you could recommend any restaurants in town."

Summer hadn't eaten at any of the restaurants in Elora. Why would she when Nancy was such a good cook, and Summer enjoyed sitting down to dinner with her and telling her about her day? Nancy had traveled all over the world and loved to share her stories, so she not only provided the food but the entertainment as well. Their plan to divvy up the cooking duties hadn't really panned out after Summer got a job, but she brought enough treats home to her landlady that they were both perfectly content with the arrangement.

"Actually, I'm new to town too. But Daphne here will be able to help you with anything you need to know." Daphne had busied herself putting on a fresh pot of coffee, but Summer grabbed her elbow and tugged her over to the counter. "I'll finish the coffee."

Before Daphne could protest, Summer had maneuvered her into place behind the counter and retreated to the coffee maker. She could hear the two of them chatting and laughing but didn't look back until Daphne cleared her throat. "What do you think, Ana?"

She shoved the basket into place and turned around. Both of them were gazing at her. "About what?"

"Trying out Tony's, the restaurant I recommended to Ryan, tonight."

Was her friend actually setting her up on a date? "Umm..."

He held up a hand. "No pressure. Daphne thought you might be interested in getting to know the town a little better, like I do. If you'd rather not do that with a stranger, though, I totally get it."

So they were two people new to Elora trying to get to know the place better? Sort of like a civic duty? "No, it's okay. I would like to try out some of the places in town. I haven't had a chance to do that yet, since my new boss is a real slave driver." She shot a heated look at Daphne.

Her friend only smiled her dimpled smile and ducked out from between them. "I need to talk to Shawn about something. I'll be in the back if you need me."

She was gone before Summer could stop her. When she turned

back to the counter, the man—Ryan, apparently—was studying her. "What time do you finish work? I could pick you up."

"No, that's okay. I'll meet you there." Summer had no intention of giving this man she didn't know her address, or climbing into a vehicle with him. Besides, if she drove herself, she could make an excuse and leave early if the evening was a disaster.

A slow smile spread across his face, as though he knew exactly what she'd been thinking, and warmth crept up her neck. "I should get to work." She reached for the cloth she'd tossed under the counter and started wiping every surface she could find.

"All right." He lifted the scone and coffee into the air. "Thanks. I'll see you tonight. 6:30 good?"

"Sure." *Please go.*

For once, he didn't settle at a table, but took his scone and coffee and headed for the door. Seriously, could the man actually read her mind? Summer shivered. That was a scary thought.

Daphne pushed through the swinging doors and Summer smacked her a couple of times on the arm with the cloth. "¿Estás bromeando?"

Daphne giggled. "No, I'm not kidding you. He's a nice, good-looking, single guy. Why wouldn't you want to have dinner with him?"

Summer pretended to scrub at a spot on the white door frame.

Her friend crossed her arms and contemplated her, a smirk on her face. "So you do want to have dinner with him. Then why are you upset with me?"

"I'm not upset." Summer leaned against the counter. "But I'm not convinced going out with a man whose last name I don't even know is a good idea. What am I going to tell him when he starts asking me about my life? I hardly remember anything after university, and that was years ago."

"Oh, Ana." Daphne wrapped her arms around her. "I wouldn't worry about that. Judging from the way he looks at you, it's not your past he's interested in."

Summer pulled away and smacked her again with the cloth. "If this all goes horribly wrong, it's on you."

"Fair enough."

The door opened and four older men pushed their way into the shop. Summer waved. "Buenos días, señores." Sam, Pete, Howard, and Bob came in most mornings about this time, ordered coffee and food, and hung out in the back corner for a couple of hours. No doubt their wives sent them over to get them out of the house, as they were all retired.

"Hola, Ana." Sam tugged off his ball cap and ran a hand over his nearly bald head. "What's on special today?"

She laughed. He asked that every time he came in. The first couple of times she'd informed him they didn't have daily specials because everything Shawn made was special. Now she simply pointed to whatever had come out of the oven most recently, since Bob preferred his pastries warm. "Carrot muffins today, Sam."

Pete clapped his hands. "We'll take four and a round of coffees please."

After she'd retrieved their muffins and drinks and sent them off, Summer watched, a smile on her face, as Howard chucked little Jamie under the chin on his way to the table the four of them always sat at. How fun would it be to have a group of friends to hang out with? She'd had that in school, but did she still? As far as she knew, no one had tried to contact her when she was in the hospital, which likely meant the answer was no. Why not? Had she been too busy with whatever career she had to spend time with people? Sadness whispered through her but Summer pushed it away impatiently.

Daphne nudged her in the ribs with her elbow and held out Summer's red coat. Summer frowned. "Are you kicking me out?"

"Yes, actually. I made an appointment with my hairdresser Wanda for you in ten minutes. She's at WonderCuts, half a block up and across the street. And it's on me. A peace offering for forcing you to spend the evening with a nice, friendly, gorgeous man with impeccable taste in..." she looked Summer up and down, a mischievous glint in her eye, "... baked goods."

Summer rolled her eyes. It was useless to even try to be mad at Daphne. The woman was off the charts on the likeability scale. Which was a little maddening. She grabbed her coat. "All right, thanks." When was the last time she'd had her hair done? Summer almost laughed. It could have been a month and a half, before her accident, or as long as seven years ago. She had no way of knowing. Regardless, it likely wouldn't hurt her to get it cut a little.

She slid an arm through a sleeve as she headed for the door.

"By the way," Daphne called after her. "It's Taylor."

Summer stopped and looked back. "¿Perdón?"

"The man whose last name you don't know. Now you do. Ryan Taylor."

Summer tugged up the zipper on her coat. Ryan Taylor. *Obvio.* Of course it was. About as un-Mexican a name as he could possibly have. Her father would not be impressed if she brought the man home to meet...

She pushed open the door so hard the bells jangled wildly. That thought was wrong on so many levels. Chief among them being that she had absolutely no intention of taking Ryan Taylor anywhere. And if she did, it wouldn't be home to meet the parents who had lied to her.

She *had* agreed to get her hair done, but only because her friend had offered it as a gift, and it would have been rude to refuse. It certainly wasn't because she had any interest whatsoever in impressing the man.

In fact, as Daphne hadn't exactly given her time to consider the scheme she and Ryan had concocted, it would probably be a good idea to make a list of pros and cons before going out with him. If the idea came out a little too heavy on the con side, she'd cancel. Nothing was set in stone. And if they did go out, she could simply have dinner with him one time then go back to eating at Nancy's house every evening. Ryan Taylor could pursue his civic duties to his new town without her.

The thought sent her stomach roiling a little.

As did the faint hint of smoke, still lingering in the air as she passed by the opening between the bakery and the building next door.

CHAPTER TWENTY

Jude toyed with the linen napkin, running it over his fingers and scrunching it up in a clenched fist. When he realized it had become a wrinkled mess, he shoved it away from him in disgust. *It's just dinner.* The fact that there could be more riding on this simple meal than on any other he'd ever eaten pretty much ensured he wouldn't be able to enjoy a bite.

He glanced at his watch. Again. 6:45. Would she show up? And why had he given Daphne a fake name? He sighed. He hadn't really had much of a choice. If Summer's father had mentioned him at all—and there was a good chance he'd been bluffing, since her parents would no doubt prefer that all memory of him be permanently erased from her mind—it wouldn't have been in a favorable way. And he didn't need to have anything else working against him in his campaign to get her back to the city. Trouble was, he'd have to try and remember to use it now with everyone he encountered in the small town, and to not call Summer by her real name either. *Ana.* He tried the name out, rolling it around on his tongue a little. It suited her, he guessed, although she would always be Summer to him.

Jude glanced at his watch again. Almost ten to seven. How long should he wait? He'd give her until seven before heading back to—

"I'm sorry I'm late." Summer pulled out the chair across from him and sat down. Jude half stood, so abruptly he nearly knocked over his water glass. A few drops spilled onto the white tablecloth as he grabbed it. *Smooth, Jude.* He sank onto his chair.

A small smile played around Summer's lips. Lips she'd applied a light gloss to, he couldn't help but notice. She'd dressed in a red blouse with rounded collars and black dress pants and wore her usual simple gold hoops in her ears. As always, she took his breath away. Had she gotten her hair cut? It looked different. Good different. For a few seconds, he simply stared at her then he cleared his throat, his cheeks warm. "It's fine. I'm glad you came."

"Me too." She glanced around the small Italian restaurant. "This place is lovely."

Is that why you're glad you came? Jude shook his head slightly. "It really is. Daphne has great taste. In restaurants and employees."

"And husbands." She deflected his comment away from herself smoothly. "Have you met Shawn?"

"No, not yet. Although I already hold the man in high esteem. He's some kind of savant in the kitchen."

Summer laughed lightly. "He really is. And he's a great guy too. A big teddy bear."

She gazed across the room, over his shoulder. He gave her a minute to get her bearings. Why had she been late? Was she second-guessing going out with him? More than likely. Summer's self-protection radar was stronger than most people's. No doubt she'd made a list of pros and cons before finally deciding to take the chance. He hid a grin. What he wouldn't give to see that list.

She scanned the restaurant, clearly buying herself time to get comfortable. When her muscles relaxed slightly, Jude leaned forward, resting his arms on the table. Time to play a little, see if he could get her to slip up and give him any information he could use. "So what brought you to Elora?"

Her smile faltered slightly. "I needed a change. I flipped through a book of maps, fell in love with the name of the place and the pictures of the mill and the river, and here I am. How about you?"

"Same. Well, except for looking at the maps. Seriously, do they even make those anymore?"

She laughed again. "They do, actually. How did you hear about the town?"

How had this gotten turned back on him? Jude shifted on his chair. "I was tired of living in the city. This seemed about as far removed from that as it is possible to be and still be part of civilization."

"I suppose it is."

A server in a crisp white shirt, tie, and black dress pants appeared at the end of their table and filled their water glasses. "Could I bring you anything else to drink?"

Jude looked at Summer. She nodded at her glass. "Water's fine, thanks."

He shifted his gaze to the server. "For me, too."

The man looked slightly disappointed as he handed them both a menu. "I'll give you a few minutes to decide."

"Thank you." Jude took his menu and lifted it in the man's direction. Summer had already flipped hers open. Evading more questions? He repressed a sigh and opened his own. With both of them dancing around their questions and answers, it could be a long evening. He studied her over the top of his menu. Not that he was complaining.

She glanced up and caught him watching her. "What are you thinking of ordering?"

He hadn't read a word on the menu, and there were no pictures, like there were in most of the places he'd been eating lately. Jude pretended to peruse the offerings. "I'm not sure, likely some kind of pasta." It was a safe bet there'd be a few of those kinds of dishes at an Italian restaurant, right? From the aromas of tomato sauce and garlic drifting from the direction of the kitchen, he probably couldn't go wrong with anything he selected. "Rigatoni, maybe? Hard to choose, since they all sound delicious. What do you think?"

"That does look great. I think I'll try the Pasta alla Norma."

The words flitted around on the page, and Jude gave up and closed the menu. The server set a basket of bread on the table. "What can I get you?"

Once they'd ordered, Jude took her menu and handed both to the man, who thanked him before heading to the kitchen. Summer intertwined her fingers on the table and contemplated him. "What is it that you do?"

He'd anticipated that question. "I'm a writer." That would explain why he was free to hang out in coffee shops during the day, right? She had no way of knowing what he did on his laptop while he was there.

She tilted her head and Jude swallowed. She wore her long dark hair up at the coffee shop, so he hadn't seen it like this in a while, dark curls splashing down over her shoulders.

He blinked. Had she asked him something? "I'm sorry, what?"

That little smile flitted around her mouth again. "I asked you what you write. Anything I would have heard of?"

"I doubt it." No books, or she could go online and discover pretty quickly he'd made his career up. "Articles mostly, for health and science magazines and websites." The lies slid a little too easily off his tongue. Hidden identities, secret pasts... how had the two of them ended up in some kind of Shakespearean drama? Time to shift the spotlight back to her. "Do you read much?"

Summer reached for a piece of bread and took her time spreading butter on it. Was she trying to remember? What must that be like, not being sure of what you liked or didn't like or anything you'd done in the past few years? He couldn't imagine.

"I do love to read, but I haven't had much time for it lately."

"I get that. Unfortunately, it seems to have become a luxury in our society."

"That's true." She set the bread down on the small plate without taking a bite. "When I was a kid and through my teens, I read all the time."

He smiled, picturing her. "What types of books?"

"Anything with horses. Mysteries. Fantasy. Pretty much anything my... that I could get my hands on."

Had she been about to say anything her parents would let her have? They'd been strict, hadn't allowed her a lot of what they considered frivolous pleasures, from what he'd heard. His fingers crumpled the napkin in his lap again. Should he press her on that? It was standard first-date conversation, so she shouldn't suspect him of having ulterior motives. Not that this was a date, exactly. "Do you have family nearby?"

The lines around her mouth tightened a little. "Only my parents, north of Toronto. No siblings."

He was about to ask more about them when the server returned with their plates and set one in front of each of them. Jude breathed in the tantalizing aroma of pasta and spices curling up from his dish. Maybe he *would* be able to enjoy it. A bit, anyway. He leaned back as the man grated pepper and parmesan over Summer's pasta and then his.

He knew her well enough to know that she'd fire a question at him as soon as the server left, trying to redirect the conversation that had wandered a bit too close to the bullseye. He had the distinct advantage here, knowing pretty much everything about her when he was still virtually a stranger to her, but he'd held the advantage with her so rarely in the past, he was going to enjoy it and not feel guilty. Besides, these were desperate times. He was prepared to use any tool in his box to achieve the ends he was working toward.

Summer met his eyes before the server was three feet away. "What about you and your family?"

That one struck the target. Of course she'd ask about that. Why hadn't he prefabricated his answers for that line of questioning?

SARA DAVISON

Summer studied him as though reading his face as easily as she'd read all those books as a kid. "Not a comfortable topic, I take it."

Jude blew out a breath. "No, although fair game, since I was the one who brought it up."

She reached for her fork. "Even so, we don't have to go there if you don't want to. Since this is simply a foray into exploring all our beautiful town has to offer and not a date or anything, why don't we agree that we both have veto rights over any topics that come up that we would rather not get into tonight?"

Ouch. That hurt a little, although he should have expected it. Summer had always been good at setting boundaries. And there was nothing ambiguous about the ones she'd just erected. "All right. We can keep things neutral." He reached for his fork. "Tell me about your bucket list."

The question wasn't as neutral as he'd suggested it might be. Having her share her hopes and dreams, if she did, might help him strategize a little. Her dark eyes locked with his for a few seconds, as though assessing his intentions, then her shoulders relaxed. "I'll give you my top five." She held up her hand and ticked off a finger with each item on the list. "Go up in a hot air balloon, learn to ski, meet Javier Hernández Balcázar in person, become fluent in French, and travel to the seven modern wonders of the world."

He blinked. How had she come up with that list off the top of her head? Had she prefabricated a few answers to possible questions herself? The hot air balloon item on the list pricked more than a little, since he knew for a fact she'd done that six months ago. He hadn't realized she wanted to learn French though, if she actually did. The fact that she wanted to meet the popular footballer Javier Hernández didn't surprise him—that was her Mexican showing. Although he hoped it was the man's soccer prowess she was interested in and not his famous good looks.

98

The skiing thing made sense too, since she was one of the most fearless people he knew. He tore a small piece of bread from the slice he'd grabbed out of the basket. "Can you even name the seven modern wonders of the world?"

"Umm..."

Ha. Not as prepared as she was pretending to be. Jude pressed his lips together.

She lifted her chin. "The Coliseum. The Great Wall of China. Uh, Machu Picchu. That statue of Jesus Christ in Brazil..."

Not bad, actually. Jude wasn't sure he could have come up with that many without more time to think about it. Or without Google.

"The Taj Mahal." She smacked the table lightly as she flashed him a triumphant smile.

"That's only five."

"Oh. What are the other two?"

"No idea. You came up with about three more than I would have."

She laughed. "If I get to see five of them, I'll be doing well."

Jude set the bread down on the small plate and stabbed a few rigatoni noodles with his fork. When he shoved them into his mouth, flavor exploded across his tongue and he barely suppressed a groan of pleasure. Daphne hadn't been wrong. This place was incredible.

Summer smiled as she twirled her pasta around a fork. "That good, huh?"

He swallowed and wiped his mouth with the napkin. "Incredible." For a few minutes, they ate in what felt like comfortable silence to Jude, other than the odd comment about the food or the ambience. Far too soon, he was down to the last few noodles on his plate and forced himself to slow down. "So which of the wonders would you visit first, if you could?"

She chewed thoughtfully, swallowed, and took a sip of water. "I think the statue in Brazil."

Interesting. "Why?"

"My faith is important to me." Summer rubbed the condensation off the side of her glass with her thumb. "So I guess that one would be the most meaningful."

Jude was almost afraid to breathe. She remembered that? Summer was being far more open and vulnerable than he would have expected, and he was terrified to say or do anything that might shut her down. "I get that," he said, softly.

"You do?"

He nodded. "Yeah. My faith is important to me, too."

For a moment she didn't speak, only scrutinized him.

Jude met her gaze steadily, watching for something, any tiny flicker of recognition in her eyes. None came. She let out a quiet laugh and looked away. "So much for keeping things neutral." She balanced her knife on the edge of the plate. "I'll have to take the rest of this home. As it is, I'll need to jog up and down the main street a few times tomorrow to work off this meal."

"Me too." He smiled and gestured to their server. As Summer packaged up her food, Jude tugged the wallet out of his pocket. He started to pull out his credit card, but realized she might notice it had a different name on it and grabbed cash instead.

Summer lifted her bag onto her lap. "We can split it."

He started to protest, but she held up a hand. "It's not a date."

So you said. Twice. No use arguing with her. If he had a nickel for every minute of his life he'd spent doing that, he wouldn't be staying in one of the cheapest motels in town, that was for sure. "Fine. 50-50. But I'm buying next time."

She'd been removing a ten and a twenty from her wallet but stopped and glanced over, a sparkle in her dark eyes that he knew from experience would have weakened his knees if he'd been standing. "That's a little presumptuous."

He lifted his shoulders. "I prefer optimistic."

Summer pursed her lips as she dropped the money on top of the bill. "All right. In the interest of familiarizing myself with the town, maybe we can do this again. As long as you understand that it won't be a—"

"Date. Got it. When?"

She zipped her bag closed. "Friday?"

Three days. Sounded like an eternity to him at the moment. "Friday it is. You choose the place this time."

"Deal." Summer pushed back her chair and rose.

Jude followed her out of the restaurant and into the cold evening air. At her car, she stopped and faced him. "Thanks, Ryan. I had a good time tonight."

He didn't like hearing the alias on her lips but managed a smile. "Me too."

She opened the car door and slid behind the wheel. "See you at the bakery?"

"You can count on it. I'm hooked now." He waited until she was in before lifting a hand. "Good night."

She nodded. "Good night."

Jude closed the door and stood in the parking lot, staring down the road long after her vehicle had turned onto the street and disappeared. Had their evening together advanced his cause at all? Maybe. He did have what he absolutely considered a date with her on Friday night. And as that was more than he'd had a couple of hours ago, he was going to call the night a win.

CHAPTER TWENTY-ONE

Díaz flopped onto the bed and lay staring up at the crack in the ceiling that started at the light fixture and crawled halfway to the door. With a heavy sigh, he rolled onto his side and reached for the small framed photo he'd set on the table beside the bed. He ran a finger over the glass. The beautiful faces of his wife Juanita and their two young daughters, Maria and Josefina, six and three, smiled back at him. His heart twisted.

It was time to check in with the boss, but he needed a few minutes with his family to fortify himself. Díaz lay back on the musty-smelling floral bedspread and clutched the photo to his chest. The three of them were his life. Everything he did, he did for them. He closed his eyes for several minutes, holding them close, then he lifted the picture, pressed his lips to it, and set it back on the table.

He had to prop three of the flat pillows against the wall that served as a headboard in order to get comfortable. When he couldn't put it off any longer, he grabbed his phone and punched in the far-too-familiar number. The boss answered with a terse, "¿Qué hay de nuevo?"

Díaz swallowed. "It's me."

"Al fin. ¿Qué está pasando?"

"She's got a place to live. With some old lady in a big house in town. And she has a job in a coffee shop."

The boss grunted. "Ha estado afanosa."

Yeah, she'd been busy. Busier than his boss knew. Unfortunately, it was his job to enlighten the one who signed his paychecks. "Yeah.

And she went out for dinner last night."

"¿Con quién?"

Díaz hesitated. His boss wouldn't like the answer. He shrugged. He was paid to tell the truth, not what anyone wanted to hear. "McCall."

He moved the phone away when the voice on the other end erupted in a response heated enough to practically singe his ear. When his boss ran out of steam, Díaz pressed the device to his ear again. "You want me to do anything about it?"

"¿Se acuerda quién es él?"

"I was a few tables away from them, but no, from what I could hear, she doesn't appear to remember him. Not yet anyway."

He winced at the loud exhalation of breath. "Entonces esperemos."

"Wait for what?"

"A que ella lo reconozca."

"So if I think she's starting to remember him, I grab her?"

"Exacto. Mendoza me contactó hace dos días."

Díaz swallowed. "Mendoza contacted you?" That was never a good thing. "What did he say?"

"Me dio un plazo de treinta días."

Mendoza had given the boss thirty days. Two days ago. Not a lot of time. And what would happen after—

The voice on the other end of the line droned on, and Díaz forced his attention back to the conversation. He'd missed a bit, but the final words, that after that they would all have to pay, turned his blood cold. Who would make them pay, Mendoza? Or his hired assassin Kendrick?

Díaz pushed to his feet and lumbered over to the window. Standing to one side of it, his back against the wall, he swiped aside the dingy striped curtains and peered out. Nothing moved in the gravel lot outside the motel. He had no proof that Kendrick knew the girl was in Elora, and no evidence that he was in town. Which didn't mean the man they called the Dragon wasn't there. In fact, Díaz had seen him. Around every corner. In every crowd. Fact was, he was starting to see Kendrick everywhere he looked. Without stepping out of the shadows, the man was already driving Díaz more than a little crazy.

The boss uttered a sharp, "Espero su llamada cuanto antes," before the line went dead.

Díaz scowled at the device. *Soon* was an ambiguous word. He'd call again when he was ready to call, not before. At the moment he had enough to worry about. His jaw tightened. *The Dragon.* Díaz wasn't sure whether the nickname had come about as a result of the man's uncanny ability to terrorize entire villages, or because his chain-smoking habit meant that he was rarely seen without a Lucky Strike clamped between his lips, smoke drifting above his head in a slow, menacing cloud.

He didn't know much more than that about Kendrick, because if anyone was willing to discuss him at all, it was in a hushed voice accompanied by furtive glances around to make sure the Dragon wasn't anywhere nearby. Not that they would know.

With an impatient hiss, Díaz let the curtain fall back into place. He couldn't allow the threat of Kendrick showing up in Elora to distract him from his job. While he'd watch out for the man, his primary task was keeping an eye on Summer Velásquez. And Jude McCall. If the boss had been given thirty days—twenty-eight now—that meant that, even if Kendrick did come to town, he wouldn't likely make a move before then.

It meant one other thing too. The clock had started to tick.

CHAPTER TWENTY-TWO

Summer stirred the Mexican chicken chili in the pot on the stove, inhaling deeply as the movement released the aromas of chili powder, cayenne pepper, and cumin into the air. In spite of its name, the dish was actually Tex-Mex, but it was still one of her favorites. They'd had a cook in their home when she was growing up, and Rosa had taught Summer how to make a few simple dishes. If Summer had added any recipes to her repertoire in the last few years, she had no idea what, so she was sticking with the ones she'd loved as a child.

"So?" Nancy plunked a plate down on the table.

Summer threw a glance over her shoulder. "So, what?"

"Come on now." Nancy planted a fist on her bony hip, bunching up her robin's-egg-blue cardigan. "Throw a lonely old lady a bone. You came in after I went to bed last night, so I've been waiting all day to hear how your date went."

Summer rested the wooden spoon against the side of the pot and carried two sets of cutlery over to the table. "It wasn't a date. And it was fine."

Her landlady pursed her lips. "Just fine?"

Summer set a knife and spoon to one side of a plate. "Well..."

"Aha!" Nancy took two glasses down from the cupboard. "So it was better than fine. Is he cute?"

Summer added a fork to the plate setting. "I'd rather not say."

"Which means he is. What does he look like?"

Summer sighed as she rounded the table. "He's tall, maybe six two or three, with this sandy-brown hair that looks all, you know," she waved a hand over the top of her head, "tousled."

Nancy paused, the glass she'd been about to set down hovering a couple of inches above the table. "Hazel eyes? Irresistible smile?"

The knife slipped from Summer's fingers and clattered to the table. "Sorry." She straightened it. "You know him?"

"I wouldn't say that. It's a small town, though. If it's the guy I'm thinking of, I did see him once." She lowered the glass. "Didn't realize that's who you were going out with. What's his name?"

"Ryan Taylor."

"Hmm."

Summer finished with the cutlery. "What does that mean?"

"Nothing. Just hmm." Her landlady pulled out a chair and sat down. "So you went to Tony's?"

"That's right." Summer dished the chili into two bowls before sliding onto the seat across from Nancy. "Daphne recommended it to us and it was fabulous."

"Yes, Anthony is a superb chef. None of us can figure out why he stays in Elora when he could be working at any restaurant in any city around the world, but no one will ask him because we don't want to put any ideas in his head."

Summer grinned. "Please don't."

Nancy folded her hands and Summer bowed her head while her friend spoke a simple blessing over the food. Summer joined in silently, thanking God for providing her with this place to live and asking for guidance for her future. Including her plan to go out with Ryan again on Friday night. Was that a mistake? She didn't want to encourage him, although something kept her from discouraging him at the same time. Loneliness, most likely. Which was a dangerous motivator.

"Amen."

Summer hid a guilty wince. She'd kind of let her thoughts wander. "Amen."

Nancy leaned over her bowl. "Mmm, this smells good." She scooped up a spoonful and ladled it into her mouth. When a look of pure bliss crossed her face, Summer beamed and reached for her own spoon. Nancy looked over at her as she dug into her bowl for more. "Still waiting for details."

Summer took a bite of the chili, buying time. It really did taste good. Not quite as good as Rosa's but pretty close. She swallowed. Nancy was still watching her, and Summer's shoulders slumped a little. "All right, I'll admit it went better than I thought it was going to. I was afraid it might be a bit awkward, since we barely know each other, but actually it was surprisingly easy. Like having dinner with a brother."

"That's how you think of him, then, like a brother?"

Summer swirled her spoon through the chili.

"That's what I thought."

She exhaled. "All right, not like a brother."

"What, then?"

"I don't know. It's hard to explain. Like someone I've known a lot longer than a couple of weeks, I guess."

"But you haven't."

"No. I never saw him before he walked into the coffee shop the day after I started working there."

Nancy pursed her lips. "Hmm."

"Nancy."

Her landlady chuckled. "Sorry."

Summer grabbed a dinner roll from the basket. "Are you actually lonely?"

"Not now that you're here." Nancy sighed. "But yes, I guess I am, sometimes."

"Have you ever been married?"

Such a dreamy look crossed her face that Summer paused in the act of buttering her roll.

"I have, actually. To a wonderful man, Patrick."

"What happened?"

"We had ten amazing years together and then, without warning, he had a heart attack at work one day and he was gone. He was forty-two years old."

Summer inhaled sharply and set down her knife. "I'm so sorry. I can't imagine losing someone you love like that."

"It was hard. I don't think I've ever really gotten over it, to be honest."

"You mentioned a son the other day. Do you have any other children?"

Nancy took a sip from her water glass and wiped a drop from her chin before setting it down. "No, just Robert. He moved out west a few years ago, so I don't really see him. Or my two granddaughters."

Summer reached across the table and grasped Nancy's hand. The older woman's fingers trembled slightly in hers. "I'm really sorry."

"Thank you." Nancy squeezed her hand.

Summer let her go and picked up the knife.

"I know what you're doing, by the way." Nancy calmly stuck a spoonful of chili into her mouth.

"What do you mean?"

Nancy jabbed the empty spoon in her direction. "You're changing the subject so I won't press you for more details about your date with Ryan."

Summer let out an exasperated breath. "It wasn't..." Her eyes met the knowing ones of her landlady. "Look, there's not much to tell. We ate, we talked, and then he walked me to my car."

"Did he kiss you?"

Summer's head jerked. "Of course not."

"Are you going out again?"

"We're supposed to try another restaurant on Friday, but I don't know. I'm thinking about canceling."

Nancy leaned back in her chair and cocked her head, red curls bouncing. "Why are you fighting this so hard?"

Summer rubbed the side of her hand across her forehead. "It's just that my life is complicated right now."

"Oh, so you're waiting until life is nice and simple, then you'll think about maybe opening your heart up to someone?"

She frowned. "When you put it that way, it does sound a little ridiculous."

"Ana, how old are you?"

"Twenty-eight."

"Well, I'm sixty-four and I have a few more years of experience than you, so maybe you'll forgive me for offering a little advice. Don't keep closing doors, darlin'. Life is precious but fleeting. I remember being twenty-eight, believe it or not. I was seeing Patrick but reluctant to get serious. Somehow I thought we had all the time in the world. If I knew then what I know now, I wouldn't have put Patrick off as long as I did. I wanted everything to be in place before we married. As far as I was concerned, we both had to be settled in our jobs, we needed to have enough money for a house, and we had to have the next few years of our lives all mapped out before we walked down the aisle. All I managed to do by trying to make things *simple* for us was rob myself of those extra years of joy we could have had together."

Summer set down the roll, her appetite gone. "That makes sense, I guess."

Nancy's smile held compassion. "I know it's scary, taking a risk. But risks are what make life exhilarating and filled with joy." She ran a piece of bread around the bottom of her bowl, soaking up the last few drops. "I'm not suggesting you jump into anything without thinking about it, but I do recommend you at least consider long and hard why you might be so reluctant to spend time with Ryan. If there's no spark, or you've seen any red flags, that's one thing. But if it's only fear, push through it. If you do, I suspect that what will be waiting for you on the other side is well worth any *complications* that might arise as a result. Besides, you know what the Bible says. If you are alone and you fall, no one will help you up, but if someone is at your side, you can help each other. Sometimes, when it's right, letting another person into your life can end up making your life simpler. Or, at the very least, a lot more fun."

"You might be right."

"I usually am." Nancy winked at her before rising and carrying her dishes into the kitchen.

Summer sagged against the back of her chair. *Was* Nancy right? Was fear keeping her from opening the door to the possibility of anything happening with Ryan? Or was she simply being careful so she didn't make a huge mistake?

Sometimes it was awfully hard to tell the difference between the two.

CHAPTER TWENTY-THREE

Summer pulled the door closed and locked it. When she turned, Ryan, a little more casual tonight in jeans and his brown leather jacket, stood at the end of the walkway, leaning against a lamppost, waiting for her. He'd asked again at the coffee shop if he could pick her up, and in a moment of weakness—Nancy's question about why she was fighting this so hard flitting through her mind—she'd agreed.

In spite of her determination to keep any interest in him beyond friendship in check, her stomach flip flopped a little as she headed down the walkway. When she was a few feet away from him, he pushed away from the pole, that slow smile that made it pretty much impossible to think of him as a brother crossing his face. "You look great."

"Thank you." Self-conscious, Summer adjusted the black scarf she had wrapped around her neck and smoothed down the front of her red Columbia jacket. "So do you."

"Are you okay to walk? Benton's is only a few blocks away."

"Sure." Did he understand that she was still a little reluctant to get in a car with him? Either way, she appreciated the gesture. "I came prepared." She tugged a pair of gloves from her pocket and pulled them on as she fell into step beside him. They chatted lightly about the weather and the houses they passed, the silences between words comfortable, even oddly familiar.

When they reached the restaurant, Ryan held the door for her and she smiled at him as she brushed by. He touched her back lightly, guiding her toward a quiet table in the back corner, and Summer bit her lip. It was getting harder and harder not to consider this a date.

Daphne had assured her that the food was excellent at Benton's, if at the other end of the spectrum from the high-end Italian they'd enjoyed the other night. The smell of hot grease accompanied them as they crossed the room and they both ordered burgers and fries. When the food arrived, Summer gaped at the giant burger—how on earth was she supposed to even get it into her mouth?

When she finally screwed up the nerve to try, ketchup and mustard dripped onto her chin while a big piece of tomato plopped onto her plate. Ryan laughed, although he wasn't having much more success with his. Summer grabbed her set of cutlery to unwrap the napkin from around it. "Is it acceptable to use a knife and fork, do you think?"

"Absolutely not." Ryan reached over and grabbed her cutlery before she could snag the napkin. "The rules explicitly state that you must use only your hands or be disqualified."

When she lunged for the knife and fork, he grasped her wrist and held it while waving for a server to come over. Summer swiped the condiments off her chin with the back of her free hand. When the young man stopped at their table, she struggled to keep a straight face as Ryan handed him both their sets. "Can you take these, please? We won't be needing them."

"Of course." The young man's forehead wrinkled, but he nodded and took the cutlery.

When he had disappeared into the back, Ryan's eyes met Summer's. "Can you believe that guy? He looked at me like no one ever asked their server to remove the knives and forks from the table before."

"Imagine that," Summer said dryly as she inclined her head toward the burger. "All right, fine. You're going to have to take what you get, then."

Ryan shrugged. "Not a problem. After all, this isn't a date, right?"

She glanced down. Their arms both rested on the table, his fingers lightly circling her wrist, her skin burning beneath his. He waited a beat before slowly pulling his hand away. Summer forced herself to meet his gaze, to level her breathing before answering him. "Right."

He waved a hand through the air. "Have at it, then."

She picked up the burger with both hands and took a bite. Ketchup dripped onto her chin, but as he had sent away the napkins with the cutlery, there was little she could do about it.

Ryan's eyes gleamed as he reached for his burger. "The one with the cleanest shirt at the end wins."

Summer glanced down at her light blue sweater. This was not going to be pretty. Good thing she had a coat to put on before they had to walk through the restaurant again. "You're on."

She settled on a strategy of taking tiny bites, which minimized the amount of drippings from the burger, and a few minutes later only a few red and yellow splotches dotted her shirt. She did have to press her lips together to keep from laughing every time she glanced at Ryan, munching away, an innocent look on his face as though he had no idea—or didn't care—that he had a big blob of relish on his chin.

Halfway through his burger, he set it on his plate. "All right, I concede. We're setting a bad example for those kids over there."

He lifted a hand to the server while inclining his head toward a table in the corner. Summer glanced over. Two young boys stared at them. As Summer watched, one pointed at them and the other giggled. Their mother, trying unsuccessfully to get them to wipe their faces, sent a reproachful glare their way.

Summer covered a laugh by coughing softly into her fist.

"Can we get a few napkins here, please?" Ryan asked the server, the same guy who had removed their cutlery, when he came over to their table.

The guy shot a look at Ryan's long-sleeved black T-shirt. His forehead wrinkled again, but he'd been well trained. He merely nodded and replied, "Of course," before heading to the front counter. A moment later he returned and set a pile of napkins on the table.

"That guy's getting a really good tip." Ryan's lips twitched as he handed half the pile to Summer. "Actually, kudos to you, too. You're a good sport."

"I don't believe in shying away from a challenge." Summer swiped at the front of her shirt.

He snorted. "Believe me, I know."

She glanced up sharply. Ryan had been rubbing a napkin over a spot on his sleeve, but he froze now, as though he hadn't meant to say what he'd said. When he looked up, his cheeks had colored slightly. "I mean, that's pretty clear. Not many women would agree to a contest that involved spilling food on yourself in the middle of a busy restaurant."

She studied him a moment. "I suppose not."

He tossed the napkin onto the table. "Are you going to finish your burger?"

Summer was pretty sure she wouldn't be eating anything for a week. "No, thanks. If I take one more bite I'll need to be wheeled out of here on a dolly."

"Me too." He scrutinized the pile of food on his plate. "Next time I think we should split one."

She blinked at his casual assumption that there would be a next time. "Sounds like a good idea."

"How about a walk?"

"Perfect." Summer gave up on her shirt and slid her arms into her coat.

The server, still looking a little unsure about the two of them, brought the bill on a tray with two peppermints. When Summer reached for it, Ryan snatched it from under her fingers. "I said this one was on me." She sighed and took a peppermint instead. He dropped cash onto the tray and pushed back his chair. "Shall we?"

He waited until Summer had gone ahead, then followed her out the door. A blast of cold air hit her when she stepped outside and Summer wrapped the scarf around her neck and tugged the gloves up higher on her wrists. Ryan grimaced. "Sorry. Maybe we should have driven."

"No, it's fine. I like the cold, actually. We didn't really have seasons in Mexico, so I enjoy them all now." The faint rumble of the waterfall behind the mill a block away drew her. "Want to walk along the river?"

In the light of the streetlamp they were passing under, he nodded. "Sure."

They walked along the stone wall Summer had followed the day she'd arrived in Elora. The path and woods appeared considerably more foreboding in the dark, but when they reached the curve of the wall that signaled the edge of the water, bright lights twinkling on the other side of the river lit up the area, giving it the fairyland feel she'd picked up from the pictures in the map book.

Still, she contemplated the path that wound along the top of the ravine, a steep drop on one side and thick trees on the other, a little dubiously. "Should we keep going?"

"It's completely up to you." Ryan's voice sounded a little strained.

Another challenge. Summer lifted her chin. "I'm game if you are."

He held out his hand in the direction of the pathway. "Lead on."

She started down the path. Lampposts every twenty feet or so helped light the way enough that she was able to avoid the tree roots that occasionally burst through the soil in the middle of the path. Concentrating on retaining her footing, she jumped when Ryan touched her elbow. "Sorry, I wanted to make sure you saw the curve ahead."

Summer looked up. The wall sloped to the right ahead of them. To the left, steps led down to a rounded area that overlooked the river. "Should we check out the view?"

"There won't be much to see in the dark." The words sounded tight, as though he had to work to get them out.

What is that about? "Might as well look while we're here." She started down the stairs. After a few seconds, his footsteps echoed on the stone behind her. At the bottom of the stairs, a low stone wall encircled a flat area. Summer reached the wall and pressed both palms to it so she could lean over the top. Soft light from the houses on the far side of the river and the headlights of cars driving over the bridge fifty yards down the gorge illuminated the area a little. Far below, the river, a ribbon of sparkling white in the moonlight, wended its way between the shores and under the bridge.

"Careful." Ryan grasped both her shoulders. A tremor passed through his fingers.

Summer straightened. He let her go when she turned around. "Not a fan of heights?"

"Heights don't bother me. You tumbling down a ravine in the dark would."

"Oh." The concern in his voice sent warmth rushing through her chest. "Sorry. I didn't mean to worry you."

"It's okay." A gust of wind swept past them, catching the ends of her scarf and sending both flapping in the breeze. Ryan grabbed for them and stepped closer.

His eyes locked with hers and Summer struggled to draw in a breath.

"By the way, I forgot to give you your prize."

She blinked. "My prize?"

"Yes, for winning the cleanest shirt competition earlier."

"Ah. What is it?"

He tugged on the ends of her scarf, pulling her closer. "This." He lowered his head. A couple of inches from her, he paused. "Okay?"

She should absolutely say no. They'd just met and she didn't know for sure that he wasn't involved with anyone else. Or that she wasn't, for that matter. It would be smart to take a little time to think about all the... *That's your problem, Summer. No pienses tanto. You think too much.* She took a deep breath. "Okay."

He pressed his lips lightly to hers. The kiss lasted only seconds but still Summer might have swayed on her feet if he hadn't been holding on to her scarf when he lifted his head.

"So," he grinned as he wrapped the ends around her neck and tucked them into the folds, "can we back away from the edge now?"

That was a good idea. In more ways than one. Summer nodded and followed him to the top of the stairs. "Should we keep going?" Her voice rasped a little when she spoke, and she cleared her throat as she inclined her head in the direction of the path.

"It only gets darker that way because there are no houses across the river here. Why don't we explore that path another time, preferably in daylight?"

"You're right, probably enough exploring for one night."

Ryan contemplated her for a few seconds, obviously catching the double meaning of her words. He didn't comment though, only smiled. "Fair enough. Let's head back to civilization."

Summer nodded and started down the path, carefully picking her way around rocks and over fallen branches. Not carefully enough. A tree root caught the toe of her leather boot and she stumbled and fell to her knees. The jolt sent a lightning bolt of pain through her head, reminding her of the head injury she'd nearly forgotten about this evening.

Ryan leapt around in front of her. "Are you okay?"

"I think so." Summer pressed a hand to the ground, intending to push herself to her feet. Instead, her fingers broke through the thin ice covering a puddle, plunging her hand into freezing water.

"Oh, Ana." Ryan held out both arms. "Here."

The fake name sounded all wrong on his lips. Summer grasped his forearms and allowed him to pull her to her feet. "It's fine." In spite of the cold, heat flared in her cheeks.

"It's not fine. Your fingers are going to freeze." Ryan tugged off her glove and shoved it into his pocket. Taking her hand in both of his, he massaged warmth back into it.

"I can't believe I did that." She should free herself from his grasp, but she couldn't bring herself to. "I'm not usually such a klutz."

He grinned. "No problem. You're not the first woman I've knocked off her feet."

The words were teasing, but Summer didn't doubt the truth of them. The idea of him having the same effect on other women that he was having on her at the moment bothered her more than she cared to admit. She tugged on her fingers but he didn't let go.

"Seriously, it's freezing out here. I've taken a few first aid courses and I know you have to keep your hand warm. Let me hold onto it until we get back to your place. Purely for the sake of preventing frostbite, of course."

"A medicinal hand hold, you mean."

"Exactly."

"Well, I *would* hate to lose a finger."

"Good call." He tightened his grip as they continued down the path. Summer kept her eyes glued to the ground, watching for other potential tripping hazards. The uneven ground continued to send shoots of pain up from the base of her skull like mini fireworks, and she breathed a sigh of relief when they reached the sidewalk. Strolling down the main street, her hand securely in his, she had to admit that this whole evening felt an awful lot like a date. Summer blew out a breath. *Give it up, Summer. You're not fooling anyone.* Not herself, not Ryan, not even Nancy, and her landlady had never seen the two of them together.

"Are your knees okay?"

She did a quick assessment. They stung a little, but she wasn't about to tell him that—he might feel as though he needed to pick her up and carry her to prevent further injury to her joints. "They're fine. Any major damage was confined to my ego."

"Really? I wouldn't have thought you'd have much ego left after wearing most of your dinner out of the restaurant."

She shot him an indignant look. "As I recall, you wore more of yours than I did mine."

"Hence you being awarded that fabulous prize."

"Which I suspect was every bit as much for you as for me."

Ryan laughed. "Busted."

Summer studied him in the windows as they walked by. Her hand was warm in his and fit perfectly. Probably best to get her mind off thoughts like that, though. "Tell me about them."

"Who?"

"All those women you knocked off their feet."

He grimaced. "Busted again. As far as I know, I've only knocked one woman off her feet."

"And where is she now?"

Ryan let out a melodramatic sigh. "She's off somewhere, far away. And she's forgotten all about me."

Summer bit her lip. He said the words lightly, but they were carried, like a piece of driftwood, on the undercurrent of a deeper emotion she couldn't quite identify. Pain, maybe? As much as he wanted her to believe it didn't bother him that the woman who had meant something to him in the past had left him, it clearly did. "I'm sorry."

They had reached the lamp post at the end of Nancy's walkway. Ryan stopped and faced her, not letting go of her hand. "What are you sorry for?"

"That this woman, whoever she is, hurt you. Although I seriously doubt it."

"That she hurt me?"

"That she's forgotten you. I'm sure, deep down, she remembers."

For a moment he didn't speak, only searched her face with such intensity in his eyes—the same intensity she'd seen the first time he came into the bakery—that her knees, already slightly sore, went alarmingly weak. She leaned back against the post, grateful for its support. After a moment, he offered her a sad smile and the intensity was broken. "Maybe."

Summer swallowed. That look wasn't anger, like she'd first thought, but sorrow. Grief, even. Obviously he'd cared deeply for this woman and she had hurt him, badly. A fierce protectiveness rose in Summer, shocking her to her core. How had she become so invested in this man's welfare? In his happiness? He was practically a stranger to her.

Although somehow he didn't feel like a stranger.

"Ana." His voice was low and soft as he took a step toward her.

She almost told him then, unable to stand him not knowing her real name. *You don't know him, Summer. He could be dangerous.* The reminder that someone was after her streaked through her and she pushed away from the post. It *was* a little strange that this man had arrived in town the same time she did. For all she knew, he could have followed her here and was playing some kind of long game with her, getting her to trust him before he carried out whatever nefarious plans he had for her. "I should go in." She yanked her fingers from his.

This time he didn't resist, only studied her for a moment before nodding. "All right."

"Thank you. I had a really good time tonight." The words came out more stiffly than she intended. His shoulders deflated slightly and she mentally kicked herself. He hadn't done anything to suggest that his intentions were anything but honorable. The head injury was making her paranoid, and that wasn't fair to him. While it would be wise to keep her guard up and not reveal too much about herself too soon, she didn't want to live in fear, either. She exhaled. "Should we try another place on Daphne's list next week? My treat this time?"

His face softened. "I'd like that." He pulled her glove from the pocket of his leather jacket. "Here."

"Thanks." She took it from him. "And thank you for the first aid treatment." Holding up her bare hand, she wiggled her fingers. "Still have all five."

"Good."

That slow smile crossed his face and it took everything she had not to lean against the post again. "See you at the coffee shop?"

"Count on it."

She forced herself to skirt around him and make her way up the walk. When she reached the door and glanced back, he stood under the lamp post, watching her. He lifted a hand and she waved in response before slipping inside.

As she hung her coat up on the tree in the front hall, she caught a glimpse of herself in the floor-length mirror on the closet door and wrinkled her nose. Between her stained shirt and the tiny rip in the knee of her jeans, the evening had taken its toll on her wardrobe.

Still—she touched a finger to her lips—in spite of the multiple hits to her ego, and her attempts to convince herself otherwise, it was the best date she could remember having in her life.

CHAPTER TWENTY-FOUR

Jude strolled down the sidewalk, barely resisting the urge to break into the dance routine from *Singin' in the Rain* as he walked past a lamp post. Approaching a dark Elantra, parked half a block down the street from Nancy's place, he slowed. Was someone sitting in the front seat? When he drew slightly ahead of the vehicle, he glanced back. A man in a black hoodie looked up from his phone and nodded at Jude.

Jude nodded back, glanced at the licence plate, and continued walking down the street. Likely no one with any connection to Summer or what had happened to her, but still, a bit odd. A vague disquiet ate away at the good mood he'd been in when he left her at the door. He'd been pretty sure no one had followed him to Elora, but someone could have tapped into the GPS on his phone without him knowing. The man looked relatively harmless, but not all criminals wore their propensity for violence like a tattoo across their foreheads. The world would be a much safer place if they did.

He'd parked his car around the corner from Summer's, knowing she'd be more comfortable walking than getting into a vehicle with him. After sliding behind the wheel, Jude tugged the phone out of his pocket and punched in a number.

"Travers."

"Evan, it's Jude. I'm calling about Summer."

"Is she okay?"

"So far. I passed a guy sitting in a car half a block from her place a few minutes ago, though. Can you run the plates for me?" Jude gave him the information.

"Hold on." Keys clicked.

A minute or two passed before Evan came back on the line. "Car's registered to a Peter Díaz. No record. No outstanding warrants. Seems clean."

The muscles that had tightened across Jude's shoulders since he'd seen the vehicle relaxed a little. "That's good news. I was sure it was nothing, but I wanted to check."

"I don't blame you. Anything else suspicious going on?"

"Not that I've noticed."

Something creaked, as though Evan had leaned back in his desk chair. "She regain her memory?"

"No, unfortunately. I don't suppose a security detail has been approved for her."

Evan sighed. "Not yet."

"Whoever attacked her is still out there, Evan. He may even be here in town."

"I know that." The chair creaked again, followed by the sound of a door closing. When he spoke, Evan had lowered his voice. "Look, Jude, I shouldn't be telling you this, but internal affairs has been conducting an investigation for weeks now. We're thinking somebody here could be on Mendoza's payroll. It's the only way to explain how he's always a step ahead of us. We have no idea who, though, so I don't want to send over just anybody to keep an eye on her."

Jude rubbed his eyes with his fingers. "That makes sense, but..."

"I know. I don't like her being this vulnerable any more than you do. Tell you what, there are a few guys here I absolutely trust. I'll talk to them and we'll try to have somebody there, if not all the time, at least driving past the places she's staying and working once in a while, checking things out, okay?"

Jude lowered his hand. "Okay, thanks."

"No problem. We're on this 24/7. You know that."

"Yeah." Jude exhaled. "I do."

"Good. I'll be in touch the second anything breaks on the case, and you let me know if you spot anything else that doesn't feel right, anything at all."

"I will. Thanks." Jude disconnected the call and tossed the device on the passenger seat. He hadn't gotten as much as he'd hoped for, but anything was better than nothing at this point. He only hoped it would be enough. He ran back over their conversation.

Vulnerable. That had never been a word he'd associated with Summer. He supposed she was though, at the moment, even if she didn't know it. And Evan was right, Jude didn't like it. He'd never associated the word with his sister, either. And look what had happened to—

Jude leaned forward abruptly and turned the key in the ignition. He wasn't going there. Not tonight. Tomorrow, though, he did have somewhere he needed to go before he chickened out.

Like he'd done every day for the past five years.

CHAPTER TWENTY-FIVE

Jude parked at the curb in front of the house with the gray siding and black shutters. *Go in.* He tightened his grip on the steering wheel. *Just get out of the car, make your way up the walkway, and knock on the door.* Something he'd done a thousand times in his life, on a thousand different doors. So simple, yet the thought of knocking on this particular door was sending his stomach into loops like the craziest ride at an amusement park. What was the worst thing that could happen?

That was the million dollar question. The answer to which he didn't even want to contemplate. *You're a coward, McCall.* Not a revelation. He'd come face to face with that truth about himself a long time ago. Sort of thought he'd dealt with that flaw in his character, but apparently not.

He barely resisted the urge to bang his head on the steering wheel. Seriously, what was he, a three year old terrified of the bogey man beneath his bed? He was a man and it was high time he started acting like one.

Disgusted with himself, Jude pried his fingers from the steering wheel and threw open the door of the car. The front walkway stretched in front of him like an endless road, the destination murky and unknown, cloaked in fog. Maybe it would be better if he came back another day.

Enough. He forced himself to take a step. And then another. With each one, his knees weakened further. By the time he reached the small set of stairs leading up to the front porch, they appeared as daunting as the climb up the outside of a Mayan pyramid.

Jude pushed back his shoulders and ascended the five steps. The floorboards of the porch hadn't been painted in a while, and they creaked beneath his shoes as he crossed them. Before he could lose what little nerve he had, he lifted a hand and rapped on the screen door. The sound echoed around the quiet neighborhood like a gunshot. In his ears, anyway.

Nothing moved inside the house. Jude took a step back. Well, he'd tried. That was all anyone could ask of him, wasn't it? He backed up another step but froze at the sound of footsteps in the hallway on the other side of the door.

His chest clenched when the wooden door opened. For a moment, the woman on the other side of the screen only stared at him. Then she pressed the backs of her fingers to her mouth. "Jude."

He swallowed the lump that had risen in his throat at the sight of her. "Hi, Mom."

CHAPTER TWENTY-SIX

His mother stepped back, cleared her throat. "Come in."

Legs weak, Jude stepped over the threshold. As he closed the door, a memory crashed through him. Of creeping out onto the porch that night and pulling this very door closed behind him. Softly, so no one would hear him. No one would try to stop him.

When he turned around, his mother stood watching him, hazel eyes filled with tears. After a moment, she let out a raspy laugh, stepped forward, and threw her arms around him. Jude hesitated before pulling her to him and resting his chin on the head that had a few more gray hairs sprinkled amongst the brown than the last time he'd seen her, five years before. The smell of lilies of the valley drifted from her. That hadn't changed, anyway.

She moved out of his embrace and hooked her arm through his. "Come in and we'll talk." She took him to the kitchen and directed him to the table by the window. "Sit. I'll make tea."

Tea. Jude grinned wryly. As far as his mother was concerned, tea was the answer to every problem. No issue in the world couldn't be resolved if both parties sat down over a steaming pot and talked things out. If she'd ever been elected prime minister, it certainly would have been the way she'd dealt with any global crisis. Which, at the moment, felt about the scale they were operating on.

He sobered. "Where's Cash and Maddie?" Just saying the names of his brother and sister reopened a wound deep down inside him. Their father had come and gone when Jude was a kid—often disappearing on some bender for days at a time. Shortly after Maddie was born he left and didn't come back. He had a new family now and they'd barely heard from him over the years. All the more reason Jude should have stuck around, not left Cash to be the only man in the family.

She set the kettle on the stove and turned to face him. "Cash is at work. He's a paramedic now and has a twelve-hour shift today before a day off tomorrow. And he doesn't live here anymore—he has his own place, an apartment on the west side of town. Maddie's in college so she's at school, but," she glanced at the clock hanging above the coffee maker, "she'll be home in a few minutes. She'll be thrilled to see you."

"Will she?"

His mother's steady gaze met his. "Yes, she will. She's missed you terribly. She cried herself to sleep for weeks after you left. So did I, for that matter." His mother turned and flung open the cupboard beside the stove. She lifted down a basket filled with various boxes of tea and Jude's chest tightened. So much hadn't changed. So how could everything feel so different?

"I'm sorry, Mom." The words sounded so futile, ridiculous even. How could three words ever begin to convey his remorse?

She set down the basket and pressed both palms to the counter. For a few seconds she didn't move then she faced him, leaning back against the counter as though she needed the support. "So am I."

He blinked. What could she possibly have to be sorry about? He was the one who left. He was the one who hadn't been able to save Tessa.

With a sigh, she pushed away from the counter and walked over to sit down on the chair beside him. Reaching for his hand, she squeezed it tight. "I know you blamed yourself for Tessa's death. But I was so wrapped up in my own grief that I wasn't able to reach out to you. It wasn't until you left that I realized how badly I had failed you. And I would have given anything to reach out to you then, to convince you to come home, but I didn't know how to find you. I tried. Cash tried too, but it was as though you'd fallen off the face of the earth."

"I know." His throat was so tight he could barely speak. "I don't even know what to say, how to tell you how sorry I am that you didn't only lose Tessa, you lost me too. At the time I thought it was for the best, that I was a constant reminder to you of what happened to her. But now I see that I was being selfish and weak. It was me who needed to escape the constant reminders, because I didn't have the courage to stay and face them like you did. You and Cash and Maddie." He lifted her hand to his cheek. It was soft and cool against his flushed skin. "I don't have any words to make that all right."

"You don't need them." She stroked his cheek lightly with her thumb. "You came home. That says everything you need to say."

Was she really going to let him off the hook that easily? If only he could do the same for himself. The kettle whistled and she tugged her hand from his, swiping a tear off her cheek as she went to make the tea.

Jude slumped against the back of the chair. Runners crossing the finish line at the end of a marathon couldn't possibly feel any shakier or more drained—physically and emotionally—than he did at the moment.

"Chai, right?"

Jude looked over at his mother. She held up the box of his favorite tea and he nodded. "You remember."

She dropped two bags into the pot, poured boiling water over them, then replaced the lid with a clank and carried the pot over to the table. After setting it down, she walked back to the cupboard and pulled out a bright red mug with a yellow smiley face. "I remember everything." She took down another mug and handed the red one to Jude.

"I can't believe you still have this."

"It's been sitting at the front of the cupboard since you left. I think of you every morning when I see it. For a long time that hurt, a lot. Gradually though, the good memories came back, slowly but surely becoming stronger than the hurt, although that never left completely. It was worth it though, worth not letting thoughts of you either turn bitter or fade away. Whatever happened in the past, you are still my son. You still hold a place in my heart that could never be filled by anyone or anything else."

He had no response for that. For a few seconds, neither of them spoke. Then she patted his hand and reached for the pot. "So, tell me everything. Where did you go? What have you been up to the last few years? Do you have a wife? Do I have any grandbabies I don't know about?"

The light was back in her eyes. Jude laughed. "No. No wife and no babies." She filled his mug and he pulled it closer and wrapped both hands around it. Where did he begin to fill her in on his life the last five years? How much could he even tell her? Knowing everything he had done since he'd left, everything he'd been involved with, wouldn't make her feel any better about him, but he was tired of secrets. Tired of hiding.

Still, he was done being selfish. He wouldn't unload anything on her simply to clear his own conscience. Not if it added to her burden in any way.

Before he could decide where to start, the front door flung open, and his sister called out, "Mom, I'm home."

His mother's eyes met his. "Give us a moment, okay?"

Jude nodded, watching her as she made her way out of the kitchen and down the hallway to the front door. How would his sister react to him being here? She'd been so young when he left, barely eighteen. A tough age at any time, but how much tougher when she'd just lost the big sister she adored? He should have been there for her.

He shot a glance at the door leading from the kitchen into the back yard. Maybe he could sneak out, come back another time. Facing his mom had been enough for one day. If he left, Maddie would have more time to come to grips with him being back in town. Maybe she wouldn't even want to see him, and if she didn't, he would respect that and stay away.

His fingers tightened around the red mug. *Seriously, Jude. When are you going to stop running away?*

He forced himself to sit and wait. The murmur of voices drifted to him from the hallway. His sister's startled cry struck him with the force of a blow and he let go of the mug with one hand to wipe away a bead of sweat that had started down one temple.

Then she was there, in the doorway of the kitchen, staring at him. Even at 23, she looked like the teenager he remembered. She wore a navy Conestoga College hoodie and jeans and her dark hair was caught up in a high ponytail.

Jude's heart thudded erratically against his ribs as he pushed back his chair and stood. For several long, excruciating seconds her blue eyes, roiling with emotion, searched his. Then she stalked across the room, clenched her fist, and pounded him in the upper arm. "You left."

"I know. I'm sorry."

"I needed you." Her voice quivered.

Jude lifted his hands. "It was stupid and selfish of me, kiddo. I'm really sorry. I know I can't, really, but if you'll let me, I want to try to make it up to you."

She raised herself slightly on tiptoes and held that position, as if debating with herself whether to stay or turn and go. Finally, she lowered her heels slowly to the floor. The intense emotion radiating off of her eased. "That's going to take a lot."

"Understood."

"I mean an awful lot."

"Like Joey's every day for a month?" Her favorite place to go for ice cream when she was a teen. Did she like it still? Was Joey's even around anymore? He repressed a sigh. He didn't only have a lot of making up to do but a lot of catching up, too.

"More like a year."

"You got it." Not that he'd necessarily be in town that long, but he'd figure out a way to make it up to his sister for abandoning her if it took the rest of his life.

She flung herself against him so hard he took a step backwards before steadying himself and wrapping his arms around her. She sobbed against his chest while he held her. For several minutes she cried, all the tears she'd needed to shed in his arms years ago, more than likely. Jude stroked her back as she wept, his T-shirt dampening beneath her cheek.

His gaze met his mother's over Maddie's head. She stood, her hand pressed to her mouth, watching them through tear-filled eyes. He couldn't believe that Maddie would trust him like that. Or that his mother had welcomed him home without hesitation. He didn't deserve either their trust or their welcome, and to receive both nearly drove him to his knees.

Thank you, Lord. Even if his family didn't believe, they'd still shown him grace, the way God had when Jude had gone, weeping, to him. The prodigal son who was fully aware he did not deserve to be called a son. Far greater grace than he deserved, but he was more grateful for it than he could say.

He pressed a kiss to his sister's head and tightened his hold on her. As it had to have been for the younger son in the story, coming home had been harder and more amazing than he could have ever dreamt, but the thing he had to do next might be even harder.

He had to face his older brother.

CHAPTER TWENTY-SEVEN

Summer lifted a slice of lemon loaf, dripping with glaze, from the platter on the counter and slid it onto a plate next to a pumpkin spice latte Daphne had made. The woman who'd placed the order had come into the bakery a few minutes after Ryan had arrived. A leggy blonde who looked like she might be more at home on a runway than in a coffee shop in little Elora. Summer was surprised she'd ordered the loaf as it didn't appear as though she'd ingested a carb in her life.

Ryan had smiled and thanked her when Summer handed him his coffee and croissant but, since there was a long line of customers behind him, they hadn't been able to talk much before he'd taken his laptop and breakfast to a quiet table in the corner. A table that Summer was studiously avoiding looking over at. The woman she'd served had no such qualms. She managed to pull her debit card out of her wallet and tap the machine to pay her bill without taking her eyes off of Ryan. As Summer watched, she gathered up her drink and food, tossed her long hair over her shoulder, and wended her way past the tables to the one closest to him.

No es asunto tuyo. She sighed. No, it wasn't her business. She and Ryan had only been out a couple of times. They weren't seeing each other, and they certainly weren't involved in an exclusive relationship. She had no right to feel this territorial about him.

"So, how did it go Friday night?" The crowd had thinned, finally, and Daphne wandered over to stand beside Summer at the counter.

"Good. The food was amazing, although the burgers we ordered could have fed a couple of small villages."

Daphne leaned back against the counter and folded her arms over her chest. "That's great, but I wasn't talking about the food."

Summer swiped crumbs off the counter with the side of her hand into her cupped palm. "I know."

"So? From the smile he gave you when he came in, I'm guessing you have a few juicy tidbits to share."

She dumped the crumbs into the garbage can. From past experience, she knew there was little use trying to keep anything from her friend. "All right, we did have a good time. After dinner, we went for a walk along the river, which was mostly great."

Daphne arched an eyebrow. "Mostly?"

"Yeah. You know that area where you go down a few stairs and look out over the river?"

"You mean Lover's Leap?"

Summer blinked. "Is that what it's called?"

"Yeah, some ancient legend about a native princess jumping to her death from that spot after her love was killed in battle or something. What about it?"

"Nothing really, except Ryan seemed a bit uptight when I leaned over the wall to see the view."

"Hmm. People do fall down the ravine sometimes. A few hikers have been killed at the gorge. He was likely worried about your safety."

"That's what he said."

Daphne pursed her lips. "That's sweet."

"It was, actually. He was sweet later, too, when I tripped over a tree root and fell."

"Oh no, were you okay?"

Summer's cheeks warmed, remembering. "It was more embarrassing than anything. Especially when I went to get up and stuck my hand in a puddle of icy water."

Daphne's hand flew to her mouth. "Ana."

"I know. Total klutz, which I'm not usually." Unless she'd become one in the last few years. Or maybe after she'd taken the blow to the head. She frowned. Was that possible?

"What did he do?"

"He helped me up and we headed home."

Daphne cocked her head. "Was that it? I mean, that's nice and all, but not necessarily sweet, and you said—"

Summer held up a hand. "I know what I said." Might as well save them both some time. "All right, he took my glove off and held my hand to keep it warm until we got home. Which, yes, was sweet."

A dreamy look crossed Daphne's face. "And romantic."

Summer shot a look at the corner in time to see the blonde flip her hair back again as she leaned close to Ryan. He said something and she laughed as though it was the funniest thing she'd ever heard. Ignoring the slight tightening in her stomach, Summer turned back to her friend. "You're married to the most romantic man in the world— why do you feel the need to live vicariously through my essentially non-existent love life?"

Daphne smiled as she looked over at the door to the kitchen. "Because I want you to be as happy as I am. And Ryan seems like a really nice guy. Not to mention that he is muy guapo."

Summer flushed. "Daphne." Ryan might be extremely handsome, but he was also very much in the room. While he likely didn't speak a word of Spanish, she still didn't want to have this conversation in his presence.

Daphne hip-checked her lightly. "Admit it, you think so too."

Irrepressible. Summer shook her head. "All right, I admit it. Él es muy guapo. Satisfied? También está muy interesado en la mujer hermosa que le está hablando."

Daphne peered around her. "He is not interested in her. She's obviously throwing herself at him and he is trying very hard to extricate himself from the conversation and get back to whatever it is he was doing on that laptop."

"Writing."

"He's a writer?"

"Apparently."

Her eyes lit up. "That's very cool. Anything I might have heard of?"

"I doubt it. He says he mostly writes articles for online magazines." Summer nudged her with her shoulder. "And could you stop staring at him? He'll know we're talking about him."

"Fine." Daphne reached for the tongs and started rearranging the food on the platters, straightening everything after the morning rush. "Are you going to see him again?"

"We're supposed to go out tomorrow night. Unless he's making other plans." Her gaze wandered again to Ryan's table and she blew out a breath. *Basta. Enough.* "Since it's slowed down, I'm going to take the garbage out to the dumpster, okay?"

"Sure." Daphne set the lid on a platter and reached for another one. "I'll keep an eye on..." She tipped her head in Ryan's direction as subtly as she did everything else, "...things here."

Summer rolled her eyes before pushing through the kitchen doors. Shawn stood in his usual place at the island, his apron and beard coated in flour. He looked up from the bowl of batter he was stirring and smiled at her. "Hey, Ana. How are things out front? My wife behaving?"

Summer grinned. "Other than trying to arrange my love life for me, I suppose she is."

He laughed. "That sounds like Daph."

She lifted the lid from the garbage can. "It's pretty quiet out there, so I'll take this to the dumpster."

"Great, thanks."

Summer hauled the bag out of the can and headed for the back door. A little fresh air would hopefully clear her mind of thoughts she didn't want to be consumed with. Namely those of the *hombre extremadamente guapo* and the woman doing her best to attract his attention.

A surge of adrenaline pumped through her and she dragged the bag across the alley as though it weighed next to nothing. She'd told herself the first time Ryan had come into the coffee shop that she shouldn't get involved with him. The fact that she was wrestling now with petty thoughts about the woman sitting in there with him proved her point.

Lowering her guard and letting Ryan Taylor in, even a little bit, had been a big mistake.

Ryan strained to hear what Summer and Daphne were talking about. It was a challenge to hear them over the irritating laugh of the woman who for some reason was seriously inserting herself into his space. In between the silly questions he felt compelled to answer or seem rude, he was able to catch snatches of their conversation. He raised his mug quickly to hide a smile. So Summer thought he was extremely handsome, did she? He'd take that. And was that a hint of jealousy in her voice when she told Daphne he was interested in the woman trying to talk to him? Should he play that up a little?

Jude sobered and set down the mug. He had no interest in playing games with Summer. Besides, he had other things to think about today. He reached for the chocolate croissant he'd ordered in an attempt to fortify himself for the coming confrontation with his brother. Jude took a bite then tossed the croissant onto his plate. Who was he kidding? As delicious as it was, he didn't need a hit of sugar to give him the courage to do what he had to do. He needed Summer.

A movement behind the counter caught his eye and he

straightened abruptly. She was heading to the back. Was she going outside? The woman at the table beside him blinked and snapped her mouth shut. He'd obviously missed everything she had just said. "Sorry." Jude closed his laptop and shoved it into the bag. "I need to get going." He stood and slung the bag over his shoulder. "Nice meeting you."

"You too." She crossed one long leg over the other. "Will I see you in here again?"

"I don't know." Jude was already a few steps away.

She called out a goodbye as he headed for the exit and he lifted a hand before shoving open the door and stepping into the crisp, winter day. A gust of frigid air blew around him, carrying a hint of smoke drifting from a nearby chimney. Or was that from a cigarette? He inhaled deeply as he strode to the corner of the building and turned into the alleyway that ran between the Taste of Heaven Café and the antique shop next door.

Summer stood in front of a large green dumpster, grasping the top of a garbage bag that had to be half her size.

"Hey." Jude called out, hoping to stop her before she tried to lift it.

Instead, she grasped the bag and hauled it over the top of the dumpster before turning to him. "Hey."

Jude stopped in front of her. "I was going to help you with that."

A hint of mischief sparked in her eyes. "I know."

He shook his head at her refusal to accept help, although he should be used to it by now. He reached for the hand she'd soaked in the puddle and examined it. "How are the fingers doing?"

When she didn't answer, he looked up and his breath caught in his throat at the way she was looking at him. Summer swallowed and pulled her hand from his. "They're fine, thanks to you." She started for the door. "I should get to work, though, and you should get back to your friend."

"My friend?"

She stopped beside the door and turned around. "Yes, the woman you were talking to inside."

Jude cocked his head. "She's not my friend. I don't even know her. And I have no interest in—"

Summer held up her hand. "You don't have to explain. I have no say in what you do or who you see."

He walked over to her. She leaned back against the wall as he stopped in front of her. "Ana." *Careful. Don't push too hard or you'll lose her.* As far as she knew, they'd only met a few weeks ago. Still, he was getting a little tired of the slow, steady approach. Might be time to take things to the next level. Jude pressed a palm to the wall beside her head. "From the first day I walked into the café, you have to know you've been the only one I see." He searched her dark eyes. Would she run? If so, it wouldn't be the first time. His chest tightened. They'd reached a crossroads. The next few seconds would determine whether he could move ahead with his plan or if they would be done.

Summer swallowed but met his gaze steadily. For a moment, nothing moved except the electricity that arced between them so strongly he could almost hear the zapping sound. Jude was afraid to breathe, in case the slightest sound or twitch broke the spell. Slowly, Summer reached up and slid warm fingers around the back of his neck, tugging him down. Right before their lips touched, she whispered, "Okay?"

He smiled. "Always."

She pressed her lips to his. The sensation was so right, so familiar, yet so shockingly powerful that it took everything he had not to gather her in his arms and pull her to him. When her fingers finally slid from his neck, Jude needed a few seconds to come down to earth and open his eyes. Whew. If that didn't fortify him to face Cash, nothing would.

"*Despampanante*," Summer breathed.

Jude almost laughed. It *had* been stunning. Better for her not to know he was fluent in Spanish though, since she and Daphne were clearly using it to speak freely in front of him. Which could get interesting. "Is that good?"

"Better than good." The gleam was back in her eyes. "And, I promise you, better than it would have been with the blonde in the coffee shop."

"There was a blonde in the coffee shop?"

Summer tipped back her head and laughed, the most beautiful sound he'd heard in weeks. She pressed a hand lightly to his chest. "I really should get back to work."

Jude pushed away from the wall and dropped his arm with a sigh. "All right, if you must. See you tomorrow night?"

"Apparently." She flashed him a smile as she pulled open the back door. He watched until she had disappeared inside. Then he adjusted the strap of his laptop bag more securely on his shoulder and started for the sidewalk. They'd survived their first moment of truth, but no doubt there would be more.

The smell of smoke still hung in the air, stronger than before. Jude sniffed. Definitely a cigarette. He glanced up and down the street but couldn't see anyone smoking. He shrugged. Not his business what people around here did.

Besides—he pressed his lips together, the light taste of Summer's cherry gloss still lingering there—there were plenty of things he'd rather be thinking about at the moment than other people's vices.

CHAPTER TWENTY-EIGHT

If he'd thought the steps leading to his mother's home loomed large, the two flights of stairs going up to his brother Cash's apartment appeared as high as Jacob's ladder—the top disappearing into the heavens. Jude took several deep breaths, blowing them out his mouth as he gripped the banister.

After he'd seen his mother and sister the day before, he'd promised to go see his brother today and asked them not to let Cash know he was in town. He wasn't sure why. Did he think Cash would refuse to open the door if he knew his long-lost brother waited on the other side? If he did, at least Jude could leave with a clear conscience. Or a slightly clearer one, anyway. That particular slate would likely never feel as though it was wiped completely clean.

Whatever his brother's reaction, Jude had to face him, had to finally be the man his family had needed him to be for years. No more running. His legs shook as he forced himself to go up one step. Then another. By the time he reached the first landing and turned to go up the second set of stairs, sweat was trickling down between his shoulder blades in spite of the coolness in the stairwell.

His stomach churning, Jude trudged up the second set of stairs, pulled open the door at the top, and started down the hallway. His brother's apartment was halfway down on the right. Several of the doors held wreaths or signs but Cash's was bare. Not surprising. Cash had always kept things sparse. His room, his life, his words.

The sound of a television drifted out beneath the door. Jude rapped three times and waited. The TV went silent before footsteps tromped across the floor. The sweat on his back dried as chills swept over Jude. The door opened and his brother, broader across the shoulders and taller than Jude by an inch or two, stood framed in the doorway. Had the guy pretty much lived at the gym the last five years?

Like his mother and sister had, his brother simply stared at Jude for several agonizing seconds. Then he crossed his arms over his massive chest. "So."

Jude swallowed. "So."

"Any idea how much I want to shove a fist down your throat right now?"

"I wouldn't blame you if you did." Part of Jude wished he would. The ache of a black eye or a broken nose would be preferable to this festering pain burning a hole in his stomach at the moment. His brother had never hit him, though. As tough as Cash came across, as much as he had always been the rock in the family—a wall of granite anyone else had to try and breach to reach any of them—he wasn't prone to violence. Of course, Jude had never asked for it as badly as he had the night he abandoned his family.

"I reserve the right to exercise that option at any point." Cash uncrossed his arms, spun on his heel, and stalked away.

Was that an invitation? Likely the warmest one he would get, anyway. Jude stepped in quickly and closed the door in case it wasn't. He followed Cash into a small kitchen. Other than a microwave and toaster, the counters were bare and clean. His brother opened the fridge door, leaned in, and grabbed two bottles of beer between his fingers. When he turned back and looked at Jude, he grimaced. "On second thought..."

He replaced the bottles, closed the fridge door, and grabbed a bottle of whiskey off a shelf above the sink. He took a glass down from the cupboard, set it on the counter, and yanked the lid off the bottle. After splashing enough gold liquid in it to fill nearly half the glass, he snatched it up and held it out to Jude. "Drink?"

Jude held up a hand and shook his head.

His brother stared into the depths of the glass a moment. Then, with a heavy exhalation of breath, he set it back down on the counter with a thud. "You're probably right—if we're going to speak clearly, best if we can think clearly."

He crossed his arms again, the movement showcasing muscles rippling beneath his black T-shirt. "Well?"

Jude swayed slightly and leaned a shoulder against the wall behind him. "I came to tell you how sorry I am."

"Twelve-step program?"

Jude blinked. "No, actually." Although he'd come closer to needing one than he cared to think about.

"Then why?"

He hadn't prepared himself for that question. The glib reply, *I was in the neighborhood*, while true, likely wouldn't set a good tone for this conversation. "I couldn't do it anymore."

"Do what?"

"Run. Hide. Not be with my family."

"That was your choice."

"I know."

"So you were what, scared? Lonely? Couldn't live with the guilt anymore?" His brother's voice vibrated with barely-contained rage.

All of the above. Jude lifted his shoulders. "Yes."

Cash contemplated him in stony silence. Jude forced himself to meet his gaze steadily. "Where did you go?"

"Toronto."

"How did you live?"

Jude rubbed the side of his hand across his forehead, remembering. "It was tough at first. For a few weeks I wandered the streets, slept in alleys or in a shelter if a bed was available. I drank a lot, trying to forget everything and everyone I'd left behind." He hesitated. *No more hiding.* "I did some stupid stuff, narrowly avoided doing time. Eventually I got it together and managed to land a job. Saved enough to go back to school and graduated a couple of years ago. Now I work as an addictions counselor in a firm with two other guys, Joe Calvin, my boss, and my partner and mentor, Rick Moser."

"So you landed on your feet."

"Eventually, I guess."

"And it never occurred to you to call and let us know that?" Cash reached for the glass he'd set down earlier and took a swig. The glass rattled against the counter when he set it down.

"I wanted to. I even started dialing, more times than I can count, but I was afraid—"

Cash's palm came down hard on the counter and Jude jumped. "*You* were afraid? How do you think Mom felt, losing a daughter and then having a son disappear off the planet? Or your little sister, who asked me every single day that first year if you'd called yet. Or me, who drove up and down the streets of every city in an eight-hour radius every weekend for months, and who has wondered for five years if you were alive or..." Cash stopped and pressed his thumb and forefinger to his eyes.

Jude's throat was so tight he couldn't swallow. He'd never seen his brother, normally cool and even-tempered, so worked up. And it was all on him. The weight pressing down on his chest was suffocating. Was it possible to die of sorrow and regret over the choices you'd made in the past? If so, it might be a good idea for him to get his affairs in order. "I'm sorry, Cash. I don't know what else to say."

His brother lowered his hand and took another drink. "In a way, I got it. I knew you'd been through something terrible and you didn't know how to handle it. But maybe the people who love you the most could have helped you through it if you'd stayed. We could have helped each other through it. Instead, we had to worry about you, too."

"You're right. I never should have left. I'm sorry." Like they had when he'd said them to his mother, the words sounded weak and foolish, but they were all he had to offer.

"Are you staying?"

His chest clenched. His future was so uncertain—could he make any kind of promise to his brother? He'd never make one again that he didn't intend to keep. "For a little while. I don't know how long. But I won't leave again without telling you I'm going and letting you know where I'll be."

Cash slammed down the glass and stalked toward him. Jude braced himself but didn't resist when his brother planted a hand on his chest and shoved him against the wall. He deserved everything Cash threw at him and more. And getting what he deserved was a lot easier than accepting what he didn't. Although what he didn't deserve kept him on his knees, which was where he needed to be.

"If you do take off again," his brother spoke through clenched teeth, pressing a little harder to drive home his point, "don't ever come back here. Knowing them, I'm sure Mom and Maddie welcomed you back with open arms, but I will not allow you to hurt them again. You leave one more time without warning and you are no longer part of this family."

Relief weakened his knees. Then he was still part of the family now. "Got it."

Cash's face softened as he slid his hand up to grip Jude's shoulder. "Don't be like Dad, Jude."

Jude flinched. That hurt more than Cash's fist down his throat ever could. And so did the truth—that he'd been on the exact same path as his father. But for the grace of God. He reached across his chest to grasp his brother's forearm. "I won't. I don't want to be anything like him. I want to be like you, Cash. That's why I came back."

CHAPTER TWENTY-NINE

Díaz sat on the bench of a picnic table, leaning back against the tabletop. He clutched a book in his hand, but his attention was on the three kids playing in the sandbox at the park. He lifted the paperback to hide a smile. One of the girls reminded him of his little Josefina. When a young boy raised a pail, leaving a bucket-shaped pile of sand in the box, she squealed and clapped her hands. His chest squeezed. *Exactly like my baby girl.*

The time his boss had been given had been sliding steadily through the small hole of the hourglass. Twenty-two days left. From habit, he scanned the area over the top of the book. He still hadn't caught a glimpse of Kendrick. Was the man in town? Had he tracked down Summer Velásquez? Díaz had been watching the girl pretty closely. A few times a dark car had driven by the place where she was staying, and more than once a vehicle had slowly passed the bakery where she worked. He hadn't been able to make out the features of any of the occupants, though. And in a tourist town, slow-moving vehicles were as likely to be visitors to Elora, gawking at the displays in shop windows and the beautiful scenery, as anyone with darker intentions.

Díaz sighed and drove his fingers through his hair. He didn't get paid enough for this. Except that the boss did compensate him quite well. The more unsavory the task, the greater the compensation, so he couldn't do anything to put his job in jeopardy. Not if he hoped to save enough money to bring his family here from Mexico.

He rested the book on his chest, imagining the moment they would come through the arrivals gate at the airport, running toward him, arms raised and yelling "Papá" as their dark braids bounced against the backs of their brightly colored dresses.

Clenching his jaw, Díaz lifted the book. No daydreaming. Not now, when the end of this job was only three weeks away. If all went well, this could be the last one. If it didn't, it might be months, even years, before he saw Juanita and the girls again. If he survived that long.

A movement at the edge of the park caught his eye and he stiffened. She was coming. Over the top of the book, his gaze followed Summer as she strolled down the pathway. He'd figured she would come through here today. When the weather was nice—and it had turned unseasonably warm the last few days—she walked to work, cutting through the park both ways.

He kept an eye on her until she reached the far side of the park. Then he closed the book, stuck it under his arm, and strolled casually across the grassy area that led to the sidewalk Summer had started down. Keeping half a block between them, Díaz meandered down the street, feigning interest in the display in every store window while keeping tabs on her progress.

A lot of people spoke to Summer, quite a few calling her by the name she'd given herself when she arrived in town. The regulars at the coffee shop—which appeared to be about half the population—were clearly coming to know her already, even though she'd only been in Elora a few weeks.

Summer smiled and spoke to all of them, and it took her close to half an hour to reach her street. Díaz waited until she had gone into the house before settling himself on a bench at a bus stop and pulling out his book again so no one would wonder what he was doing sitting there. An hour later, he closed the book and stood. If she'd been going out with McCall again, she would have come out by now, so likely she would be home now until morning.

That meant he could call it an early night and head back to the motel. With a final glance at the house, Díaz started down the street. None of the cars parked along the curb had anyone inside. Maybe he'd been imagining the vehicles that had passed by as though its occupants were watching her house and work, like he was.

He turned the corner and trudged in the direction of the Torchlight Inn, a twenty-minute walk away, contemplating his situation as he walked. Summer and McCall had been spending quite a bit of time together, which made Díaz's job both easier and harder. Easier because he could keep an eye on both of them at the same time, harder because his antenna needed to be up every second. If Summer's memory came back, if she started showing any hint at all that she remembered McCall, Díaz would have to act fast.

And he would need to make sure that, if Kendrick had tracked her to Elora, he didn't come out of the shadows and get to her first.

CHAPTER THIRTY

Summer slid onto the bench beside Daphne and scanned the room. Shawn and Daphne's church was in a small stone building with stained glass windows and rows of wooden pews. Mercifully, these ones had padded seats and were surprisingly comfortable.

Quiet music played over the sound system and something eased inside her, a feeling of anxiety she hadn't realized she'd been feeling since she'd walked into the place. Or maybe since the cop had first told her, weeks ago, about the attack in her home. The knots in her shoulders and stomach loosened. However she had come to her faith, she was deeply thankful she had. Being in this room, studying the biblical scenes etched in every window, listening to the worship music, being surrounded by other people who shared her faith in the same God, and, most of all, the large wooden cross hanging on the wall behind the pulpit, filled her with peace.

The sense that she wasn't alone, that God was with her and that she belonged in this community of believers, wrapped itself around her like the old knitted afghan on Nancy's couch and she relaxed into the warmth of it. Although it had taken her a few weeks to work up the nerve to come, she needed this, to feel part of something greater than herself. When the worship leader welcomed everyone and announced the first song, she stood with everyone else. She didn't remember hearing the words before, but she followed along on the screen and soon caught on, even joining in, a little tentatively, on the chorus. Beside her, Daphne's voice rose, clear and lovely, mingling with Shawn's bass. Summer smiled, glad that she had allowed her friend to talk her into coming.

After three songs and a handful of announcements, the minister walked up the steps to the stage and took his place behind the pulpit. He looked to be in his early-forties, with a kind face and enough muscles on him to suggest that he didn't spend all his time studying theology textbooks. He greeted everyone then opened his Bible and read a passage from it. The words were unfamiliar to Summer, even strange, something about offering their bodies as living sacrifices. Still, the power of the words he was speaking in a strong, deep voice, full of conviction, flowed through her like electricity through a wire, infusing her with energy and light.

She strained to catch every word, wishing she'd brought a Bible so she could follow along. Did she own a Bible? Maybe, if she'd had more time to look around her home, she might have found one. Daphne nudged her with an elbow and Summer looked down. Her friend was reading along from hers and she held it closer to Summer so she could see the passage as well. It helped to be able to study the words for herself.

The section talked about members and the body and sounded like they might be referring to the same thing Summer had been thinking about earlier, that everyone in the room was part of a larger community. A community designed by God to use their strengths—the Bible called them gifts—to help each other. Kind of how she and Daphne and Shawn worked in the café.

Shawn definitely had gifts he used in the kitchen, while Daphne's lay more in how she interacted with all the people who came through the door. Summer did much of the hands-on work, cleaning and organizing in order to give Daphne more time to talk to the customers. Many of them seemed to come in as much to share their problems with her and receive comfort, commiseration, or advice as to indulge in Shawn's amazing baking. When she put the passage in that context, it made complete sense to her that the church should work the same way.

The last part of the section shocked her a little. Hating evil and doing good sounded right. She certainly hated the evil that someone had done to her and that the threat still hung over her head so she had to hide away here and be concerned about her safety. And she appreciated the good she saw in others—Nancy's generosity, Shawn's gentleness, Daphne's sweetness, the way Ryan made her feel safe and special. Something inside of her, the work of God, most likely, had to be good too, for all of those people to care about her.

But she tripped over some of the other instructions. Be patient in tribulation? She had only a vague sense of what tribulation was, but it felt as though what she was going through might fit into that category. And God wanted her to be patient about it? Did that mean she was supposed to sit around waiting for something to happen? Or could she be patient but still take steps to protect herself, to try and remember the past so she could help the police find the man who had done this to her and bring him to justice?

No sooner had that thought passed through her mind than the pastor read that they were not supposed to repay evil for evil but to live in peace with everyone, at least as much as possible. And to leave vengeance up to God and never try to avenge themselves. Really? After someone had attacked and nearly killed her in her own home, she wasn't supposed to try and go after him but let God deal with him?

For a few seconds that concept burned in her chest. Then the heat subsided, as though cool drops of rain had spattered down over it. Maybe it wasn't so much that she *couldn't* seek revenge but that she didn't have to. It wasn't her responsibility. That job fell to one much greater, more powerful, and more perfectly just than she was. It was possible that the directive wasn't meant to tie her hands but to lift from her the weight of attempting to exact revenge for herself, from feeling afraid or angry or bitter. She bit her lip. Could it be that God's commandments weren't intended to enslave her—like she'd heard so

151

many say and that she had believed when she was growing up—but that they were designed to free her?

Summer felt the burden she'd been carrying around since she'd left the hospital lift from her as clearly as if she'd shrugged off a backpack filled with rocks and dropped it to the ground. The next breath she took was a deeper one than she could remember inhaling in weeks.

The final song was another she didn't know. Still, the words rang so true to her that by the second time through the chorus she had lost her tentativeness and allowed them to pour out of her. They spoke of how, as children of God, they were no longer slaves to fear. Was that how she had been living? Summer had tried her best not to let fear overwhelm her since finding out about the man who had assaulted her. Still, she was confronted now by the truth of those words, the idea that she couldn't fight fear on her own, but could only overcome it through the freedom that God offered.

She *had* been afraid. Afraid of who might track her down and what he might do to her if he did. Afraid that someone would go after her parents or the people in her new town, especially anyone she had grown close to. Afraid of giving her heart away in case the person she gave it to betrayed her in some way, smashing it into pieces.

God, help me with my fear. Take it from me. I don't want to be a slave to it anymore. Before the words had died away in her mind, she felt that burden being lifted too. Something she couldn't have begun to describe to anyone else—not in any language—flowed through her, like a beam of sunlight shimmering in the air. Ethereal yet driving back the darkness all around it.

Daphne touched her elbow, drawing Summer back into the moment. The service had ended and people were filing out of their pews. "Are you good?" Her bright blue eyes searched Summer's.

She smiled. "I'm good. Very good."

"Great." Daphne grinned, dimples appearing in both cheeks.

"Want to stay for coffee, get to know a few people? I'll introduce you to the pastor."

Summer had determined before coming to church that she wouldn't stay, that simply coming to the service would be a solid first step and she could gradually ease into the rest of it if she felt it might be for her. Now, though, she was surprised at how much she wanted to stay. At how interested she was in meeting the people she'd spent the morning with, hearing the same words, reading the same Bible, singing the same songs.

Although she couldn't remember being in a church before, she was struck suddenly by the overwhelming and incredibly warm feeling—one she wasn't sure she'd ever experienced—that she belonged.

CHAPTER THIRTY-ONE

"Cash barbequed, so Maddie and I will do the dishes." Jude's mother stacked the empty dessert plates. Jude held the screen door open for her and she smiled at him before carrying them into the house. His sister gathered up the empty coffee cups from the table and crossed the porch to the door. She nudged him in the chest with her shoulder. "Not sure why you don't have to help with the dishes, but whatever." Her voice held a hint of laughter, the way it always had before—

Jude slammed the brakes on that thought.

"Jude just came home. We'll give him a few days before we put him to work." Their mother's voice carried out onto the porch.

"Yeah. So stop mouthing off and go get those dishes done." Jude ruffled his sister's hair and she made a face at him before flouncing into the house. Still grinning, he closed the door behind them. The day had been oddly warm for early March, so they'd seized the opportunity to eat out on the wraparound porch.

"Cigarette?" Cash pulled a half-full pack from the pocket of his jacket and held it out.

Jude shook his head. "No thanks. I quit a while ago."

"Seems like you quit a lot of things."

His head jerked. Was that a dig at his lengthy absence from the family? "What do you mean?"

Cash lifted his chin in the direction of the table where the beer he'd set by Jude's plate still sat, untouched. "Never known you to let a bottle get warm."

"No." Jude propped both elbows on the porch railing. "Guess I never did." Regret over his past threatened to wash over him again but he pushed it back.

"Find a woman?" Cash tapped the packet against his palm until a cigarette tumbled out.

Jude swallowed. *Here we go.* "That's part of it." He straightened and turned to lean back against the railing. If he was going to open up to his brother after all these years, he'd do it face to face. "The bigger part is that I found Jesus."

"Why, was he lost?" Cash struck a match. His face lit with an orange glow as he brought it close to light the cigarette. Inhaling deeply, he flicked the match out onto the lawn where it hissed against the slush. "Sorry, bad joke."

"It's all right, I get it. Something like that would have sounded completely crazy to me too not that long ago. Thing is, now that I understand it, it's not crazy at all."

Cash propped a shoulder against the gray siding and blew out a puff of smoke. "What is it then?"

Jude mulled over the question. His faith was so many things to him—how could he give his brother a simple answer? "Life-changing about sums it up."

"Other than requiring you to give up all your former guilty pleasures," his brother held up the pack of cigarettes before shoving it back into his pocket, "how has it changed your life?"

Jude nudged a curl of paint lifting off a floorboard on the porch with the toe of his running shoe. "I used to think I had it all figured out, you know? Big jock in high school, captain of the hockey team, everybody thought I was so cool, that I had everything together. I guess I did too, or convinced myself I did anyway, until..." A sharp pain gripped his chest and he rubbed the heel of his hand over the spot. "Until what happened with Tessa."

In the soft wash of the porch light, a shadow passed over Cash's features. He lifted the cigarette and took another long draw, the round end glowing red. "Yeah, that changed us all, I guess."

"It didn't change me as much as it opened up my eyes to see myself for who I really was. I realized I had nothing figured out. That I wasn't cool, I didn't have my life together, and I certainly wasn't a big man. I was, in fact, the smallest of men, not in control of anything, least of all myself. And I couldn't take that. Couldn't take seeing that truth in the eyes of everyone who looked at me. So I took off. It was easier to run from everything than to face it. Which was the biggest truth of all—I was a coward through and through." Jude studied the cigarette his brother clutched between two fingers. Man what he wouldn't give for a smooth, calming drag on that little baby right about now.

Tearing his eyes away, he drove his fingers through his hair. "You're right. I did meet a woman. I walked into a coffee shop on my way to work one morning, same one I walked into every morning, so often the barista always had my drink waiting for me when I arrived. Same drink. Same people. Same everything every day."

"Until one day." Cash dropped the cigarette butt onto the porch and ground it under the toe of his boot.

"Exactly. One day—it was a Friday morning in September, two and a half years ago—I walked in and started for the counter where the guy was already holding out my drink for me. Then I saw her sitting in the corner and I froze. I mean, it was like something out of a romance novel. Like being struck by lightning. She was beautiful, with long, dark curls that hung halfway down her back and these incredible, almost-black eyes. It was more than that, though. Something I couldn't have explained in that moment, but it paralyzed me."

"And you'd never seen her there before?"

"No, definitely not, or I would have remembered. So there I was, standing in the middle of the coffee shop like some kind of marionette with no one working the strings, until the barista, a high school kid named Josh, called out my name. I blinked as if I'd been in some kind of trance and stared at him until he lifted the drink and I came out of it enough to walk the rest of the way and grab it from him."

"Let me guess. You left without talking to her."

Jude offered him a wry grin. "You know me too well. Like I said, coward. So yeah, I took the drink, sent her one last, fleeting glance, and strolled out of the place as if I wasn't walking away from the best thing that might ever happen to me in my life."

"Was she there the next day?"

"She wouldn't have been, no. She lived on the other side of the city and only happened to be in the neighborhood to meet a friend. She'd never been in that coffee shop before and likely would never have set foot in it again."

Cash's forehead wrinkled. "So how do you know all that?"

"Because I went back. I got halfway down the block, still thinking about her and lamenting the lost opportunity to meet her, and suddenly this hot, burning rage, aimed at myself, billowed up inside me. I spun around, stalked back to the shop, and walked straight over to her table."

"And the rest is history."

"Not quite." Jude let out a short laugh. "She wasn't at all interested. Too busy with her career and figuring out her own life to get involved with anyone. Or so she claimed."

Cash blew out a breath and sank down onto the bench below the front window. "This is going to take awhile, isn't it?"

"I can give you the condensed version. She was pretty firm in her rejection, and normally I would have walked away, but I couldn't bring myself to do it. So I made a classic, chick flick move. I grabbed a napkin and a pen from the counter and scribbled my name and number on it. I went back to her table, told her I usually didn't do this sort of thing but that I had felt a real connection with her as soon as I

saw her. When she merely lifted a shoulder, not giving me the slightest
bit of encouragement, I dropped the napkin on her table, slid it over
to her, and asked her to think about it."

Cash snorted. "Begged her, more likely."

His brother really did know him. "All right, begged her." He didn't
care then and he didn't care now if that made him sound weak. He'd
have gotten down on his knees that day, in the middle of that crowded
coffee shop, if he'd thought it would help. Given the cool wariness in
those dark eyes staring at him over the rim of her paper cup, he'd
assumed it wouldn't. "And then I left. Which, considering it was my
signature move, was the hardest thing I'd ever done."

"I take it she called."

"Not for nine of the longest days of my life, but yes, she did."
Warmth spread through Jude's chest as he thought back on that time.
What if she hadn't? His throat tightened and he swallowed hard.

"I'd like to meet her. Are the two of you still together?"

"That is a long, complicated story. One better saved for another
day."

Cash nodded. "So how does Jesus fit into this narrative? Was this
mystery woman some kind of missionary or something? She drag you
to church? Force you to convert before you could date her or what?"

Jude laughed. "No, nothing like that. Faith wasn't really part of
either of our lives when we met. In fact, we dated for weeks without it
ever coming up in conversation. But she is really into music, and one
night we were strolling down a side street in Toronto and passing by
one of those old stone churches with the stained glass windows.
Someone was playing a massive organ inside and you could hear it out
on the sidewalk. She pulled me up the steps and we slipped into the
back row and sat there listening—it was incredibly beautiful."

A light breeze ruffled his hair and Jude closed his eyes, almost able,
even now, to hear that music playing in the dark.

"What happened then?"

"When the music stopped, a guy in robes walked to the pulpit carrying a huge Bible. Normally that would have been it for me, so I don't know whether the music had gotten to both of us or what, but neither of us moved. We stayed and listened to everything the pastor had to say and for the first time in my life it made perfect sense to me. He talked about how broken we all are, and lost. He was talking in general terms, but it felt as though he was speaking directly to me. Then he said that Jesus had come and given his life for us so that everyone who was lost could be found. It struck me hard. I couldn't argue with the fact that I was lost—I had been for a long time and was deeply aware of it. And I knew I couldn't find my way out of the darkness I was wallowing in on my own because I'd been trying to for years. Someone else had to show me the way.

"It hit her just as hard. We went back the next Sunday and the next, and it continued to feel as though the words were spoken right to me. When the minister asked at the end of one of the services if anyone wanted to come forward and give their life to Christ, we didn't even discuss it, just looked at each other then got up and went. And nothing has been the same since."

"Huh." Cash fumbled with the pack of cigarettes until it came loose from his pocket and dumped another one into his hand. Neither of them spoke as he stuck it into his mouth, cupped his hands around it and the matchbook, and lit it up. He took a long draw on it and leaned against the back of the bench. "So it helps you, believing in God?"

He gestured toward the bottle of beer on the table. "A lot more than that ever did."

Cash glanced over but didn't respond.

Jude tipped his head back, gazing up at the half moon surrounded by stars. *God, help him to see. Help him to understand. I can't do it. Only you can.*

159

"Is that why you came back?"

Jude sighed. "It's not why I came to Elora—that's part of the long story I mentioned earlier. But it is why I came back home. I needed to see all of you, tell you how sorry I am, and ask for your forgiveness. I don't really expect it, and I wouldn't blame any of you if you couldn't give it to me, but I needed to stop running away and finally face up to what happened. To what I had done."

"It wasn't your fault."

His brother's quiet words drifted across the space between them, enveloping him as softly as the tendrils of smoke wafting around Cash. They loosened something inside of Jude, part of the wall he'd built to maintain a safe distance from anyone who tried to get close. Fear clutched at him. Was he ready for that wall to come tumbling down? What would happen to him—to his heart—when it did?

Cash propped an elbow on the arm of the bench. "I mean it. Tessa knew she wasn't supposed to be out on the ice and she chose to go anyway. If you had kept trying to get to her, you both would have gone through and likely drowned. None of us blame you for not saving her. We never did."

Jude's heart thudded so loudly in his ears he could barely hear what his brother was saying. He pushed away from the railing. "It's getting late. Better say goodnight."

Cash stabbed the butt into the ashtray on the windowsill and pushed to his feet. "Running again, little brother?"

Jude stopped on the top step. "No. Just need a little time to think things over. I'll be back."

"Good." Cash reached for the handle of the screen door.

"Cash."

His brother turned around. "Yeah?"

"Thanks."

Cash nodded. "See you tomorrow?"

"I'll be here."

His brother grabbed the still-full bottle of beer from the table and pulled open the screen door. "Don't want you falling prey to temptation now."

Jude watched him disappear into the house and close the wooden door. He pursed his lips. He *had* been tempted to take a drink, almost as tempted as he was to walk off this porch, disappear into the night, and never return.

But either move would drag him back down into the pit he'd been rescued from, and he had no desire to spend time in that black hole ever again.

CHAPTER THIRTY-TWO

This is a really bad idea. Somehow, Díaz didn't care. For three weeks now he'd walked past the Taste of Heaven Café, the aromas emitting from the building proving the place was aptly named. He was sick of smelling and not tasting. Tired of being so close to something that good and not able to close his fingers around it, take a bite of it, enjoy the rich sweetness of it.

That frustration pretty much summed up his entire life. Ever since he was a kid standing with his nose pressed up against a restaurant window or a teenager crouched on a street corner, sniffing the tantalizing aromas as eager customers handed over money to vendors and received a taco or tamale wrapped in paper in exchange, he'd felt this frustration. And never more so than now, when the promise of a new life for him and his family hung in front of his face like a carrot dangling before a racehorse, driving him forward but never allowing him to reach his goal.

So, if he wanted a cup of coffee and one of those muffins he'd smelled while hanging out in the parking lot behind the building or walking past it on the other side of the street, he was going to have them. And he didn't care anymore who saw him do it. Summer Velásquez wouldn't know him from Adam, and neither would anyone else in town. Only Jude McCall might recognize him from the car parked outside Summer's place, and he was still asleep in his motel room, last Díaz checked.

In ten days, the clock would run out for his boss. Díaz had no idea what would happen then, but he had a pretty good idea it wasn't going to be a lot of fun. Might as well take advantage of these last few days, indulge himself a little, before he really had to earn his pay.

Striding to the front door of the café, he yanked it open and headed for the counter. Summer flashed him a smile as he approached. "Good morning."

"Buenos días." No sense pretending he spoke only English, as he couldn't lose the accent if he tried. Which he had no desire to do.

Her eyes lit. "¿Hablas español?"

He got that a lot. After winning or losing the gene pool—depending on how you looked at it—when he'd inherited his Canadian mother's pale skin, blue eyes, and light-brown hair, few people who saw him suspected him of having a Hispanic heritage until he opened his mouth. Then they were mostly confused. Sometimes even hostile. He'd grown up in Mexico, where his father was from, but he hadn't been accepted there either. A foot in each world, he'd straddled the border between the two countries for as long as he could remember, never quite sure where he belonged.

"Sí."

"¿De dónde eres?"

He hesitated. Here's where it got tricky. If he told her exactly where he was from, she'd realize he'd grown up outside the small town where she and her family had lived when she was younger. That would likely result in an extended conversation he might not be able to extricate himself from. Not without drawing more attention to himself than he wanted. If he made something up, she might ask questions he wouldn't be able to credibly answer. *Venir aquí fué un error.* Díaz mentally kicked himself. It *had* been a mistake to come in here. What was he thinking, risking everything for a muffin? "México." He stepped back and pretended to study the baked offerings covering every inch of the counter. Maybe she'd take the hint and not press the issue any further.

"Yo también. ¿De qué parte eres?"

"Del sur," he said, curtly, still surveying the selection of items. He wasn't from the south, but if he told her the north, where she was from, she would certainly ask for more details.

From the corner of his eye, he saw her smile dim. Good. She'd obviously gotten the message.

"¿Qué se te ofrece?"

Ah. That was more like it. What *could* she get for him? He'd been sure he wanted a muffin, but now that he was here, the doughnuts, croissants, loaves of lemon and banana bread, and assorted scones all looked so good he couldn't decide. His gaze landed on a cinnamon bun covered in white icing and he smiled. Juanita's favorite. He pointed to the platter. "Un rol de canela y un café, por favor."

Summer nodded and grabbed a plate and a set of tongs. She lifted a bun onto the plate with the tongs and set it on the counter before going for the coffee. The cinnamon bun was still warm. Spice-laden steam curled from it as a splotch of icing dripped onto the plate. Díaz's mouth watered. He was wrong. It hadn't been a mistake coming in here. In fact, it might be the first truly right thing he'd done since he'd asked Juanita to marry him.

"Que lo disfrutes." She set the paper cup down, hard enough that a few drops sloshed through the tiny hole in the lid.

"Gracias." He most certainly would enjoy it. Díaz grabbed the plate and cup and scanned the small coffee shop. The most prudent thing would be to leave, to not give Summer Velásquez any more time to memorize his features than she already had. But he'd thrown caution to the wind already, why stop now? The armchair by the fireplace looked too appealing to resist and he strolled over and dropped down on it, setting the plate on one arm and the cup on the floor at the side of the chair. The bed in his motel was lumpy and overly soft, so he hadn't slept well in weeks. Díaz sank into the chair with a groan of pleasure. Good call not to head back out into the sub-zero temperatures just yet.

Grasping the fork Summer had set on the plate, he used the side of it to cut into the cinnamon bun then shoved the bite into his mouth. If the people sitting at tables near him hadn't glanced over at his first groan, he'd have emitted another. The bun might have been the best sugary treat he'd ever tasted. Díaz closed his eyes and reveled in the sweet cinnamon taste on his tongue. After several seconds, he bent forward to retrieve his coffee cup and took a swig.

He was so immersed in the sensory experience that he barely noticed the jingling of bells. When he tilted back his head to take another drink, he nearly spewed out the mouthful of hot liquid. McCall was here. It was only eight in the morning—what in the world was he doing up and about this early? Díaz cursed softly in his head. If McCall saw him in the café, no doubt he'd put two and two together and figure out that he was following Summer. Maybe he'd even be able to fit all the pieces into place and guess why. Which would be very bad.

Thankfully, the man hadn't shot so much as a glance around the place as he'd strolled toward the counter, his eyes on Summer. Díaz grabbed the cinnamon bun. Still clutching his cup of coffee, he pushed to his feet and casually strolled for the door. McCall said something to Summer, who laughed as she poured him a cup of coffee. Neither of them looked at him as he passed by, a few feet away. If either of them glanced at the door when the bells jangled, Díaz didn't see them. He didn't look back as he reached the sidewalk and scurried down the street.

When he was a few blocks away and confident that no one had followed him, he ducked into an alleyway and leaned against a wall so he could take another bite of the bun. No way he was wasting that, not when treats like those had been denied him growing up. His wife and daughters still rarely got anything like this to eat. Which would change when he brought them here to live. A smile crossed his face as he swiped the back of his hand across his chin, wiping off a drip of icing. Once they were all together again, he'd take them out for cinnamon buns every Saturday morning if they wanted.

None of them would go hungry or rush out of a place so they wouldn't be seen and recognized. As soon as he finished this, his last job for the boss, and brought his family here to be with him, everything would be different. They would be safe. He'd have gotten hold of the dangling carrot and everything else he'd ever reached for in his life and never been able to grasp.

CHAPTER THIRTY-THREE

Summer set the novel she'd been reading on the arm of the chair. A fire crackled in the woodstove and she breathed in the fragrant scent of maple and sighed. She and Nancy had come into the living room after dinner and Summer had been curled up in the chair for almost two hours, absorbed in her reading. She couldn't remember the last time she had felt so relaxed.

Nancy looked up from her knitting. "Everything okay, darlin'?"

"It's pretty much perfect. I'm not sure I've ever spent an evening like this in my life." Summer yawned and stretched her arms above her head. Charles Dickens, sitting on her lap, lifted his head and meowed in protest at the movement. "Sorry, kitty." She scratched the big calico cat behind its ears and he lowered his head again, purring loudly.

Nancy rested the knitting needles and wool across her knees. "You didn't have nights like this in your home growing up?"

If the question didn't hurt so much, Summer might have laughed. "Not like this, no."

"What was it like for you?" The words were gentle, as though Nancy understood they might cut a little and was trying to make them as painless as possible.

Summer exhaled. "In Mexico, and then again in Toronto, my parents and I lived in a big, cold house, kind of like a castle, only nothing like a Disney one or anything. Much more cold and sterile. And my parents didn't spend a lot of time with me—if they spoke to me at all, it was usually to tell me not to make so much noise when I was playing or to turn down my music. Mostly, when I think about it, the word that comes to mind when I think about my childhood is *quiet*."

"Funny, the first word that came to my mind was *lonely*."

Summer winced. "Yeah, I guess it was that too."

Nancy tilted her head and contemplated her. "How did you manage it, then?"

"Manage what?"

"To grow up to be such a sweet, loving person?"

She shook her head slightly. "I don't see myself that way."

"Well, I do. And when I was in the Taste of Heaven Café the other day, Daphne certainly gave me the impression that's how she sees you. And from what she said, so does a certain handsome writer who's taken to hanging out there whenever you're working. So there you go, you're outnumbered."

Summer's cheeks warmed at the mention of Ryan. What else had Daphne and Nancy talked about? "Of course, if you count my parents, it would be a tie."

"Then we'll let Charles Dickens be the tie-breaker. What do you think, Charlie, is our Ana a sweet and loving person or not?"

The old cat stretched a little before settling himself a little more comfortably on Summer's lap. Nancy laughed. "There you go. You can't argue with a cat. They have impeccable instincts about people. They're much more reliable than humans are at judging one another. Or ourselves."

"I'm sure that's true." Summer gently shifted the cat to the side of the chair. "I should probably get to bed, though. I need to be at work early in the morning."

"I suppose I should, too." Nancy set her knitting on the couch beside her and stood. "It gets easier, you know."

Her right foot had gone to sleep and Summer tapped it on the floor. "What does?"

"Believing the things the people who care about you say about you. Accepting their love."

"Does it?"

Nancy rounded the coffee table and stopped in front of her. "Yes. But only if you decide to let them in. That's the scary part, I know, but it's also the part that makes life worth living." She wrapped her arms around Summer and pulled her close.

Summer couldn't remember either of her parents ever hugging her. The gesture was as warm and comforting as the crackling of the fire and, after a few seconds, she allowed herself to give in to it completely.

When Nancy stepped back, she patted Summer lightly on the cheek. "Good night, sweet girl."

"Good night, Nancy. And thank you."

"For what?"

"For making me feel so welcome, so cared for."

Her landlady's face crinkled into a wreath of smiles. "You are cared for, darlin'. I'm glad you can feel that. The way I see it, you need some hugging, and I've got lots of hugs stored up and no one to give them away to. We're a match made in heaven, is what I believe."

"I think you may be right."

"I am right. It's no accident that you're here, you know. God knew we needed each other. Knew we needed to be each other's family."

Unable to force words through a throat that had gone tight, Summer could only nod before heading up the wide staircase to her room. Nancy's words echoed around in her mind, finding a place to settle in. She was right. Summer did need to learn how to let down her guard and allow people to get close to her. For a long time, when she was a teenager and in her early twenties at least, she'd guarded her heart as closely as her parents had guarded her when she was growing up. Likely because her early attempts to reach out to them, to show them affection and ask for it in return, had all been rebuffed. What kid wouldn't stop asking, eventually?

Still, if people like Nancy and Ryan and Daphne could see good in her, could believe that she was worth spending time with, possibly even worth loving, then maybe it was true. She wasn't sure what had happened during the years she couldn't remember that had changed her so much, but she suspected it had a lot to do with her newfound faith. And possibly whoever it was that had introduced it to her?

Summer frowned as she closed the bedroom door behind her and leaned against it. The frustration of not knowing who that was, of having no idea who had been in her life the last few years, who had coaxed her to open up her heart and let them in, was maddening to her. Would she ever know? Would her memories return one day and, with them, the life that she suspected had been a lot fuller and richer than the one she could remember?

A fierce anger swept through her. The man who had broken into her home had stolen a lot more than her peace of mind. He'd stolen that life from her. Her jaw clenched. How dare he? If only he was standing in front of her now. Enough rage pumped through her body that Summer was sure she wouldn't have any trouble neutralizing the ongoing threat he posed. Permanently.

Except that wasn't her job.

The anger drained from her as though someone had pulled a giant plug as the pastor's words from last Sunday came back to her. Vengeance was God's to exact, not hers. *God, don't let me forget that. Help me to give up my desire to get back at this person, whoever he is, and trust that you will take care of him for me.* She pushed away from the door and dropped to her knees beside the bed, lowering her face into her hands. *And please help me to remember.* Something good, *someone* good, had happened during the years she had lost. All at once she knew it, deep in her bones, as strongly as she knew that she believed in the one she called on now.

But if her memories didn't come back, whatever or whoever it was would be lost to her forever.

CHAPTER THIRTY-FOUR

Jude wet his fingers under the tap and shook off the water before running them through his hair. Ever since he'd followed Summer to town, he'd been a little concerned that someone might recognize him. It wasn't a huge threat. They had only moved to Elora a couple of years before he'd left, after his mother had fallen in love with the place on a shopping excursion with friends. Even after moving here, he'd continued to work at a factory in the nearby city of Cambridge, where he'd grown up, so he hadn't gotten to know a lot of people in Elora.

Still, he'd taken to leaving more stubble on his face than usual, hoping that would help. And he tried to stay alert at all times, when he wasn't distracted watching Summer, anyway. The café was the most dangerous place. If someone called out his name while he was sitting there, he'd have to do some fast talking to explain why he'd told her his name was Ryan. Thankfully, it hadn't happened yet, although he had lowered his head to his hand and ducked behind his laptop a couple of times when someone came in who looked familiar.

Small towns. It had been so long since he'd been here that he'd almost forgotten what they were like. Although he had driven through Elora once, with Summer. After he'd told her about what had happened with Tessa, and that his mother, brother, and sister lived here, she'd wanted to see the town. She had tried to get him to stop and see his family then, but he hadn't been ready. Had that memory, even buried deep, influenced her decision to come here somehow?

He sighed. Caffeine. He needed caffeine. Grabbing his leather jacket, he swung open the door of the motel and stopped in the doorway. Cash waited for him in the parking lot, a hip propped against the side of his silver Ram truck. He pushed away from the vehicle and met Jude halfway across the parking lot. "Going somewhere?"

"I was thinking of grabbing a coffee."

Cash jerked his head toward the truck. "Thought we might go to the cemetery. We can get coffee on the way."

For a moment Jude didn't move, his brain warring with feet that felt welded to the gravel lot. *It's time, Jude. Past time.* He nodded curtly and followed his brother to the truck.

Cash stuck the key into the ignition. "Tim Horton's okay?"

Not really. The popular chain coffee shop didn't hold a candle to the Taste of Heaven Café—or its employees—but he wasn't ready to take Cash there. Not yet. Jude slammed the door and reached for the seat belt. "Sure."

The truck rumbled south up a hill to the coffee shop and into the drive-through. Then, coffees and breakfast sandwiches in hand, Cash and Jude headed for the outskirts of town, to the small cemetery where their mother's parents were buried, their sister next to them.

When his brother pulled the Ram into the small parking lot, Jude stuffed most of the sandwich into the paper bag, his stomach churning. He tossed the bag onto the seat and took a deep breath. When he reached for the handle, Cash stopped him with a hand on his arm. "Mom sent this." He let go of Jude and reached over the back seat to grab a pot with a bright red poinsettia from the floor. He lifted it over the seat and held it out to Jude.

Jude took it from him. "Aren't you coming?"

"I'll give you a minute. Tessa's stone is at the far end of the fifth row."

Which I should know. Jude nodded and pushed open the door, clutching the poinsettia to his ribs as he jumped to the ground. The late-winter air held a hint of the snow about to fall from iron-tinted clouds, and he zipped his jacket up to his throat.

Thankfully, the cemetery was small and he didn't have any trouble finding his sister's grave. A light dusting of snow covered the top of it and Jude wiped it off then dried his fingers on his jeans. He'd fled before his sister's funeral and had never been to her grave. Heat crawled up his neck. What right did he have to be here now?

Jude set the poinsettia at the base of the stone and ran trembling fingers over the lettering etched into the marble. *Tessa Rose McCall. Forever in our hearts.* He touched the dates, the small, thin line that represented her life from birth until the day she had disappeared beneath the ice. Twenty-one years. A line that couldn't begin to capture Tessa—her athletic achievements, her sense of humor, her random, profound musings on life, her sense of adventure, her refusal to let anything, even rules laid out for her own good, stop her from doing something she wanted to do. His stomach roiled.

"I'm sorry, Tessa. Sorry I didn't go down those stairs after you that day. Sorry I couldn't save you," he murmured, swiping away a tear that had started down his cheek. As ashamed as he had felt since that terrible night, as much as he blamed himself for her death, he'd never had the chance to tell her how desperately sorry he was. Saying the words, here, at her final resting place, even knowing she couldn't hear them, did help. A little.

On some level, Jude knew Cash was right, that Tessa had made choices that had ended up costing her everything and that he wasn't entirely to blame. Still, he struggled with letting go of the burden of responsibility that had pressed down on him for five years.

Cash came up beside him and clapped a hand on his shoulder. "You okay?"

Jude sighed. "I guess so."

"Still can't let it go, can you?"

"I'm trying."

Cash crouched down and straightened the poinsettia pot, settled it a little more firmly in the snow. "When you said that thing about going to the front of the church and praying, what was that about?"

Jude blinked at the abrupt change in topic. Did his brother really want to hear more about that? "Repentance. Forgiveness. Reconciliation."

"So you repented and God forgave you."

"Exactly."

"But you still can't forgive yourself."

He mulled that over. How could he? Jude exhaled. "I guess not."

His brother straightened. "So your court is higher than God's."

Jude frowned. "What do you mean?"

"It sounds like God made a decision that day, that you were worthy of forgiveness. Only you've been overruling that decision ever since."

He couldn't breathe. Was that what he'd been doing? Overruling God's decision? Refusing to accept the judgment that had exonerated him, the mercy that had commuted his sentence? Did his inability to let go of the past mean that he believed the one who had taken the punishment for him did not actually have the right or the power to do so?

Cash raised his hands. "Look, you know God better than I do, but if half of what I've heard about him is true, it seems he should get the final say, not you."

Jude had heard a lot of good sermons since he and Summer had started regularly attending church, but his brother's had to be one of the best. Not bad for an unbeliever. Cash was right. Jude *had* been refusing to accept God's grace. His forgiveness for Tessa's death. *God, help me.* Pressing a hand to the top of the stone, he closed his eyes. *I can't carry this burden around any longer.*

No wind from on high swirled around him, no thunder crashed, but a slight, barely discernible breeze brushed across his cheek and the weight he'd been shouldering for years lifted slightly.

When he opened his eyes, his brother was watching him. "So you're good?"

"Better, anyway. Thanks for dragging me here. I needed to come."

"We all need a push sometimes."

"Some of us more than others." Jude offered him a rueful grin.

"Ready to head out?"

"I think so." He brushed the last of the flakes off the top of the stone. *Goodbye, Tessa.* Sadness coiled through his chest, but he straightened his shoulders as he followed Cash to the truck.

They drove in silence for a few minutes, until Cash shot him a sideways glance. "I've got time now."

"For what?"

"That long, complicated story you mentioned."

"Ah." Jude rested his head against the back of the seat. He'd had dinner with his family twice more since the night Cash had barbequed, but he and his brother hadn't had an opportunity to delve any deeper into his relationship with the woman he'd met in the coffee shop that day. Although his family had welcomed him back, insisted they had long forgiven him, he and Cash still circled each other a little when they were together. Feeling each other out like boxers at the start of a round, not yet locking in and tackling in earnest all that lay between them, everything they had missed in each other's lives the last five years. Maybe it was time.

He shifted to face his brother. "All right. The name of the woman I met that day is Summer Velásquez and she's the most amazing person I know. I pretty much knew from the first moment I saw her that she was the woman I wanted to spend the rest of my life with. For the last two and a half years, we've spent every spare minute together. And six months ago, I asked her to marry me."

Cash's eyes widened. "Really. What did she say?"

"Remarkably, she said yes."

"Huh. So far this doesn't sound that complicated."

"Hold on. That part's coming." Jude straightened in his seat. How could he put this so he didn't come across like a complete idiot? He contemplated that for a moment and realized he couldn't. "At first, I was over the moon. We started making plans and I was counting the days until she was my wife. Then I got thinking."

"Never a good idea."

"No kidding. I started going over and over my past and how much it had messed me up. All I could think about was how I didn't want to ruin Summer's life like I had Tessa's, or force her to wade through the garbage I still wrestled with every day. The closer we got to the wedding date, the more I panicked."

Cash signaled and turned at the next corner, heading back to town. "What did you do?"

"A week before we were supposed to get married, I went to her place and told her I still wanted to marry her, but that I needed more time to figure out everything in my head." The conversation they'd had that night, in Summer's house, flashed through his mind. Every word he'd said came back to him, crawling over his skin and biting into his flesh as though he'd stepped into a nest of angry fire ants. Yep. He'd been an idiot. No two ways about it. And the next day someone had broken into her house and nearly killed her.

He clenched his fists on his knees, still not able to even think about that.

Cash looked over at him. "Did she understand?"

Jude let out a short, humorless laugh. "No, I think it's safe to say she did not understand. She was furious and told me that if I still had doubts at that point, there was no sense in us even thinking about a future together. Tried to give me back my ring, although I refused to take it. Then she kicked me out of the house."

"Ouch."

"Yeah, it was pretty bad. I tossed and turned all night, castigating myself before deciding I had to go back the next day. Blame it on cold feet, recant everything I had said, and tell her that, even though I still had stuff to work through, I wanted to be with her. I had to be with her. And hope and pray she would listen and agree to take me back."

When he didn't speak for a few seconds, Cash lifted a hand. "And?"

Jude swallowed. "Before I could, someone broke into her home and attacked her."

Cash wheeled his truck over onto the shoulder of the road. Shifting the vehicle into park, he turned to face Jude, his face grave. "Did he rape her?"

The first thought he'd had too. The one that had paralyzed him. "No, thank God. He beat her up pretty good though and shoved her down the stairs."

"But she lived."

"Yes, but she was badly injured. Brain trauma. For two weeks she was in a coma."

"And you stayed by her side."

"I didn't, actually." Jude rubbed his hand across his forehead. "I never even got to see her. Her parents, who hated me from the start because I wasn't Mexican and had done everything they could to keep us apart, wouldn't let me anywhere near her. Somehow her father knew about the fight we'd had and he threatened to tell the police I was the one who attacked her if I tried to see her. When she did wake up, she had no memory of the last seven years or so, so even if she heard I'd tried to get in, she wouldn't have known who I was so she wouldn't have stood up to them on my behalf."

Cash slumped against the seat. "Okay, I'll give you complicated. When did all this happen?"

"She was attacked on January third. Woke up from her coma on the twentieth, and left the hospital February second. The plan had been for her parents to take her to their place, but the night before she was supposed to be released into their care, she fled to Elora."

"Why?"

"I'm guessing because a police officer came to see her in the hospital that evening and told her the guy who'd attacked her was still out there somewhere. She likely hoped this would be a safe place to hide out until the police could track down the person who did this."

"Huh."

"What?"

"Given that you're guessing all of this, I take it you still haven't talked to her?"

"Actually, I have. A few times. But she doesn't know me."

"And you haven't told her who you are."

He shrugged. "She's been through a lot of trauma. I don't want to add to it in any way. Besides, I keep hoping, if we spend time together, it will come back to her."

"Define 'spend time together'."

When Jude didn't answer, Cash straightened. "You're dating her, aren't you?"

"We've gone out a couple of times."

"Have you kissed her?"

Jude rubbed a thumb over a small coffee stain on the arm rest.

His brother studied him. "Given the other vices you've stopped indulging in, I'm assuming you haven't slept with her."

His head jerked. "Of course not."

"Okay, easy. I'm trying to fully assess the situation."

And me. God, help him to see you when he looks at me.

Cash shook his head. "From what you've told me, this woman doesn't appreciate people keeping things from her. Why wouldn't you tell her?"

"Like I said, her parents hate me. Her father informed me that he told Summer I was the one who attacked her. If that's true and I tell her who I am, she'll go on the run again. I think it will be a lot easier on her if she regains her memory on her own."

"And if she doesn't, you'll still win, won't you?"

"Meaning?"

"If you can get her to fall in love with you again, but not remember what an a—" Cash cleared his throat, "a moron you were the night you told her you weren't ready to marry her, that leaves you in better shape than before, doesn't it?"

Heat surged through Jude's chest. "Are you suggesting it was a good thing for me that the woman I love was attacked and nearly murdered in her home?"

"No, of course not." Cash's voice softened. "I'm only trying to get you to admit that your reasons for not telling her the truth might be more about you than her."

Jude blew out a breath, his chest cooling a little. "Oh." Had Cash gotten a lot wiser over the years, or had Jude forgotten how perceptive his brother was?

Cash tugged a pack of cigarettes out of his coat pocket and tapped one onto his palm. Jude stared at it. As much as he got the appeal, he didn't like seeing his brother smoking. With all the stuff Cash saw at work, how could he still do it?

Cash tossed the pack onto the dash. "You're right."

"Statistically, it had to happen at some point." Jude lifted a hand into the air, palm up. "About what?"

His brother held up the cigarette. "I shouldn't be smoking. And actually," he grabbed the pack and shoved the cigarette into it before tossing it back on the dash, "I've been thinking about quitting. I figure if you can do it, I certainly can."

"That's likely true. Although, I still have to take it day by day. Giving up smoking was one of the hardest things I've had to do, other than walking away from my family and then going through all this with Summer."

Cash shook his head. "Man, I thought Renee and I had problems."

Jude frowned. "Why, what's wrong with you two?" Cash and Renee had been together since high school.

"Another long and complicated story. Let's deal with the romantic problems of one McCall brother at a time, shall we?" He glanced at the pack of cigarettes. Jude reached for it and shoved it into the inside pocket of his jacket. "Don't want you falling prey to temptation now."

"You know I can take those away from you any time I want."

"I know."

Cash smiled grimly as he put the truck into gear and drove onto the road. "Do they have any leads on who might have attacked her?"

"I don't think so. I know a guy on the force, and I'm keeping in touch with him, but he says they don't have anything solid at this point."

"I'd like to meet her."

"You would?"

"Of course."

Jude pondered the idea. Could they pull it off? "We wouldn't be able to tell her you're my brother." Other than keeping yet another thing from her, that shouldn't be too much of an issue. Like Maddie, Cash took after their father with his dark hair and blue eyes, while Jude's sandy-brown hair and hazel eyes came from their mother's side. They didn't look all that much alike, really. He and Tessa had resembled each other a lot more, enough that people often mistook them for twins, even though he'd been almost three years older.

Cash shrugged. "Whatever. I don't have as much to lose as you do if and when she finds out you've added one more lie to your list."

Jude hunched down in his seat and crossed his arms. "I'm not lying to her—I just haven't exactly been giving her the whole truth."

"Or any of it."

"That's not true. A lot of what I've said to her is right. I even told her I've only swept one woman off her feet and when she asked where that woman was now, I said she'd forgotten all about me."

Cash's eyebrows rose. "Sounds like a dangerous game you're playing."

"It's not a game to me. None of this is."

His brother clasped Jude's forearm. "I know it isn't." He returned his hand to the steering wheel.

Jude looked out the window, concentrating on the mailboxes sailing by, the snow-covered fields broken only by the odd dead corn stalk or tree stump. "You'd have to call me Ryan," he mumbled, his cheeks warming. "Ryan Taylor."

When Cash didn't respond, Jude braced himself and turned to him. A smirk had crossed his brother's face. "Anything else I need to know?"

He sighed. "Summer's going by Ana Santos here in town."

"Of course she is." Cash rolled his eyes. "I think I might need a cheat sheet. Can I still be Cash?"

"You better be. You haven't been away from town for the last few years. I'm sure that any females we run into or who overhear us talking will know who you are."

The smirk disappeared. "What are you talking about?"

"Oh, come on. Have you seen yourself? You don't exactly blend into the background. I'm sure there's been a spike in women calling 911 since you became an EMT in town. In fact, if I was a betting man, I'd wager that's one of the issues you and Renee have, am I right?"

Cash didn't answer.

"That's what I thought."

"Anyway," his brother drew out the word, "can I meet this Summer, or Ana, or whoever she is?"

"I guess you can, if you really want to. She works at the Taste of Heaven Café downtown."

"Okay, Friday's my next day off. I'll pick you up at nine and we'll have breakfast there. All right?"

"Sure." Jude focused on the road ahead of them as they drove across the bridge and into Elora. Was it all right? It was a small town, and his brother knew where Summer worked now. Even if Jude changed his mind about taking Cash there, he couldn't stop him from going any more than he could stop him from taking back his cigarettes if he wanted to.

Besides, part of him really wanted Cash to meet Summer. Cash's opinion meant a lot to him. After all the mistakes Jude had made the last five years, he had a long way to go in earning back his brother's trust and respect. And maybe meeting the incredible woman whose heart he had won once, and hoped to again, would be a good first step in that journey.

CHAPTER THIRTY-FIVE

Summer followed Nancy into the one small grocery store in town. Nancy had slung a basket over one arm, and she glanced back at Summer. "What are you thinking for supper?"

Summer lifted her shoulders. "It's my turn to cook. If we get corn, potatoes, and chicken, I could make sancocho, which is a kind of stew."

"Mmm. Stew sounds good. It's freezing out there."

The temperature had definitely dropped the night before. The short-lived warm spell, the hint that spring wasn't that far off, had ended abruptly as the mercury plunged. The idea of a pot of hot, thick stew bubbling on the stove was definitely appealing.

Nancy nodded to the butcher shop at the back of the store. "You get the corn and potatoes, and I'll grab a package of chicken."

"Sounds good." Summer stood and watched her landlady for a moment. Almost everyone she passed by greeted her or stopped to chat with her. Summer grinned. It might be awhile before she saw Nancy again, since pretty much everyone in town seemed to know her. Warmth rushed through her chest. How had she been fortunate enough to end up in the home of this amazing woman? She'd only known Nancy a few weeks, but it already felt like a lifetime. Her landlady filled a hole in her heart that Summer hadn't been entirely aware she'd had.

She had never been close to her mother. She'd tried, over and over, to win her affection, to hug her and tell her she loved her, but her mother couldn't seem to receive it. It was as though she had erected a wall around her heart, a barrier to anyone getting close to her. If she had been hurt in the past, or harbored some kind of fear of intimacy because of something that had happened in her life, she'd never shared that with Summer.

Her father hadn't shown much interest in her either. Summer had wondered often why they stayed together, or why they had ever had a child, as neither seemed to have any need for the companionship of family. Or any other people, come to think of it. Their home had been more of a fortress than anything, and rather than loved or cared for, what she'd felt most growing up was guarded. And not in a good way, like a priceless treasure. More like a prisoner.

She shrugged off the moroseness that threatened to settle around her and wandered down the aisle between the freezers that lined both sides. Past a hundred different kinds of pizzas in colorful boxes and every type of frozen potato imaginable until she reached the bags of vegetables. Her hands were still chilled from being outside, so she contemplated the options, choosing the one she wanted before opening the door, grabbing it, and closing the door again quickly.

Tossing it into the black plastic basket she'd grabbed at the door, she made her way around the end of the aisle to the produce section. Summer studied the potatoes, stacked like sand bags on the shore of a threateningly high body of water. She decided on a bag of Yukon Golds which, contrary to their name, had actually been created at a university half an hour from Elora, according to Nancy. Might as well support the local economy and ingenuity. She reached for the bag.

"Excuse me."

Her attention shifted to a man standing a few feet away, holding a vase filled with miniature pink roses.

"If you were mine, would you appreciate getting something like this for a gift?"

Her skin crawled. If she was his what? The man had short dark hair and a neatly trimmed beard. He was tall, well over six feet, with a long, dark wool coat draped over broad shoulders. His handsome face was marred only by a slightly crooked nose. Something about the way he presented himself—with a self-assurance that bordered on cockiness—made him appear out of place in the small town. The way he was looking at her raised all kinds of red flags in her mind.

Better not to engage. Summer waved a hand lightly. "It's lovely." She lifted a two-pound bag of potatoes into her basket and turned away.

A crashing sound spun her back around. The man had dropped the vase and it had shattered on the cement floor. Red-tinged water flowed in tiny rivulets in all directions. He contemplated the mess for a moment before looking up. His dark eyes locked on hers. "Beautiful things are so easily broken, aren't they, chica?"

Chills skittered across her flesh. Summer tore her gaze from his. *I need to get out of here.* Without a word, she whirled around and strode toward the far side of the store where she hoped she would find Nancy. When she spotted the back of her landlady's head of red hair halfway down the baking aisle, her muscles relaxed a little and she hurried to join her.

Nancy smiled when Summer came alongside her, but her smile quickly disappeared and she tipped her head to one side. "What's wrong?"

Summer blinked. "Nothing, why?"

"You look like you've seen a ghost."

"I do?" She pressed the back of her hand to one cheek. Her skin felt cool and clammy beneath her fingers. "I'm fine." She grasped the handle of the basket with both hands. "I had kind of a weird encounter with someone, that's all."

Nancy's eyes narrowed. "Who?"

"Some guy. No one I've seen before."

"What did he say?"

"It wasn't what he said, exactly, but how he said it." Summer let out a short laugh. "It really wasn't anything. I'm only imagining there was something sinister going on, I'm sure. Although he did break a vase of flowers, and I'm not entirely sure it was an accident." She was starting to regret bringing it up. No doubt she was making far too much of the encounter.

"I thought I heard a crash." Nancy set a small bag of flour in her basket. "Look, if you felt something sinister, that was likely your subconscious telling you something was off. Don't take that lightly." She started for the end of the aisle. "I'm ready to go, but point this person out to me if you see him, okay?"

Summer trailed after her, not anxious to run into the man—whoever he was—again. He'd called her chica. The word sparked something deep inside, something that hissed and flashed like a downed electrical wire. Other than the fact that it had been spoken in her native language, did that word mean something to her? Did the man?

As far as she knew, she'd never met him. But she could have encountered him any time in the last few years and she wouldn't know it. They passed the produce section. Summer was almost afraid to look, but when she did, the man was nowhere in sight. An employee in a full-length green apron swept up pieces of glass. A woman squeezed a tomato while a child, a young girl with blond ponytails, pointed out apples to her father who dutifully stuck them into a plastic bag. The scene was so normal that Summer released a pent-up breath and shook her head, attempting to clear it of the image of those dark eyes piercing hers.

He was a man buying flowers for his wife, that was all. The vase had obviously slipped through his fingers. These things happened. Summer slid a hand through the crook of Nancy's arm and guided her to the checkout. "Whoever he was, he's gone. I really don't think it was anything except my imagination playing tricks on me."

Nancy didn't look convinced as she unloaded items from her basket onto the black conveyor belt. "Even so, be careful, okay? I don't want anything happening to you. Charles Dickens and I would miss you terribly."

Summer managed a weak smile as she set the potatoes on the belt. As much as she wanted to reassure her landlady, Summer was far from convinced herself that Nancy and Charles Dickens had nothing to worry about. The encounter with the stranger had shaken her out of the false sense of security she'd been lulled into since arriving here.

Which was likely for the best. She needed to put her guard up, be more aware of what was going on around her and who was in the vicinity. If she spotted the man who'd dropped the flowers again, Summer would need to either confront him or call the police. She was done with sitting around waiting for something to happen.

The thought she didn't want to consider, but should, was that it would likely be wise for her to find another place to live. If she was in danger, so was Nancy, and the last thing she wanted was to be responsible for anything happening to the woman who was rapidly becoming a very important part of her life.

CHAPTER THIRTY-SIX

Bells jangled as Jude pushed open the door to the coffee shop. He still wasn't convinced it was a good idea, bringing Cash here. Kind of felt like he was playing that dangerous game his brother had warned him about. It didn't matter now, though. They were here and Summer had already looked over and smiled at him. Suddenly he didn't care at all if it was a good idea, them being here.

"Have you been to this place before?" Jude started for the counter.

"A few times, yeah. Not for a couple of months, though."

They stopped in front of the display case. Summer was ringing up someone else's order, so Jude concentrated on studying Shawn's offerings, overwhelmed, as always, by the choices. From the corner of his eye, he could see Cash eyeing Summer. Would his brother like her? He shook his head. Of course he would.

She finished with the customers ahead of them, a young woman with a toddler on her hip and an older woman, likely her mother. The three of them headed to a table by the fireplace as Summer shifted over to stand in front of Jude. "Hey, Ryan."

"Hi, Ana." He tilted his head toward his brother. "This is Cash McCall. Cash, this is Ana Santos."

Cash held out his hand. "Good to meet you."

Summer shook it and smiled at him. "You too."

It was surreal, seeing two of the people he cared about the most in the world meeting each other for the first time. Jude had never allowed himself to even imagine this moment when he and Summer were together in Toronto.

189

Cash propped an elbow casually on the counter. "How do you like Elora so far?"

"I love it. I grew up in a small town in Mexico, but I've been in the city so long I've forgotten what it's like to be in a place where everyone knows your name."

"And your business."

Summer laughed. "That too."

The door opened behind them and Cash straightened. "I'll take a coffee and a blueberry streusel muffin, please."

"Sure." Summer turned to him. "Ryan?"

"I'll have the same." The good thing was you couldn't go wrong with anything you ordered here. That's why he usually let Summer decide for him. "It's on me." He handed Summer a twenty. She retrieved his change and reached for the tongs. "I know how Ryan likes his, but what do you take in your coffee, Cash?"

"Just black, thanks."

She nodded and set the muffins on the counter before heading for the coffee machine on the back counter. Jude didn't look over at his brother, afraid his face would give away too much if he did. When she set their mugs on the counter, Jude reached for one of the coffees and a plate. "See you tomorrow night?"

"Looking forward to it. Nice meeting you, Cash."

He lifted his mug in her direction. "You too."

They headed for a table in the back corner. Jude took a sip of coffee and set down the mug. "What do you think?"

"It's good." Cash held up the muffin he'd already taken a bite out of.

Jude tilted his head.

His brother set the muffin down and brushed the crumbs off his fingers onto the plate. Before he could say anything, Jude held up a hand. "Actually, you can tell me later. This place is too small. And I know for a fact that you can hear people talking at the counter from over here."

"How do you know that?"

Jude gave him a sheepish look. "I listen to her and Daphne sometimes. If they're talking about me, they speak in Spanish and don't usually worry about keeping their voices down all that much. Especially Daphne."

"No." Cash grinned. "Daphne's never been too worried about that. I didn't know she spoke Spanish, though."

"Apparently she does."

"Do you?"

Jude shot a look at the counter. Summer was busy waiting on an older couple, but he didn't want to take any chances. He lowered his voice. "Yeah."

"Fluently?"

He shrugged. "I was hoping to win over Summer's parents. Which turned out to be a waste of time, although I'm not sorry I learned it."

"Because now you can eavesdrop."

He shot Cash a heated look. "No, because Summer appreciated it when I spoke in her language."

"Spoke? Past tense?"

"That's right. She has no idea Ryan can speak Spanish."

"And why haven't you told her?"

Warmth crept up Jude's neck.

"So you can eavesdrop."

His brother had him there. "It has come in handy on occasion."

"Uh huh." Cash reached for his coffee. "How do you manage to keep it all straight when you're with her?"

"I have to stay on my toes. I've come close to blowing it a couple of times, but so far I don't think she suspects anything."

"How is it you're able to take so much time off work?"

Jude winced. "I'm not, really. I mean, my boss isn't happy about it, apparently. Although he's been as sympathetic as can be expected, given what Summer has been through. He's a trauma counselor, so if and when she does remember what happened to her, he wants to see her. He believes he can help her work through the attack."

"Sounds like a good idea."

"I think so. We're a ways from that, though. At the moment I'm only hoping I have a job to go back to."

"You know, there's a drop-in center here in town that offers counseling." Cash said the words nonchalantly before popping a bite of muffin into his mouth.

Jude studied him. "Are you suggesting I move back to Elora?"

"It's a thought. Mom and Maddie are thrilled to have you here."

"What about you?"

"I don't hate the fact that you're in town." Cash took a swig of coffee then met Jude's gaze over the rim. "I really did miss you, you know."

His chest squeezed. "I missed you, too. All of you. And I have to admit it's been pretty great, being home. All of you have made it far easier on me than I deserve, but I appreciate it."

"Think about it."

"I will. I can't make any kind of plans at the moment, although I also can't keep going without an income for much longer. Something's going to have to give soon."

Cash set down his coffee. "If you need a loan, just ask."

"Thanks, I appreciate it. It's more than the money, though. Like you said, it's been hard to keep everything straight when I'm with her. One of these days I'm going to slip up and call her by the wrong name, or mention something she doesn't realize I know about her, and I'm going to have a lot of explaining to do. The longer this goes on, the more difficult it's all going to be for her to accept when she does find out everything."

"Yeah, I can see that. Out of curiosity, what does Ryan Taylor do for a living?"

The warmth in his neck intensified. "He's a writer."

"I thought you hadn't told her any outright lies, other than your name."

That stung a little. "I guess that is one, although I do write a lot of articles on addictions for a couple of different online magazines and our company's blog. And it was the only way I could think of to be here all the time."

Cash shook his head. "What a tangled web we weave."

Jude pushed his plate away, his appetite gone. "Look, I've never been in a situation remotely like this before. Most people haven't. I'm feeling my way through, doing the best I can."

His brother sighed. "I know you are. I'm worried about you, that's all. I'm hoping all of this doesn't blow up in your face when Summer finds out the truth. And I'm concerned about this guy you mentioned who could be after her. Is there any chance he'll find out she's here in town?"

Jude blew out a breath. "There's a chance. That's why I've been spending so much time around her." Before Cash could say anything to that, he added, "One of the reasons, anyway. I'm hoping and praying that the Toronto PD will be able to figure out who he is and find him before he can track her down."

"I hope so, too." Cash pushed a couple of muffin crumbs around the plate with his finger. "Have you talked to Dad since you've been back?"

Jude's head jerked. "No. I haven't spoken to him in ages. Do you keep in touch?"

"I call him once in a while. More in the last couple of years."

"Why?"

Cash set his muffin down on the plate. "His wife died two years ago."

"Ah." A pang shot through Jude's chest. So much loss. "I'm sorry to hear that."

"I was too. It was a shock, one of those cases where she was diagnosed with cancer in the fall and was gone by Christmas. I think it really shook Dad. He actually seems to be trying to get himself together, to be there for their kids."

His stomach twisted. "How old are they?"

"I think Haddon's twenty-one, Brooke's nineteen, and Lily is eighteen."

"Have you met them?"

Cash shook his head. "No. But since you've been back, I've been thinking that maybe we should try to see them. I mean, they are our brother and sisters. And they've been through a lot."

"Yeah. Maybe." He wouldn't mind meeting his half-siblings. He'd thought about them a lot over the years and wondered what they were like. Not sure he was ready to see his dad, though.

"We don't need to decide about that today. You have enough to deal with at the moment." Cash stuffed the last bite of his muffin into his mouth and washed it down with his coffee. "Anyway, I should get going. Mom wants her bedroom painted and I promised I'd do it today."

"Need some help?"

"That'd be great, if you don't mind. She promised me dinner in exchange for my services."

"Sounds good to me." Jude carried the plates and mugs over to the counter. Summer was dishing a brownie onto a plate for a customer, so he set them down and lifted a hand. She flashed him a smile before turning back to the man she was waiting on.

Jude followed Cash out the door and into the cold. It had been a long winter, but the soft wind that brushed by him carried with it the faint smell of rain and damp earth. Spring was coming. He clung to that thought as he trudged up the street in the direction of his brother's truck.

CHAPTER THIRTY-SEVEN

"It's definitely Cash and Jude's turn to do the dishes tonight." Maddie pushed back her chair, the legs scraping across the wood.

"Watch the floor, please, Madison." Her mother sent her a look of mild reproof as she picked up the nearly-empty platter of roast beef. "And your brothers don't need to clean up. They've been working all afternoon."

"That's fine. We can do them." Jude grabbed the gravy bowl and a dish of carrots and stood up.

Cash shot him a look. "Speak for yourself."

Their mother rested a hand on Jude's back. "Are you sure?"

"Of course. A small price to pay for a home-cooked meal." He kissed her on the cheek. She smiled at him as he grabbed two water glasses and carried them over to the counter.

Cash slid an arm around her shoulders and guided her to the door. "Go sit down, Mom. Read. Watch something. Whatever. You've done enough for today."

"Well, all right. If you insist." She untied the apron around her waist and tossed it over the back of a chair before disappearing into the living room.

Jude contemplated the dishes piled next to the sink. "No dishwasher, huh?"

Cash chuckled. "Nope. Mom still likes to say…"

"… that's why she had us." All three of them said the words at the same time and Jude grinned.

Cash carried a stack of plates over to the counter, elbowing Maddie in the arm as he passed by. "You go do your homework then."

She made a face at him. "I was planning on it. I don't need you to tell me what to do." Maddie tugged the phone out of her pocket and typed something on the screen with her thumbs.

Jude watched the two of them from the corner of his eye as he cleared the table, his chest a little tight. He didn't feel like an outsider anymore, but he didn't feel as though he'd made it back into the inner circle either. His sister and brother were so easy with each other, so familiar. He'd been like that with them too, most of his life. Would they ever get back to that place? He flipped on the tap and squirted liquid detergent under the running water.

Cash nodded toward the stairs. "Put your phone away and go do it then."

She shoved the device into the back pocket of her jeans. "Whatever you say, *Dad.*"

"You're lucky I'm not your dad," Cash's voice held affectionate teasing, "or you know what I'd do?"

"How in the world would I know that?"

Stunned at the raw pain in her voice, Jude smacked the faucet off and turned around. Cash slowly lowered the plates to the counter and walked over to her, grasping her upper arms lightly. "I was going to say ground you for a month, but suddenly that doesn't seem very funny. What's up, Mads?"

"Nothing." She blew the bangs out of her eyes. "I'm fine. Too many midterms and assignments, that's all. I'm tired."

Still holding onto her arms, Cash studied her for a moment. "You know Jude and I are always here for you, right?"

"I know. Thanks. But I'm fine." She pulled away from him and strode over to her backpack hanging on a hook on the wall. After slinging it over one shoulder, she glanced back. "You can both stop looking at me like that. I said I'm fine. I'll see you later."

Jude pushed away from the counter. "Maddie?"

She stopped in the doorway. "Yeah?"

"Joey's tomorrow?"

Her shoulders relaxed a little. "Sure."

"Good. I'll meet you here after school, okay?"

"Okay." She waved and disappeared out the door.

Cash grabbed a towel from the handle of the stove, a troubled look on his face. Jude turned the faucet back on. "What was that all about?"

"I have no idea. I don't think I've ever heard her mention Dad before."

"If she hadn't told us she was fine like a hundred times, I'd be a lot less worried. She's obviously hurting."

"Yeah, more than I realized." Cash reached for a glass in the dish rack. "It's good you're going to spend time with her."

Jude set the pile of plates Cash had brought over into the water. "I need to get to know her again. She was so young last time I saw her, a kid."

"Unfortunately, she's not a kid anymore. Which she informs me at every possible opportunity."

"Does she have a boyfriend?"

Cash grabbed a plate and swiped a towel over it. "Not at the moment. She did, for a while. *Damien.*" He said the name as though it tasted rotten in his mouth.

"You didn't like him?"

"Not at all. I could never understand what she saw in him since he didn't treat her nearly as well as he should have. The night I saw him grab her wrist, I cordially invited him outside for a little chat. After that, he wisely decided not to come around here anymore."

"How did Maddie react?"

"She had a few choice words for me about interfering in her life. Not as many as I expected though. She's not stupid. I think she knew he wasn't remotely good enough for her, only she wasn't sure how to end it."

Jude ran the platter under the running water and set it in the dish rack. "What about Mom? She's still young. Does she ever date?"

"No. She has a lot of friends that she does stuff with, and she goes to a book club once a month. Volunteers at the hospital a few hours every week. And she works part-time at the library. She keeps busy." Cash lifted the platter and shook water off of it. "You could ask them these questions yourself, you know."

Jude sighed. "I know. But..."

"What?"

"It's all stuff I should know about them. If I ask them, it drives home the fact that I missed out on so much of their lives, which I don't know how I'll ever make up to them."

Cash leaned a hip on the counter and contemplated him. "Something you're going to have to figure out sooner or later, little brother, is that you can't."

The words hit him like a palm thrust to the solar plexus. Since the day he'd screwed up the courage to knock on the door of this house, he'd been focused on how to make it up to his family for taking off on them for so long. He swung around, his hands dripping soapy water on the floor. "What do you mean, I can't?"

"You lost five years with us, Jude. That's time none of us can get back. What has been done in the past can't be undone, no matter how much we've changed or what we do in the future."

"So there's nothing I can do to make up for it."

"Nope. That's what forgiveness is for."

Jude stared at him. Everything that had happened since the night Tessa died, every single thing he had said or done, flashed through his mind like a movie montage. An intense cold crept through him. All of it had either been to forget what had happened or to try to somehow compensate for Tessa's death and his cowardice. And it had all been for nothing. Cash was right. Nothing he said or did could ever make up for what had happened in the past.

"You're white as a sheet." Cash tossed the towel over his shoulder and gripped Jude's elbow. "Do you need to sit down?"

"No." Jude shook his head. "Give me a minute." It was almost too much for him to wrap his mind around. If he couldn't do anything to make it right, then he was free to stop trying. He didn't consider himself stupid either, but he'd been acting that way. As though he'd owed someone a million dollars, and even after they'd forgiven the debt he kept trying to pay it back, a few measly pennies at a time.

What Cash had said to him that day at Tessa's grave had impacted him, but it had clearly not fully sunk in until this moment. Now he got it. The only real option he had was to stop striving to make things right and simply accept the forgiveness that God and his family had offered him. Jude slumped against the counter. He really could stop carrying this load around. The burden he'd carried for so long it felt like a part of him.

God, help me to let go. I don't even know how. The sensation that slowly filled him, like mist rolling across the surface of the water, was so unfamiliar he couldn't even name it at first. When he did, he pressed a damp palm to his denim shirt, overwhelmed. Lightness. The load that had lifted slightly in the cemetery was gone.

He still owed it to his family to be here, to avoid repeating the mistakes he'd made in the past, and with the help of God do better in the future, but that was all. He needed to move forward. They needed him to move forward. And now he could, free and clear. All those songs they sang in church about chains being gone suddenly meant more to him than they ever had.

His brother watched him warily. Jude met his gaze. "Anyone ever tell you you'd make a great preacher?"

Cash let out a short laugh as he released his arm. "No, I can't say they have."

"Well, you would."

"The fact that I haven't set foot inside a church in years might be a little off-putting to whoever might be thinking of hiring me." He picked up a glass and rubbed it with the towel.

"That could change." Jude said the words lightly as he turned back to the sink. The last thing he wanted to do was show up at the house after five years and start pressuring his family.

"Anything's possible." Cash set the glass upside down on a shelf.

That wasn't a no. Jude suppressed a grin as he scrubbed the bottom of a pot. He'd take it, anyway.

One step forward at a time.

CHAPTER THIRTY-EIGHT

Jude pulled open the door of Joey's and waited until Maddie had gone in before following her. The place hadn't changed much over the last five years. It still had the same fifties vibe, with Buddy Holly playing over the speakers and black-and-white checkered tiles covering the floor beneath red leather booths. It felt like coming home and the sensation filled him with conflicting emotions.

He wandered over to the counter and gazed at all the choices, even more here than at the bakery. Unfortunately, here he had no one to choose for him. The thought made him miss Summer, although he'd see her later that night because they'd decided to go to a movie at the small theater in town. Like she had the day he'd come home, his sister stood in front of the counter, balancing on the balls of her feet. Clearly her stance when she was trying to make a decision.

Jude walked over to drape an arm around her shoulders. "What'll it be, Maddie?"

"You're buying, right?"

"Of course."

"In that case, I think I'll have a scoop of moose tracks and a scoop of chocolate chip cookie dough in a waffle cone."

The sheer amount of sugar in a cone like that was dizzying to Jude, although, given what he'd consumed the last few weeks at the Taste of Heaven Café, he really didn't have the right to judge. "Go for it."

His sister ordered while he contemplated the brown barrels filled with ice cream of every color, combination, and design. He finally settled on a dish of black cherry, kind of boring but about all the sweet he could handle at the moment. The young kid in a white top and pants, white cap on his head, handed Jude his dish, almost dropping it because he couldn't take his eyes off Maddie long enough to pay attention to him. When he did glance up, Jude gave him a look that had him scrambling to find a cloth and get busy wiping up the drops of ice cream around the containers.

Jude followed his sister to a booth on the far side of the ice cream parlour. The song playing over the speakers set in the ceiling switched to "Great Balls of Fire" as they settled onto the red benches across from each other.

"You know that guy?"

"What guy?"

"The one that served us the ice cream. He couldn't take his eyes off you." The protectiveness that rose up in him was a few years late, but he couldn't have kept it at bay if he'd tried. Which he didn't.

She frowned. "He was doing his job."

"Yeah, okay."

"Look," she pointed her cone in Jude's direction. "I already have Cash scaring off every guy who has the audacity to look at me or say hi, I don't need you doing it too. Got it?"

"Sorry, no promises."

She rolled her eyes. "Whatever."

"So tell me about school." Jude stuck the pink plastic spoon into his ice cream. "What are you studying?"

Maddie licked one side of her cone. "Pre-health sciences."

"Really." How could Jude not have known that? He clearly hadn't spent enough time with his sister since coming back to town. "What are you planning to do with that?"

"I'm not sure yet. I've been thinking about either nursing or becoming a paramedic."

"Like Cash."

"Yeah, I guess. He loves to inform everyone that I'm considering it because I idolize him and want to be like him. I tell him he's full of it, but maybe there's something to it. Don't tell him this or I will deny ever saying it, but I do admire him, a lot. And I think what he does is pretty cool."

"Tough job, though." The thought of Maddie seeing everything his brother had to see all the time made his stomach churn. He hadn't earned the right to say much about her choices, though. Not yet.

"I know. That's why I haven't completely decided yet." She turned the cone and caught a drip sliding down the far side with her tongue. "What do you do?"

"I'm a counselor."

"Like a shrink?"

"Kind of, although I'm not a doctor. I work with people who are struggling with addictions."

"Wow." She cocked her head and studied him. "That's pretty cool, too."

"It can be. Tough sometimes as well. I hear lots of heart-wrenching stories." *And lived a few of them.* Not that he particularly wanted to get into any of that with her. Unless she asked. He'd tell her anything she wanted to know about the five years he'd been missing from their lives. A lot of it wasn't for the ears of kids. But, as Cash had pointed out, she wasn't a kid anymore. Which was going to require a major mind shift on his part.

"So where did you go when you left?"

"Toronto."

"Why?"

He shrugged. "It was the easiest place I could think of to get lost."

"Why did you want to get lost?"

Jude sighed. "I was a mess after Tessa died, Maddie. I blamed myself for what happened, and I believed that everyone else blamed me too. And I couldn't take that. It was easier to leave and find a place where no one knew me, where I could blend into the crowd and become just another street person no one gave a second glance to."

Her blue eyes widened. "You lived on the streets?"

"For a while, yeah."

"Did you ever get beat up or robbed or anything?"

Not a time of his life he particularly wanted to re-live, but Jude wasn't going to keep anything from her. Not anymore. "I did, a few times. It's a rough way to live. Everyone's in survival mode, and when that's where you're at, you'll do pretty much anything to get what you have to have."

"Like drugs?"

His stomach clenched. They were going to go there. "Yeah, like drugs. Or alcohol, or food, or a warm place to sleep. Whatever the need of the moment is." Would she fall for the redirection?

The eyes that studied him confirmed Cash's assertion. His sister wasn't stupid. "So you did drugs."

He expelled a breath. "I did, actually. Not a lot, and not for long, but enough to know it's not a path I ever want to be on again. And enough to give me the desire to help anyone I can to get off of it."

Ice cream dripped from her cone onto the table, but Maddie didn't seem to notice. She leaned forward slightly. "Obviously you've done some stuff that wasn't the brightest, but I want you to know that I admire you, too. For getting your life together and for having the guts to come back here. I'm sure none of that was easy."

Jude's throat tightened. When had his baby sister become such an incredible woman? He'd been pretty sure that, when he told her the truth, he'd drop even further in her eyes. Why did he always have to underestimate the people who cared about him? "Thanks, Maddie. That means a lot to me."

She nodded and lifted her cone to lick all around the edges, catching the drips. "So what now?"

"What do you mean?"

"How long are you going to be in Elora?"

"I don't know, actually."

She cocked her head. "Don't you have to go back to work?"

"I'm kind of on a leave of absence at the moment."

"To see us?"

"Partly. Also because I have a friend in town who may be in trouble."

"What's her name?"

Jude grinned. "Why do you assume it's a woman?"

"Because if you're being this knight in shining armor, swooping in to save someone, it's most likely a woman."

"Well, you're partly right. Her name is Summer. But I'm not sure she needs—or wants—me to swoop in and save her. She's pretty capable of taking care of herself."

"But you're here anyway."

"Yep."

"Do you love her?"

"Yes."

"Are you going to marry her?"

Jude leaned against the back of the padded seat. No discussing the weather or sports or anything nice and superficial like that with his sister. "I don't know. It's complicated. Like I said, she's in trouble at the moment. Until that gets resolved, neither of us can think about the future."

"What kind of trouble?"

She was severely testing his determination to be completely honest and transparent with her. Jude stabbed the spoon into his ice cream a couple of times without taking a bite. How much should he tell her? He let go of the spoon. "All right, here it is. She was attacked in her home a couple of months ago and the guy may still be after her. She came here to get away from him, and I followed her to keep an eye on her until the police can figure out who he is and arrest him. Which will hopefully be soon."

"Wow. She must appreciate you looking out for her like that."

"She likely wouldn't, actually, if she knew that was what I was doing."

"She doesn't know?"

"No. The truth is, she doesn't even know me. When she was attacked, she suffered a brain injury. She doesn't remember the last few years of her life."

Maddie sagged against the back of the seat. "Are you making this up?"

He let out a short laugh. "I wish I was, but no."

"Is her memory loss permanent?"

"No one knows. Her memories could come back any time, or it's possible they never will. All we can do is wait and see."

"Have you talked to her?"

"Yes. We've actually gone out a few times. We're seeing a movie tonight."

"So you're trying to get her to fall in love with you again."

"I guess I am, yeah."

"Do you have a picture of her?"

Jude pulled out his phone and scrolled through the photos before turning the screen toward her.

Maddie stared at it for a minute. "Oh, well. Good luck with that."

He laughed as he stuck the phone back into his pocket. "Thanks a lot."

She grinned. "I'm kidding. You guys would have some pretty cute babies together."

Ouch. That sent a piercing dart right through to his core. Jude rubbed a hand over his chest.

Maddie took another lick of her ice cream. When she looked at him, she wrinkled her nose. "Sorry. That was insensitive."

He shook his head. "It's okay. But the thought of bringing Summer home to meet you guys, marrying her, having kids with her... it's all stuff I haven't let myself think about for a long time. At the moment, I don't even know if we can get back anything close to what we had."

"You will."

"How do you know?"

"Because you're a great guy. You're smart and sweet and funny and, according to all my friends in high school, you're not exactly ugly. Plus, she fell in love with you once, right? That love still has to be there, somewhere. So it's only a matter of time before she realizes it."

Jude contemplated her. "How can you say all that about me after what I did, abandoning you and Cash and Mom when you needed me the most?"

Maddie set her cone on a napkin and focused all of her attention on him. "Jude, *you* were in survival mode. You were doing what you had to do to get through this horrible thing that had happened to you. That isn't who you are." She reached over and gripped his hands with her sticky fingers. "This guy, the one who had the courage to come home and face everyone, and who's risking his life now for a woman who doesn't even know who he is, that's the real you. And if this Summer can't see that and fall for you all over again, then she doesn't deserve you." She pulled back her hands.

His throat had tightened to the point where he could barely swallow. "I hate to tell you, Maddie, but you just made your life a whole lot more difficult."

"What do you mean?"

"I mean that I can't begin to conceive of the guy who could possibly be good enough for you now, so between Cash and me, it may be a long time before any of them get close enough to even say hi to you again."

CHAPTER THIRTY-NINE

The movie theater was small and quaint, like the rest of the town. Summer crossed her legs and balanced the bag of popcorn on the armrest between her and Ryan. She had no idea whether the movie was any good. Several times they reached for popcorn at the same moment. Every time the touch of his fingers against her skin sent shivers of electricity racing through her.

What was she doing? With everything that was going on in her life at the moment, the last thing she needed was to get caught up in any kind of romantic entanglement. Somehow though, no matter how many times she told herself that, she couldn't stay away from this man. Something she didn't fully understand drew her to him. Had her looking up every time bells jangled in the café, hoping to see him walking in. True, her life was complicated. And true, it wasn't exactly the perfect time for her to fall for Ryan Taylor. Yet, she had.

And there it was. The thing she couldn't keep denying to herself. She was falling for him and she was falling hard. Good thing Nancy had given her that talk about the foolishness of waiting until life became nice and smooth and simple before taking a leap like this, because those words were all that were keeping her from complete, hyperventilation-level panic.

Ryan set the nearly empty bag of popcorn on the floor and reached for her hand in the near darkness of the theater. When his warm fingers closed around hers, Summer swallowed. Well, maybe Nancy's words weren't the only thing helping her through this. The truth was, not only could she not fight against her desire to get involved with

Ryan anymore, she didn't want to. The thought was as freeing as it was terrifying.

The movie ended and credits rolled across the screen. Ryan looked over at her and smiled but didn't let go of her hand as they stood and made their way out of the theater. "Do you have time for coffee?"

She nodded. "Sure."

They strolled outside, beneath stone walls and arches draped in twinkling mini lights. A Hallmark movie moment. She smiled at the thought. As much as Summer had gotten used to the noise and chaos of the city, her heart was definitely warming up to Elora. In fact, she was starting to wonder how she could ever go back to living in Toronto again. She glanced at Ryan, walking beside her. What if she hadn't decided to come to this particular small town? She might never have met this man who, in spite of his admission that he didn't do it often, had definitely swept her off her feet.

That thought sobered her, enough that she stopped walking. Ryan had mentioned another woman, one who had hurt him by forgetting all about him. Where was that woman now? Had he ever gotten over her loss? Was there any chance she could come back into his life? The thought of losing him to this mystery woman caused an intense ache in her chest. What had she done, letting herself become this vulnerable? If there was anything she hated, it was feeling vulnerable.

"Ana?"

She blinked rapidly, pulling herself back to the present. Ryan squeezed her hand. "Are you okay?"

"Yeah, sorry. Lost in thought there for a minute."

He drew her over to a bench and tugged her down beside him. "What were you thinking about?"

"Only that, if I hadn't randomly picked Elora out of a map book in a gas station a few weeks ago, I would never have ended up here and I might never have met you."

He shifted on the bench to face her. When he spoke, his voice was soft. "Do you really believe it was random?"

She could easily lose herself in the hazel eyes that met hers. He was right. She shook her head. "No, I guess I don't."

"Neither do I."

Ryan let go of her hand and wrapped his arm around her. Summer rested her head on his shoulder. A few flakes of snow drifted down from the sky, swirling through the air in the light of the streetlamp. Other than that evening reading a book in front of the fire with Nancy, she couldn't remember ever feeling such complete peace.

Ryan pressed a kiss to the top of her head. "What did you think of the movie?"

"I don't have a clue what was happening on the screen. Was it any good?"

He laughed. "I have absolutely no idea."

She sat up and smiled at him. "Next time we might as well stay home and sit on the couch, save the thirty bucks."

His eyes gleamed. "That works for me. More privacy, too." He lifted the hand that had been resting on her shoulder to run his thumb down the side of her face.

Summer swallowed. Probably best to go get that cup of coffee now. "Should we walk?"

"All right." He stood and reached for her hand again. The Taste of Heaven was closed, so they walked past it and stopped at another small coffee shop a few blocks away. One that didn't offer nearly as many tantalizing desserts as Shawn and Daphne's place did. Which was just as well.

Summer studied the menu board. "We should probably get them to go so we can walk back to Nancy's place. I have an early morning tomorrow."

"Sounds good."

She decided on a decaf latte while Ryan ordered a black coffee. When she pulled a ten-dollar bill out of the purple wallet she'd tugged from her bag, he started to protest, but she held up a hand. "It's my turn to pay."

He covered her fingers with his. "All right, on one condition."

"What's that?"

"You agree that this is a date."

"Fine." She started to hold her hand out to the cashier, but Ryan didn't let go of it.

"I want to hear you say it."

She stared at him for a moment before relenting. "Okay, this is a date."

"Did you hear that?" Ryan let go of her and turned to the cashier, a teenage guy with blond hair hanging over his eyes who couldn't look less interested in the drama playing out in front of him. "We're on a date."

"Congratulations," the kid said in a complete monotone, holding out his hand for Summer's money.

She bit her lip to keep from laughing as she gave it to him. Ryan slid an arm around her shoulders as soon as they stepped outside. "Did you see how excited that guy was for us?"

"Yes, he could barely contain himself. My guess is he didn't even know what you were talking about. I'm pretty sure kids don't call this sort of thing dating anymore."

"What sort of thing?"

"You know, hanging out, holding hands at the movies, sharing popcorn."

"Kissing?"

She tilted her head to look up at him. "I suppose."

He leaned down and brushed his lips against hers. More sparks of electricity hummed through her. Definitely Hallmark material.

He straightened. "Hmm."

"What?"

"I think I could get used to this dating thing, or whatever you want to call it." He tightened his hold on her and took a drink from his takeout cup.

Summer could definitely get used to it too. She wrapped both hands around her own cup, allowing the warmth of the liquid and of Ryan's arm to flow through her. As long as she could keep from worrying, not only about everything that was going on in her life at the moment, but about Ryan's mystery woman, she actually might find her happily ever after in this small town.

CHAPTER FORTY

Although the stone stairs were slippery and covered in snow, she skipped down them as lightly as a schoolgirl playing tag with her friends. Jude gritted his teeth. Where was she going now? He was tired and not in the mood to play games.

"Come on, it's only fifty-nine steps, you can do it." Her voice, playful and teasing, floated up to him, carried on an icy breeze that drove into the exposed skin on his face and neck like a thousand tiny daggers.

He didn't want to go down fifty-nine steps. After the day he'd had, climbing all those stairs to the top again would feel like trudging up the last five hundred feet of Everest with a giant pack on his back.

She'd reached the bottom. From the first step, he followed her with his eyes, tracking her journey by the flashes of red that appeared between openings in the trees and rocks. He frowned. Why was she wearing a red dress down to the river? And why hadn't she put on a coat? It was the middle of winter—she had to be half-frozen.

Should he call her? Ask her to come back? He let out a hiss of frustration, knowing he would be wasting his breath and that he would need every bit of it if he was going to have to go down and retrieve her.

Wearily, he stepped onto the second cold stone. The heavy thud sent a wave of angry tingling up his leg. He was half frozen himself, and he had his black ski jacket on, although his head and hands were bare. How could she stand the cold in her sleeveless red dress? He settled into a stomping rhythm as he descended the stairs and eventually reached the bottom. To get to the edge of the river from here, he had to follow her footsteps down another slope, fraught with stones and tree roots hidden under a layer of snow.

Shaking his head, he started down, testing each step to make sure no buried hazard would trip him up and send him hurtling the rest of the way to the bottom. Adrenaline and anger pumped through him, energizing him to scramble down to the shore.

He stopped and peered down the path that wound along the river. Where was she? Another flash of red up ahead caught his eye. His sister had stopped at the edge and stood gazing out over the ice-covered expanse. Her long, dark hair cascaded down the back of the red velvet dress. She wouldn't go out on the ice, would she?

The adrenaline coursing through him thickened to sludge. Of course she would. She had never encountered a rule that something inside her wasn't compelled to challenge. In a way, he envied her that, the way she lived her life with absolute abandon, unhindered by the boundaries and regulations that kept the vast majority of the population hemmed in.

Tonight, though, that instinct of hers to disregard rules put in place for her own safety was sending twin tendrils of fear and fury winding through him.

As he watched, she stepped forward, her black, lace-up boot hovering above the ice.

No. He tried to call out the warning, the command, for all the good it would do him, but the fear had tightened up his throat and no sound emerged. He lunged forward, desperate to stop her.

His hesitation at the top of the stairs had cost him precious ground, and he was too far behind to reach her before she stepped onto the ice. She glided forward, the dress swirling around her until she appeared to be nearly dancing as she moved, floating over the glass-like surface. He neared the spot where she had stepped onto the river. Already she was fifteen feet out.

A loud crack stopped the heart in his chest. Before he could take another step, the ice beneath her feet shattered and she disappeared into the black, bone-chilling water beneath. He did call out then, not words but a primal, guttural cry for help from any being within hearing, natural or supernatural.

Dropping to his belly, he crawled toward the gaping hole, his palms scraping and burning on the ice. Silence draped over the river. Even as he slid toward her, he knew he was too late. She was gone.

Gasping in a deep breath so ragged it scraped like shards of glass against his windpipe, Jude shot upright in bed. Beads of cold sweat slithered down his back between his shoulder blades, and he clutched the sheet so tightly the knuckles of both hands ached.

Pressing his eyes shut, he forced himself to breathe in slowly and evenly for several moments, until the painful thudding in his chest eased. Flashes of red still pulsed behind his eyelids, brief glimpses of the dress his sister had worn down to the river in his dream. She'd never owned a dress like that, as far as he knew, and wouldn't have worn it to clamber over rocks and trees in the dead of winter if she had. So what did that mean?

Releasing the sheet, Jude turned onto his side, punched the pillow up beneath his head, and rested his heated cheek against the cool cotton. Gray light filtered between the crack in the heavy curtains. Barely dawn. Was there any chance his traumatized psyche would allow him a couple more hours of sleep? He closed his eyes, concentrating on blocking out the images that continued to force their way into his tortured consciousness.

A revelation struck him then and his eyes flew open, fresh terror gripping his chest. His sister didn't own a dress like that, but he knew who did. He'd seen it on her at a Christmas party three months earlier and the sight had taken his breath away. Jude drew in another shuddering breath. He'd had that dream dozens of times, maybe hundreds in the five years since Tessa had slipped below the surface of the frigid water that fateful night. This was the first time that she hadn't been the one in his nightmares.

The woman in the red dress was Summer.

CHAPTER FORTY-ONE

Still shaken by his dream, Jude followed Cash into the one gym in town. He hadn't worked out in weeks and guessed that, next to Cash's regimen, his was going to look pretty pathetic. Still, he had to start somewhere. It had been too long.

After forty-five minutes of cardio on the treadmill and step machine, the two of them headed over to the weights. Jude's white T-shirt clung to his chest and back. Cash rolled up his sleeves before lying down on the bench and gripping the bar above his shoulders. Jude adjusted the weights on the ends of his bar, trying not to let the fact that he was about to pump about half of what his brother was bother him. Like earning his way back into the inner circle with his family, it would take time, but he'd get there.

He stretched out on the bench next to Cash. For twenty minutes they worked on arms and abs. Jude pushed himself to near-exhaustion. If he was lifting far less, he could at least hold out as long as Cash did. Finally his brother set the bar into the holders with a clang, sat up, and reached for a towel.

Relieved, Jude sat up too. Something on Cash's shoulder caught his attention and he studied the drawing of a small bird. Not the kind of tattoo he'd have pictured his brother going for. "Nice ink."

Cash glanced down. "Oh yeah." He looked a little sheepish. "It's a wren."

It took a few seconds for the light to come on. "Oh, as in Renee."

"Yep." His brother shifted around to show him his other shoulder. "Maddie and I got this one on our left shoulders about a year after Tessa died. It helped us both to do it. Something you might want to think about."

Jude's throat tightened at the sight of the red rose. Tessa's middle name and her favorite flower. He'd never seriously considered getting a tattoo, but he loved the significance of this one. "I might do that."

Cash wiped himself down and then stood and ran the towel over the machine. "That's it for me."

Jude stood too and remarked, casually, as though he could go for a couple more hours, "Already?"

His brother's lips twitched. "I'm game to hit the treadmill again if you are."

Calling his bluff. Jude swiped his towel over the bench. "I would, but I'm supposed to go out with Summer tonight. I better head back to the motel and get ready."

Cash fell into step beside him as they made their way to the change room. "How are things going with you two?"

"Good. Great, I think."

"No hint that she has any idea who you are yet?"

A twinge shot through his chest. "Not yet, no." He shoved open the door of the change room. "What did you think of her?"

Cash shot him a look as he pulled open his locker. "Do you really want to play that game?"

Probably not. "I wasn't talking about her looks. I want to know what you thought of *her*."

"Oh. Then from what I could tell, she's great. Kind of hard to get a definite bead on her when we had such a brief conversation, but I could definitely see why you were so drawn to her from the beginning. There's something about her, something real and authentic. Which is pretty remarkable, given that she has no idea what she's been doing the last few years and is pretending to be someone else at the moment." He pulled out a black sports bag and closed the locker door. "Plus, she's gorgeous."

Jude punched him in the upper arm and Cash laughed. "I warned you."

"I guess you did." Jude slung his own bag over one shoulder. "Speaking of gorgeous, you still haven't told me what's going on between you and Renee."

Cash pulled on his coat. "I'd need a week."

"How come the two of you aren't married yet?"

His brother sighed. "You'd have to ask her that."

"What do you mean?"

"I'd marry her tomorrow. In fact, I've likely asked her a dozen times over the years, including a couple of weeks before you showed up at my door. She always turns me down."

"Why?"

"The last time she said something about not being ready, but I didn't buy it. She's been acting strangely for awhile now. We haven't been seeing that much of each other because she's so busy doing her residency, but this seems to be more than that. I'm trying to figure out what's going on, but it's tough, because at the moment she won't talk to me or return my texts."

"What are you going to do?"

His brother picked up the bag he'd set on a bench. "There's not much I can do. I'm trying to be patient and trust she'll talk to me when she's ready."

The two of them made their way through the machinery to the front door of the gym, a journey that took about ten minutes because almost everyone greeted Cash as they walked by. Several women flirted openly with him. Although Cash was good at lightly deflecting those kinds of interactions, they did give Jude a little more insight into the challenges Cash and Renee faced.

"Jude?"

He'd been waiting for Cash to finish a conversation and the female voice caught him by surprise. He spun around. A petite woman in spandex and a skimpy tank top, strawberry-blonde hair caught up in a ponytail, swiped a towel across her forehead as she gazed at him.

"Justine, hey." Jude struggled to keep his voice neutral. Running into someone he knew in a town this size had been almost inevitable. The fact that it was someone he'd dated, briefly, was a worst-case scenario, though. At least he wasn't in the café or somewhere else with Summer.

"I haven't seen you in forever. How are you doing?" She draped the towel around her neck and hung onto both ends of it as she took a couple of steps closer to him.

A loaded question. "I'm good. I've been living in Toronto for a few years, just back for a visit."

"For how long?"

Jude threw a look at his brother over his shoulder. Cash was watching the two of them, a smug look on his face, and didn't appear remotely inclined to rescue him. He turned back to Justine. "I'm not sure yet."

"Well then, give me a call if you want to get together while you're around." She sashayed past him, almost brushing against him as she did. "We can reminisce about old times."

"Yeah. Maybe." *Or maybe not.* His ex-girlfriend had been a pretty big partier, from what he remembered. So had he, as far as that went. In fact, they'd met at a bar shortly after his family moved to Elora. Not something he would have wanted to be around anymore, even if Summer hadn't been in the picture.

She glanced back, her ponytail swishing against her neck. "See ya, Cash."

"'Bye, Justine."

His cheeks warmed at the amusement in Cash's voice. Jude headed for the door, not bothering to see if his brother was following. When he reached the sidewalk, he stopped for a moment, breathing in the crisp air. Cash stopped beside him. Jude shot him a look. "What?"

He shrugged. "Maybe you don't *blend in* to the background as well as you think you do."

"Maybe not as much as I had hoped I did, anyway."

"I'm kind of surprised this hasn't happened before, given the size of this town."

"Me too. Although I have been on guard for anyone I know. I've seen a couple of people from a distance but managed to avoid them."

"How long do you think you can keep that up?"

Jude slumped against the brick wall of the gym. "Not much longer, I'm sure."

"Well, on the bright side, if Summer does find out you've been lying to her and dumps you, there's always Justine."

Jude pushed away from the wall. "That's very cute." He slung an arm around his brother's shoulders as they started for Cash's truck, trying to hide a wince at the pain that shot through his arm at the movement. "Pathetic, isn't it?"

"What is?"

"Us. Your long-time girlfriend isn't talking to you and mine doesn't know who I am. We're quite a pair, aren't we?"

Cash snorted a laugh as they reached the truck. "We definitely are. A pair of losers, at the moment." He nodded at Jude's arm. "Take a bath in Epsom salts tonight. That'll help with the pain in all those muscles you'd forgotten you had."

He never had been able to keep anything from his older brother. Clearly that hadn't changed. "Thanks for the advice."

"Anytime. See you tomorrow?" His brother rounded the front of the vehicle.

"Sure. And Cash?"

He stopped on the other side of the truck. "Yeah?"

"It's going to work out with Renee. No way she's going to walk away from you and everything you guys have."

"I hope you're right."

Jude watched him for a moment as he pulled the keys out of jacket pocket and hit the remote to unlock the doors.

Even with the five years he'd missed seeing the two of them together, Jude believed the truth of what he'd said to Cash. He and Renee had started dating in the tenth grade. As far as Jude knew, Cash had never even looked at another woman. He'd known since he was fifteen years old—half his life—who he wanted to be with. Everyone who'd spent ten minutes with the two of them could see they were meant to be together. What could have happened to change that?

Another question, one Jude didn't want to spend a lot of time contemplating, was if Cash and Renee couldn't make it, who could?

The two of them had far more history than he and Summer did. Whenever Jude had seen them together, which was a lot, they'd seemed so happy, such a perfect fit. He thought about their parents. Presumably, at some point, they'd been happy too. What had happened to them?

That one was a little easier. Their dad had turned out to be a selfish drunk. At what point had his mother realized that he wasn't the man she had fallen in love with? How must that have made her feel? His chest clenched. Somehow he'd never given that much thought.

In spite of everything, their mom hadn't turned bitter. She'd remained positive and kind and steadfast, offering them as stable and loving a home as she possibly could have. Even now, after losing Tessa and not knowing where Jude was for so long, she had stayed strong and managed to maintain her sweet nature.

Jude admired her more than anyone he knew. And his greatest desire was for her—for all of his family—to find the faith he and Summer had found. He couldn't push them, though. All he could do, for his mother, for Cash and Renee, for Maddie, was pray for them. And then live his life in a way that showed them how much that faith had changed him and how it was helping him, every day, to become the man he desperately wanted to be.

CHAPTER FORTY-TWO

Summer stumbled into the kitchen and went straight for the coffee pot. She shouldn't be this tired. It was her day off and she'd slept in until nine. Since her alarm usually went off at six a.m., that was quite a change.

Still, she was in desperate need of a hit of caffeine. After filling the machine with water and dumping in a few spoonfuls of her favorite hazelnut vanilla coffee, she stabbed at the power button and waited a few seconds until the machine started to gurgle. Ten small bottles of various colors and designs, filled with what looked like sand, lined the windowsill above the sink. Each one was labeled with a year between 1984 and 1993. Summer contemplated them. What was their story? She'd have to ask Nancy about them sometime. The air was chilly and she rubbed her arms with both hands. Why was it so cold down here?

A meowing sound coming from the dining room snagged her attention. She'd heard water running in Nancy's ensuite shower when she passed the master bedroom on her way downstairs. Her landlady must have slept in as late as she had. Poor kitty must be starving. She grabbed the cat food, filled the small metal bowl on the counter, and carried it through the doorway between the two rooms. "Here you go, Charles Dickens. I'm sorry your breakfast is so late this—"

Summer froze. The door leading from the dining room into the backyard stood open, ice-cold air pouring into the room. What in the world? Had Nancy been down here earlier? Even if she had, why would she leave the back door open? The same creepy feeling that sent her stomach roiling when she watched a Hitchcock movie swirled around her, so strongly she could almost hear the sinister organ music. Had someone been in the house? She glanced around the room. Were they still here?

She swallowed and forced herself to cross over to the door and peer outside. No one appeared to be out there. Should she close and lock the door? If whoever had come in was still here, maybe they should leave that exit readily accessible.

With Nancy in the shower, as vulnerable as Janet Leigh in *Psycho*—Summer shivered at the thought—it was up to her to check out the house. *Tranquila. Stay calm.* She concentrated on inhaling and exhaling until the thudding in her chest eased slightly. A gust of cold air swept through the room, stirring up a faint odor Summer couldn't quite identify. Bumps rose on her arms. *Necesito algo con que defenderme.* Yes, a weapon. Great idea. A Glock would come in very handy right about now. She frowned. Where had that thought come from? Would she have any idea what to do with a Glock if she had one? Summer shook her head. It was a moot point. She didn't have a gun and, as far as she knew, had never owned a pistol in her life. A knife would have to do.

As quietly as possible, she set the dish of food down, hoping that would keep the cat busy and quiet for awhile, and closed the back door, leaving it unlocked. She tiptoed into the kitchen. Her fingers trembling slightly, she slid the kitchen drawer open and pulled out the sharpest-looking knife. After closing the drawer with her hip, she turned and made her way out into the hallway, gripping the knife tightly.

Now that she was armed, something clicked in Summer's brain. The fear dissipated and she shoved back her shoulders as she moved, nearly soundlessly, down the hallway, her back pressed to the wall. She checked out the living room, study, and downstairs washroom. No one waited behind any of the doors or crouched on the far side of a piece of furniture. Nothing appeared to have been disturbed. *I need to check upstairs.* She started down the hallway. When a knock sounded on the front door, she swung toward the noise, holding the knife out in front of her in both hands. The shadowy outline of a man in the window of the door tightened up her stomach. Was it whoever had snuck into their house in the night? She shook her head. Unlikely he would come to the front door and announce his presence.

Whoever it was knocked again. Still clutching the knife, Summer hid it behind her back and made her way to the door. She shoved aside the red and white striped curtain. Ryan. Her muscles relaxed as she pulled open the door. "Hey."

The slow smile that got to her every time crossed his face as he held up two paper cups. "Thought you might need coffee since you're not at the café today."

Adrenaline still pumping through her, Summer couldn't muster a smile in return. The sound of Nancy singing drifted down the stairs. With Ryan standing there, the rich smell of coffee drifting from the cups in his hands, sunlight pouring through the door, and Nancy's off-key singing filling the air, the idea that someone might be lurking around their house seemed suddenly ludicrous. Likely her landlady had gone out to retrieve something earlier that morning and come in through the back door. If she hadn't shut it tightly, the wind could easily have pushed it open. No doubt Summer had blown the entire thing out of proportion. She took a step back. "That's sweet, thank you. Come in."

Ryan stepped over the threshold and held out one of the cups. "Here you go."

Her right hand still bent behind her back, she reached for the coffee with her left. He gave her a funny look. "Everything okay?"

"Of course. Why?"

He raised an eyebrow. "You have your hand behind your back. Any particular reason?"

She forced as innocent a look onto her face as possible. "Nope." Any chance she could keep the knife out of sight until they were back in the kitchen and then slip it into the drawer when he wasn't looking? "Let's go sit at the table."

"Ana."

She swallowed. Even if he didn't know her real name, Ryan still looked at her as if fully aware that she was keeping something from him. And it didn't appear as though he was going to budge from his spot inside the door until she told him what it was. Summer sighed. Warmth crept into her cheeks as she brought the knife out from behind her back and held it up to show him.

He frowned. "Why are you carrying a knife like a weapon?"

It might be easier to show him than tell him. "It's probably nothing, but something did happen this morning that freaked me out a little. Come into the dining room."

She spun around and headed down the hallway, his footsteps echoing on the wood floor behind her. When they passed through the kitchen, she tossed the knife into the drawer before leading him into the adjoining room. Summer stopped and gestured toward the back door. "I heard Charles Dickens meowing in here a few minutes ago. When I brought his food in, the back door was wide open."

"Really?" Ryan strode across the room and peered through the window in the door. "Where's Nancy?"

"Still upstairs. I didn't think she'd been up that long, but maybe she came down earlier to grab something and didn't shut the door tightly."

"Do those look like her footprints?"

Summer walked over to stand beside him. She studied the prints that crossed the yard and up onto the back deck and another chill swept over her skin. "No, actually. They look too big to be hers." But if Nancy hadn't been the one to leave them, then who had? And where was that person now? She looked up at Ryan, her eyes widening. "There are no footprints leading away from the house. Do you think whoever did this is still inside? I looked all around the main floor, but..." *Nancy.* She whirled around. "I need to check upstairs."

"Wait." Ryan grabbed her elbow. "I'll go."

She shook her head. "I can't sit around down here waiting. I'm going up. You can come with me if you want to."

He looked as though he wanted to argue but pressed his lips together and nodded. They retraced their steps down the hall and up the wide staircase. Nancy was still singing away loudly in her room, so Summer assumed the master must be clear. She and Ryan walked quickly through the other bedrooms on the floor, checking under beds and in closets. Nothing. Finally they searched her room but didn't come across anything out of the ordinary.

"I think the house is clear." They stopped in the middle of the area rug and Ryan cupped her shoulders, searching her face. "Are you okay?"

"Yes, of course. It all seems silly now."

"I don't think it's silly at all. Someone did walk across the backyard. And since whoever it was didn't leave that way, there are only two explanations. Either they're still in the house, which we've pretty much established they aren't..."

"Or they left through the front door."

"Exactly."

Summer whirled and headed for the hall. Ryan followed her down the stairs to the door and, when she pulled it open, moved to stand beside her in the doorway. The front porch was covered by a shingled overhang, and the wood slats below were largely free of snow and ice. Summer had shoveled the stairs and front walkway the day before, so no clear footprints stood out like they did at the back. She grabbed her boots and tugged them on so she could join Ryan, who'd stepped out onto the porch.

"See anything?" She wore the plaid flannel bottoms and black T-shirt she'd slept in. The front of the house was largely blocked from the wind. Still, the air carried an icy enough bite that she hugged herself tightly as she walked to the top of the stairs.

"Not yet." He started down and she followed. With her eyes glued to the front walk, she missed seeing a small patch of ice on the bottom step. When her boot slipped to one side, she braced herself with both hands against Ryan's back to keep from falling. He turned and grasped her forearms. "Are you all right?"

"Yes." She shook her head. "Just incredibly clumsy lately. Sorry." Something caught Summer's attention from the corner of her eye and she glanced down. "Look." She tugged herself free from Ryan's grasp and bent to examine the partial print in the snow at the edge of the sidewalk. "Looks the same as the ones out back, doesn't it?"

He nodded. "I think so, yes. The police will be able to determine that for sure."

She straightened. "You think I should call the police?"

"Of course. Someone was in your house. You can't take that lightly."

"I should check with Nancy first, make sure it wasn't her. She could have pulled on her husband's old boots or something if she had to go outside for something."

"If she didn't, you'll call the police, right?"

The thought of uniformed officers swarming through their house on what was supposed to be her one quiet day this week sent a rush of irritation through her. Her jaw tightened. It didn't appear as though anything in the house was missing. Why on earth had someone come into the house? To show them he could? That thought sent shudders through her. What if it was the same man who had broken into her house before? Had he found her? If so, she wasn't the only one in danger. She'd put Nancy in the path of this psychopath. The last of the warmth drained from her body.

"Ana? What is it?" Ryan sounded alarmed. When she didn't respond, he reached for her hand and tugged her toward the porch. "Let's get you inside and warmed up."

She followed him into the house, but the shivers rolling through her had little to do with the outside temperature. Ryan led her down the hallway and into the kitchen. "Sit down. We'll have our coffee, and when Nancy comes down we'll figure out the best thing to do."

Summer sat, woodenly. Ryan took the chair across from her. He still held her hand and now he reached for her other one. "Look at me." When she did, he rubbed the backs of her hands with his thumbs. "Everything's going to be fine, I promise."

She nodded. Sitting here, in the bright sunlight, his strong fingers grasping hers, she could almost believe him. "Here." He let go of one of her hands and moved the coffee he'd brought closer to her. "Drink this."

Summer lifted the paper cup to her lips and took a sip. The aroma curled around her and she breathed deeply. That had to be one of the best smells in the world. So much better than...

She lowered the cup to the table. The scent she had breathed in earlier, in the dining room, the one that she hadn't quite been able to pinpoint, came to her now, like a memory roused by the new aroma drifting in through her nostrils. With absolute certainty, she knew what it was she had smelled.

Cigarette smoke.

CHAPTER FORTY-THREE

Jude paced the huge, fenced-in backyard behind Nancy's house, his phone pressed to one ear. *Come on. Come on. Come on.* After what seemed like an eternity, a voice came over the line. "Travers."

"Evan, it's Jude."

"Jude. I'm glad you called. I have news."

"Me too."

"What's going on? Is Summer okay?"

"So far, yes."

"What does that mean?"

Jude kicked at a chunk of ice in his path. "Someone was in her house last night."

"In her house? Did he attack her again?"

"No. When she went downstairs this morning, the back door was wide open. There were footprints across the yard and up the stairs but nothing going back out. We did find prints leading away from the front entrance though, that looked to be from the same boots. The police here in Elora are checking that out now."

After a few seconds of silence, Evan blew out a breath. "So, if it was the same guy, he was letting her know he's found her and can get to her any time."

"That was my take, yes. You need to get people here now."

"Look, Jude, here's the thing. We're following a hot new lead. I'm pretty sure this investigation is about to break wide open. When it does, we'll know who's after Summer and we can take him down."

"How long is that going to take?"

"I don't know, twenty-four, forty-eight hours at the most is my guess. I can't come there myself, I need to be on this. I'll try to get someone else there, but in the meantime, can you keep an eye on her?"

"I'm not going anywhere. But if you could send someone, that would be great."

"I'll do my best. You likely won't know they're there, though. They'll want to keep out of sight to avoid scaring this guy off."

Scaring this guy off sounded pretty good to Jude. He had to trust the police on this, though. "All right. I'll stay with her."

"Great. I'm not leaving the office again until this is all wrapped up. Believe me, I want that as badly as you do."

Jude seriously doubted it. "Okay. Thanks, Evan."

"I'll be in touch."

He shoved the phone into the back pocket of his jeans and ran a hand over his head. Great. Protective detail. He was an addictions counselor. What did he know about fending off sociopathic killers with guns?

Jude lowered his hand. He may not know a lot about defending himself from dangerous criminals, but he did know two things. He would gladly give his own life to keep Summer safe. And he knew exactly where to get a gun.

CHAPTER FORTY-FOUR

Jude rapped on the front door of Nancy's place. He didn't have a hard and fast plan, but he needed to talk to Summer and Nancy before he could come up with one. The best idea would be for him to stay in the house, preferably on the main floor so if this guy came back he'd have to get past Jude to reach the second floor. He had no clue, though, whether either of the women would agree to that. He was a virtual stranger to Nancy and Summer wouldn't like the idea of needing a man around to protect her.

Jude would do everything in his power to persuade them both. Failing that, he was looking at a couple of arctic-temperature nights in his car out on the street. Even then, he wouldn't be able to cover both the front and back of the house. Slightly better than nothing, but not ideal. Footsteps sounded in the hallway before Summer brushed back the curtain and peered out. He was glad to see her taking minimal precautions, at least. And even gladder when she smiled, let the curtain drop back into place, and pulled open the door. "You came back."

"Yeah, sorry I had to take off. I needed to grab a few things." He held up the overnight bag he'd hastily shoved a few clothes into before leaving the motel to return here.

Her smile faltered a little. "Are you going somewhere?"

"I was hoping to talk to you about that, actually."

She contemplated him for a few seconds before stepping back. "Come on in."

"Thanks." Jude kicked the snow off his running shoes before

stepping into the front foyer and closing the door behind him. He flipped the lock with a decisive click. When he faced her again, Summer's eyebrows had risen, but she didn't comment on the action.

"Would you like a cup of tea?"

"Tea would be great, thanks." Jude stripped off his coat and hung it on a chair in the hallway. After tossing the bag onto the seat of the chair, he followed Summer into the kitchen.

She plugged in the kettle and leaned against the counter. "So what's going on?"

"I talked to the police." Cash's voice rang in his head, like it had done all his life. Jude lifted his chin. It wasn't a lie. He *had* spoken to the police. If she assumed he meant the Elora police and not the Toronto PD, that wasn't his fault. Entirely.

Summer regarded him with interest. "So did I. They said to keep the doors locked and they'll drive past the place every hour or two all night. I'm sure we'll be fine."

"That's good, but I'm still concerned. This guy was pretty brazen. And you likely had your back door locked last night, didn't you?"

She bit her lip. "Actually, I'm positive we did. I remember checking it before I went up to bed. Which is weird, right? The police said there was no sign of a forced entry."

"Does Nancy keep a spare key outside anywhere?" Even if she didn't, a professional could pick pretty much any lock in seconds. Jude kept that thought to himself.

"Not that I know of. She's gone to play bridge with friends of hers, but I can ask her about that when she gets home." The kettle whistled behind her and Summer pushed away from the counter and poured the boiling water into the pot. She carried it and two mugs over to the table and sat down. "Are you going to tell me?"

"Tell you what?"

"What the bag is for."

Jude drew in a breath. "The thing is, I'm worried about you and Nancy. I'm sure the police here will do everything they can to track down the guy who came into your house, and hopefully they'll find him soon. In the meantime, I was hoping you'd consider letting me sleep on your couch."

She leaned against the back of the chair. "Why would you want to do that?"

Did she really not know? "Like I said, I'm worried about you. I wouldn't be able to sleep if I wasn't here. To be honest, if you won't let me stay in the house, I'll sleep in my car, but it would be a lot more comfortable in here."

She narrowed her eyes slightly, as though trying to figure him out. "That's a lot of trouble for you."

"I don't mind." Throwing caution to the wind, he reached across the table and clasped her hand. "In case you haven't figured it out, I care about you. A lot. There's something powerful between us. I felt it the first time I came into the coffee shop." No need to specify which one of those he was referring to either. "I hope you feel it, too. I don't know what I'd do if anything happened to you."

For a few seconds, she didn't move or speak. Jude felt the silence like the hush that fell over a courtroom right before the head juror delivered the verdict. When Summer did speak, her voice was low and quiet. "I do, actually."

"You do what?"

"Feel it." She tugged her hand from his and poured tea into both their cups. "Still, it seems like too much to ask you to sleep on our couch."

"It isn't. And you didn't ask. I offered." Jude wrapped his fingers around the mug she slid across the table to him. "I'm sure it will only be for a night or two."

She chewed the inside of her lip, the way she always did when contemplating a problem. He didn't have the time or patience for her to make one of her pros and cons lists, so hopefully that habit would help her decide on the spot. Thankfully, it appeared to as she eventually sighed. "I guess it's okay. If you really don't mind. And as long as Nancy doesn't object. Only for a night or two, though. If nothing happens during that time, I think we can assume that whoever it was has moved on."

Which wasn't likely. "Great. Thank you."

"I'm the one who should be thanking you." She lifted her mug in his direction. "I really do appreciate it. I'm sure Nancy will too."

She must have connected the dots and realized the person who had strolled through the house while they were sleeping could very well be the same one who had almost killed her, and a genuinely serious threat, otherwise Jude was confident she'd never have agreed to him staying.

The muscles that had tightened while waiting for her response loosened a little. He couldn't relax, though. Not until the guy who was after her was safely behind bars. If he let down his guard, Summer could pay the price, and Jude couldn't let that happen.

Not to another woman he loved.

CHAPTER FORTY-FIVE

So McCall had moved in. Díaz shifted on the seat, tired of being cooped up behind the wheel of his tiny car. Since he'd already been spotted once, he'd parked almost two blocks down the street today and had a hard time seeing exactly what was happening, but he'd been able to gather that much.

Something had happened the day before. When he'd driven by in the afternoon, three police cars were parked in the driveway and on the street in front of the place Summer was staying. He'd seen her outside, so nothing had happened to her. Not yet, anyway. Had Kendrick done something? Left her some kind of message? That was exactly the kind of thing he would do. Díaz still hadn't seen any sign of the man. Unfortunately, that didn't mean he wasn't around.

If the boss hadn't come up with the money for Mendoza yet, time was running out. This was day twenty-nine of the thirty-day extension Mendoza had offered. And if Díaz had learned anything from past experience, it was that Mendoza was a big believer in enforcing deadlines. After tomorrow, it was anyone's guess what would happen, but if Kendrick was the one sent out to exact retribution for non-payment, it was more than likely that it was Summer who was in his sights.

Díaz snatched up his phone from the passenger seat and punched in a series of numbers. The boss answered after the third ring. "Dígame."

"It's me."

"¿Qué pasó?"

237

"McCall has moved into the house with Summer. The police were here yesterday so something happened, but I don't know what."

"Kendrick?"

"Possibly. I'm going to stay here today, see if I can spot any sign of him."

"Está bien."

Díaz hesitated. At the moment, his boss had complete control of his future and the future of his family. How could he ask if payment had been made without causing offense and possibly suffering the consequences? "Do you have any idea what might happen after tomorrow? It would help if I knew what I was watching for."

His boss grunted. "Solo esté listo."

Díaz frowned. Be ready? Be ready for what? "¿Para qué?"

"Te diré si necesito que la agarres."

He massaged his temple with the fingers of his free hand. Okay. Grab her at the boss's signal. He could do that. "And bring her to you?"

"Sì."

"Fine. I'll wait for your signal."

"Muy bien." The line went dead.

Díaz tossed the device back onto the passenger seat and grabbed the take-out cup of coffee he'd picked up. Not at the café—he hadn't made the mistake of going there again—but at the far more anonymous chain coffee shop. He took a sip and nearly spat it back out. Cold. Grimacing, he forced himself to drink every drop. It was going to be a long couple of days and he needed to be alert and ready for whatever was coming. Whether or not he was able to carry out his orders, Summer Velásquez would likely suffer. But if he failed, or didn't survive, his family would also suffer. And he would do whatever he had to do to make sure that didn't happen.

CHAPTER FORTY-SIX

Jude set down his fork. "That was amazing, Nancy." The ham and scalloped potatoes had been nearly as good as his mother's.

She beamed at him. "Thank you. It's nice to have people to cook for again. It's been too long." Her smile dimmed a little, as though memories of those past meals—or whoever she had made them for—carried hurt along with them. What was her story? Would he ever be able to sit and casually talk about life with her? Until she knew who he really was, it felt like a betrayal to ask her to share too much.

Summer pushed back her chair. "You cooked, so I'm on for dishes."

"I'll help you." Jude stacked their three plates and carried them to the sink.

Nancy set the platter of ham and a dish of green beans on the counter. "I think I'll head up and take a bath then, call it an early night."

Was that a wink? What did she think he and Summer were going to do down here alone, make out on the couch? He shot a look in the direction of the living room. Actually, not an unappealing thought. At all. When he met her gaze, Nancy was watching him, a smile playing around her lips. "Well, good night then. Ryan, were you okay last night? Warm enough?"

"Absolutely. I was fine." He had been. The big couch in front of the woodstove had been surprisingly comfortable, which wasn't a good thing. He'd planned to stay awake as much of the night as possible, but ended up falling asleep around two in the morning and not waking up until Summer came down at six thirty, ready to go to work.

Opening his eyes and seeing her had been a pretty great way to start the day. His chest tightened. If it were up to him, they'd get married so he could start every day like that, but he had no idea whether they would ever be able to get back to that place. Not after everything that had happened. And could happen still.

He gave Nancy a hug. When he pulled back, his eyes met hers. "Thanks, Nancy." He meant for a lot more than dinner, which she seemed to understand.

She nodded. "My pleasure." She pulled Summer into an embrace. "Good night, darlin'."

Summer flung her arms around her landlady before pressing a kiss to her cheek. "Good night, Nancy."

Jude watched the two of them. Obviously they'd grown close over the weeks that Summer had been here. It had been a stroke of luck that he'd seen Nancy's ad online the day they had arrived in Elora. Jude shook his head. Luck? He knew better than that. Luck had nothing to do with it. God had clearly had a hand in bringing those two together. Summer's mother was so cold and closed off that Summer had never really known what it was like to have someone like that in her life offering her unconditional love and support. Somehow she'd grown into a woman capable of offering her heart to others without reservation, as he'd been fortunate to experience first-hand before he'd blown it. She hadn't learned that from the people who had raised her, though.

Maybe he'd had something to do with it. She was pretty guarded when they first met. Even though she'd been the one to call him, he'd still had to work extremely hard to break down her walls and get through to her. But it wasn't until she'd given her life to God that they'd come tumbling down altogether.

He pulled open the door of the dishwasher and set their plates in the rack. God had obviously led Summer to Elora too, even though she couldn't have remembered him telling her about his connection to the place. Not consciously, anyway. His chest squeezed. Was anything about him or their past together registering with her on any level?

"Ryan?"

He blinked, yanked from his thoughts of the past. Nancy had gone, and Summer was holding out a clean, dripping pot to him, a quizzical expression on her face. It took everything he had not to reach for her and pull her close. "You were a million miles away. What were you thinking about?"

Jude grabbed a towel hanging on a hook and took the pot from her. He was tired of keeping things from her, exhausted by the constant effort of remembering what he was supposed to call her, who she was supposed to be, who he was pretending to be. Trying to ascertain what she remembered about herself, about them. And worrying about what might happen next. He was pretty close to not being able to do any of it anymore. At least this he could be honest about. He set the pot on the counter and tossed the towel down beside it. "You."

Her dark eyes widened slightly. "What about me?"

Jude stepped closer. "I was thinking about how blessed I am to have found you."

"Oh." She bit her lip but didn't react as he took another step, stopping in front of her and resting his hands on the edge of the sink on either side of her. Summer swallowed. "Can I ask you something?"

"Yes. Anything."

"What does that word mean to you, exactly?"

"Blessed?"

"Yes."

"It means that meeting you, having you in my life, is a gift from God to me. And not one that I take lightly." Jude brushed a long dark strand of hair back from her face. How much did she remember about her faith? Was the spiritual level, a relationship with God, stronger and more real than any conscious memory?

Her face softened. "Good. That's what it means to me too." She tipped back her head a little, her eyes locked on his.

Given the clear invitation, Jude didn't bother asking this time, but lowered his head until their lips met. Moving in closer, he took her face in his hands and deepened their kiss. Weeks of holding himself back, of being forced to be apart from her and then slowly, slowly inch his way back into her life, culminated in this moment. He poured everything he felt into the kiss, into the hands touching her soft, warm skin. *Remember me.* He begged her silently, calling to the person she was, to the love they shared and that had been lost down deep inside of her the day of the attack. *Remember us.*

Finally, reluctantly, he ended the kiss. When he pulled her head to his chest and wrapped his other arm around her, she didn't resist, but rested against him, her cheek against his thudding heart.

They stood like that for several minutes, until she lifted her head and smiled. "Wow."

Jude laughed and kissed her again, lightly. "No kidding."

She ran a finger down his cheek, sending tingles of warmth shooting through him. "Who are you, Ryan Taylor?"

Good question. "Someone who is falling for you, Ana Santos. Utterly and completely." He let her go while he still had the strength to do so and reached for the towel. "Should we finish up here?"

"We should, although you're retreating so quickly I'm not sure we'll be able to."

He stared at her. "What does that mean?"

"It means that you have a tendency to be evasive when I start asking you questions about yourself. Why is that?"

Because I'm scared of letting something slip that I'm not supposed to know about you but do because I know almost everything there is to know about you. Which was true, but it was a response that would cause the kind of trouble he'd been trying to avoid since he'd come to Elora after her. He sighed. "That isn't intentional. What do you want to know?"

She turned around and dipped her hands into the water. "Where did you come from and how did you happen to arrive in town right around the time that I did?"

He gulped a little. Jumping into the deep end. Jude took the dripping bowl she handed him. "Like I told you before, I've been in Toronto for a few years. I grew up in a small town, though, and the big city finally got to me, so I came here." Choosing each word carefully was a bit like navigating through a mine field. A wrong step could cause an explosion and who knew what kind of damage. He didn't want to lie to her anymore, though, which meant telling the truth in a way that didn't give too much away. He had to mentally test every sentence before saying it out loud to make sure it didn't contain anything that would arouse suspicion.

"Why Elora?"

He studied her profile as she turned on the tap and ran another large bowl under the water. She spoke lightly, but the words carried more weight than she was letting on. This wasn't casual conversation. "You know Cash, the guy I introduced you to when we had coffee a few days ago?"

"Yes." She held out the bowl for him.

Jude took it and shook off the excess water over the dish rack. "I've known him a long time. Since I had a connection in Elora, it seemed as good a place as any to land." It struck him suddenly, the next question she would ask. He needed to head her off at the pass. "Also, I have family here in town."

She swung her head to look at him, surprise flashing in her dark eyes. "You do?"

"Yes, but," he scrubbed the towel over the already-dry bowl, "I had a falling-out with them a few years ago. One of my reasons for coming back to town was to see if we could find a way to reconcile."

Summer set the last pot on the rack and dried her hands on his towel. "Have you seen them?"

"Yes, a few times."

"And?"

"We're making progress."

"I'm glad to hear that." She rested her hands, still warm and slightly damp from the water, on his forearms. "I'd love to meet them sometime."

Jude swallowed. Not only because of her words, but because the feel of her hands on his skin was weakening any resolve he had not to move too quickly with her. It was killing him, being well into the book of their story when, as far as she could remember, she'd only read the first few pages. "I'd love that too. Maybe when I'm on a little surer footing with them."

"Of course." She smiled. "Thank you for sharing that with me. I feel like I understand you better now."

"Good. I do want that, you know."

"I do, too." She raised herself up on her toes to press her lips to his. Jude kept a tight grip on the bowl and towel, but he did allow himself to close his eyes and sink deep into the feel and taste of her. The faint scent of coconut drifted from her dark, shimmering curls, and he breathed it in.

When she pulled away, the smile she offered him weakened his knees. He hadn't seen her smile at him like that for so long, he'd almost forgotten the way that look brushed across his skin like a physical touch and burrowed deep inside him. The last time she'd looked at him that way was the night he'd turned up at her place to try and explain to her why he wasn't ready to marry her. She'd flung open the door, flashed him that smile, then thrown her arms around his neck and held him.

Minutes later his words had driven that smile from her face.

Jude couldn't think about that tonight. Like he'd decided he needed to do with his family, he had to keep moving forward with Summer. Although he hadn't allowed himself to truly consider the possibility that she might never regain her memory, the possibility did exist. And if that was the case, the past didn't matter anymore. All that mattered, all the two of them could share, was the present and any future they might have together.

He returned her smile. "Wow."

She laughed. "No kidding." She stepped out of his arms. Jude set the bowl in the cupboard and hung the towel over the rack to dry.

"I guess I should call it a night. I have church in the morning." She hesitated. "Would you be interested in coming with me?"

He hadn't been to church since her attack. Suddenly there was nothing he wanted more. And not only for the chance to spend more time with her. Jude nodded. "I'd like that. I went to a great church in Toronto but haven't found one here yet."

Summer flashed him that smile again. Seriously, she had to stop doing that, or he wouldn't be responsible for his actions. "Great. I'll see you in the morning, then." She started for the door.

"I'll be here."

She stopped and turned back. "Thank you for that, for being here. It does make me feel better."

"Good. Me too." He stood for a long time after she had gone, staring at the doorway and remembering the feel of her lips on his, the warmth in her eyes when she looked at him. The feelings that coursed through him were so strong he hardly knew how to handle them. How could he have ever hesitated, even for a second, to marry her? If it wouldn't freak her out completely, he'd go upstairs right now and ask her to spend the rest of her life with him.

Focus, Jude. He blew out a long breath. Good advice. Someone was still out there, still after her. Maybe even watching the house right now. He couldn't forget that, not for a second.

Jude almost wished the guy *would* show himself. After tonight, he was ready to face whoever it was, ready to tear him limb from limb if tried to get to Summer. Jude clenched his fists.

The sooner whoever it was did step out of the shadows, the sooner he and Summer could get back to writing the rest of their story together.

CHAPTER FORTY-SEVEN

Jude planned to stay close to the café today, sit inside for a while and then watch from down the block somewhere. Ever since he'd found out a stranger had been in Summer's house, he'd sensed that something big was about to happen. Evan still hadn't contacted him, so the case must not have broken open yet. How much longer could they all go on like this, knowing the clock was ticking down toward some kind of event but not knowing when or where it would happen, or what it would look like when it did?

Maybe this *was* the event. The waiting. The not knowing. The apprehension. It was possible that whoever had broken into Nancy's house did so solely because he knew it would throw everyone involved into a crazy turmoil. This could very well be his sick and twisted end game.

Or it might not be.

So they waited. Him. Summer. The police. On edge but trying not to give this man the satisfaction of causing them to live their lives in fear.

Jude tugged on jeans and a long-sleeved navy T-shirt. Summer had already gone to the café and he was anxious to join her there as soon as possible. A light spring mist filled the air. He left his leather jacket on the chair inside the door and pulled on the wind-breaker he'd grabbed from his motel room the day before, after he'd gone to church with Summer.

The service had been great. A little less formal than the church they'd attended in Toronto, but filled with the same sense of being in the presence of God. He definitely planned to go with her every week. He yanked up the zipper on the wind-breaker. Making any kind of plans for the future at the moment felt a little futile.

When he strode down the porch steps, a dark car was driving past the house, slowly. The driver didn't speed up when Jude walked toward the sidewalk, which meant that, if it was someone watching the house, it was probably one of Evan's guys. The thought made him feel better about leaving Nancy alone in the house.

The café was busy. Summer handed him a coffee, but he shook his head when she asked him if he wanted anything to eat. "I think I better lay off the sweets for awhile. Cash runs laps around me at the gym and, frankly, I'm getting a little tired of it."

She laughed as he headed over to his usual table and opened up his laptop. For a couple of hours he sat there, pretending to work but really watching her over the top of it. Thankfully, he'd managed to avoid running into the blonde woman again, but the mother, daughter, and grandson were there, as well as several other regulars Jude recognized. Having his laptop open limited the number of people coming over to talk to him, but he did get a lot of waves, nods, and friendly smiles from customers he'd seen there before. Ah, life in a small town. He really had missed it.

Finally his rapidly cramping muscles drove him to his feet. He packed everything up and walked over to the counter. This late in the morning, the line-up had finally dissipated, and Summer came over to him, running a cloth over the counter as they spoke. "Did you get your work done?"

"For now." Jude set his laptop bag down on the counter.

"Good. I'd love to read one of your articles sometime."

"Maybe. I don't really have anything ready for anyone to read at this point."

She stopped scrubbing the counter. "Older articles are fine. Maybe tonight after dinner we could go online and look something up."

"Yeah, we'll see." Jude shifted his weight from one foot to the other. Why was she pushing this? Was she starting to get suspicious about the writing story? Possibly she'd noticed he wasn't really typing when he was sitting there. Which of course he could have and should have been doing. Or maybe she'd looked him up online and not been able to find anything he'd written. His stomach tightened. If she believed—or could even prove—that he'd lied to her about one thing, everything he had ever told her would be called into question. And if she started to believe she couldn't trust him, the next logical step would be to ask him to leave her home. *Hang in there with me, Summer. Only another day or two.*

She was still watching him. "It's been two days."

"Since what?"

"Since you offered to come and stay at our place for two days. I'm pretty sure whoever was in the house the other night is long gone by now."

Jude wished he could be as sure. Someone got into line behind him. "Now isn't a good time to talk about this. Why don't I come to your place this evening and we'll discuss how to proceed from here. Okay? I'll even cook for you and Nancy."

He waited through a long few seconds of silence, during which the customer behind him heaved out two or three heavy sighs, clearly wondering why nothing was happening in front of him.

Finally, Summer tossed the cloth under the counter. "Fine. We'll talk about it tonight."

"Okay, thanks." Although her tone of voice was not encouraging, he loved the way the words sounded, as though they were already a married couple who needed to discuss something when they got home. Would that ever be them?

Before she could change her mind, Jude hauled his laptop bag off the counter and slung it over his shoulder. "See you at home." He couldn't resist saying the words, in case he never got the chance again.

As he'd hoped, an almost imperceptible smile softened her features. "See you."

He moved out of the way so the impatient man behind him could leap toward the counter. Summer was running out of patience with having a bodyguard. Not surprising. But if he played his cards right, if dinner was good enough, he might be granted a reprieve. For one more day.

If nothing happened tonight, though, given the way Summer was looking at him, his time would definitely run out.

CHAPTER FORTY-EIGHT

Summer wasn't sure what to think. All morning she'd been glancing over at Ryan and she hadn't seen his fingers moving over the keyboard once. Come to think of it, she wasn't sure she'd ever actually seen that. Had he lied to her about being a writer? And if he had, what else had he lied about?

After she left work at 6 p.m., she strolled down the street in the direction of Nancy's house, taking her time getting home. Ryan would be there, cooking in her kitchen. Given the growing suspicion in her mind, she should be apprehensive about that. Maybe she shouldn't have even told him he could go to their place, knowing that would leave him and Nancy alone in the house. Somehow, though, the thought of him there, preparing food, eating with them as though he belonged there, sent warmth into her chest instead of trepidation.

Which wasn't good. She'd grown complacent again, even though someone had broken into their house. It had been so comforting having Ryan around that she'd allowed her emotions to take over. A mistake like that could hurt her. After dinner tonight she would tell him to go. And then, until this situation with the man who had attacked her was resolved, she should definitely restrict the amount of time she spent with him.

Summer reached the walkway of Nancy's place. For a moment she stood there, contemplating the old house. Light spilled from the front windows. Inside, she knew, it would be warm and cozy. They would enjoy good food and laughter, and Ryan's presence, his touch when he brushed by her or handed her something, would do strange things to her insides, and chances were she'd forget that she was supposed to be wary around him. That she was considering evicting him from the property as soon as they'd finished eating.

She took a deep breath, fortifying herself. *God, help me. If I can't trust Ryan, help me to see that. Protect Nancy and me from anyone who might be threatening us, whether that person comes into the house invited or uninvited. Give me strength and courage.*

Straightening her shoulders, she climbed the steps to the porch and pushed open the door. Voices and laughter and the clanging of dishes drifted from the kitchen. Summer removed her boots, hung up her coat, and headed in that direction.

The sight of Ryan in black jeans and a wine-colored T-shirt, stirring a pot on the stove, hit her even harder than she'd expected. She was cold and tired, not only from her long day but from the lingering effects of her injury and the weeks of anxiety that had followed. A ridiculous urge to walk over to him and throw herself into his arms, allow him to hold her until the last of the chills left her body, gripped her.

He looked over at that moment and his eyes met hers. They softened as though he could read her thoughts, and he set the spoon down on the stove and came toward her.

Move, Summer. No lo dejes que se acerque. If she did let him touch her, she wouldn't want him to let go.

Her feet remained rooted to the floor. Ryan wrapped his arms around her and pulled her close. "Welcome home," he breathed, close to her ear.

And somehow, in spite of her best intentions, it felt as though that's exactly where she was. For several moments she allowed that feeling to cocoon her, helpless to break their connection.

He was the one who stepped back, finally, and searched her face. "Are you hungry?"

At the mention of food, she became aware suddenly of the smells drifting in the air. Sautéed onions and cilantro? "You made chicken enchiladas?"

He took her hand and led her to the table where Nancy was setting out knives and forks. "Yes. Is that okay?"

Okay? Enchiladas were her favorite food in the world, although there was no way he could have known that. Except that she was Mexican, of course, so... lucky guess. Maybe. "More than okay. I love enchiladas."

When he let go of her hand to go back to the stove, her fingers felt as cold as they had the night they broke through the puddle into icy water.

Still clutching a handful of cutlery, Nancy gave her a one-armed hug. "How was work?"

"Good. Busy."

"You must be exhausted."

Ryan glanced over his shoulder at that. "Sit down and relax, Ana. Dinner's almost ready."

His concern warmed her almost as much as his embrace had. She couldn't remember anyone ever being that worried about her when she came home after a long day. Her parents would grill her sometimes, but that was always about whom she'd been with and what she'd been up to—an attempt to confirm that she hadn't done anything she wasn't supposed to be doing rather than an actual interest in her well-being. Summer had to admit it felt kind of nice to be cared for like this.

She sank onto a kitchen chair. It felt good to get off her feet, too. And the sense of being taken care of only increased when Ryan brought over plates and bowls loaded with food. Any lingering apprehension dissipated into the warm, spice-laden air in the kitchen as the three of them sat around the table talking and laughing.

As a last-ditch effort to perform her due diligence, Summer swallowed another delicious bite of enchilada and wiped her mouth on her napkin. "When we're done cleaning up, can we take a look at one of your articles, like you promised?" *Promised* was a bit of a stretch, but she was determined to use any weapon in her arsenal to find out if he had been telling the truth about his profession.

"Absolutely. Except that *we're* not cleaning up, I am. You've been on your feet enough today. As soon as I'm finished here we can sit down and I'll show you some of my work."

Any hint of the hesitation he'd shown in the café that morning regarding what he did for a living was gone. Had she imagined it? Her mind could very well be inclined to play tricks on her these days, given the trauma she'd put it through. Or, to be more accurate, that the man who'd pushed her down the stairs had put it through. Yes, that was it. Brain injury. She hadn't used that lame excuse for awhile. Maybe it was time to pull it out and dust it off.

"I can help. I don't need to sit around doing nothing."

"No, you can't help. But you could go upstairs and take a bath, or put your pajamas on, or read a book, whatever it will take to get you to relax. I'll meet you in the living room when I'm through in here."

"But..." Her protest was weak. A bath did sound incredibly appealing.

"I need to go too, I'm afraid. Bridge night at Theresa's." Nancy carried over a bowl of refried beans and one of lettuce that she set on the counter.

"Good. Both of you go. I'll take care of the clean-up. It's the least I can do to thank you for making me feel so welcome in your home the last couple of days."

"Keep feeding us like this and you can stay as long as you like." Nancy kissed him on the cheek before sailing out of the kitchen.

Summer met Ryan's eyes. He lifted his shoulders. "I didn't tell her to say that."

"She's a pushover. Give her a nice meal and flash a little of your charm her way and she's putty in your hands."

"But you're not." His lips twitched as he walked toward her.

"Definitely not." The words she'd intended to sound forceful came out more like a question and his smile widened.

"So if my cooking doesn't do it, or my charm," he took a step closer, close enough that she could feel the warmth of his body even though he wasn't touching her, "then what will it take to win you over, I wonder." Ryan rested a hand on her cheek, stroking her skin with his thumb. His touch was incredibly gentle, like a feather brushing over her, yet the effect on her was immediate. Her heart pounded against her ribs and her knees went so weak she had to grasp the back of the kitchen chair to stay on her feet.

"A lot more than that." As soon as the words crossed her lips, she knew they'd been a mistake.

A gleam ignited in his eyes. "I accept your challenge. Because I can do a lot more than that." He kissed her behind her ear and along her jaw, his lips leaving a trail of blazing heat in their wake. He paused then spoke in a low voice, "If you want me to stop, just say the word."

Her head was spinning. Summer gripped the back of the chair so tightly her knuckles went white. "Which word?"

He pulled back and that slow smile crossed his face. "Stop."

"Oh. That word."

He waited a heartbeat before pressing his lips to her skin again. "Tell me I can stay." He whispered the request, his breath warm against her skin. A shiver passed through her, but she shook her head. He kissed the other side of her face along the same pathway, his fingertips brushing across her throat. "Tell me."

"No." Her breathing had grown shallow and the word came out as a hoarse whisper. Clearly undaunted, he pressed his lips to hers. His hands slid along her jaw, into her hair as he pulled her closer.

Summer tried to think clearly. She still wanted proof that he'd been telling her the truth. And she needed to know that he wasn't... His kiss grew deeper, more demanding, and she gave in to it with a low groan. His skin smelled of soap and a faint, masculine musk and she couldn't breathe in enough of it to satisfy her.

After a moment, he lifted his head, his hands still buried deep in her hair, his thumbs massaging the back of her head. "Tell me."

She closed her eyes. "One more night."

CHAPTER FORTY-NINE

Either taking a bath or slipping into pajamas would be a bad idea after what had transpired in the kitchen. Summer carried a book from the shelf in Nancy's study into the living room and settled into an armchair. By the time Ryan had finished up in the kitchen and come into the room carrying his laptop bag, the words on the page had grown blurry.

"You look exhausted." He set the bag on the coffee table in front of the couch. "Why don't you go to bed? We can take a look at my writing tomorrow."

Oh no, he wasn't going to put her off again. She may have been a pushover in the kitchen, but she was absolutely going to stand her ground now. And keep a good three feet between them at all times. And while she may have agreed to him staying in the heat of the moment, if she found out he had lied to her, that agreement would be immediately rendered null and void. She straightened in the chair. "I'm fine. I really want to see it."

"All right, if you're sure. But I warn you it's not exactly scintillating stuff."

"That's fine. I've had enough scintillating for one evening."

Ryan pulled the computer out of the bag and opened it up. He typed something into the search engine. "Here you go."

She held out her hands for the laptop and he handed it to her and stepped back. It was unnerving, how well he could read her, as if he knew instinctively she wanted—needed—space between them. Summer scanned the screen. It was an article written by a Ryan

Taylor—no picture, she noted—on the root causes of addiction in teens. He *had* lied. Not about the writing though but about it not being scintillating. The piece was well-written and fascinating. Hmmm.

Summer handed the laptop back to him.

"Well?"

"It was good, actually. Can I see another one?"

He contemplated her for a moment before slowly turning the laptop around, typing into it again, and handing it back to her.

Summer made him show her five different articles before she was satisfied. Two of them did have his picture in the top corner, which she felt better about. "Thank you for showing those to me." She pressed a fist to her mouth to stifle a yawn. "I think I better get some sleep now."

"So I passed?"

She blinked. "Passed what?"

"Whatever test you just put me through." His voice held an edge she hadn't heard there before.

"I wasn't testing you. I'm genuinely interested in your work."

Ryan pressed his lips together as though he'd been about to respond to that with a crude and not entirely inaccurate word, given that they both knew she'd been making him jump through hoops for the last fifteen minutes. He managed to restrain himself and settle for, "Really."

"Yes, really." She stood, not enjoying the fact that he was towering over her. Her eyes met his steadily.

Neither of them moved for a long moment, until he closed the laptop with such a loud snap she had to force herself not to jump. The sadness she'd seen in his eyes the night he talked about the woman who had hurt him drifted into them now. "You can trust me, Ana. Don't you know that by now?"

That look. That look was her kryptonite. She was powerless against it. Only she couldn't let him know that or he would have the upper hand forever. She lifted her chin. "Of course." The words came out cooler than she'd intended.

Ryan shoved the computer back into the bag. "You're right. You should get some sleep." His words were cool too, and stung her as much as hers had clearly stung him.

Her throat thickened but, not sure how to repair the damage she'd done, she nodded. "Good night, then."

"Good night." He stepped out of her path as she walked, on unsteady legs, to the door. She didn't stop until she had gone into her room and closed the door behind her. Leaning back against it, she closed her eyes, determined not to give in to a sudden urge to throw herself on her bed and weep.

She'd done what she had to do tonight and she couldn't feel badly about that. Except that she did feel badly. She felt horrible, in fact. Deep down, for reasons she didn't fully understand, she did believe that she could trust Ryan. Right now, though, with this ongoing threat hanging over her head, that was the problem. She couldn't trust him. She couldn't trust anyone.

Because that trust could end up costing her everything.

CHAPTER FIFTY

Jude sank down onto the couch. Propping his elbows on his knees, he scrubbed his face with both hands. *Are you kidding me?* After what had gone on between the two of them when they were doing the dishes last night, and tonight in the kitchen, he'd foolishly allowed himself to think that they had found their way back to each other. That they might actually have a future together. Exactly the type of thing he'd been trying to avoid thinking about.

So what had happened between the kitchen and the living room that had changed everything?

It wasn't so much that she'd insisted on seeing a sample of his work—he got that she was being careful right now and wanted a little confirmation—but demanding five showed the depth of the lack of trust she was feeling, which hurt. She remembered she had a faith, so the relationship she had with God existed in such a deep place that even a serious head injury hadn't been able to touch it. Not that he expected their relationship to be on the same level, but wouldn't what they'd shared together still be there, somewhere inside? He exhaled loudly. Maybe it was. He'd seen flickers of it in her eyes, as though she felt drawn to him without fully comprehending why. Those flickers had given him enough hope to keep trying to reach her.

Jude hadn't even been lying to her about the pieces, not exactly. He wasn't a full-time writer, and he hadn't worked on anything since coming to Elora, but he had written the articles he'd shown her and they had been published various places on-line. Of course, he'd had to go in that afternoon, cut and paste seven or eight of them, and re-post them under the name Ryan Taylor. So, okay, he couldn't claim that he was being completely forthright with her even now.

Given that, did he have any right to complain when she didn't fully believe something he'd told her?

He slumped back on the couch. Maybe it was time to tell her who he really was. She'd had more than a month to get to know him again. Even if he had been using a different name, he'd still been himself. And he'd won her back. At least, he'd thought so until twenty minutes ago. They couldn't go on like this. As he'd told Maddie, Summer might never regain her memory. Was he planning to go through the rest of his life as Ryan Taylor?

If he told her the truth about himself, maybe she would be free to go back to using her real name too. Summer. He loved the sound of her name on his tongue and longed to start calling her that again. And he would give anything to hear her say his name. He would be able to introduce her to his family and let her know that Cash was actually his brother. It would definitely make his life less complicated. If nothing happened between now and then, he was going to come clean in the morning.

Restless, he pushed to his feet and wandered over to the window. Peering out into the blackness, he could make out two vehicles parked at the curb along the street. One, a dark sedan, was stopped a half a block to the east. The other sat a block away in the other direction. Jude couldn't tell from his vantage point if either had anyone in it. Should he go out and stroll by them? Try and figure out if they were the good guys or the bad guys?

Probably not the best idea. They were safer here, in the house. Although likely not at the moment with him standing in front of the window making himself an easy target. He backed away and crossed over to the couch.

Summer was safer with him here. Unless, of course, he started thinking about how they were alone in the house and she was upstairs getting ready for—

Don't go there, Jude. That was dangerous territory. Besides, he needed to keep his mind clear. *God, help me stay focused. Keep my thoughts on what they should be on, not on what they shouldn't.* He was extremely grateful that Summer had allowed him to stay, even if it had taken him exploiting nearly every weakness he knew of hers to get her to agree. Not that it had been any hardship for him. He had such a strong sense that something was about to happen in the next twenty-four hours, he likely would have sat on the front porch all night if she'd kicked him out.

So he appreciated being here. But he did need to keep his mind off the thought of her upstairs in bed, at least until Nancy got home. Which could be an hour or two yet.

Jude grabbed the cell phone out of his pocket and stabbed in a number. It rang twice before a voice came over the line. "Moser."

"Hey, Rick."

"Jude. Are you okay?"

He let out a short laugh. "Define *okay*."

"What's going on?"

"Too much to get into at the moment. I wanted to check in, though. Let you know I've been working through some stuff. I've been spending time with my family."

"Really. How's that going?"

"Great. They've been amazing."

"And Summer?"

Jude propped his feet up on the coffee table. "That's a little more complicated."

"You want to talk about it?"

A floorboard creaked on the second floor and he tipped back his head and stared up at the ceiling. "Trying to get my mind off her at the moment, actually."

"Ah. Hence the long-overdue phone call."

"Sorry about that."

"Don't be. You drinking?"

He blew out a breath. "No."

"Thinking about it?"

"Not much. Although I have been seriously considering picking up my relationship with cigarettes where we left off."

"But you haven't."

"No." If nothing gave soon, though...

"Praying?"

"Every single day."

"Good. That's the only crutch you need."

"I know."

A pause, then, "Anything I can tell the boss man?"

Jude ran his fingers through his hair. It was longer than he usually kept it. Getting a haircut hadn't been on his to-do list the last few weeks. "Nothing definite yet. I have a feeling we might be about to have a breakthrough here, though. I should be able to contact him in the next few days." *If I'm still alive.*

Moser, his therapist, colleague, and friend, depending on the need of the moment, sighed. "I'll try to hold him off a little longer. No promises, though."

"I don't expect any. I appreciate everything you've done."

"I'm always here for you. You know that."

"I do, thanks."

"Keep in touch."

"I will." Jude disconnected the call and tossed his phone onto the coffee table. Well, that had killed ten minutes. Now what?

He bent forward and tugged his bag out from under the bed. Shoving aside a pile of clothes, he pulled out his Bible. Afraid to stretch out on the couch in case he fell asleep, Jude dropped down on the armchair Summer had vacated and opened the book. He knew the passage he wanted and turned the pages until he'd found Psalm 91. The verses, with their promises of protection, spoke to him more in this moment, when threatening forces hovered all around them, than they ever had, although it was one of his favorite chapters. Jude read the sixteen verses over and over, drawing strength and comfort from the words. God was their refuge and fortress. What could provide more safety and peace of mind than that? And he promised to send his angels to guard them.

Jude leaned his head against the back of the chair. The sense that they weren't alone, that, whatever happened, God was with them, nearly overwhelmed him. And even if the worst happened and one of them was killed—as much as the thought of anything happening to Summer hurt his heart—he knew where they would go. They would be in the presence of God. And even death couldn't separate them. Not forever. The peace that drifted through him in the wake of that thought pushed back the hurt of his conversation with Summer and the trepidation he'd been feeling about what could happen to them. She was in God's hands, not his. And so was he.

Díaz straightened up so quickly behind the wheel that lukewarm coffee splashed out of the hole in the lid of the takeout cup and splattered over his pants. He muttered a curse word and snatched a handful of napkins out of the fast food bag on the seat beside him. Dabbing at the splotches, he bent forward to peer through the windshield.

McCall stood in the front window of the tree-hugger's place. Could he see him this far down the street? What about the vehicle parked a block up? Díaz had been watching it carefully since it pulled to the curb and stopped. It had been there nearly an hour now and no one had gotten out. Unlikely it was Kendrick, since sitting out in the open was definitely not his method of operation. Probably a couple of kids making out or something, but their presence still made him nervous.

Especially since this was day thirty. As far as he knew, the boss hadn't made a payment. What that meant for Summer Velásquez, or him, or McCall, he had no idea.

But Díaz had a feeling that sometime in the next few hours they were all about to find out.

CHAPTER FIFTY-ONE

Summer ran a brush through her hair then tossed it into a basket and pressed a hand to the counter on either side of the sink.

She'd lain awake for hours last night, deeply aware of Ryan sleeping a floor away. Several times she'd thrown back the covers, thinking she would go down and talk to him, try to make amends. Each time she'd stayed in bed, reminding herself how she had felt when he'd kissed her in the kitchen, when he'd touched her, and that sadness in his eyes. All of which made her incredibly weak. And she couldn't afford to be weak. Not now. Not when the person who had attacked her in her home could be here in town.

When she'd heard the front door open around eleven, then the murmur of voices, she'd relaxed a little. Having Nancy in the house lowered the chances that she would lose her resolve and go down to talk to Ryan. That thought had triggered a revelation. Maybe it wasn't Ryan she couldn't trust. Maybe it was herself when he was in the room.

What did the man who was after her want? Would he come back? What if Nancy got caught in the crossfire? Or Ryan? Both thoughts terrified her. She had to stay alert so that, if something did happen, she would be the target, not them. Sometime in the wee hours of the morning a truth had struck her, so hard that she had bolted upright in bed. She needed to leave. Being here was putting people she cared about in danger. She had a little money saved from working at the café and she had a car. The best thing for everyone involved would be if she waited until Ryan and Nancy were busy and then sneaked out of the house and took off. She had no idea where she would go, but she'd figured it out the last time. The most important thing was that the people she'd met since coming to town were safe.

Since she couldn't sleep, she'd gotten up around four in the morning and packed her suitcase, then set it on the floor on the far side of the bed. The thought of leaving Elora without telling either Nancy or Ryan, or having any idea if or when she would see them again, sent pain twisting through her stomach. Still, she didn't need a pros and cons list to tell her that she had to do this, that she didn't have a choice.

A quiet knock on her door brought her head up sharply. Summer pushed away from the bathroom counter and crossed her room to the door. "I'm coming, Nancy. I was just—" She pulled open her door and froze. "Ryan." The sight of him, his copper hair tousled and his hazel eyes gazing intently into hers, reminded her of the thought that had crossed her mind when he first walked into the café. Movie star man. He'd been that for her. Not only because of his looks, but because he had been so sweet and kind, had made her feel so important to him. A romantic hero with enough flaws to make him real and human. She was truly going to miss him. Summer bit her lip, pushing back a wave of emotion she couldn't afford to indulge in.

"Sorry to disappoint." His grin tempered the words. "Nancy did send me up here though, to let you know that breakfast will be ready in ten minutes." He glanced into the room.

Summer pressed a hand to her stomach. Could he see the suitcase? "Okay, thanks. Tell her I'll be right down." She started to close the door, but Ryan shot out his arm to stop it.

"I wanted to talk to you anyway." He brushed past her and into the room. "Apologize for last night."

She shook her head. "It's fine. You were right. I shouldn't have pushed you so hard to show me your work. That crossed a line." Her stomach tightened. He was edging deeper into the room. Did he suspect something? Hear the guilt in her voice or see it in her eyes? Entirely likely, since he seemed to be able to read her in a way no one else in her life ever had.

She searched her mind for something to say that would get him to leave. "Anyway, please tell Nancy I'll be right down. As soon as I get dressed."

His gaze traveled the length of her. She'd already tugged on a pair of jeans and a pale yellow button-up shirt so she could pack her pajamas. "I mean, get changed. I think I might need something a little warmer for—"

Before she realized what he was going to do, Ryan spun around, strode to the wardrobe in the corner, and flung open both doors. Nothing hung on the bar except empty hangers.

"Interesting." He turned around. "What exactly were you planning to change into?"

Summer's jaw worked, but she didn't answer.

He bent down, picked up her suitcase, and tossed it onto the mattress. "Seriously? You were going to run?"

She crossed her arms over her chest and lifted her chin. "You have no right to tell me what I can do or where I should go. I'm free to leave anytime I want to."

Ryan's gaze bore into her, but she refused to look away. Finally he lifted both hands. "Whoever broke into your house is still out there. You could be walking right into his trap if you leave. I care about you. A lot. Does that not give me any say at all in whether or not you do something that could put you in extreme danger?"

Summer uncrossed her arms. "That's the thing. I'm already in danger. But if I stay here, so are you and Nancy. And I don't know what I'd do if..." She stopped and swallowed. "I can't be responsible for anything happening to either of you."

Ryan came back around the bed, walked over to her, and took her face in his hands.

Sé fuerte. Stay strong. She may as well have told the stars to stop twinkling in the night sky.

His eyes, light brown with tiny flecks of green she hadn't noticed before, probed hers. "If you're doing this for Nancy and me, doesn't that give us the right to an opinion? Please come down and have breakfast with us. We can discuss this together and figure out a plan." He pressed his lips to her forehead. "You don't have to do any of this alone. Not when you have people here who love you and want to help you."

She blinked rapidly. Was he saying that he loved her?

"All right?"

Even if she'd been able to withstand the feel of his touch against her skin or the earnestness in the eyes that searched hers, she couldn't resist the pleading in his voice. Her shoulders slumped. "All right."

He kissed her forehead again. "Thank you. I'll go help Nancy finish getting ready. I'll see you downstairs."

She nodded and watched him as he left her room and disappeared into the hallway. So much for her brilliant plan. Her car keys hung on a hook in the kitchen, so even if she changed her mind, there was no way she could grab them and leave without him knowing. And maybe the three of them *could* figure out a plan together. While she'd do anything to make sure neither of them got hurt, she didn't want to leave them, either.

With a sigh, Summer trudged out of her room and pulled the door closed. As she descended the stairs, Ryan's voice and Nancy's laughter carried up to her. In spite of herself, warmth rushed through her chest. At the bottom of the stairs, she took a step toward the kitchen, anxious to be with them. Ryan's leather coat, draped across the chair inside the door, caught her eye and she sighed. More than likely he was going to end up staying a while longer. Might as well hang his coat up in the front hall closet.

She grasped the soft leather with both hands. The hint of musk she'd smelled on Ryan the night before drifted from the coat and she lifted it to her face. Something dropped onto the floor and she lowered the jacket and glanced at the object lying on the round carpet. The blood flowing through her veins went ice cold.

A pack of cigarettes.

CHAPTER FIFTY-TWO

Summer stormed into the living room. How dare Ryan, or whatever his real name was, follow her to this town, pretend to want some kind of relationship with her? What kind of a sick person did that? Spent that much time grooming his quarry to... to what, trust him? Fall in love with him? Did he derive some kind of perverse pleasure from watching her fall under his spell? How far had he planned to take this thing anyway? Was he trying to make sure she was completely and utterly vulnerable before he finished the job he had started back at her house?

She shuddered and dropped to her knees in front of the couch so she could yank his bag out from underneath it. After shooting a quick glance at the doorway, she set the bag on the couch and unzipped it.

Summer shoved aside clothes, a shaving kit, and a Bible. Where was his wallet? She needed to see his ID, find out who this guy really was. The back of her hand knocked against something hard and she unzipped the side pocket of the bag and reached in. Her fingers closed around something round and cold and she tightened her grip and drew it out of the bag. Her eyes widened. A gun.

Until she saw it, felt the cold metal against her skin, she'd held out hope that she was wrong, that Ryan wasn't the man who had shoved her down the stairs. But why else would he have a gun? And she knew that whoever had been watching her, whoever had broken into Nancy's house, was a smoker. All those times she'd smelled cigarette smoke outside the café, inside her home, even... She pressed a hand to her chest. The first day when she'd arrived in Elora and had seen the cigarette butt beneath the tree. Had Ryan been watching her even then? The two pieces of evidence together were so incriminating there was no other plausible explanation.

Still clutching the weapon, Summer scrambled to her feet. She had to get Nancy away from him and then she could confront Ryan, demand that he tell her exactly who he was and what he wanted from her. And if he didn't, well, it would be pretty easy to plead self-defence if she ended up having to use the gun to protect herself and Nancy. A shudder moved through her at the thought, but she quelled it immediately.

Concéntrate. Ryan was good. Somehow he knew exactly what words to use, how to look at her, where to touch her to get her to soften towards him. She couldn't allow him to do that now.

Clutching the pistol against her thigh she crept to the doorway of the living room and peered out. Dishes clattered in the kitchen and she could hear water running in the sink. They were both still in there. Summer took a step into the entryway and stopped. Something about this felt all wrong. She hadn't known Ryan long, but somehow it seemed a lot longer. There was something between them, something powerful that she'd have thought would have taken a lot longer to develop. At least, she had believed there was. Even though he was right and she had been testing him the night before, deep inside she believed that he would pass, that she could trust him. Was it a coincidence that he had a pack of cigarettes in his pocket—even though she'd never seen him with one—when she'd been smelling smoke around her, even in her home?

She ran shaking fingers across her forehead. With her head injury, could she even trust her instincts? Irrational paranoia could very well be a lingering effect from her attack. The cold metal of the gun pressed against her leg and she lowered her hand. No. This was more than paranoia. The cigarettes she might be able to explain away, but not the gun. If he did happen to have a reasonable explanation for carrying a weapon around, well, he could tell it to the police.

Her jaw tight, Summer strode across the foyer and stopped in the doorway. Ryan stood in front of the stove, flipping pancakes. Nancy leaned over the sink on the far side of the room, filling the kettle.

Summer gripped the pistol in both hands. It felt so natural, as though she had held a gun before. Had she? When she raised the weapon, something happened, like a switch going off in her brain. Every bit of anger and apprehension and doubt dissipated, replaced by a calm, chill detachment.

She took three steps into the room and stopped, pointing the weapon directly at Ryan. "Nancy, can you come over here please?" Her voice was cool and even, with barely a trace of an accent.

Both of them turned to look at her. Ryan's eyes went immediately to the gun and the color drained from his face. Nancy set the kettle down on the counter. "Ana? What are you doing?"

She gestured with the weapon. "Come over here and I'll explain."

Nancy's brow furrowed as she made her way to Summer.

Ryan set the lifter down slowly and turned off the burner on the stove. "This isn't what you think."

"What I think is that you have been playing some kind of sick game with us."

"No, I..." He took a step toward her.

Summer released the safety on the gun. He stopped and lifted his hands in front of him. She kept her eyes laser-focused on him. "Nancy, call 911. Tell them we have the man who was in our house the other night."

"What? You think Ryan broke into our place?" Nancy lifted the phone off the base attached to the wall behind her.

"I know he did."

Ryan shook his head. "Nancy, wait." He took another step toward them.

Summer's finger tightened on the trigger. "Take one more step and I will shoot." He stopped.

Nancy clutched the receiver but didn't dial.

Keeping his hands in the air, Ryan swung his gaze back to Summer. "Let me explain, please."

"What possible explanation could you have for bringing a gun into our house?"

"It isn't my gun."

"Then whose gun is it?"

"Look at the way you're holding it. Whose do you think it is?"

Her jaw tightened. "Don't play games with me, Jude. You know I hate it when you treat me like a client on your couch and answer my question with a..."

She froze.

Jude eased his hands down, his eyes not leaving hers. *She remembers.*

"Who is Jude?" Frowning, Nancy moved closer to Summer.

Summer lowered the Glock to her side. "He is." She waved a trembling hand in Jude's direction.

He took a step toward her, but she held up a hand to stop him. Her eyelids flickered. How must that feel, years of memories flooding into her mind all at once? Pretty much like standing at the bottom of a dam when it burst, sending millions of gallons of water crashing over her with destructive force, most likely. As though she might actually be physically swept away. He'd give her a minute to get her footing.

She drew in a shuddering breath. "He's my fiancé. No." Summer stopped and shook her head slightly. "Ex-fiancé." She pressed her eyes shut. Jude's heart sank. He knew exactly which memory assaulted her now. And Cash was right, as usual. On some level Jude might have been hoping that was one memory she didn't regain.

She opened her eyes and glanced down at her finger before slowly lifting her head to meet his gaze. "We were engaged and then he told me he didn't want to marry me."

Nancy's head spun toward him, the orange baubles in her ears swinging wildly. "What?"

Jude swallowed. "I didn't tell you I didn't want to marry you—that would have been a lie. I'd never wanted anything so badly in my life. I told you I needed more time."

She pressed the fingers of her free hand to her temples, as though trying to push back the confusion. "Why?"

"I didn't even know at the time. But I do now. I was scared. The night Tessa..." he stopped and gripped the counter, needing the support, "... the night she died, something happened inside me. I blamed myself and I couldn't let it go. I carried that guilt around with me for five years, struggling to figure out how I could possibly make up for the past. I couldn't marry you because I couldn't see a way to move forward into a future with you. But then Cash said something to me..."

Her head jerked and he stopped. "Cash is your brother."

He sighed. "Yes." As his brother had suggested she would, she'd clearly added that to the long list of lies he'd told her. When she didn't say any more, he pushed on. "Anyway, what he said helped me to finally figure out that I can't make up for what happened, that I don't have to. God has forgiven me and so has my family. I've even been able to forgive myself, something I never thought would happen. I can finally move on." He edged closer to her. "I'm sorry I hurt you, Summer. I hope you can find a way to forgive me too." If he needed to, he would get down on his knees and beg, like he would have the first day he saw her, and not care how it made him look.

She stepped back. "You lied to me."

"I know. I'm sorry." Why did those words always have to sound so small in the shadow of what he had done?

Nancy frowned. "Who is Summer?"

She sighed. "I'm Summer." She rubbed her forehead with the side of her hand. "I'm sorry, Nancy. I lied too. I recently suffered a head injury and didn't remember the last few years of my life. I came to Elora to try to get away from..." She dropped her hand and shifted her gaze back to him. Likely it had just occurred to her that if Jude wasn't the one following her, someone else still was.

"From what?"

"My parents, for starters. And the person who attacked me, in case he planned to come back and finish the job."

Nancy's face blanched. "Attacked you?"

"Yes. But now I realize that I never should have come here. I never should have involved you in all of this. It was selfish and—"

"Stop." Nancy grasped her elbow. "It was the good Lord himself who brought you here. I'm not one to question his ways and you don't need to be apologizing for them either. Don't you worry." She returned the cordless phone to the base. "And now that we have established who everyone is," she shot a look at Jude, who dipped his head in mute apology, "we can figure this thing out together."

"Thanks, Nancy." Summer set the gun down on the counter and reached for the phone. "I know exactly where to start. I need to call the detective sergeant."

Nancy let go of her. "The police?"

Jude nodded. "She's a detective with the Toronto PD. Hence the gun."

Nancy's eyes widened. "You're a cop?"

"Yes." Summer hit the button to get a dial tone.

Jude closed the distance between them and stopped her with a hand on her arm. She looked down at it and back at him and he withdrew it. "Look, I know you're angry with me, but you have to listen. It won't help to call the DS. I've been communicating with your partner. They're working night and day to try and find out who did this to you and figure out if he has tracked you down here. Some of your colleagues have been driving past the house and the café whenever possible."

"Evan knows I'm here?"

"Yes. They're close to breaking this case open. We need to wait to hear from him."

She hesitated before replacing the phone. Her eyes narrowed. "Speaking of tracking me down, how did you know where I was? I made sure no one was following me and I dumped my phone back at the house. There's no way you could have known where I..." Her dark eyes widened and she snatched her car keys from the hook on the wall and whirled toward the front entryway.

"Summer." He had to stop her from going outside, out in the open where she would be a target, like he had been standing in the window the night before. Jude took off after her, calling her name again, but the only response was the slamming of the front door.

Jude's footsteps pounded down the porch steps, but Summer didn't look back. Her car was parked at the curb across the street. He'd planted a trace on it—or in it—somewhere and she was determined to find it to prove it. Once she did, he would have a lot of explaining to do about everything he had kept from her since he'd shown up in Elora.

She stalked down the driveway and around to the front of it and crouched to feel inside the bumper. In seconds her fingers closed over a small plastic device and she yanked it out and straightened. Jude stopped a few feet from her.

Summer held the device out in his direction. "You tracked me."

SARA DAVISON

"I had to. I couldn't risk losing you."

She shoved the device into the pocket of her jeans. "Why didn't you tell me who you were?"

"I couldn't. I had no idea what lies your parents had told you about me. When I tried to see you, your father confronted me. He said if I didn't leave you alone, he would tell the police it was me who attacked you. And he claimed he'd already told you that."

"He hadn't. And it wasn't. He could never have proved it was."

"It would have been hard for me to prove it wasn't, without your testimony. No evidence was found at the house, but it wouldn't have been that hard for your father to go in and plant some. Not only that, but he had a recording of you and me talking the last time we were at your place. You were clearly trying to end things with me and I was arguing with you, doing everything I could to persuade you not to. That alone would have made me look like a possible suspect."

The fight went out of Summer and her shoulders slumped. "After I kicked you out of my house, why did you follow me here?"

"I had to make sure you were safe."

"Even though I didn't know who you were?"

His eyes met hers. "Yes." After a few seconds of silence, he cleared his throat. "I love you, Summer. I'm hoping and praying you'll give me another chance to prove to you how much you mean to me. I don't want to do this life without you."

Summer studied him. Could she believe him? Trust that he wouldn't push her away like he had before? Her eyes searched his. How often had she wished she could read them, see what he was thinking and feeling, but they'd been closed, indecipherable. Her breath caught. They were open now, meeting hers steadily. The tortured look that had so often hovered in them was gone.

It was Jude. He was the one. The one who had changed her life so much over the last few years. Who had taken her hand and walked

278

with her to the front of the church that day. And the one who had loved her more deeply than anyone else ever had, who had showed her she was capable of loving, too. Yes, he'd hurt her. But now he was the one who had changed.

She took a step toward him. "I—"

A strong arm wrapped around her neck, choking off her air supply and dragging her around the far side of the car.

Jude, his face ashen, started toward her, but the man behind her pressed the sharp tip of a blade to the side of her neck. "One more step and she's dead."

Summer clawed at the man's arm, desperate to draw in a breath. Black spots danced in front of her eyes. His thick Spanish accent confused her. Who was he? The man who had attacked her in her home didn't sound like that.

His arm loosened when they reached the back door on the passenger side, but the knife stayed pressed to her skin. He grabbed the keys from her hand, hit the remote, and yanked open the door. "Get in."

Before she could move, a gunshot split the air, echoing around the quiet neighborhood. The man behind her lurched back a step before dropping onto the sidewalk. She shot a horrified glance at him. It was the man who had come into the café awhile ago, the one who refused to engage in conversation with her even though he spoke Spanish. Now she knew why.

Her gaze shifted to the row of hedges in front of the house across from Nancy's. A tall man emerged from the shadows, appearing to drag them with him as though he had the ability to meld into them completely. Was that how he'd stayed hidden from her for so long? The sunlight caught his face and she repressed a shudder. The guy who had broken the vase of roses in the grocery store sauntered toward her car, the pistol in his hand pointed directly at her. He removed the cigarette from his mouth with his thumb and forefinger and flicked it onto the road.

Summer's body went completely numb as an image of this man standing in the doorway of her bedroom, clutching a Beretta, slammed through her mind. He'd come back to finish the job.

"Come here, chica. And bring me the keys." He gestured for her to go to him. When she hesitated, he swung the pistol in the direction of the front lawn. "Now. Or I shoot the old lady."

Summer's gaze met Nancy's. Her friend had stopped halfway down the walkway, her flowered skirt billowing in the cool March wind. "Summer, no. Don't do it."

I can't let him kill her. Or Jude. Summer bent down and grabbed the keys lying in the grass. She strode to the man and, when he opened the passenger side door, lowered herself onto the seat. He slammed the door behind her. Keeping the gun trained on Nancy and his eyes on Jude, he rounded the front of the car and pulled open the driver's side door. Summer gasped when Jude lunged toward the man. The deafening crack of the pistol firing sent her heart rate into overdrive. Jude dropped to the pavement.

Summer fumbled for the door handle, but the man dove into the car and shoved the weapon against her temple again. She let go of the handle. He slammed the door, ripped the keys from her fingers, and shoved one into the ignition. In seconds he had roared away from the curb and was speeding down the street.

Summer twisted in her seat. Jude lay sprawled on the street. Her chest clenched. If he was dead, what more did she have to lose?

The fear drained from her and she turned a cold, hard gaze onto her captor.

Absolutely nothing.

CHAPTER FIFTY-THREE

Jude pushed back the blinding pain that shot from his hip down to the ankle of his left leg as he forced himself to his knees. Biting back a gasp, he grasped the hand Nancy held out and staggered to his feet. "Where are your keys?"

"In the kitchen. I'll get them."

Jude didn't argue. Pressing a hand to the side of his leg, he hobbled toward Nancy's car in the driveway. Faster than he would have thought she could move, she bolted from the house and back down the walk, tossing him the keys when she was still a few feet away from him. Jude caught them, wincing as the jerking movement sent fresh pain slithering down his leg. He snatched the phone out of his back pocket before sliding behind the wheel.

Jude stabbed at the buttons on the device, bringing up the app that would follow the tracer Summer had stuck in her pocket. When it flashed across the screen, he set it in the drink holder. Clutching the key in fingers smeared with blood, he shoved it into the ignition and turned it. The engine roared to life. Jude shoved the transmission into reverse and backed down the lane. Squealing onto the road, he shifted to drive and took off in the direction the man had taken Summer.

He thought he caught occasional glimpses of the car before it disappeared around a corner again but concentrated on following the small dot moving along his phone screen. As he rounded a corner, a pedestrian leapt out of the way of his vehicle. His angry shouts followed Jude halfway down the block. Although it nearly drove him out of his mind, he let off on the accelerator slightly. Killing someone else in an attempt to save Summer wasn't right, and although he wouldn't mind the police getting involved in this situation, he didn't want to stop to talk to them or get involved in some kind of high speed chase either.

He shot another look at the screen. The dot had stopped moving. Jude frowned. Were they at a stop light? He glanced back and forth between the device and the road, but the dot didn't move. Part of him was glad, since he had almost caught up to it. But why had they stopped? Had they gotten into an accident? Was Summer fighting him? Knowing her, it was entirely likely.

Jude studied the spot where the vehicle had stopped moving. It struck him, suddenly, where it was, and shock reverberated through his entire body. *No.*

Summer glared at the man behind the wheel. "What do you want from me?"

He smirked. "This may be hard for you to believe, but I don't want anything from you. All of this has very little to do with you, in fact."

"Then why do you keep coming after me?"

"You'd have to ask your parents about that."

She jerked as though he'd hit her, again. "My parents? What do they have to do with this?"

"They owe a very big debt. One they have proven they cannot pay. So you are the one who is going to have to pay on their behalf."

"But..." Summer calculated her meager earnings since arriving in town, and the savings that still sat in her bank account. "I hardly have any money."

If his eyes weren't so hard and cold, the look he shot her might have been one of amusement. "You aren't going to pay with money, chica."

Her throat tightened. "Then what?"

"You'll find out when we get there." He glanced in the rear view mirror.

"When we get where?"

"First to my car, on the other side of the river, then out of this little hick town. After that you will have to wait and see." He glanced in the mirror again and swore.

Summer twisted to look out the back window. Her heart leapt. Was that Nancy's car a few blocks back? Who was driving it?

The man pushed a little harder on the accelerator. "Your boyfriend is very persistent."

She narrowed her eyes, trying to see who was behind the wheel of the car behind them. Was it really Jude? The vehicle was still too far away for her to tell, but she doubted Nancy would drive like that. And if it was Jude, then he wasn't dead. Although... she shifted around in her seat and her gaze fell on the Beretta still clutched in the man's hand. If he kept following them, that might not be the case much longer. She had to do something.

She spun sideways on the seat and thrust out one foot, connecting with the man's head. It slammed against the driver's side window. The car veered into the opposite lane, but he jerked it back. The car they'd narrowly missed hitting swerved and laid on the horn.

The man let out a string of curse words as he shot out his arm, the side of the gun connecting with her jaw. Pain exploded in Summer's head and the world spun around her.

"That was a big mistake, chica."

She pressed the back of her hand to her throbbing jaw. "Stop calling me that." She glanced back again. Nancy's car was catching up to them.

The man shot another look in the mirror and his face hardened. "Your little friend is becoming far too much trouble, so I think we need to end this right now. There is more than one way to get across the river. I know exactly where we can go and he will not follow."

He pressed down harder on the gas pedal and the car shot up the main street, past the café. At the top, he spun onto a side street and followed it until it curved at the end. Jerking the wheel, he pulled the vehicle left into a parking lot and stopped.

Summer peered out her window. Where were they? And what would the man do now? Her stomach tightened.

He shifted to face her. "Here's what's going to happen, *chica*." He emphasized the word and she gritted her teeth. "You are going to come with me and do exactly as I say. If you fight me anymore, I will take this gun," he held it up to show her, "and I will put a bullet through Jude McCall's head. And this time I will make sure he is dead. Do you understand me?"

When she nodded, he shoved open his door. "Wait." He rounded the front of the car, yanked open her door, and grabbed her by the wrist. "Let's go."

Knowing the only way Jude might possibly survive this was if she did what she was told, Summer climbed out of the car and followed him.

Jude jerked the steering wheel, turning Nancy's car onto the side street at the top of the hill. When he reached the curve, he swung into the parking lot at the top of the gorge and skidded to a stop. The man who'd taken Summer strode across the lot at a near run, dragging her with him. They were heading straight for the stairs that led down to the river. *I can't.* A deep cold seized Jude. *Then you will lose her too.* He hefted the door open with his shoulder and leapt out of the car. As he sprinted across the lot, the man pulled her to the top of the stairway and the two of them disappeared from his sight.

Fifty-nine. Fifty-nine. Fifty-nine. His stomach roiled. By the time he reached the top of the stairs, the man and Summer were halfway down. Jude started to go down the first step and stopped short, as though an invisible wall had risen in front of him. *Not now.* Heart pounding, he forced himself to shove through, the barrier shattering like a wall of glass, thousands, millions of shards pricking and slashing him as he descended another step. When he took one more and came down hard on the stone, he stopped short at the pain that streaked through his leg. Jude clutched the rickety wooden railing as darkness threatened to overtake him. For a few seconds he concentrated on taking in as deep a breath as his traumatized body would allow, then he went down the next step. Clenching his teeth until they ached, Jude managed the next few stairs. Eight, nine, ten. Forty-nine to go. Summer and the man were approaching the bottom of the staircase.

Jude stumbled on the next step and pressed his lips together to keep from howling as he clutched the railing and hauled himself upright. Who was this guy and what did he want with Summer?

Shoving back the pain, Jude went down a few more steps. Twenty-two, twenty-three, twenty-four. The pair ahead of him had reached the bottom of the stairs and started along the path leading to the river. Where was he taking her? The man still clutched Summer's wrist and hauled her along the shoreline. Why wasn't she fighting him?

Jude gritted his teeth and continued his descent. By the time he reached the last step, his vision had blurred. He pressed a hand to his stomach and gulped in several breaths of air to push back a surge of nausea. Ahead of him, Summer tripped over a rock and nearly fell. The man jerked her to her feet. Heat coursed through Jude and he started after them.

Warm liquid flowed down his calf. Jude glanced down. A scarlet stain spread along the side of his jeans, nearly the length of his leg. How much time did he have before he passed out? He pressed on, picking his way over large rocks and avoiding patches of ice on the narrow pathway.

A wave of dizziness gripped him and he stopped and leaned against a large rock, his eyes pressed shut. When he opened them, the man had dragged Summer out onto the ice. Several cars were parked in a lot on the other side of the river. Was that where he was trying to go? If they got across before he caught up to them, Jude would have no way of following them. Not that he had any idea what he'd do if he did catch up to them. If he could manage to avoid being shot again, he and Summer might be able to take the man down. Why hadn't he gotten Nancy to grab the Glock when she went back for the keys? *Focus, Jude.* For now, he had to concentrate on getting to them before they slipped out of his grasp and were gone.

Spurred on by the thought, he took several more steps down the path. When he reached the edge of the river, he stopped again, struggling to breathe. *I can do this. I can do this.* Summoning every ounce of strength he had left, he stepped onto the ice.

Twenty feet from shore, the man whirled around suddenly, yanking Summer around with him by the wrist. "I'm very impressed, Mr. McCall. I didn't think you would have the courage to come down here after what happened with your sister. But since you have defied expectations..." The man lifted the gun and pointed it at Jude.

Summer suddenly yanked free of his grasp and drove her elbow into his throat. The man shouted and started to swing his weapon in her direction, but she clasped her hands together and brought them down on his arm. The pistol clattered to the ice and spun around in circles.

Shoving back the fog swirling around in his brain, Jude lunged forward. Summer scooped up the gun, spun around, and smashed it against the man's temple. He fell backwards, his head cracking against the ice. He didn't move again.

"Summer!"

Jude slid forward a couple of yards, desperate to get to her.

She took a step toward him. Ice cracked beneath her shoe. The sound tore through Jude like another gun shot. *Not again.* "Summer, stop. Don't move."

She froze, ten feet from him.

"Lie down, slowly."

Summer complied. When her knee hit the ice, it cracked again, louder this time. Jude inched forward as she carefully lowered herself to the ice. "Okay, now what do I—"

With a thunderous crack, the sheet collapsed beneath her. Summer dropped into the icy water.

Jude's heart thudded erratically in his chest. *God, help me. I can't do this again.* Terror clawed at his throat until he could barely draw in a breath. *I'm coming, Tessa.* He squeezed his eyes shut and opened them again. The mist swirled through his mind now, heavy and dark, and he fought for coherent thought. *It's not Tessa, it's Summer, and she needs you.*

Shoving back the fear that threatened to paralyze him, Jude lowered himself to the ice and shimmied toward the black hole where Summer had disappeared. *God, don't take her. Please. I can't lose her too.* He drew close to the opening and forced himself to move more slowly.

A hand broke the top of the water, grasping the jagged edge of the hole. *She's alive.* Jude gave up trying to move cautiously and scrambled toward her. The ice groaned beneath him. Her fingers, unable to find a hold, scratched across the frozen surface. Thrusting his arm above his head, Jude snagged them right before they disappeared below the black waves and then slid his hand along her skin until he could grasp her wrist. Summer's head broke the surface. She gasped for air and flailed with her free arm, breaking off another chunk of ice.

"Summer." Jude waited until her eyes met his. "I'm going to get you out. Don't fight me, okay?"

She nodded and held out her other arm to him.

Before he could grasp it, something hard and cold pressed against the back of his head. "Let her go."

Jude froze. Consumed with thoughts of Summer, he hadn't seen the man who had abducted her clamber to his feet and make his way over to them. He couldn't let go of her though. She'd be too cold to climb out herself and within seconds would slide below the surface and be gone.

"If you pull her out, I will shoot her and then I will shoot you and send you both to the bottom of the river. She has become too much trouble to me. This ends now."

God, I don't know what to do. Send some of those angels I read about last night. Please. He couldn't bring himself to let go of her wrist, even if doing so might spare his own life. What good was living if Summer was gone too?

A blast shook the air, echoing off the sides of the ravine. The man behind him staggered a few feet away before collapsing. The ice beneath Jude shuddered. He twisted his head to look back at the shore. A lone figure stood on top of the ravine. Evan. One angel, then. That was good enough for him. A cracking sound brought him back around. *I have to get her out. Now.*

Summer's head was submerged, but he clutched her wrist in fingers rapidly growing numb. He leaned back, straining as hard as he could until her head broke the surface and her other hand slashed through the air. Forcing his fingers to do what his brain was commanding them to do, Jude managed to grab hold of her other wrist. Slowly, slowly, he tugged her from the icy lake, pieces breaking beneath her, until she was out of the hole far enough to push herself forward with her feet.

Jude slid backwards until they reached the shore then he wrapped his arms around her as she collapsed onto his chest. "It's okay. I've got you. You're okay." She shivered uncontrollably and he ran his hands frantically up and down her back. Neither of them had grabbed a coat before leaving the house and her thin shirt clung to her skin.

The wail of a siren, this time one of the sweetest sounds Jude had ever heard, filled the air. Summer lifted her head and met his gaze. Her lips were blue and her teeth chattered, but she managed to get out, "Yo tampoco quiero vivir sin ti," before she collapsed back onto his chest.

Jude slid his hand around the back of her head and pulled her close. Over her shoulder he caught a glimpse of paramedics and firefighters rushing along the shore toward them. He closed his eyes, slowly giving in to the encroaching darkness. Relief flooded through him, warming him in spite of the half-frozen body pressed against his. Partly because of the people rushing to their assistance, but even more so because of her words. She didn't want to live without him either.

That was all he needed to know.

CHAPTER FIFTY-FOUR

Nancy had fussed over her until Summer had asked her to go get them both a cup of tea from the cafeteria. She had almost drifted back to sleep when a brief knock on the door of her hospital room was accompanied, virtually simultaneously, with someone flinging open the door and tumbling into the room. "Ana!"

Summer struggled to sit up. "Daphne." A weary smile crossed her face. Exactly the medicine she needed at the moment.

Daphne flung a bouquet of flowers on a chair and stampeded toward her. Before Summer could react, her friend had flung her arms around her and pulled her close. "Are you okay?"

"She'd likely be better if you weren't accosting her, Daph." Shawn followed his wife into the room, considerably more sedately, clutching a white box under one arm. Summer grinned. They really were perfect for each other, those two.

Daphne let go of her and stepped back abruptly. "Sorry. But I was so worried after Nancy called and told us everything that was going on, including that your name is actually Summer and Ryan's is Jude. I had to see for myself if you were all right."

Summer winced. "I'm sorry about all that confusion. I am fine, I promise. It was an experience, but between Jude and the police and God, everything turned out okay." *I hope.* Her smile dimmed as she wondered again how Jude was doing. Likely he was still in surgery, but she'd give anything for an update.

As though he could read her thoughts, Shawn touched the blanket over her foot. "Is Jude all right?"

Summer swallowed. "As far as I know. He was shot in the leg, so I'm guessing he's in surgery, but no one is willing to tell me anything about him."

"I know a few people who work here. Want me to ask around? See if I can find out anything?"

She could have wept at the offer. "Would you?"

"Of course." Shawn set the white box down on the table beside the flowers. "A few of your favorites."

"They're all my favorites."

He flashed her a grin. "That's what we like to hear." He headed for the door. "I'll come back as soon as I hear anything."

"Thanks, Shawn."

As soon as he was gone, Daphne pulled a chair up to the side of the bed and plopped down on it. "Are you really okay?" Her bright blue eyes searched Summer's.

"I am, but I'm worried about Jude."

Daphne's forehead wrinkled. "Nancy didn't give a lot of details on the phone, so Shawn and I are still trying to figure out who everyone actually is."

Summer expelled a breath. "Ryan Taylor is actually Jude McCall, my..." What should she call him? Ex-fiancé didn't give off the right impression, even if that was exactly what he was. "... boyfriend."

Daphne's eyebrows rose nearly to the blonde bangs sweeping across her forehead. "But you didn't remember him because of that head injury."

"Exactly. He followed me here to Elora because he was worried that the guy who attacked me in my home might follow me here. Which, of course, is what happened."

"And you're Summer..."

"Velásquez." Summer held out her hand. Daphne took it and pressed it between both of her plump ones. "I'm sorry I lied to you about that. I came here to hide, so I couldn't use my actual name."

"I get it. It's nice to finally know the real name of my sister, though."

Summer blinked.

"That's right. I've decided we're going to be each other's sisters, since neither of us has one. You can choose your own family, you know, especially if the one you're born into turns out to be a dud."

She laughed. Daphne her sister and Shawn her brother-in-law. "I love that idea."

"Me too." Daphne patted her hand. "And that means you get to be an aunt in a few months, too."

Summer's mouth dropped open. "Really?"

"Yep. I've known since shortly after you started working with us, but I was afraid to tell anyone because of what happened last time. A couple of days ago we told Shawn's son Cory, who was pretty thrilled to find out that, at twenty-three, he was about to have a baby brother or sister. You were next on my list of people to tell, so now you know."

"Daphne." Summer tugged her hand free and threw her arms around her friend. Her sister. "I'm so happy for you and Shawn."

"Thank you." When Summer let her go, Daphne sat back on the chair with a little bounce. "I'm happy for us, too."

"That's exactly what I needed to hear right now."

Daphne gripped the armrests and leaned forward. "I'm sure it must be terribly hard, waiting to hear news about the man you love. If Shawn had been shot..." She stopped and cocked her head. "What is it?"

"What makes you think I love him?"

"Oh, come on. It was clear to me from the minute Ryan or Jude or whatever his name is walked into the Taste of Heaven that the two of you were meant to be together. Even those first few weeks, when you didn't know you knew him, there was obviously something strong between you." She drew in a sharp breath. "When you get out of the hospital, you guys should get married and have a baby and we can raise our kids together."

Shock jolted through Summer. "Espérate, Daphne. Slow down. I don't think Jude and I are there right now. The last time we were engaged, it didn't go so well."

"Wait." Daphne flung out an arm, knocking the white box off the table. She grabbed it before it could hit the floor and set it back on the table. "You two were engaged?"

"Yes. Until the night before I was attacked. Then he came to me to tell me he wasn't ready. So what would make me think that he's ready now?"

Daphne reached for her hand again. "Summer, I know I've been discreet about it, but I've been watching the two of you together."

Summer pressed her lips together.

Her friend let out a long-suffering sigh. "All right, I don't do discreet. The point is, I've been watching. That man is deeply, madly in love with you. And I'm pretty sure—now that you remember everything that happened between the two of you, and maybe even before you remembered—you feel the same way about him. ¿Estoy equivocada?"

Summer stared at her for a few seconds, until her shoulders slumped. "No. You aren't wrong."

A smug look crossed Daphne's face. "There you go."

Shawn tapped lightly on the door before walking into the room. Summer straightened quickly. "Did you find out anything?"

He walked over and stood behind Daphne, resting his hands on her shoulders. "Not a lot, only that Jude's out of surgery. He's going to be in recovery for a while."

"Okay, that's good to know. That's all they told you?"

"I'm afraid so. They don't like to give out information to anyone who isn't family."

Daphne scowled. "We're practically family."

He squeezed her shoulders. "I know, sweet. Unfortunately, the hospital doesn't recognize 'practically family'."

"It's okay." Summer tugged the blanket up higher as a coolness skittered across her skin. What if Jude wasn't all right? Daphne had reminded her how much she had loved him before her attack and how much she loved him now. More, if possible. She didn't know everything that had happened to Jude since coming to Elora, but he was different. She hadn't seen a trace of the blackness that had surrounded him occasionally, that had pressed down on him in dark moments. He'd worked through something, even more than he'd shared with her in the kitchen. She hoped and prayed they'd have a chance to talk about that so she would be able to understand why he had appeared to hold back from her before but now seemed to be all in. *God, help him to be okay. We have so much to talk about, so much life to live. Help me not to worry, but to leave him in your hands.*

The prayer helped. The fear she'd been feeling eased and the coolness dissipated.

Shawn patted Daphne's shoulder. "We should go, Daph. Let Summer get some sleep. And you should rest, too."

Summer smiled. "Yes, Daphne told me your news. Congratulations."

"Thank you." Shawn nodded toward the white box. "Enjoy, okay?"

"I always do."

Daphne bent down and hugged her again. "Let me know when you're home. No need to come back to work, though, until you're absolutely ready." She straightened and pressed a hand to her chest. "You are coming back to work, right?"

"I'm not sure. Everything is up in the air at the moment. Can I tell you as soon as I have a chance to talk to Jude and we figure out where we're going from here?"

"Of course." She winked at Summer. "I'll be dying to hear how that conversation goes."

"I'll let you know. And maybe I can tell you my story then too. I think I'm ready to share it now."

Dimples flashed in Daphne's cheeks. "I can't wait to hear it."

Shawn slid an arm around his wife's shoulders and guided her to the door. The room, as it always did, felt emptier and quieter after Daphne had left than it had before she arrived. That woman trailed laughter and sunshine with her wherever she went. No wonder Shawn was so head over heels in love with her.

Like Jude is with you and you with him? Summer lay back against the pillow, contemplating Daphne's assertion. She hadn't had a moment to analyze where she and Jude stood with each other since her memories had come back. Now that she did, she could only come to one possible conclusion, one that drove the last of the cold out of her body.

No, Daphne was definitely not wrong.

CHAPTER FIFTY-FIVE

Jude shifted slightly on the hospital bed and winced. He'd woken up in recovery a couple of hours ago and was going crazy lying there, wondering if Summer was okay. He needed a distraction from both that question—which nobody here seemed to want to answer even though he'd asked every single person walking by, some more than once—and the throbbing pain in his thigh where they'd removed the bullet.

They'd brought his belongings into the tiny cubicle, and he reached over to the small table beside the bed, lifted his shirt, and grabbed his cell phone. He punched in a phone number and waited through a couple of rings before his brother answered. "Hello?"

"Cash, it's me."

"Hey. Everything okay?"

Jude hesitated. "I'll tell you, but before I do, let me start by saying that I'm all right."

When he spoke, Cash's voice was tight. "What's going on?"

There really was no good way to break it to him. "I got shot."

He held his breath through three seconds of silence before his brother spoke again. "Are you actually *trying* to shorten my life, Jude?"

Jude laughed. "No, I promise I'm not."

"What happened?" The couch creaked as though Cash was getting to his feet.

"The guy who attacked Summer showed up at Nancy's place this morning. He took her hostage at gunpoint. When I tried to stop him, he shot me in the leg and took off with her. I followed them and he drove to the top of the gorge and dragged her down the steps and out onto the river."

"Before we go any further with this, is Summer okay?"

"I think so. She's somewhere in the hospital too."

"Shot?"

"No, she..." Jude stopped and rubbed his eyes with his thumb and forefinger. "She fell through the ice."

"No."

"I know. It was crazy. I even started getting messed up in my head about who it was I was going after. Anyway, the guy tried to stop me, but the police arrived and took him down and I was able to pull her out in time."

"Wait. So all those sirens I kept hearing earlier today, those were about you?"

"I guess so."

Cash blew out a breath. "Did you have surgery?"

"Yeah, it went well. I'm in recovery now. Can you come and talk to some of your buddies here, get them to let me out of this place?"

His brother let out a short laugh. "I doubt I can do that, but I can come, yes. I'll bring Mom and Maddie too."

"Okay. And Cash?"

"Yeah?"

"Mom doesn't know anything about Summer. Can you fill her in on the way in case she meets her here at the hospital?"

"Sure."

"And I know I've put her through a lot the last five years. Please lead with the fact that I'm going to be perfectly fine."

"I can, although, from personal experience, I'll tell you that all that does is raise about a million red flags."

"Sorry."

"It's all right. There's no good lead-in to news about being shot."

"I guess not. But speaking of news, the other breaking headline is that Summer remembers."

"Everything?"

"Yeah. It all came back to her this morning, right before that guy showed up."

"Wow, that's amazing, Jude. Really."

"I know. She made it clear that I have some explaining to do, but I'm hopeful we can work everything out."

"Does that mean we can all be ourselves tonight?"

"Yes, thankfully."

"Good to know. I'll head out now." Keys jangled in the background. "Is there anything you want me to bring you?"

"Actually, there is. Can you go to the motel and see if they'll let you into my room? If so, grab me a change of clothes and..." He hesitated. Should he bring it here? He couldn't wait until he was out of the hospital to ask Summer—again—to marry him. He needed to know that as soon as they were both strong enough to get out of this place they could start their life together. "There's a blue ring box in the top drawer of the dresser. Can you grab that too?"

A short pause, then, "I thought you refused to take that back from her."

Jude exhaled. "I did, but I went to her place and took it from her room before coming to Elora."

"Ah. Okay then, I'll grab that. And I'll be able to get in. I know Melanie, the woman who works the front desk there, from the gym."

Meaning the chances of Jude getting his stuff were pretty good. "Thanks."

"No problem. See you soon."

Jude set the phone on the table. For a long time, when he was in trouble, he hadn't had anyone to call. It felt pretty good now to know that, whenever he needed him, his big brother would be there. So good that he didn't know how he'd been able to go so long without that. Of course, he could have called Cash any time after leaving home. He'd known that, even in his darkest hours. He hadn't lied to his brother when he'd told him he'd almost called, more times than he could count. And he should have. Although, if he had, Cash would have come and gotten him and maybe he never would have met Summer or figured out what he wanted to do with his life.

Jude sighed. God was in control, and he was not. And he was perfectly fine with that.

CHAPTER FIFTY-SIX

Summer was ready to tear her hair out by the roots. "I'm going to lose my mind." She flopped back against the pillow.

"Which would be a shame, since you've only recently gotten it back." Nancy calmly handed her a cup of tea.

Summer made a face at her. "That's very funny."

"I thought so." Nancy fluffed the pillows up behind her back—her earrings and clunky orange necklace clattering as she did—and gave her a quick hug. "He's going to be fine."

"I'm sure he is, but I'd really like to hear that from the surgeon."

"Well, I keep bugging them at the nurse's station, and they keep telling me they can't give me any information because we're not family. I have a strategy, though. I plan to hound them until I wear them down and they give me an update purely to shut me up."

Summer had an entirely different strategy in mind. She set the cup of tea on the table beside the bed and clasped Nancy's arm. "I appreciate you being here, but why don't you go home and have a nap? I can call you when they release me."

Nancy's eyes narrowed. "Oh no. You're only trying to get rid of me so you can sneak out of bed and try to find Jude. I'm not going anywhere." She picked up her bag of knitting and plunked herself down on the chair in the corner.

Summer blew out a breath. Jude was here in the building somewhere. So close and yet he might as well be a hundred miles away, since no one would let her see him or tell her how he was doing. Now that she'd finally recovered her memories, the two of them could—

Summer gasped and pressed a hand to her mouth. The woman who had forgotten all about him. It was her. *She* was his mystery woman. Only now she remembered.

A knock on the door interrupted her thoughts and she lowered her hands to the blanket. "Come in."

She'd been hoping for a doctor, but a thrill still shot through her when she saw who it was. "Evan!"

"Hi, Summer." He walked to the side of her bed, bent down, and kissed her on the cheek. "Are you okay?"

"I'm fine. Thankful you showed up when you did."

"Me too."

Summer looked over at Nancy. "Nancy, this is my partner, Detective Evan Travers, from the Toronto PD."

Nancy rose from the chair and shook his hand. "Nice to meet you."

"You too."

She gestured to the small white box on the table beside the bed. "Would you like something to eat?"

Summer opened the box and held it out to her partner. "They're from the bakery where I've been working, the best you'll ever taste. Even better than Aunt Dolly's on Yonge Street."

"That's a ringing endorsement, for sure." Evan examined the choices before grabbing a white-chocolate-macadamia-nut cookie. "Thanks." He pulled a chair closer to the side of the bed and sat down.

Summer clasped her hands on top of the blanket. "Have you heard anything about Jude?"

"Actually, yes." He frowned. "Pretty tight security around this place. I had to flash my badge around to a few different people before they'd tell me anything."

"Is he all right?"

Evan broke off a piece of the cookie. "He's going to be fine. He's out of surgery and the doctor said everything went really well. They don't expect there will be any permanent damage."

She sagged against the pillows. *Gracias a Dios. Thank you, God.* "Did they say when he could go home?"

"He lost a lot of blood, so they want him to stay a day or two at least, keep an eye on him." He shoved the cookie into his mouth.

Summer blew out her breath. "That makes sense. Thank you. I was going crazy not knowing what was going on with him."

"I'm sure." He glanced at Nancy and then back at Summer.

Summer cleared her throat. "Nancy, would you mind giving us a few minutes?"

"Of course." Nancy gathered up her knitting and stuck it into the bag. "I may slip home for that nap, now that we know how Jude is. Call me when they release you and I'll come back and pick you up to bring you home."

Home. Summer couldn't remember that word every being associated with anything but cold silence and loneliness. Until she met Nancy. "That sounds great. Thank you."

Nancy paused before pulling open the door. "Keep an eye on her, Detective. She's supposed to be resting, but if I know her, she'll be sneaking out of here the first chance she gets."

"Don't worry. I'll make sure she doesn't leave the room."

Summer shot him a look, but he grinned and winked at her as Nancy slipped out into the hallway. When she'd gone, Evan inclined his head toward the door. "She seems to really care about you."

"She does. I'd say she's become like a mother to me except that, as you know, my mother is nothing like that."

"I do know, and I'm glad you have Nancy in your life now."

"Me too." She unclasped her fingers and gripped the metal bed railing. "So what's going on? Who was the guy who was after me and what did he want?"

"Are you sure you're feeling up to getting into all this right now?"

"Absolutely. I'm in desperate need of a distraction at the moment."

"Okay." He ran a hand over his short, blond hair. "The guy's name was Alexander Kendrick. He worked for Luis Mendoza."

Her eyes widened. "The drug lord in Mexico?"

"Yes." He took another bite of the cookie. "Mmm."

"Told you." Summer shifted slightly, getting more comfortable. "He said I should ask my parents why he was after me. Do you have any idea what he meant by that? Did my father owe money to Mendoza or something?"

Evan sighed. "Not your father, Summer. Your mother."

She blinked. Her mother? "I don't understand."

"Back in Mexico, your mother kept the books for Mendoza and his cartel. Apparently she was a favorite of his. He called her *El Diamante*, because he admired how cold and ruthless she could be."

The words sent shock billowing through Summer in waves. *El Diamante*. The Diamond.

Evan touched her hand. "What is it?"

She shook her head slightly. "The day Kendrick broke into my house, he told me he had every right to come after the diamond. I thought he was looking for jewellery, but he must have meant her. Mendoza sent him to attack me in order to send a message to my mother, didn't he?"

"It looks that way. What Mendoza didn't know back then was that your mother was taking a cut of the drug money when it came in. Apparently, over the years she managed to bilk Mendoza out of millions of dollars. When she realized he was starting to become suspicious of her, she and your father fled to Canada with you."

A cold nearly as deep as the one that had gripped Summer earlier crawled through her now. *This isn't happening.* No wonder their houses had been fortresses. Her parents had been trying to protect themselves from the retribution of a drug lord. "Am I still in danger?"

"I don't believe so. Kendrick is dead. And we've been working with the Mexican authorities to bring down Mendoza for months. Two days ago we arrested Sam Garcia, a narcotics officer for the PD."

Summer nodded. "I met him a couple of times."

"Turns out he was our mole. He worked for Mendoza, letting him know about planned drug raids and essentially running his operation in Toronto. He's been talking non-stop since he was taken into custody. Based on his intel, the Mexicans carried out a raid early this morning on Mendoza's compound. They took Mendoza into custody, along with most of his top people. The cartel has been effectively shut down and Mendoza will be going away for a long time."

Summer's head was beginning to pound and she massaged her temples with her fingers. "I can't believe this is happening." She dropped her hands to the blanket. "What about the guy who grabbed me first. Do you know what he was after?"

"Yeah. That one is on me. Guy's name is Peter Díaz. Jude actually reported that he'd seen him sitting outside your place a few weeks ago. I ran the plates though and he was clean, so we both assumed he was some random guy who'd pulled over to use his phone or something."

"So who is he?"

"Believe it or not, he's actually been looking out for you."

She frowned. "What do you mean?"

"When you moved out of your parents' place, they hired him as a kind of bodyguard. He's been keeping tabs on you ever since, including getting inside your house at least once and bugging your place."

Summer closed her eyes. "That's how my father got the recording of my fight with Jude that he planned to use to make it look as though Jude was the one who attacked me." The thought that everything she'd said in her home, everything she and Jude had said to each other, had been recorded and listened to made her feel as violated as she'd felt when Alexander Kendrick stepped into her bedroom. She opened her eyes and clenched the blanket in both fists. "What about Díaz? Is he dead too?"

"No, actually. He survived. He'll be in the hospital for awhile, but they think he'll make a full recovery."

"Will he be charged?"

"That's up to you, actually. He did grab you and threaten you with a knife. If you want to press charges, that's absolutely your right."

"But you don't think I should."

Evan shrugged. "Of course I'm not happy that he choked you or held a blade to your throat, but even that appears to have been a somewhat overzealous attempt to protect you. Your mother, whom he refers to as the boss, ordered him to bring you to them if he suspected either that Kendrick was about to make a move on you or your memories came back, which of course both happened this morning. The excessive force was likely a result of the fact that not only was Jude right there but that Díaz is also fully aware of your ability to fight back and he was terrified of failing to carry out his orders."

Summer shook her head. "Why do you think he should be let off?"

He reached into the inside pocket of his jacket and withdrew a piece of paper that he unfolded and held up. Díaz stood in the photo, smiling, his arm around a beautiful woman with long, dark hair. Two young girls stood in front of them in braids and yellow and pink dresses.

Summer shifted her gaze to her partner. "His family?"

He nodded and folded up the paper. "I was right about the fact that he was clean. Before today, the only other time he committed a crime was when he broke into your house, although even then he used the key your mother gave him and did it on her orders. I spoke with him before I came to see you. All he wanted to do was make enough money to bring his wife and daughters to Canada. He's devastated that he might have ruined any chance for them to be together."

Summer bit her lip. Sounded like Peter Díaz and his wife and daughters were as much victims of her mother's machinations as she was. "I'm not going to press charges."

"I think that's a good decision."

"And I'll make sure *the boss* pays him what she owes him. Hopefully that will be enough for him to start the process of bringing his family here."

"I hope so. I may check in on him from time to time, see if there's anything I can do to help. Make sure he gets a legitimate job and stays on the right track."

She nudged his arm. "Softie."

He stuck the paper back into his pocket. "Don't let it get around."

"What about my parents?"

"I'm not sure what's going to happen to them. It doesn't appear as though either of them has broken any laws here, but the Mexican authorities did inform us that they have launched an investigation into your mother. It's possible she will be extradited to Mexico, but that will depend on whether or not they feel they have enough evidence to charge her with anything. Or whether they will consider that stealing drug money from a cartel even constitutes a crime. No evidence that your father, who was a fairly low-level lackey of Mendoza's, has done anything illegal, except possibly in being complicit in your mother's crimes. Certainly she had to explain where all that money came from and give him a good reason for them having to leave the country, so he's likely aware of everything she's been involved in."

"I'm surprised they let me stay in Elora this long if they knew where I was."

"Díaz told me they thought you'd be safer here than at home, unless Kendrick found out where you were. And we subpoenaed their financial records. They have been making a concerted effort to come up with the money, even put their house up for sale, but in the end they fell a couple of million short, apparently."

A headache pulsed through her temples. Summer reached for her glass of water and took a sip. "The diamond. That fits, actually. Remarkably well."

Evan swallowed the last bite of cookie and brushed crumbs from his fingers. "In a way, I can see how it happened, how she got so hard and cold. She had to have seen a lot of horrific things. At some point she must have learned how to block out that part of her that felt anything in order to survive."

"That makes sense. She certainly never did seem to feel anything, not for my father, or for me. I've always struggled to understand why they got married, or had a child."

Evan pursed his lips.

"What?"

"I found their marriage certificate and your birth certificate in their file. They were married at a justice of the peace six months before you were born."

"Ah." That was new information. Like all of this, she supposed. "So, she probably didn't want either of us. Except, given her Catholic upbringing—which she appears to have adhered to sporadically, at best—she got stuck with us both."

"That's something you'll have to ask her about, I guess."

"Oh, believe me, I will."

"It's her loss, you know."

"What is?"

His smile was sad. "The fact that she has never appreciated what an incredible daughter she has."

Summer held out her hand and he grasped it. "Thank you for that. It's tragic, isn't it?"

"Which part?"

"The way they lived their lives. All that money, and it never bought them a moment of happiness. Or peace."

"Maybe it's not too late."

She contemplated that. "Maybe not." Was anyone beyond the reach of redemption? In human terms, maybe, but in God's? Likely not. Summer squeezed his hand before letting him go. "Where do you suppose Kendrick was trying to take me?"

He winced. "Given his MO, and Mendoza's, our best guess is that he planned to drive to your parents' place and execute you in front of them."

Oh. Summer swallowed hard. "I guess I owe you and Jude even more than I thought."

"You don't owe either of us, Summer. You know I'd do anything for you. And obviously Jude will, quite literally, take a bullet for you. Not to mention that, even if neither of us had been there, I have no doubt that at some point you would have been able to take that guy down yourself."

She offered him a wry grin. "Maybe. It would have been fun trying, anyway."

He chuckled. "In any case, I'm happy it all worked out the way it did."

"Me too." She kneaded the blanket with her fingers. "Will any of this affect my job, do you think?"

"Of course not. You aren't responsible for your mother's actions. In fact, the DS told me to let you know that as soon as you feel ready for active duty again, you're welcome to come back."

She nodded. "Tell him thanks. I'm not sure what I'm going to do yet, but I'll let you know as soon as I decide."

His eyebrows rose. "You're not sure? What, small town living get to you?"

Summer lifted her shoulders. "I don't know. Maybe." The truth was, *this* small town had gotten to her, and she wasn't at all sure she was ready to leave it.

"Well, selfishly, I hope you come back. I'd sure miss having you for a partner. But whatever you decide, I hope you're happy, Summer. You and Jude."

"Thank you. I think we just might be." Which would mean that she had found her happily ever after here, like those girls in the movies always did. She managed a smile at that.

Evan pushed to his feet. "Tell you what. If you promise not to leave the room so I don't get in trouble with your friend, I'll see if I can find a doctor and make a case for you getting sprung from here."

"That would be great, thank you. Give my love to Tracy. Tell her I'm sorry I haven't called for awhile."

Evan grinned. "Pretty sure my wife understands, given that you had no memory of her. She'll be thrilled to hear you do now. And she'll want to get together with you soon."

"I'd like that."

"So you know, she did try to see you in the hospital and to drop off a card and flowers. She couldn't get past Díaz, though, who was stationed outside your door. Apparently your parents had ordered him to keep everyone but the medical staff out of your room. Díaz told Tracy they didn't want anyone disturbing you while you were recovering, but I suspect it had more to do with controlling who went in and out in case Mendoza sent someone after you. Even I couldn't get in, since your doctor didn't give the PD permission to talk to you until the night you left the hospital."

"That would explain why no one came to see me." The memory of all the friends she had warmed her. As soon as she and Jude figured things out, she needed to contact every one of them.

"I'm afraid so." He tapped the top of the bed rail with his palm. "Take care of yourself, okay?"

"I will." Summer watched him as he crossed the room. When he was gone, she leaned back against the pillows and reached for her tea. It was only lukewarm, but still it soothed her a little as it slid down the throat that had gone dry as she'd talked to Evan. A hundred thoughts whirled through her mind, but she could only manage to pin down one.

She needed Jude.

CHAPTER FIFTY-SEVEN

Jude crossed his arms. "I'm not leaving the building, but I need to go upstairs."

The nurse, a red-headed man about Jude's age, stood next to the bed, his arms crossed too. "I'm sorry, sir, but you aren't going anywhere."

Really? Challenging him to a battle of wills? He'd been with Summer Velásquez for the last two and a half years—he was an expert in that kind of warfare. Jude tossed back the sheet and thin beige blanket. "Look, whether or not you help me, I'm getting out of this bed right now."

"You most certainly are not." Summer strolled into the room. Even in jeans and a burgundy hoodie, her dark hair caught up in a loose bun on her head, she stole his breath away. "You are going to do whatever this nice man tells you to do so that you can get out of here soon and come home."

The nurse offered her a grateful smile. "Good advice. I'll be back in an hour with your next dose of pain medication." He crossed the room and disappeared into the hallway.

"Summer." Jude held out his hand. When she sat down on the chair beside his bed and clasped it in hers, he searched her face. "Are you okay?"

"I'm fine."

Heat rose in his chest as he reached out and gently ran a finger along the bruise on her jaw. "He hit you?"

"Apparently he objected to me kicking him in the face while he was driving."

311

"Summer." What was he going to do with her? *She's not in your hands.* Which was true. And likely something he was going to have to remind himself repeatedly in the future. He tugged the back of her hand to his mouth and kissed it. "Not exactly what I had in mind when I bought you those kick-boxing lessons for Christmas last year."

Amusement flitted across her face. "What did you think I was going to do with them?"

"I guess I try not to think about that part." Jude sobered. "¿Estás bien? Dime la verdad."

"I am telling you the truth. I'm okay. Better than okay. The doctor said a couple more minutes and hypothermia would have definitely set in, so you…" She stopped and stared at him, her eyes wide.

"What is it?"

"You speak Spanish."

Jude pressed his lips together. Something else he'd kept from her. Even used to his advantage. Would she hold that against him?

She pulled her hand from his and pressed both palms to her cheeks. "The things Daphne and I said…"

"You mean like how handsome I am?" He shrugged. "It wasn't anything that I didn't already know."

Summer rolled her eyes. "Since you are still recovering, I suppose I'll let you off the hook. Although, speaking of recovering, there is another issue we need to discuss."

Only one? He could handle that. "What issue?"

"Have you started smoking again?"

He blinked. "Why would you ask…?" Ah. Cash's cigarettes. The guy that abducted her had been smoking when he came after her. No doubt she'd smelled smoke around the café before, too, like he had. Whoever he was had been watching her even then. Jude's fist clenched, but he forced himself to relax. She was safe now. "That's why you went looking through my bag, isn't it? You found the cigarettes in my pocket."

"I was hanging your coat up and they fell out. So? Do I need to use my kickboxing skills on you next?"

He grinned. "No. They aren't mine. Cash is trying to quit, so I took the pack away from him a while ago. Kind of forgot they were there, actually." Probably a good thing, given his state of mind the night before.

She studied him a moment before nodding and folding her arms on the bed rail. "Okay. Enough about me. How are you doing?"

"I won't object when that nurse comes back with my pain medication, but overall I'm doing great, now that you're here."

"Really?"

"Sí. Puedes confiar en mí."

Her dark eyes locked on his. "I do trust you."

That went a long way toward healing the pain of the evening before. He reached over and brushed the backs of his fingers across her cheek. "Bienvenida, Summer. Welcome back. I missed you."

She smiled faintly. "It's good to be back, believe me."

"Have you been released?"

"Yep. I'm free to go." She settled back on the chair as if going anywhere was the last thing on her mind.

"Did Evan find you?"

A shadow passed over her face. "Yeah."

"Bad news?"

She sighed. "I'll tell you all about it, once I have a chance to sort it out in my head. Right now I only want to enjoy being here with you."

"Fair enough. I'm sorry I wasn't able to come up and see you."

"Given that you were being operated on to have the bullet you took for me removed, I'm willing to overlook it. This time."

He glanced down at his leg. "Really hoping there's no next time."

"Me too."

"And you saved my life as well. That guy was about to take another

313

shot at me, and I'm pretty sure this time it wasn't going to be a warning."

"But you could have gone through the ice when you came after me, so—"

Jude held up both hands. He'd missed sparring with her. If he wasn't exhausted and in pain, he'd happily dive right in. "I saved your life, you saved mine. Can we call it even?"

She smiled. "Sí. Claro."

"Gracias." Jude started to shift a little onto his side, wanting to face her, but abandoned the attempt when pain shot down his leg. "Summer." He might never get tired of being able to say her name. "Lo siento. Can you forgive me for lying to you?"

She took his hand and wove her fingers through his. "It would be pretty hypocritical of me not to. I lied too, after coming here. To you and Nancy and Daphne and Shawn, all the people I care about. I have a lot of making up to do for that."

He shook his head. "No, you don't. As Cash told me once, that's what forgiveness is for."

She nodded. "You're right, and I will forgive you. On two conditions. That you forgive me, and that you promise you'll never lie to me again."

"I do and I won't." A smile crossed his face as he studied her.

"What?"

"The way you said that, it sounds as though you're imagining a future for the two of us."

She lifted his hand to press the back of it to her cheek. "I've always imagined a future for the two of us, Jude. From the moment you passed me that ridiculous napkin with your number on it in the coffee shop."

"Then why did it take you nine days to call me?"

Summer lowered his hand and studied their clasped fingers. "For the same reason you asked for more time before you could marry me, I guess. I felt as though I had nothing to offer you. I really had no idea how to love someone because I had never been truly loved. And that scared me, because even though we'd only spoken for a minute or two, I knew you were someone who deserved great love." She rubbed her thumb over the back of his hand and his stomach tightened. She knew his weaknesses, too. "In the end, though, I couldn't get you out of my mind, and I decided I had to take a chance. I've been thankful every day since, because you taught me how to open up my heart and love another person completely and utterly. You make it pretty easy, in fact."

"You make it easy for me to love you too. Even when you're driving me crazy."

Summer laughed and the last of the tightness gripping his chest eased.

Someone knocked lightly on the door and they both looked over. Summer let go of his hand and stood as Maddie and his mom came into the room. Cash followed them and closed the door. "Jude." His mother made a beeline for him and he lifted his hand. "I'm okay, Mom. Honest." She stopped next to him and rested a hand on his shoulder, scrutinizing him as though judging the truth of his words for herself.

Maddie stopped at the side of the bed. "Did you really get shot?"

He almost laughed at the mix of concern and awe in her voice. "I did, yes."

She gripped the bed rails. "Life's not going to be boring with you around, is it?"

Jude grinned.

Cash stuck a hand into his coat pocket. "The two of you certainly gave this little town lots to talk about, anyway. Three people shot, one abducted, that's the most excitement in one day Elora has ever seen. I wouldn't be surprised if they named a street after you." He looked across the bed. "Hey, Summer."

"Hi, Cash."

Jude nodded at his sister. "This is my little sister Maddie, and this," he reached for his mother's hand, "is my mom, Leanne. Everyone, this is Summer."

Summer's smile was warm. "Nice to meet everyone. Jude's told me a lot about you."

His mother let go of Jude's hand, rounded the bed, and pulled Summer close. "We McCalls are huggers, I hope you don't mind."

"Not at all."

Jude watched the two of them, his heart swelling. His mother stepped back and held Summer at arm's length. "Are you okay?"

"I'm fine, thanks to Jude."

"Good." Jude's mother didn't let her go. "Is he actually okay?"

Summer nodded. "The surgery went well. If he takes it easy and does what they tell him to do, they'll release him in a couple of days."

"Oh, he'll do what he's told." His mother sounded fierce as she lowered her arms to her sides.

Jude held up both hands in protest. "I'm right here."

Cash chuckled. "Give it up, Jude. You're outnumbered now. You *will* be doing what the medical staff tells you to do." He held out a bag. "Here's the stuff you asked for."

"Thanks." Jude took the bag and tossed it onto the table beside him. The small blue box, the one he'd taken from Summer's room the day she stopped by her house to pick up her car, tumbled out of the bag and he grabbed for it, biting back a groan at the pain that shot through his leg. Gritting his teeth, he opened the drawer, intending to drop the box in.

Summer's lips quirked. "Is that for me?"

He stopped with the drawer partway open and looked over. "As a matter of fact, it is."

"Aren't you going to give it to me?"

Jude glanced at his family. "You want to do this now? In front of everyone?"

She lifted her slender shoulders. "Why not? The last time it was only the two of us in that hot air balloon, and as romantic as the proposal was, the engagement didn't end very well. Maybe it would be a good idea to do things differently this time."

Suddenly he wanted very much to share this moment with Cash and Maddie and his mom. "I can't get down on one knee."

"Been there, done that."

Maddie snickered.

Jude pushed up onto his elbows and his mother straightened the pillows behind his back. "All right, but years from now, I want you to remember that you asked me to do it this way." *Years from now.* That thought sent a rush of warmth through his chest.

"Got it."

Maddie clasped her hands in front of her chest as Jude opened the box and grabbed the ring. He held it out to Summer. "Summer Velásquez, te amo. There's nothing I want more than to spend my life with you. ¿Te quieres casar conmigo?"

A smile lit up her dark eyes. "Sí. Yes, Jude McCall. I will marry you." She held out her left hand and he slid the ring onto her finger. When he finished, he tugged her down and kissed her, not caring that his entire family was standing around watching.

When he let her go, his mother and Maddie swarmed around her, admiring the sapphire ring he'd picked out for her what felt like a lifetime ago.

Cash held up his hand and Jude clasped it. "Congratulations, little brother. I'm really happy for you."

"Thanks, Cash." Jude tilted his head. "Things with you and Renee any better?"

317

Cash waved a hand through the air. "Not really. But today isn't about me and Renee, it's about you and Summer. Let's focus on that."

Jude shifted his attention to his fiancée. He really hoped she wasn't planning on a long engagement, because the only thing he wanted in the world right now was for her to be his wife and for them to start their life together. She met his gaze and gave him that smile of hers that touched some place deep inside him, and suddenly he forgot everything else, including the throbbing in his leg.

They'd both been lost but, through the grace of God, had found their way back to each other. He had no idea what would happen in the future—what they would do or where they would live. At the moment, none of that mattered to Jude.

All he knew was that, wherever they ended up, if Summer was there, he would be home.

Dear Reader,

Thank you for taking the time to read *Lost Down Deep*. As with all my stories, my hope and prayer is that it had an impact on you in some way. That, as you read, you were reminded of the powerful truth that, whatever you are going through, you are never alone.

One of the questions the book explores is: On what level does our relationship with God dwell? Summer loses the memory of the last few years, during which time she came to faith in God. What does that mean for her? Is that faith lost, or does it exist on a plane other than conscious memory? In *Lost Down Deep*, I propose one answer, but I leave it to you and God to determine for yourself what you believe.

Jude's return to his family is, of course, a type of prodigal son story. His situation was extreme, but are we not all, on some level and at various points in our lives, prodigals in need of forgiveness? In the words of the great hymn, "Come, Thou Fount of Every Blessing," I am deeply aware that I am "Prone to wander, Lord, I feel it; Prone to leave the God I love." I don't understand how we can so easily drift away from our loving Heavenly Father, but I do know that I am grateful beyond words that, when we return, He is waiting with open arms to welcome us home. One of my favorite passages in the Bible is Psalm 103:13,14: "As a Father shows compassion to his children, so the Lord shows compassion to those who fear him. For he knows our frame; he remembers that we are dust." Being deeply aware of how much I need God's compassion—how often I need him to remember that I am dust—these verses bring me tremendous comfort.

Whether or not we have a loving earthly family, those who believe can rest in the knowledge that we have a spiritual family that spans all of time and the entire globe. And we have an eternal home waiting for us. When we arrive there, the pain of abandonment, loss, betrayal, or heartache that we have endured will vanish as though it never existed.

In the meantime, my hope and desire for each of you is that you experience the deep love and acceptance of God here on earth and the peace, joy, and hope of knowing that one day he will welcome us home to dwell with him forever.

Sara

Acknowledgements

First and foremost, to the One who gives the stories and who always welcomes the prodigal home.

To my family and friends, especially Michael, Luke, Julia, and Seth. Without your support and encouragement I'm quite sure I couldn't—and wouldn't want to—do this.

Thank you to early readers and all who offered invaluable insight and guidance in shaping and polishing this story, including members of my writer's groups and Bev and Helena, my writing retreat partners. It takes a village to write a book, and I am deeply grateful for mine.

Special thanks to Ines for helping to ensure the Spanish was accurate, and to Yolanda, who also advised me on the Spanish and who read the manuscript for cultural sensitivity. If any errors or inaccuracies in the portrayal of the Mexican culture are perceived by readers, I offer my sincere apologies. I have nothing but respect for the Mexican people, the country, and the culture.

And to my beautiful Mosaic sisters and readers. We were created to be in community, and the Mosaic community has come to be one of the most valued in my life and career. Thank you for your unwavering support, encouragement, and advice!

Let's Connect!

I would love to connect with you further. You can find me at the following places:

Website: www.saradavison.org

Twitter: @sarajdavison

Facebook: @authorsaradavison

For news and encouragement about upcoming books, contests, giveaways, and other activities, sign up for Sara's monthly newsletter.

If you've enjoyed *Lost Down Deep*, please consider leaving a review. Your words bring hope and encouragement to the author as well as to other readers.

Discussion Questions

1. Have you ever been betrayed by someone close to you, like Summer felt she was by her parents? How did you deal with that?

2. On what level do you believe our relationship with God exists? Even though she has lost the memory of the last few years, during which time she came to faith in God, Summer does know deep in her bones that she has a relationship with him. Do you believe this is possible? Why or why not?

3. When Jude faces his family for the first time in five years, he realizes that, "He deserved everything Cash threw at him and more. And getting what he deserved was a lot easier than accepting what he didn't." Have you ever struggled with accepting forgiveness for something you have done? Why do you think it is so hard for us as humans to accept forgiveness? Can this be a barrier to us experiencing God's grace and forgiveness?

4. Nancy fills the void in Summer's life left by a cold, detached mother, and Daphne informs her that, "You can choose your own family, you know, especially if the one you're born into turns out to be a dud." Do you have someone in your life to whom you are not related by blood, but whom you have chosen to be part of your family? How did that come about?

5. On a lighter note, when Summer first walks by the Taste of Heaven Café, she inhales the scents of chocolate, fresh-baked bread, and coffee, and suggests that the combination must be

what heaven smells like. Of the three, which aroma is your favorite, and what kinds of emotions, memories, or experiences does it invoke for you?

6. Due to circumstances beyond the control of either of them, Summer and Jude are forced to lie and keep secrets from people they care about. Have you ever had to do this? What happened? Are there ever times when it is acceptable to lie?

7. Jude refers to Elora as "His Ninevah. The place God had been telling him to go for a long time and he'd been resisting." Have you ever felt God calling you to do something and you resisted? What happened?

8. Do any of the items on Summer's bucket list (go up in a hot air balloon, learn to ski, meet Javier Hernández Balcázar in person, become fluent in French, and travel to the seven modern wonders of the world) resonate with you? Have you done any of them? Do you have a list of things you would like to do, people you want to meet, or places you want to go in your lifetime? What are your top five?

9. Summer struggles with the command in the Bible not to seek revenge, until she concludes that, "Maybe it wasn't so much that she *couldn't* seek revenge but that she didn't have to. It wasn't her responsibility. That job fell to one much greater, more powerful, and more perfectly just than she was." What do you think about these statements?

10. When Summer hesitates to get involved with Ryan, Nancy tells her, "Don't keep closing doors, darlin'. Life is precious but fleeting." Have you ever let fear prevent you from doing something that, deep down, you really wanted to do? Were you able to overcome it? What happened?

Other Books
BY SARA DAVISON

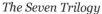

The Seven Trilogy

Bookstore owner Meryn O'Reilly and Army Captain Jesse Christensen are on opposite sides of a battle. When the army is sent in to keep an eye on believers, Jesse is equally amused, intrigued, and terrified by Meryn's spirit. Jesse's worst fears are realized when Meryn commits a crime and faces consequences he cannot protect her from. As the world descends into chaos, Jesse and Meryn face the greatest barrier to their love yet—a barrier that may prove too strong to breach.

Children are disappearing in the night. When Detective Daniel Grey comes to see diner owner Nicole Hunter to enlist her help, she realizes everything—and everyone—she has clung to so tightly may soon be ripped from her grasp.

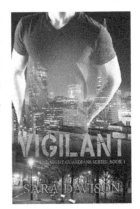

Detective Daniel Grey is back in town and Nicole isn't sure how she feels about that. Someone is working hard to disrupt her present with reminders of the past she has worked hard to forget. As much as she might want to push Daniel away, Nicole needs him closer now than ever before.

But the one she trusts to keep her and her son safe has a secret that may prove to be the biggest threat of all.

Coming soon to

THE MOSAIC COLLECTION

The Mischief Thief by Johnnie Alexander

Two wrongs don't make a right . . . except when they do.

For con artist Chaney Rose, life hasn't been easy. In desperate need of cash, she readily accepts a gig from an unethical attorney to recover Mischief, a stolen racehorse. Hunting for clues, she breaks into the suspected thief's home only to be caught—with a few pilfered items in her pockets—by the police detective who's tailing her.

By-the-book Adam Thorne was fired from his church ministry because of his father's involvement with the valuable racehorse.

He arrives home to find a detective arresting the young woman who broke into his house. In a burst of Les Miserables-inspired charity, he claims he gave Chaney the stolen items.

Adam needs Chaney's help to find his father who has disappeared along with Mischief. But when Chaney learns that Mischief's owner intends to kill the horse, she needs Adam's help to expose the cruel plan before it's too late.

Can a con artist with a conscience and a minister without a ministry team up to do the wrong thing for the right reason?

CHAPTER ONE

"The best way of successfully acting a part is to be it."
~ Arthur Conan Doyle ~

The shadow, in the squat outline of a broad-shouldered man with a slight paunch, slid across the wrought iron table where Chaney Rose read a dog-eared paperback.

"Fancy finding you here," the shadow said. "You don't mind if I join you, do you?"

Chaney minded very much. But before she could respond, the shadow shifted as Detective Benjamin Grant settled into the seat next to her. He leaned back, propped his ankle on his knee, and stared at her behind tinted sunglasses that hid his eyes. He wore khakis and a pale green polo shirt sporting the Orlando Police Department's logo above his heart.

Except he had no heart. Only a stone where his heart should be.

His easy smile, no doubt meant to be charming, didn't fool her. Chaney slid her sunglasses from the top of her head to hide her own eyes and closed her book.

"What are you reading?" He bent his neck to read the spine. "*Black Beauty*. A classic, isn't it? Not sure I ever read it, but I think I saw the movie."

She inwardly scoffed at his vain attempt to make a connection. Before he decided to paw through it, she slipped the book into the tote hanging on the back of her chair. The very thought of him touching one of her beloved books made her want to gag.

"Why are you bothering me?" she asked.

He flung out his arms in an expansive gesture, palms open and fingers spread apart. All innocence. As if.

"The Dogwood Diner here is one of my favorite places to stop and get a cold drink on a hot day."

As if she'd been summoned by him to appear at that exact moment, a waitress suddenly stopped at the table. A multitude of rings sparkled on her tanned fingers. "Hey, Detective. The usual?"

His expression, half smirk and half grin, clearly said, *I told you.* His gaze shifted from Chaney to the waitress. "That'd do me just fine, Gail. How are the boys?"

"Growing like weeds."

"Boys'll do that." He looked at Chaney and pointed at her to-go cup. "Want a refill? Something to go along with your drink? My treat."

He surely couldn't believe she'd ever take as much as a pressed penny from him. But despite how much she wanted to throw her drink at him, toss the table, and run away, her grandfather's lessons on the art of hiding in plain sight glued her to the chair. Only an amateur would cause a scene or do anything to be remembered by the other diners.

Though it was probably too late to hope for that since the detective had parked himself at her table. Who could help noticing the gun belt strapped around his waist when he loomed over her? At least he hadn't slapped his handcuffs on her.

Yet.

She darted a smile at the waitress. "I'm fine, thank you."

"I'll bring you a refresh anyway." Gail's rings sparkled in the sunlight. "The ice melts fast out here and no one likes watered-down soda. Let's see, you had a Pepsi with lemon slices, right?"

"That's right." Now, please, go away.

"I'll be back in a jiffy with those drinks." Gail's broad smile covered both of them.

When she left, Chaney glanced at Detective Grant, sensing him studying her behind his dark lenses. His amused expression made her feel as small as a mouse trapped by a cat. She wasn't fooling him with her outward poise and disinterested air. He'd been highly trained, too, and it would be a mistake to underestimate him. Though his training had taken place at an academy and during years patrolling the streets of the City Beautiful. While hers had begun before she'd taken her first steps. A cute and happy pawn in her grandfather's arms.

She leaned forward and, with her elbows on the table, rested her chin on her clasped hands. "Don't you have anything better to do than follow me around? No drug deals going down? No jaywalkers to ticket?"

"At the moment, no." He flicked a spot of dust from his pants leg then stared at the businesses across the street. "Interesting view you've chosen."

She followed his gaze and consciously relaxed her shoulders while mentally preparing for his interrogation.

"Let me guess." His tone was as off-handed as if they were discussing the latest movies or the warm February weather. Anything inconsequential. But she was determined not to be tripped up by his easy-going manner. "Giaquinto's Jewelry. I can practically see all those diamonds and precious gemstones glistening from here. An in-and-out snatch-and-grab for someone who knows what she's doing."

"You're right. Jewels are easy to steal." Chaney copied his off-handed tone. "But hard to fence. That is, unless you don't mind someone else knowing your business."

He nodded, that slow annoying nod of his, which seemed so patronizing. As if he understood when he couldn't understand. She'd done her homework on Benjamin Grant. Decorated officer. Married with three young children. When had he ever gone hungry? Or been left on his own to survive?

He turned his attention back to the other side of the street. "Surely not the bank? That kind of heist wouldn't be easy for a gal on her own. And you are on your own now that your cousin is behind bars."

He couldn't have cut her any deeper if he'd used a knife. Though her guilt was already eating her up inside. She casually swept back her long bangs.

"Not impossible, though," she said, her tone easy. "And banks provide ready cash. As long as the bills are unmarked."

"But?"

"Too many variables. Besides, I don't have time to plan a bank heist."

"What's the rush?"

"As if you didn't know." Chaney peered past the detective's shoulder at two middle-aged women who were taking their time choosing a table and seats that would provide at least some shelter from the mid-day sun. A slender, sharp-nosed punk, probably in his early twenties and wearing a long thin coat, approached them. He said something and one of the women laughed.

"Let's see then," Grant continued. "That leaves the bookstore, the insurance agency, the dry cleaners, and the shoe store." He turned back to her, his smile and tone confident. "And the hotel. Plenty of marks inside those walls."

The luxury four-story hotel with its restaurants, banquet rooms, and meeting spaces, anchored the city block. It catered primarily to a convention crowd. No doubt that's where the two women, who had finally settled at a table, were staying. They wore lanyards around their necks, giving away their names and new-to-town status. Perfect marks.

"Most tourists carry debit cards and credit cards," she said dismissively. "Those don't help me much."

"And yet that's why you're sitting here, isn't it?" Grant leaned closer, as if to see past the dark lenses they both wore to hide their eyes—those windows to the soul—and see inside her. "You're keeping an eye on who's coming and going. Sizing them up. Waiting for the perfect opportunity."

The punk laughed, bent over one of the women, then walked toward Chaney's table.

"The perfect opportunity appears to be now." She stood and took the lid off her drink. "Watch my bag, will you?"

Before the detective could answer, she strode toward the man and lightly bumped into him. Soda and ice spilled onto his coat as the cup fell to the ground. As if to keep herself from falling, she grabbed hold of his arm. "I'm so sorry," she said apologetically then laughed. "I am such a klutz. No harm done is there? Except to your coat. You must let me have it cleaned for you."

She kept up a patter of apologies and offers to help while the punk tried to extricate himself. When she stepped back, he hurried on his way. After he turned the corner, she faced the detective and held up a necklace in one hand and a cell phone in the other.

Grant frowned and started to rise.

"Stay there," she ordered.

When he sat back down, she strode to where the women were looking at their menus.

"Are these yours?" She placed the necklace and the phone on the table.

The women stared at the items then both started talking at once. Uncomfortable with the attention, Chaney held up her hands. "Just be careful who you talk to. And keep an eye on your stuff."

She glanced at their lanyards and stifled a giggle. "After all, you're not in Kansas anymore."

"How did you know we're from Kansas?" the older woman asked.

"Just a lucky guess." Chaney grinned and pointed at the woman's lanyard. "Enjoy the rest of your stay."

She returned to her seat, picking up the fallen cup along the way, and removed her sunglasses. No more hiding.

Grant eyed her for a moment then removed his own. "Impressive. But if you'd given me a head's up, I could have arrested the guy. Gotten him off the streets."

"I would have loved recording a video of you chasing that loser." Her lips curled into a mischievous grin. "I'd have sent copies to all the news stations, to your boss, to the mayor. Even put it on the city's Facebook page."

"So you think you did me a favor by letting him go? Is that it?"

Chaney slid a wallet across to him. "This should help you find him."

He opened the wallet and held up the side showing the punk's driver's license. "What do you know? Home address right here." He checked the bills. "About thirty dollars. If I weren't an honest cop, I'd give the cash to you as a thank you."

"If I'd wanted it, I'd have taken it before giving you the wallet."

"Touché." The detective unlocked his phone and placed a call.

As he was reciting the punk's name, address, and description, Gail arrived with their drinks. "A Pepsi with lemon for you," she whispered. "An Arnold Palmer for the detective." When she put the ticket on the table, Grant picked it up, pulled a five from his pocket, and mouthed a thank you.

After Grant finished the call, Chaney handed him a phone. "I got this, too."

"His?"

"His."

"How did you . . . ?" Grant shook his head. "I was watching, closely watching, and I didn't see you take a thing from him."

Pride surged through her despite the warning in her head. *Never take anything from a cop. Not even a compliment.*

"I'm good at my job."

"Except it's not a job, Chaney. You're an intelligent and, okay, I'm just going to say it, you're also easy on the eyes. You could do something else with your life besides break the law."

"When did I break the law?"

"Are you denying it?"

She pressed her lips together. Detective Grant wasn't some small town yokel who could be easily manipulated. Better not to talk at all than to say something she'd regret.

He glanced behind him at the women.

"You didn't have to retrieve their valuables." He shifted in his seat, stared at nothing as he worked his jaw. She'd rattled him. *Good.*

"Doesn't that violate some 'honor among thieves' kind of code?" he asked.

"If he'd stolen the necklace from the older woman, I might have let it go."

He studied her expression, but she refused to be intimidated by his stare. She leaned back in her chair and crossed her arms.

Finally, he shrugged. "Care to elaborate on that?"

"Look at the way they're dressed."

"Business clothes. Look expensive."

"They are expensive. And expensive clothes are usually tailored. You might not have noticed, but the brunette's sleeves are a little too long and the shoulders don't sit right. Either she's borrowed that outfit or gotten it from a thrift store."

"Nothing wrong with that."

"I didn't say there was. It's just . . ." She pressed her lips together again. She was saying too much. And yet she wanted to make him understand that she had her own code. But could he step outside of his black-and-white world to enter the gray area where she operated? Even for a minute?

"Look at her shoes."

"Her shoes? What about them?"

"The heels are worn down. She's obviously had them a long time."

"Let me see if I've got this straight. You recovered her stolen necklace because she doesn't have new clothes and new shoes."

"She's wanting to look her best. That necklace *is* her best. Maybe it's the only jewelry of any real value that she has. Besides, it was a locket. It probably has sentimental value." Chaney looked the detective square in his eyes. "No one should take that away from her. No one."

Grant didn't flinch from her direct gaze but seemed to be sizing her up. Finally, he took a long sip of his drink then leaned forward. He gripped his cup. "Taking someone else's property is always wrong. Even if they have a lot of it or it doesn't have sentimental value. This isn't Sherwood Forest and neither you nor your cousin is Robin Hood."

"We never claimed to be."

"I guess not. At least Robin Hood gave his stolen bounty to the needy."

When she didn't respond, he stood. "I'm going to get statements from those women. Wouldn't mind having an official one from you, too."

"You want me to go to the police station? No, thanks." She stared at the luxury hotel. Despite what she'd said earlier, the guests who stayed there were pigeons waiting to be plucked.

But instead of sitting at the bar inside that hotel and sizing up enough marks to get the money she needed, she'd sat, lost in Black Beauty's world, at this sidewalk table. And as much as she'd like to think otherwise, it wasn't because she had a sense that Detective Grant was somewhere near by watching her. She'd been able to hide her surprise at seeing him, but the truth was, she'd been shocked when he sat next to her.

She had slipped up. Allowed her worry over her cousin Marshall to dull her observational skills . . . something she couldn't afford to do. Especially not now when she was desperate for money. Five thousand dollars. Minimum.

"Stay out of the hotel, Chaney," Grant said. "All the hotels."

"Are you going to keep following me to make sure I don't?"

"I wouldn't have to stay on your tail if your cousin wasn't so loyal." Grant smiled, but the expression in his eyes remained serious. "Usually I admire loyalty, but in this case . . . let's just say, I wouldn't have to follow you if you were in a cell next to Marshall."

"You've got nothing on me."

He stood and loomed over her, his shadow blocking the sun. "Not yet," he said with a smile as he put on his sunglasses. "Just give me time."

The story continues. Read more at bit.ly/MosaicMischief

About Johnnie Alexander

Johnnie Alexander creates characters you want to meet and imagines stories you won't forget. Her award-winning debut novel, *Where Treasure Hides* (Tyndale), is a CBA bestseller. She writes contemporaries, historicals, and cozy mysteries, serves on the executive boards of Serious Writer, Inc., co-hosts an online show called Writers Chat, and interviews inspirational authors for Novelists Unwind. She also teaches at writers conferences and for Serious Writer Academy. Johnnie lives in Oklahoma with Griff, her happy-go-lucky collie, and Rugby, her raccoon-treeing papillon.

Made in the USA
Coppell, TX
15 December 2020